HOME SWEET HOME

HOME SWEET HOME

APRIL SMITH

ALFRED A. KNOPF   NEW YORK   2017

THIS IS A BORZOI BOOK
PUBLISHED BY ALFRED A. KNOPF

Copyright © 2017 by April Smith

Library of Congress Cataloging-in-Publication Data
Names: Smith, April, [date] author.
Title: Home sweet home : a novel / April Smith.
Description: First edition. | New York : Alfred A. Knopf, 2017.
Identifiers: LCCN 2016015836 (print) | LCCN 2016021941 (ebook)
ISBN 9781101874219 (hardcover) | ISBN 9781101874226 (ebook)
Subjects: LCSH: Families–United States–Fiction. | Domestic fiction. |
BISAC: FICTION / Family Life. | FICTION / Coming of Age. |
FICTION / Romance / Western.
Classification: LCC PS3569.M467 H66 2017 (print) |
LCC PS3569.M467 (ebook) | DDC 813/.54—dc23
LC record available at https://lccn.loc.gov/2016015836

Jacket photograph by Stuart McClymont/Getty Images
Jacket design by John Vorhees

Manufactured in the United States of America
First Edition

For my teachers
Tillie Olsen and
Richard "Coach" Scowcroft

The pale, cold light of the winter sunset did not beautify—it was like the light of truth itself. When the smoky clouds hung low in the west and the red sun went down behind them, leaving a pink flush on the snowy roofs and the blue drifts, then the wind sprang up afresh, with a kind of bitter song, as if it said: "This is reality, whether you like it or not. All those frivolities of summer, the light and shadow, the living mask of green that trembled over everything, they were lies, and this is what was underneath. This is the truth."

—WILLA CATHER, *My Ántonia*

HOME SWEET HOME

Rapid City, South Dakota, is a small municipality on the western edge of the state. Originally settled by a band of disillusioned gold miners, a sense of melancholy disappointment still prevails. Despite generations of civic promoters, commerce has never taken hold along its restored frontier streets. December, especially, does not come easily here. In the winter months, temperatures can hang below zero, in the teens if you're lucky, and continuous storms bring gale-force winds, keeping up a moan of desolation that is peculiar to this place, as if speaking the unspeakable when human voices fail.

On Christmas Eve day, 1985, there had been snow on the ground but the sky was clear. During the night the weather changed. Heavy rain began to fall around the same time the police switchboard became flooded with 911 calls. For two more days the skies stayed blustery, then the rain turned to sleet, which pelted the windshield of Jo Kusek's rental car as she made her way from the airport. Twenty years ago she'd left South Dakota, vowing never to return. As if in retribution, the prairie was drawing her back, this time in the face of a horrific event.

The windshield wipers swept the sludge away in crescents. Jo watched as the familiar road became muddled, then sharp, then obscured again by a layer of ice. And that's how it would be for the days ahead, as she tried to grasp what had happened to her family. The whole town was in shock. Her sister-in-law, Wendy Kusek, had been bludgeoned to death with her own steam iron by an intruder on the night of December 24. Jo's brother, Lance, and their son, Willie, had been savagely attacked as well and were barely clinging to life.

The Kuseks lived on West Boulevard, a genteel enclave of the city's most affluent. Around seven p.m., one of them had opened the front door of their saltbox house painted a jaunty blue, assuming it was an early visitor for the annual holiday dinner. The dining room table was decorated with fine china and fresh pine boughs, and a good-sized fire was still blazing in the hearth when police arrived some fifty minutes later, summoned by panicked guests. Locked out, with no answer at the door, they'd gone around to the windows and seen the Kuseks lying motionless on the floor in what looked like a massacre.

The community hospital that Jo remembered as a small brick building with an ivy-covered portico had become a lumbering medical center. She parked in a cavernous underground lot. Hatless in the frigid air, too distressed to even zip her parka, she followed the arrows to the fourth-floor surgical wing, where she was directed by a solemn nurse to a characterless brown-and-green waiting room.

Murmuring sympathies, a small crowd of people she had known all her life rose to greet her. Cattlemen and ranch wives. The garage owner. Her father's political supporters and the Democratic state chairman. Jo saw fear in their shell-shocked eyes, and not just of the killer or killers, who were still at large. Everyone there had been close to her family, and now they were wrestling with their own guilty consciences. What had been their part in the events leading up to this incomprehensible act?

Newspaper and TV reporters were being kept in a separate room. The turnout was familiar to people who knew the Kuseks' story. The national press had swarmed Rapid City before, during her parents' trial. Once again the family made sensational news. Then they'd been fighting for freedom. Now, one by one, they were fighting for their lives.

State Trooper Randy Sturgis, retired, was the first to get to Jo. They hugged wordlessly. He'd also been first to befriend the Kuseks when they drove out from New York City, a young family in a secondhand station wagon, back in 1950. Thirty-five years later, he was the same lanky beanpole, but his hair had turned all white and she could feel a tremor as his hands gripped hers.

"Don't lose hope," he said.

Jo nodded, although she felt nothing.

"The doctor said they really won't know," he added in a husky voice. "Not for a couple of days."

"Where is the doctor? I have to talk to him—"

"Jo—" He stopped her. "They're calling in the state investigators. I promise you, we'll get whoever did this."

Jo imagined that they would. After so many years, somebody hated her family enough to murder them. The sheriff must have had a pretty good idea of who that could be. Rapid City was still a small town, after all.

ONE

DREAM

The station wagon was stuck in the mud and Jo's parents were trying to fix it. This was before State Trooper Randy Sturgis showed up to rescue them. Jo was four and her brother, Lance, still a baby. They had driven almost two thousand miles from New York City, passed through Sioux Falls and crossed into the grasslands, a couple of hours shy of their destination at the Crazy Eights Ranch. The highway here was newly built, and every time the sun came out the road became a beckoning river of silver.

Jo's father had been driving. He was a lawyer who still wore his hair city-style, slicked back with Vitalis, and he had a dashing mustache that made a thin line over soft, ample lips. He was a confident fellow of thirty-seven, big-boned and good-looking, with a narrow face, sandy hair, eyes typically narrowed in thought, and a long, straight aristocratic nose. His plain decency made Calvin Kusek someone you would trust. Foreman of the jury. The passenger who takes charge when the subway car breaks down. He was sure of himself in a quiet way that inspired others to follow.

It was early spring, 1950. The world as Cal Kusek saw it had lost its innocence and was facing grave dangers. Just last year Truman announced that the Soviet Union had detonated an atomic bomb. Now both sides had it. A believer in old-fashioned cracker-barrel democracy,

Cal was fed up with Senator Joe McCarthy running roughshod over civil rights, yet gaining in power. Unstable times called for levelheaded choices, which is how the Kuseks came to leave Manhattan for the heartland of America.

"I always imagined the prairie would be flat and dull," Jo's mother, Betsy, had said. "But this is beautiful."

"Isn't it, though?" Cal agreed. "Real live Nature! The way it's *suppos'd* to be!" he added in a carefree voice that made the endless days in the car sound like a song.

The trip had started on a buoyant note. When both kids had finally quieted down in the backseat and the steel cables of the George Washington Bridge were winging by overhead, the Kuseks touched hands in the natural way of married people and, without having to say a word, affirmed their love and the rightness of their purpose, heading west in order to find a better life for their children.

From the beginning they'd been a matched pair. They were tall and physically alike. Her looks may not have been as striking as his, but she was slim and athletic; her long legs fit his stride. She did her blond hair in waves and had a breakout laugh. Coline "Betsy" Ferguson was the one to call on a dime if you were desperate to complete a foursome. She'd show up with no complaints about it being last minute—and it wasn't because she didn't have dates; she was just that kind of friend. Calvin was a dreamer, an attorney fighting on behalf of the workingman. Betsy had gone to jail in support of her union. They both dug oysters and rhythm and blues. A month after they'd met, they were practically engaged.

And why not? It was wartime. Cal joined the army and became a pilot in the Eighty-Second Airborne Division at the rank of second lieutenant. He flew a transport plane from his post in North Africa. On the home front, Betsy got a degree from the U.S. Cadet Nurse Corps and worked in a veterans' hospital. They were married on a three-day pass. When the war was over and Jo was born, they found a studio apartment on the Lower East Side, which in 1946 meant the first move toward a house in the suburbs, but the Kuseks discovered they were out of step with the flush of postwar prosperity.

Rationing was over, and the thrill of making sacrifices was gone. Everyone wanted *new, new, new* in a mad rush for status: desirable apartments, the latest appliances, jazzed-up cars, and televisions for all. The streets of Greenwich Village, so romantic during their engagement, had taken on a dirty, hard, bohemian edge, overrun by society's outcasts, who wallowed helplessly in booze and marijuana, and radical beatniks, who wanted to tear everything apart. Uptown, it was the opposite. To get ahead, you had to conform.

Now a family man, Cal could no longer afford the low-paying job of a union lawyer. Brandishing his Yale Law School degree, he landed a position at the distinguished law firm of Berle, Berle, and Brunner, whose senior partner, Adolf A. Berle, a Democrat, was doing vital work to rein in corporate greed under new government regulations. Berle had been appointed to President Roosevelt's Brain Trust, the advisers at the heart of the New Deal. The prospect of being close to this tough-minded leader who fought for civil liberties was electrifying.

But Cal Kusek got nowhere near the famous man. As a new hire, he was assigned scud work that never went to trial. Like everyone else he wore suits and ties to work, with a white shirt and a hat, and was relegated to a cubicle in a musty bullpen of cubicles that spanned the thirty-first floor. He never saw the light of day and went home on a packed subway train, disillusioned by the incremental crawl up the ladder of success . . . to where? He wanted to get his hands around the throat of things like corruption and race prejudice, not just file papers. When Lance was born, they saw two choices: Cal could swallow his pride and stay with the firm, and Betsy could go back to work in order to afford a bigger place . . . or they could change their lives.

The decision to leave New York had been based on a postcard: an ordinary, two-cent postcard stamped Rapid City, South Dakota. It had arrived in response to a letter Cal had written to an army buddy, Sergeant Scotty Roy, a parachutist who'd jumped out of Cal's airplane during the catastrophic Allied Invasion of Sicily. Their drop point was farther inland, so Cal hadn't known the extent of the disaster until he returned to North Africa, where he learned that navy gunners had mistaken the American squadrons of C-53s for German bombers and dozens of U.S. transport planes had gone down, destroyed by friendly fire. Soldiers were shot dangling from their parachutes. Pilots aborted and brought the damaged aircraft back punctured by thousands of bullets and with their holds washed in blood.

When Cal had written care of the Crazy Eights Ranch, he didn't know if Scotty Roy was alive or dead, or in God knows what shape—if he'd had the luck to survive the ground fighting. But the crazy kid who'd always wanted to fly was their only contact west of the Mississippi, so Cal took a chance, writing that the open plains of South Dakota Scotty had so rapturously described seemed to fit what he and his wife, Betsy, were looking for. Could they come out for a visit and see for themselves?

Scotty had replied ASAP. *"Great to hear from you, come on out, you are welcome here. Stay as long as you want. Mom and Dad say hello. S. Roy."*

Like pioneers before them, the Kuseks took barely more than their savings and the optimism of youth. Cal would become a "Lincoln lawyer" and serve the rural community, taking a personal approach to the practice of law, one client at a time, and maybe from there he'd venture into local politics. For Betsy, nursing would always be a part of her life, but first she would be a mother and a working partner on the ranch. They envisioned open space and fresh air, raising their own food, getting involved in the schools, teaching their kids the right values. Both were eager for hard physical labor, believing that devotion to each other and their children would sustain them in the end.

The Kuseks realized if they drove across the continent, it wouldn't be for a visit, it would be for keeps. If their final destination turned out not to be the Dakotas, they'd try Washington or Oregon. If not cattle ranching, then a fruit tree orchard or a vegetable farm. The appeal of South Dakota was that they were practically giving land away out there. During the Depression, so many ranchers had gone belly-up and defaulted on their taxes that counties were selling foreclosed properties for as little as twenty bucks an acre.

They'd decided to take it slow on the trip out west, to sit back and enjoy the scenery. Later they would put their shoulders to the wheel, but for now the task was done. They'd managed to loosen their family ties bit by bit, enough so they could say their good-byes to Cal's family in Pennsylvania and Betsy's widowed father and sister, Marja, who lived in the Bronx. Their efficient partnership had taken care of every detail in the huge effort of moving. If they could find an inch of space in the overloaded station wagon, they could relax and be tourists in their own country.

They were free.

· · ·

The plan was to leave the city by ten a.m., but somehow it was five hours later, and Lance had missed his morning nap. He'd been cranky until he blessedly dropped off to sleep, his big blond head lolling against the window, pale translucent eyelids trembling in the warmth of the spring sun. Cal insisted on smoking his pipe, which caused Jo to announce over and over that she was "vomitatious." Jo, named for the independent heroine of *Little Women,* was working on coloring books. She wore her favorite overalls and her hair, sandy brown like her dad's, had just gotten a new pixie cut. She was a determined child, even at age four seeming to know her own mind, whispering to her baby-self as she chose her crayons, then approving them in her "grown-up" voice.

Somewhere around Paterson, New Jersey, Lance woke up crying and fussed for the next three hours, so that they had to make several rest stops to reshuffle the seating arrangements. Every time he was settled, Jo would innocently push him off the backseat, raising squalls of tears, so Betsy had to ride with Lance in her arms while he tried to squirrel away and grab the steering wheel. At least it was convenient for wiping his stuffy nose, which was turning into a cold.

It was dark by the time they found a motel, since most were still closed for the winter. After tripping over a loose step on the porch, the proprietor—half drunk, with a tubercular cough and falling-down pants—managed to open a frigid bungalow that hadn't seen fresh air since last year's Labor Day. When they discovered the room was too tiny to accommodate both their luggage and a rusty folding cot the owner had grudgingly dragged over, Betsy burst into exhausted tears, and Cal ended up sleeping on the cot with his feet sticking out the open door.

Tourism abandoned, the objective became getting to South Dakota as fast as possible. For seven days they drove with purpose, on turnpikes and toll roads, blacktops and main streets, stopping every few hours because the secondhand engine would be overheating again, until they crossed the Missouri River and realized that they were entering the promised land.

The sky was huge and their spirits rose. The prairie was hardly flat, but filled with vivid moss-green folds undulating across millions of acres of open plain—no markers, no fences, just the ageless tracks of winding creeks, spectacular as the African Serengeti, they imagined, and filled, it seemed, with as many wild animals. Herds of golden antelope sprang across their vision, and everywhere the air was filled with birds: chickadees, finches, flashing clouds of swooping terns, and, grandest of all, great blue herons, eagles, and hawks coasting high up on the thermal currents. Pitch-black cows and their babies wandered beneath the bare cottonwood trees, foraging on clumps of winterfat and sage, and the Kuseks stared in awe at their first sight of real cowboys.

They passed through empty towns with stunted names: Presho, Murdo, Kadoka, Wall. They spotted a family of wild mustangs, and man-made ponds with windmills to draw the water that was blanketed by hundreds and hundreds of squawking ducks and geese. In the distance there were flat-roofed farmhouses, but often, because the road had gone this way since the gold rush, they'd see miners' shacks so old that nothing remained but charcoal studs and air.

Finding their destination became a game. Cal would veer off sharply, calling, "That's it! That's our house!" while Betsy, trying to keep hold of Lance, would cry, *"Cal, don't!"* and Jo would jump up shouting, "Where? Daddy! Stop! You passed our house!"

"Uh-oh! Daddy made a mistake," Cal would answer. "That house isn't nice enough for us. Let's keep looking."

"Okay!"

This went on until a dark gray storm line manifested on the horizon and quickly grew into a towering thunderhead—so fast that Cal and Betsy barely had time to roll up the windows. The clouds were ugly beasts, sheared off at the top, with columns of black rolling undersides coming directly at them. A forked lightning strike hit the ground and everything turned chalk white, then a burst of rain came down so hard that Jo screamed and took cover, crying, *"Mommy!"* It sounded like when you spilled a can of marbles on a bare wood floor, only this was a giant pelting them with pails of marbles and thunderously shaking the car. A solid curtain of water obscured the view through the windshield. Cal struggled to keep the car steady, but the hardtop was flooded. The danger now was out-of-control vehicles coming toward them, whose headlights they couldn't see, so when they glimpsed a turnoff through the downpour, they took it.

Immediately they felt good hard gravel beneath the tires, and with relief continued on a little ways. Then the road turned bumpy, and without warning the gravel ended and gave way to slushy mud, causing them to fishtail wildly back and forth between the gullies on either side. Betsy, wide-eyed, clung to Lance, and Jo was thrown across the backseat. Cal gritted his teeth and fought the wheel, until they came to a gentle, almost anticlimactic stop. All at once they felt the right rear end of the wagon sink, and they couldn't go any farther.

Betsy struggled out of the car, still holding Lance in her arms. Instantly, like a slap in the face, the wind blew the door shut. *You're not wanted here,* it said. This was not the fresh fall wind that flew along Fifth Avenue, streaming the bright colors of department store banners and knocking off ladies' hats. This wind was burly and powerful, more than thirty miles an hour without a pause; this wind owned the prairie. Always had and always would, and everything that was there was because of it—what could grow and what couldn't, where the rain fell or was sucked up by drought, which direction the buffalo took to graze and how the Native Americans followed their migration.

Betsy felt a vertiginous sense of space. The wind took away all boundaries. It stripped you of past and future. Were her feet still on the ground? Nowhere was there evidence of humankind. Everywhere she turned she found the disorienting absence of buildings, of knowing where you are in the city by the crosshatches of the grid. Cal was coming around the hood to assess the damage. The only anchors in this new frontier were the trustworthy face of her husband and the baby's needful cry.

The car was tilted sidelong in the weeds. Jo, ordered to stay inside, was making circles of breath on the window, while Cal crouched beside the rear tire, which was sunk into the clay—not mud, he discovered, and much more slippery. It clung to everything and hardened quickly in the blowing air. Within moments their shoes were caked and their clothing was splattered with streaks. Where they'd turned off was a quarter of a mile away; they could no longer see the main road. They were in the middle of mauve-and-straw-colored alfalfa fields. The storm was holding off, leaving a sky of soft gray clouds that gusted beads of hail. The temperature was close to freezing and the wind kept on. Even outside for a short time, Betsy's hands were numb with cold and the baby's face bright red. The first hint of fear crept into her throat.

With clumsy fingers, she changed Lance's diaper on the front seat, found two sweaters and put them both on him. She took the keys from the ignition and gently closed the door, absurdly telling Jo, "Play with your brother." At least they'd be safe in the car. She opened the trunk and dug out their summer coats from the picnic ware and children's books they'd packed so carefully—useless stuff, she realized, unless they wanted to burn them for warmth. Another jolt of fear. Cal was prowling along the ditch. She brought him a light tweed blazer she'd found in the car.

"What are you doing?" she asked.

"First of all, we need something for traction."

She joined his search, but it was futile. There were no structures that might provide wooden planks to slip under the tires, like you would in a snowstorm back east; there weren't even trees.

"Cal! What are we going to do?"

"We'll get out of here," he promised.

"I didn't see any gas stations, did you?"

"Not for the last fifty miles," he said calmly.

Betsy didn't answer. She had only one bottle of formula left, but didn't want to burden him with that particular worry. It was four thirty and getting dark. It looked like another storm on the way. The wind that was bringing the developing rain seemed even stronger than before as if to test their resolve to make this move, here and now.

She clutched the thin summer coat around her, incongruously Easter yellow.

"I'm scared for the kids. Lance is just getting over a cold—"

Cal interrupted. "Look at the facts, Betsy. Don't go by emotions—what do your instruments say?"

She tried to laugh. "For God's sake, we're not flying an airplane!"

"The facts are . . . nobody's hurt, the kids are fine. There's nothing out here that can harm us. A big hungry bear is not going to come out of the woods, because there aren't any woods," he said, going for humor. "We'll get by, and in the morning I'll walk to the main road and flag someone down. Relax, honey. There's a bottle of Scotch in the glove compartment."

"Can't give the baby Scotch," Betsy observed drily.

"Hey, wait a minute. Hold the phone. There's something."

Cal's attention had been caught by the only object standing upright in the landscape of bowed grass. Twenty yards away the remnant of a cattle gate was hanging at an angle on its frame.

"Help me get that off."

It was made of pipe and discouragingly heavy. They pulled and twisted, and Cal took a tire iron to the hinges. They got it loose and dragged the thing toward the car, but Betsy's palms were freezing to the metal and she couldn't keep up. Finally Cal said, "Let me do it." He picked the gate up and heaved it over his head like some angry god dressed like a professor, staggering to the car, where he threw it to the ground and kicked it into position behind the sunken tire.

"You get in," he told Betsy. "Put the gear in reverse. When I tell you, hit the gas. Gently!"

They worked for fifteen minutes, easing backward until the tire mounted the metal rungs, nursing forward and gaining traction, but the gate kept slipping sideways. They'd reset and try again, but the spinning wheels dug deeper and finally it was just too cold to be out there. Inside the car, they saw in the mirror that their faces were windburned and their eyes bloodshot red. Cal turned the engine on so they had some heat, but Betsy was shivering so hard, she thought she'd never be warm again. Jo's teeth were chattering, but she laughed and pointed to their shoes, which had turned to solid blocks of clay.

"You have dinosaur feet!" she said.

Clay was everywhere—smeared on their noses, encrusting the seats, floor, dashboard, and no doubt jamming up the drivetrain under the car. Cal took a map from the glove compartment, along with the pint of Scotch. It was hard to pinpoint their location. It hardly mattered. They weren't going anywhere.

The Christmas lights that had adorned the blue Kusek house with the peaceful repose of a holiday evening were overwhelmed by scarlet police car flashers. The well-to-do enclave on West Boulevard had become a crime scene, ringing not with church bells but with sirens. Two ambulances left carrying bodies on stretchers. A coroner's van pulled up and parked. Coats on top of pajamas and boots over bare feet, neighbors stared in disbelief until the freezing rain drove them inside. Above the clouds the stars were tranquil, but in the pale net of lamplight that fell on the city streets below, a wound had been opened in this city, crimson red.

Wendy Kusek had been found dead at the scene. When Lance and their ten-year-old son, Willie, arrived at the emergency room of Mercy Medical Center, they were unconscious. Their pupils were dilated and they had difficulty breathing. IV lines were started and the patients were intubated for respiratory support. The doctors began their assessment of further injuries. They noted skull fractures, blood loss, and shock.

But when Jo Kusek arrived at the hospital from Portland, Oregon, her brother and nephew were no longer in the emergency room and there was confusion about whether they were still in surgery. It took her asking, "Where are they? Where are they?" of every person passing by in scrubs to determine that they had been transferred to intensive care. Former state trooper Randy Sturgis, who had become her protecting angel, walked Jo down from the surgical wing.

"Has anyone called Wendy's parents?" she asked.

He nodded. "It was a big snafu. They'd just left Illinois for vacation in Florida. I believe a relative got ahold of them and they turned right around."

Jo clutched at her stomach in a spasm of grief. "Lance will be devastated. Wendy is everything to him."

They'd reached the air-locked doors to the ICU. Only next of kin could go inside, so Randy Sturgis waited in the hallway.

Jo entered the cold hush of the critical care zone. A balding male nurse stood like an oracle behind a gray desk that seemed to be floating in a soft pool of light. Knowing that every word he said would carry the revelation of life or death, she walked toward him in slow motion, dreading his pronouncement, fixed on his clear, expectant eyes.

The word he spoke to her was "unstable."

On hearing this, Jo, too, seemed to lose her footing and become unbalanced. Without any awareness, her right hand had begun to claw at the smooth surface of the desk like an animal trying to escape.

"What does that mean? Unstable?"

"They're both on ventilators, which are breathing for them," the nurse explained. "They're getting IV fluids, and their brain functions are being assessed."

"Why is that?" she managed.

"They've received significant blows to the head."

"Is that how Wendy died? My sister-in-law?"

"I honestly don't know. The medical examiner has the last word on that."

"I can't believe it." Jo was tearless, still in shock. She shook her head. "How can this be?"

The nurse said, "I'm very sorry for your loss."

"Do you have any water?"

"I'll get you some," said the nurse, and returned with a plastic cup. Jo drank it all before she could ask, "What is the prognosis for my brother and Willie?"

"Really, it's impossible to tell," he said.

The nurse had a pleasant, clean-shaven face and a neutral way of relaying terrifying news. Her mind went blank, and in the next instant she couldn't remember anything he'd told her.

"What did you say about the brain functions again?" she asked.

"We don't know what's going on in the brain, which is why they're doing CAT scans."

"Nobody told me about the CAT scans . . . ," Jo murmured.

"Would you like more water?"

Jo shook her head. "I want to see them."

"The initial evaluation by the neurosurgeon is still ongoing," the nurse replied steadily. "He'll be out to talk to you when he's done, and then he'll let you know more. You're welcome to have a seat. There's coffee."

Jo did what she was told and sat in a chair. The tiny waiting room was darker and more comfortable than the public area in the surgical ward. The upholstery was new. Burgundy and navy. There was a low table with games for children to play with. She was alone, but her nervous system could not relax. She'd been on high alert for almost twenty hours.

Early yesterday morning the phone had rung in the Portland apartment Jo shared with her boyfriend, a firefighter named Warren Vitelli. It was not unusual for Warren to get an emergency call to duty, but when he realized it was from the Rapid City Police Department, and that it was for Jo, he snapped on the lights and their lives were changed forever.

It was Christmas Day. He couldn't leave because of work and she couldn't get a flight until the following morning. Then the plane had sat on the ground in Portland for ninety minutes while a crew was located to clean the toilets, because that was a federal regulation, the pilot announced, over boos and jeers. Upon landing in Denver, Jo had less than ten minutes to make the connecting flight. A tragedy was unfolding, but it would take too long to explain, so she commandeered an electric cart, gave the driver five bucks, and begged him to go to her gate, where she leaped off just as the doors to the aircraft were closing.

At the terminal in Rapid City, waiting on the tarmac to deplane, there had been another delay. Trapped in the aisle with winter-coated travelers clutching oversized gifts, Jo had been stymied into an unfocused daze when she was jolted awake by a woman's voice asking, "Are you all right?"

The woman was unremarkable in every way—middle-aged, a dark coat and dark hair, and an unexpected smile was all Jo would remember. She realized that she must have looked totally miserable, clutching the handle of her carry-on and ready to sprint.

"There was an accident, and I have to get to the hospital," Jo offered.

"I'm sorry," said the woman. "Are you from here?"

Jo nodded. "I grew up outside of Rapid."

"We live in Custer," the woman said, naming a nearby town. "I'll pray for your loved ones."

The line began to move.

"Thank you," said Jo, totally taken aback, and then a second miracle occurred. Another woman, younger, who'd been waiting in the aisle in front of them, overheard their conversation. She turned around and said, "I'll pray for them, too," before hurrying off the plane.

In the broad-minded city where Jo was living now, strangers didn't pray for you. They didn't ask if you were okay or facing the unthinkable.

As she sat alone in the waiting room outside the intensive care unit, Jo wondered where those openhearted ladies were when she was growing up. She already knew the answer, and it didn't make her feel any better.

2

It had stopped hailing long enough for State Trooper Randy Sturgis to spot the station wagon stuck by the side of the road, down on the turnoff where he often checked in on Wolf Harrington, who had been his high school math teacher, now in his eighties and confined to a wheelchair. It wasn't graveled good up there, he knew, and the road would be a sea of muck, so he turned off the highway and stopped a dozen yards in.

At that time Randy Sturgis drove his own car for the department, a maroon 1948 Plymouth Special Deluxe, which didn't have a siren or revolving lights, just POLICE gamely written on the doors. He grabbed his flashlight and walked through the misty dusk to where he discovered there were people huddled inside. The husband got out and shook his hand—an outsider, for certain, with New York license plates and a nice sport jacket just about ruined.

"Glad to see you," Cal said.

The officer was tall enough to tower over him. He was also unusually thin, but you couldn't see that beneath the gleaming rain-soaked slicker. He had two-tone hair, white at the temples and black toward the crown, but you couldn't see that, either, beneath his waterproofed hat covered in transparent vinyl film that gave off a *pop!* with every raindrop. The forehead was high, the brows ordinary, but his eyes were wide in unguarded amazement. You had the impression that nothing in the course of duty—not a bloody double murder or a speeding ticket— would change that look of good-natured, childlike bewilderment.

"Stuck in the mud?" he asked with a friendly smile.

"Yes, sir," Cal replied. "We've tried several times to get out, but no go. Would you happen to have a rope?"

"I do have a rope, and ordinarily I'd be happy to give you a tow, but that would make two of us stuck."

"My family's inside," Cal said. He wanted to snap his fingers in the man's face to get some kind of reaction.

"How're they doing?"

"The kids are pretty hungry."

Randy Sturgis ran the flashlight beam over the half-buried tires.

"Tourists, are you?"

"Visitors." Cal realized he had to break through somehow. "Say, I'm a friend of Scotty Roy, at the Crazy Eights Ranch—"

Immediately Randy Sturgis straightened up.

"So that's *you*. You're the pilot!" he said, shaking Cal's hand all over again. "You're a hero, Scotty says—"

"I just did my job. There were a lot more deserving heroes than me over there—"

"—and you're staying with the Roys till you find a place of your own," Randy Sturgis announced, giving Cal his first taste of small-town hearsay.

"Just for a while. We're hoping to—"

"You know, we got Ellsworth Air Force Base, you might want to go up there sometime, they'd be happy to put out the welcome mat for a veteran, show you around."

"Sure thing," Cal said, blinking rainwater out of his eyes.

"Let's get you out of here. Best bet would be to get the wife and kids to my car and I'll take you up to the Roys'. Think we can manage that?"

They grabbed one suitcase, wrapped the children in blankets, locked the car, and trekked through the flooded wash toward the faint red pulse of the Plymouth's running lights. When they had all squeezed in, Randy Sturgis reached behind his seat and came up with a green metal lunch box.

"Here, you take these," he told Betsy, passing her a wax paper bag filled with doughnuts. "Fresh this morning." He laughed merrily. "Probably seems like a long time ago."

"Another lifetime," Betsy agreed, offering a doughnut to Jo, who was wide-eyed and stunned to silence by everything that had happened. "We just can't thank you enough."

"We got nice people here. We all pitch in and help each other. No other way to do it, really."

By the time Trooper Sturgis knocked on the door of the main house at the Crazy Eights Ranch it was past nine o'clock at night, but Chris "Dutch" Roy answered, fully dressed in wet jeans and a sheepskin vest over a wool shirt. He was a big, heavyset man, barrel-chested, six foot five, and took up the light in the doorway. He'd been tending to broken gutters, he explained, looking curiously at the rain-soaked refugees huddled on his porch.

"You know this fella?" Randy Sturgis asked ironically when Scotty Roy appeared behind his father.

"Like hell I do!" Scotty shouted, bounding out to shake hands with Cal.

He was noticeably shorter than his dad, with those oddly bright light blue eyes, and as wiry and high-strung as Cal remembered of the wild airman who'd jockeyed to be first in line to parachute into the dark. The body heat just came off him. He was in jeans, a white undershirt, and stocking feet.

"Great to see you," Cal said sincerely. "Been a long trip."

"Don't I know it! Look at you! You made it! And who do we have here?" he asked, squatting down eyeball to eyeball with Jo, who leaned shyly against Betsy's leg.

"She's tired," Betsy explained, caressing her daughter's hair.

"Do you like baby chicks?" asked Scotty.

Jo nodded sleepily.

"We've got baby chicks and goats and maybe even a few calves, what do you think of that? Hey, Mama! They're here!"

When Doris Roy came into the entryway, the resemblance to her son was almost comical. She was a robust little woman with smooth pink skin who wore her short white hair in tight ringlets like a poodle. Her teal-blue eyes were as startling as Scotty's, but it was her take-over energy that was most like his.

"Randy, I hope you parked away from the truck."

"Yes, ma'am," the trooper said.

"Dutch ain't so good at backing out."

Her husband frowned. "Since when?"

She ignored him. "Come on in, you all!"

Betsy hesitated at the threshold. "Are you sure, Mrs. Roy? We don't want to mess up your clean floor."

The older woman grabbed Betsy's arm and pulled her into the warmth of the house. Along the way they passed an oversized living room, a hodgepodge of mismatched sofas, easy chairs, and magazine tables, with deer heads mounted over a stone fireplace—the kind of place meant for a lot of people to eat great quantities of food. They settled around a big oak table in the kitchen. Doris and Scotty were like little indoor tornadoes, producing leftover macaroni casserole, whiskey, milk, and homemade ginger snaps, even an old crib and baby blankets from the storeroom. Cal asked about Scotty's sweetheart, a girl he'd said he was engaged to marry, which seemed to take him by surprise.

"Oh, that broke off," Scotty said shortly, and Cal wondered if he'd forgotten over the years, or maybe, under the influence of the African sun, and the gin they used to drink on top of the old railway cars, Scotty had made the whole thing up.

Doris handed Betsy a pile of linens.

"Don't you worry, dear, you're almost there," she said, apologizing for the cabin not being all set up, but they hadn't known when to expect them. "You're lucky to have such a beautiful family," she crooned.

"We're lucky you can take us in," Betsy replied gratefully. "And that Mr. Sturgis came along and was nice enough to help."

"People here are nice," Doris agreed.

"I hope so," Betsy said. "We left our worldly goods in the car."

"Harrington's road," Randy Sturgis put in.

"Oh, don't worry, stuff like that don't happen here. Not like New York City," Dutch said, smiling with big teeth. Despite his vigor, he looked worn down by outdoor work, with ruddy, veined cheeks and tired eyes beneath a pair of bushy eyebrows gone to gray.

"We'd better get the kids to bed," said Cal.

"Come down in the morning," Dutch said heartily. "After breakfast I'll give you the nickel tour."

The children, dead asleep, were carried through the heavy rain to the ranch truck, along with the crib, and Scotty drove half a mile over potholes and logs to a pitch-black maw that turned out to be the darkened shape of a stucco-sided log cabin. He said it was built by homesteaders in the 1890s.

The cabin had two rooms, including the kitchen, and a corrugated tin roof that magnified the snap of every raindrop like a drum. Raw, unpainted wallboard had been coarsely nailed in places to the logs. He flipped on a light and said, "Oh, hell!"

"What's the matter?"

"They been in here again."

Cal asked, "Who?"

"Local kids," Scotty said dismissively, kicking cigarette butts and beer cans into the fireplace.

"What's that?" exclaimed Betsy, pointing to the head of some poor animal on the floor, maybe a raccoon, with patches of fur stuck to the skull and a piece of spine sticking out.

"Probably a cat."

Betsy watched, horrified, as he kicked it into the fireplace as well.

"A house cat could do that?"

"Cougars," Scotty explained. "You better keep watch on the baby."

Betsy sought Cal's reassurance with a worried expression. *Is that a joke?* He shrugged.

"So the cougars and the hoodlums just kind of wander in and out?" Cal wondered, pleasantly enough.

Scotty didn't answer, absorbed in pointing out the features of the cabin. There was cold running water and a privy out back. No phone, and a generator for electricity.

"You got your kindling already cut," he said, indicating they could start a fire in the iron stove. "I'll be back at six a.m.," he promised, adding generously, "You might as well sleep in."

Cal used his last drop of energy to put up the crib. There were two cots with thin cotton mattresses on bare springs. They pushed them together, tore off their damp clothing, and climbed in with Jo for warmth. Cal fell asleep instantly, but Betsy's eyes stayed wide, thinking about the raccoon head and where the rest of the body might turn up, alerted by the constant wind.

The wind was big and it was everywhere. She was afraid that it would shake the house, but the stucco and logs held firm. Sometimes the wind sounded like a distant train whistle, changing pitch as it tore across the grasslands. Sometimes it was very close and regular, like a big, breathing animal just outside the door.

3

Everything was golden, Jo thought, when she woke up in the Roys' cabin the next day, even the walls, which were made of logs like her Lincoln Logs play set, only huge. There was a friendly little fire in the black stove, which Jo knew not to touch. Mommy and Lance were still asleep, but Daddy wasn't there. She wondered where he'd gone, and if he was the one who'd made the fire, so they'd be warm while he was away. The sun was coming through the windows and Jo was glad the big rain was over. She remembered being trapped in the car when it wouldn't go. She'd rubbed a clear spot on the glass so she could see the familiar shapes of her parents, her mother holding Lance like she always does, but they were blurry and far away, and she had been alone and cold in the car, telling stories to herself.

She felt small as an ant when Daddy wasn't there. He was big and kind as a papa bear and always knew where they were going and how long it would take to get there. She ran a finger along the blanket that was covering her. It was made of squares. Inside every square there was a tiny Christmas tree. Jo slipped out from under the blanket very quietly because it wouldn't be any fun if they woke up, there would be all kinds of *"projects"* her mother would make her do, but for now she could sneak all over the new house, playing her favorite floating game, where she had to fly like a fairy around the whole room by only stepping on the furniture. Her bare feet were not allowed to touch the floor—not even once—because there was a huge ocean of deep water down there.

She started out on the sofa, making sure to jump on every cushion. At the end of it she came to a flat wooden arm that made a natural step to the seat of a chair and then to the top of the kitchen table, which was made of silvery metal folded at the corners, like a package, and hammered in with nails.

It was exciting to be up there, like at the top of the monkey bars in the park. First of all, as Jo liked to say in her grown-up voice, like Daddy, *"First of all,"* it was right next to a window that had high curtains with bears walking on them, and she could touch the bears if she stood up on the table, because, first of all, no matter what you did, that table didn't shake. It had a boat on it that was really a lamp, two pink pigs that were really salt and pepper shakers, but the most interesting thing was her mother's black purse, which happened to be open—which it never was—a cave of hidden pockets as forbidden as the dangerous water that was rising quickly up the white legs of the table.

Spicy smells were coming out of the purse. Jo sat cross-legged on the table to examine it. Dollar bills were soft and had a special aroma like face powder. She knew they were kept in *Mother's wallet,* but that would be at the bottom. She'd have to wiggle her fingers way down into the cave to get it and there might be snakes. Thinking about this made Jo hesitate, but the earthy scents kept drawing her closer, knowing that dollars meant toys, and if she had enough dollars she could have as many toys as she could want, and none for Lance. Then a frightening lady's face was looking at her right through the tall window! Was the lady a giant? Jo was afraid the lady could see *"exactly what you've been up to!"* but she didn't seem angry. The lady was motioning for Jo to come outside, so Jo climbed off the table.

The front door was easy to open. It didn't have two locks like the door in the other house in New York City. Outside the wind was blowing everything, even her hair, but it wasn't cold wind, it was hot. She put her hand up to shade her eyes from the sun. All the way to the bright blue sky there was yellow grass that was blowing with a crackly sound. The lady came from around the back of the house. Now Jo could see why she was tall enough to look through the window. She was riding a real live horse! It was amazing to see an old woman wearing a cowgirl hat on a horse. The horse's feet snapped sharply on the ground and its head went up and down, and then it stopped and stood perfectly still. It had large spots in two colors: brown and white.

Jo stared in wonder. The lady was very high up, as high as the roof. She was dressed in dungarees, and she was wearing gloves.

"Is your dad at home?"

Jo shook her head sadly. "I don't know where he is."

"Do you remember me?" the lady asked.

The child didn't answer.

"I reckon you don't. You were very tired."

Jo was fascinated by the gloves. They had silver buttons and leather fringes, and Jo recognized right away that they were magical. They could make the horse fly, and the girl who wore them would have the power to ride that flying horse. In that way, Doris Roy and her deerskin riding gloves would become part of Jo Kusek's earliest memories of South Dakota: the golden light; the queenly figure towering above, framed by an aura of sun, wearing a talisman that could give you powers, arousing in the child her first exotic, unnamable feelings of lust.

"My name's Doris and I live in the main house down the road," the lady said. "I bet I know *your* name."

"No, you don't."

"Jo-Anne."

"You're wrong. It's Jo."

"Joe? Not Jo-Anne? Just Joe? I don't believe it! That's a boy's name."

"It's my name, too," the girl insisted, stamping her foot like the horse.

"Well, all right then, Miss Jo!" Doris Roy said with some amusement. "Where's your mama?"

"In the house."

"Run and get her."

Jo turned and saw that her mother was already coming out the front door with Lance on her hip. Jo squinted up at the lady, expecting something bad to happen because there she was, alone and out of the house, but instead the lady offered to let Jo pet her horse.

"What's his name?" Jo asked.

"His name is Pete. He's part dog, likes to be scratched behind the ears."

Jo stretched up. "I can't reach."

"Easy," Doris told Pete.

The horse flicked his ears, relaxed and lowered his head almost to the ground. His eyes drooped when Jo found the sweet spot. She smoothed his wiry hair. He had bangs, like hers. And eyelashes. She stuck a finger in his nostril and he sneezed gooey green stuff all over her nightgown.

Doris said, "That means he likes you."

Betsy had panicked when she couldn't find Jo in the cabin, thrown on a robe, and raced outside. Now she was surprised to find Scotty's mom sitting on a horse, all decked out in cowboy gear and, despite her small stature, looking dominating in the saddle. She wore a washed-out light green checkered shirt, and her white curls were neatly coiled beneath a huge black cowboy hat, while Betsy looked and felt like a mess, hair undone, brainless and exhausted from endless days of driving that had culminated with yesterday's battle with the mud and rain.

"Doris!" Betsy managed. "Good morning! What are you doing out here?" she admonished Jo, not wanting to seem completely disorganized in the older woman's eyes.

"It's all right," Doris said. "She's saying hello to Pete."

"Pete likes me," Jo said, looking up at her mother with a bashful smile.

Doris said, "I take it my son Scotty ain't here with your husband?"

"He was here earlier. They left to dig out the wagon."

"That'll be a job." Doris tightened the reins and the horse woke up. "Never mind. I'll go over to the Gibsons'."

"Is something wrong?" Betsy asked.

"There's a cow stuck in a draw."

Jo broke out in high-pitched giggles.

"What's so funny?" asked her mother.

"A cow can't fit in a drawer!"

Betsy and Doris both cracked up laughing.

"A cow *is* too big for a drawer," Doris said. "But this is what we call a *draw*—"

"Like with crayons?"

The two women were howling and wiping their eyes.

"No," Betsy managed, "it's a place in the ground like a giant crack—"

"See that bunch of trees, way out there?" Doris chimed in. "That's what we call a *draw*. You can't tell from here, but it's got water in the bottom of it because of the rain."

"If you can't see it, how do you know the cow got stuck?"

"Well," said Doris, leaning forward on the saddle horn, "I was out checking fences and I heard her bawling. They do that, go down for a drink and can't get back on their feet, just like some men I know," she added with a wink.

"Will the cow be okay?"

"We'll need a truck to pull her free. We could use Fred Gibson's truck. He'll be home—he's got testicular cancer," Doris explained matter-of-factly. "You want to see that cow get saved?" Doris asked.

"Me?" said Jo, pointing to herself.

"If you mind me, you can watch."

"Can I, Mommy?"

Betsy tried to picture a cow being pulled out of mud by a truck and whether that was a safe place in this unknown territory for her little girl. She was so discombobulated that she found it hard to think.

"But we don't have the car—" she began.

"She can ride with me over on Pete."

Jo was staring at Betsy with a look of frozen excitement. "Can I?"

Lance was fussing, so Betsy put him down, then grabbed him up again before he could toddle off the porch.

"Do you want to go and watch?"

Jo nodded hesitantly, waiting for her mother's reaction. For a moment, neither of them moved, equally immobilized by the lightning speed with which their lives were changing. Jo was old enough to know she had to wait until the light turned green and hold her mother's hand on the street. To look through the peephole and say, *"Who is it?"* before opening the door, and to never let her baby brother touch an electric outlet; but what were the rules in the middle of nowhere?

"Go on and get dressed," Doris ordered from on high. "Does Jo own any kind of pants?"

"Yes!" said Betsy, releasing her daughter into their new world with a decisive smile. "Yes, in fact, Jo prefers pants. You have to learn to ride a horse sometime," she told the girl.

"I *do*?" Jo's eyes were huge.

"Doris will take good care of you. What a marvelous adventure!" Jo ran into the house.

"She's a pistol," Doris said admiringly. "How're *you* getting on?"

"My head's still spinning. I don't know where to start."

"You'll get yourself going. Not a lot of choice in the matter."

"When we get settled, we'd love to have you over for dinner," Betsy said, wondering if people here had dinner parties, and how she could possibly pull one off with a wood-burning stove.

Doris stretched in the saddle, easing her hips.

"How did you and Calvin come to meet?" she asked.

"He got me out of jail!" Betsy answered brightly.

Doris laughed. "What'd you do, get a parking ticket?"

"I was a salesgirl at a department store. We went on strike and got arrested. He worked for the union. It was my first job."

"Your first job, you had to go along," Doris said sympathetically.

"No, the union was right. We deserved a lot better."

Doris Roy didn't answer. Her bright blue eyes scanned the distant horizon.

"I recall that years ago they tried to organize the meatpackers," she mused slowly. "Out in Sioux City. Railroad, too. Unionizing. Doesn't stick."

The sun was only halfway to zenith and already puffs of heat were rising from the earth. Pete was dozing. Neither woman spoke.

Betsy found herself at a loss. "So how did you meet Dutch?"

"I met Dutch at a square dance," Doris announced. "You don't have those," she added loftily.

Having dressed herself in her trusty red corduroys, Jo bounded from the cabin, climbed the porch rail, and mounted up in the saddle in front of Doris, leaning back against her cushiony chest.

"Bye, honey," Betsy called. "Have fun!"

Jo wasn't listening. It was the first time she had seen the world from between the ears of a horse, and she wasn't looking back.

"I want to steer!" she demanded, and the two of them took off at a lope as smooth as a carousel. Betsy watched her daughter disappear in the arms of Doris Roy.

4

It was afternoon when the station wagon appeared on the road from the main house. Cal got out of the car carrying groceries. Betsy was sitting on the porch. She'd pinned her hair up but it still whipped across her eyes. Lance was propped against the steps, playing with rocks in his own small whirlpool of dirt.

"You look like real pioneers!" Cal shouted over the moaning wind.

Closer, he could see that Betsy was using a screwdriver to chip away at the clay that had hardened around their shoes.

"Got the car out," Cal reported. "Imagine this: the garage owner, his name is Ken Addis, refused to let me pay."

"Why not?"

"Scotty told him—and everybody else—that we served together, and Ken has a policy that he won't take money from veterans. Isn't that amazing?"

"In a million years that would never happen in New York." Betsy stood to take the groceries. "*And* you found a *store*!" she said with mock ecstasy.

"It's not the A&P," he warned, kissing her.

She'd always liked the way he kissed. He had sweet lips, firm and tender, and did none of that tonguing stuff men think is the point. Lightly, he brushed the back of his hand against her breast.

Betsy smiled against his cheek. "Don't do that . . . unless you mean it."

"Who said I don't mean it?" Cal looked around suggestively. "Where is Jo?"

"She's with Doris. I thought they'd be back by now."

"I'll go get her," Cal said, nuzzling his wife's neck. "Later."

Maybe it was a warning note in the wind or Betsy's habit of being discreet in front of the children, but she pulled away, alert.

"What's the matter?" he asked.

Betsy looked chagrined.

"I think I might have said the wrong thing to Doris."

"What on earth did you say?"

"She asked how we met and I told her about the union."

"What's wrong with that?"

"I don't know, she got all huffy. This ain't exactly a union town," Betsy said playfully. "I'm afraid she was offended."

Cal took that into consideration.

"We have to be ourselves," he decided. "That's the whole point. They'll get used to us, we'll get used to them. It'll all work out."

He gave her a reassuring hug before getting back in the car. Betsy nodded and tried to shake it off, but knew she'd be nervous until every-one was back safe and sound in the cabin. In order to occupy her mind, she decided to give Lance a bath. He was too big for the sink, but she managed to sit him down on a towel placed over the edge and sponge-bathe his muscular little body clean of prairie grime, leaning him back in the crook of her elbow to carefully pour water from a measuring cup over his hair while he slipped all over the place, pleased with herself for not getting baby shampoo in his eyes, although she herself was soak-ing wet. Wrapped in the towel, rosy and warm, he smiled as she sang, *"Lance, Lance, put on pants,"* and got him into pajamas and gave him a bottle, her body relaxing along with his as she watched his eyes slowly soften into sleep.

She laid him in the crib and turned on the lamps, as it was already dark. She examined the cans of soup, Vienna sausage, and other items Cal had bought. He'd picked up a copy of the *Rapid City Journal* and, thank God, a package of beer. She cracked one open and took a long, cold swallow, glancing at the front page.

She was astonished to see that the headlines were all about Senator Joe McCarthy's attack on Owen Lattimore, accusing Lattimore of being a top Russian spy. The newspaper's editors gave a lot of space to McCarthy, rehashing his March 8 testimony before the Senate Subcommittee on the Investigation of Loyalty of State Department Employees. *You'd think they'd be more concerned about the price of corn than chasing phantom Reds,* Betsy thought.

"Good Lord," she mused aloud. "The press loves this lunatic."

It went on to say their own senator from South Dakota, Karl E. Mundt, had introduced a bill *"to crack down on Communist conspiracies that threatened to overthrow the government of the United States and set up a dictatorship."*

Why was she surprised that the spores of anti-Communist hysteria had taken root here, right under her feet? She was certain that she had not been wrong about Doris Roy's allergic reaction to the mention of workers organizing. It was the same die-hard point of view as her father's: belonging to a union was a step away from socialism, which meant it was a hair's breadth from spying for Russia, which is why Betsy had never told her father that for a brief period of time, when she was a salesgirl at Gimbels department store, she'd been a member of the Communist Party.

Her stomach tightened and she felt very much alone in hundreds of miles of pitch-dark prairie, far from her youthful flirtation with the party, yet maybe not. Her own thoughts turned against her, and she began to defend herself from invisible accusations, which was ridiculous. She'd quit the party just after she met Cal. She'd grown out of those ideas by then. She scolded herself to stop. It was harmless nostalgia, another life, before marriage, before children, when she was a brave, romantic, trusting young girl on the other side of the country.

She saw herself walking down Thirty-Third Street on a steamy summer morning in 1941. She'd ridden the subway down from the Bronx, carefully dressed in a navy-blue rayon shirtwaist and pumps, blond curls tucked beneath a wide-brimmed hat, determined to play her part. She waited on Broadway for the light to turn. Boys pushing garment racks raced by. Businessmen pressed around her, sweating through their shirts, hatless, suit jackets over their arms. On the other side of Herald

Square the picketers were packed in tightly—fifteen hundred strong, the papers said. The swarm of placards proclaiming STRIKE! made the word jump out through the full-leaved trees.

At the store, Betsy Ferguson was another obedient clerk in a starched white blouse. She had always been tall for her age, with rangy arms that made her a high scorer in basketball, but in the store, like everybody else, she played it dumb as the mannequins in the window. For nine hours a day she kept up a courteous smile, then limped back to the subway crippled by foot cramps from standing all day without breaks. A six-day workweek paid $14.50. The girls were kept in line by a network of spies and store detectives and forced to ask permission to get a drink of water.

When Betsy first was hired, dark-haired, blue-eyed Elaine O'Grady, who worked in Fashonia Dresses on the fourth floor, had been the kindliest of the girls, explaining what was what. She warned Betsy about employees who were stools for management, squealing on whoever was in the union or a member of the Communist Party. Elaine was both. Later, when she was slipped a handbill about a meeting, Betsy understood that her new friend was risking her job.

Elaine O'Grady had come honestly to her beliefs. Her mother and baby brother died in the influenza epidemic of 1917 when she was two years old. Her father placed her in a Catholic home for children in Queens and disappeared forever. She lived there until she was released at age sixteen.

"I took my little bag and walked a couple of miles to a boardinghouse," she'd told Betsy on a lunch break in the park. "It was the worst year of the Great Depression, but I didn't know a lot about it because we were well fed and insulated by the nuns. I didn't realize how terrible it was until I saw things for myself—desperate people looking for jobs, doctors driving taxicabs, people who'd lost all their money jumping off buildings. I thought, *What kind of bleak, horrible world have I been sent into?*

"I met a fellow at the boardinghouse who was a member of the Young Communist League. I'd never heard much about Communism, but I would listen to anyone who could explain the reasons for the awful situation I was in. What he said made sense. YCL became my family."

Betsy was so inspired by Elaine's courageous story of facing the world alone that she joined not only the union but the Young Communist League as well, which turned out to be one party after another—beach parties, boat parties—it even had a girls' all-city basketball team!—a marvelous social club made up of smart young activists full of juice, looking for answers, as eager as Betsy was to create a world without the ups and downs of boom or bust, uncertainties, poverty, and war. It fit with Betsy's idea of herself: that she was always ready to lend a hand, and here were people united by causes larger than themselves, while others—like the bosses at Gimbels—cared only about the dollar. The union asked, *"Which side are you on?"* and Betsy knew.

She crossed the street to the park across from the strikers. It was breathlessly hot, even in the shade of the maple trees. On benches set against banks of rhododendrons, an array of New Yorkers sat stupefied, dreading each degree of rising temperature. There was birdsong. The baking sidewalk tiles released the stench of pigeon rot and the ground-in residue of a million, million footsteps. In another hour the humidity would be in full bloom—the kind of humidity that made you grateful for the dirty warm drafts of the subway.

Yet the men on strike wore suits and neckties and the women proper summer dresses with heels. It was important to convey that retail workers were protesting peacefully and were not a bunch of roughhouse troublemakers. Just now Betsy could hear through the traffic the high voices of female picketers singing, *"I am a union woman / Just as brave as I can be / I do not like the bosses / And the bosses don't like me . . ."* But their innocent gaiety was held back by rows of coppers on steadfast brown horses and police vans.

Betsy joined Elaine and the picketers as they continued their slow waltz around the block. Selling expensive clothes to rich women did not fit Elaine's socialist ideals, but it paid for her split of a one-bedroom apartment shared with three other gals, and supported her real life, which was writing a novel. It was to be a raw exposé of the life of a working girl inside a big department store, she explained. She was incessantly writing in a spiral-bound book, even as they marched, and almost bumped into a lamppost when the column of protestors in front of them stopped short.

There was some kind of ruckus going on at the main entrance. Strikers were yelling at Gimbels customers trying to enter the store not to cross the picket line. Long-simmering resentment between low-paid shopgirls and uptown ladies broke into open war. There were screams and threats. Someone threw a bottle of red ink at a gray-haired shopper, ruining her white linen suit.

"This is disgraceful!" she cried. "I'm going to call the mayor!"

A whistle blew.

Shouts of *"Here they come!"*

Mounted police plunged into the crowd, swinging nightsticks. Armored motorcycles appeared, roaring around the block. Police trucks equipped with tear gas blocked off the streets. People ran. Uniforms and detectives bored through the crowd, clubbing anyone in their way with blackjacks and fists, pushing people off their feet. It seemed hundreds of sirens were screaming at once. Strikers grappled with hired thugs. The orderly demonstration became a fighting mob of bloodied heads and faces.

Betsy and Elaine tried to duck into a doorway, but they were pulled apart. Big hands clamped around Betsy's arms. Up close, the cops looked larger than life. Their taut faces and heavy pistols made her legs tremble in surrender.

Elaine shouted, "Stay strong! A union lawyer will get you out! Remember why we're doing this!"

She was dragged in one direction and Betsy the other, marched to the curb and forced into a police wagon with other striking workers. Inside it was dark and smelled like a sewer. There was a metal grate down the middle, one side for men, one for women. It already held several common criminals a lot worse off than the strikers were. Betsy could make out a young black girl wearing a summer halter dress that showed scrawny shoulder bones. Her mouth was cut. She pressed a cloth against her lips but it was already soaked with blood that pooled freely on the floor. Another woman had a blanket over her head. Beneath it was a feral, dirt-stained face. She was carrying on an argument with Jesus in a guttural voice that wasn't human. Staring emptily through the grate was a middle-aged white man wearing a threadbare suit, tie, and brown cap, unshaven, with haunted rheumy eyes.

"Where are they taking us?" Betsy wondered out loud.

"Downtown," answered a union member on the other side of the divider, a gray-haired older fellow wearing a loud red sport jacket and crumpled porkpie hat. "First time, sweetheart?" he whispered hoarsely.

Betsy nodded, staring wide-eyed. He'd been smashed across the nose and his entire face was swollen purple.

"Don't name names. Never give 'em a straight answer," he mumbled, swaying listlessly with the movement of the wagon.

"I swear I won't," she promised.

The injured girl moaned a high-pitched, keening cry. The despondent man had a racking cough. The rest of the strikers huddled in silence, forsaking their defiant songs. The siren went on and the van picked up speed, going south until they reached the Women's House of Detention, a severe monolith that rose like a fortress on Tenth Street in the heart of Greenwich Village. The men would go on to the Federal Detention Center on West Street, and after that, she could not imagine.

Betsy climbed out with her female comrades to an alley filled with the familiar New York City smell of wet asphalt and rotting garbage. Clothing ripped, bodies bruised, shoes and purses somehow gone, they tried to muster dignity as they were led to a steel-plated door. Inside they were escorted down a grimy passage that wound around to the booking desk, where the benches were full of despairing women waiting to be processed, among them the black girl from the van, slumped against the wall. Her slack arms showed bluish needle marks.

They made Betsy stand beside a giant yardstick to have her mug shots taken, side and front. Then a matron called her name and marched her down a corridor that reeked of industrial paint and soured milk. She was burly as a wrestler, with an iron grip on Betsy's upper arm as she steered her into the lockup—rows of cells where inmates, dressed in stiff white prison-issue frocks, were listlessly sprawled on their bunks under the weighty blanket of stultifying heat. All at once they stirred, and then every prisoner was on her feet at the bars, calling *"New bitch!"* and worse, a clanging roar of obscenities that accompanied Betsy on the long walk to the holding area.

The matron turned the key in a huge lock that opened an empty cell. There was a toilet with no stall. Betsy decided she'd rather die than use it.

"Now what?" she asked.

"You're here until they decide what to do with you."

The matron's footsteps echoed briefly on the steel floor, quickly overcome by the screeching taunts of the inmates. Betsy sat on a concrete bench and tried not to stick her fingers in her ears. She stared at the bricks in the wall, four times the size of subway tiles, as if to emphasize that everything here was bigger than you. Mortified by defeat, she wondered desperately what had happened to Elaine and the others, if union headquarters even knew that she was here, when a lawyer would show up, and what her father would say when she was finally allowed to make that phone call.

The thought made her stomach go sour. Her father, Albert Ferguson, was an angry man. He'd owned a shipping company that went under during the Depression. A few years later her mother, Rosslyn, died of bone cancer within weeks of being diagnosed. His wife's death broke his will. An alcoholic spiral drove him to his knees and he never got up, but he held on to his hatreds, especially of unions. Betsy had had to lie to get out of the house for meetings. He'd disown her completely if he knew she'd also joined the Young Communist League.

The Tudor mansion in Scarsdale had been sold, and the remaining three Fergusons moved to an apartment on the Grand Concourse in the Bronx. Betsy had dropped out of Hunter College and given up her dream of becoming a doctor. Instead, she took the Gimbels job to support her father and disabled sister, Marja, who had contracted measles at six months old and was partially blind. It was Marja's handicap that had inspired Betsy to become a doctor and, poignantly, Marja's care that had forced her to abandon it.

Tension from the worry that her absence was undoubtedly causing her father and sister was the hardest thing to endure—an unending drumbeat that made her want to jump out of her skin. Hours later, an orderly came through and put a ham sandwich and a cup of pop through the bars. She still hadn't heard the charges or been allowed to call home. Abruptly a different matron appeared, this one with glasses and a sucked-in frown.

"You," she said.

Back at the booking desk, a telephone was plunked down in front of Betsy.

"Three minutes," the matron commanded.

Betsy was so shaken that she had to dial her home number twice.

"Papa?" she said when he answered. "I'm sorry for calling late. I know you must be worried—"

"I'm not worried, I'm *hungry*! Where are you?" he demanded. "It's way past dinnertime."

She pictured him picking up the phone in the living room, rye on the rocks in the other hand—bald, thin except for a portly middle, still dressing every day for business in a crisp white shirt she'd ironed for him and a pin-striped vest.

"Papa, there's food in the fridge. There's a roast left over from yesterday, just look. Can you please put Marja on?"

"Hi, Betsy," came her sister's voice. "Did the subway break down or something?"

"Marja, I'm in trouble."

"Why? What happened?"

"I'm in jail."

"What are you talking about?" Marja squealed, sounding like she was on the edge of hysteria. "Why would you be *in jail*?"

"I was arrested on the picket line."

"Oh, no—"

"I'll be out in a couple of hours—"

"Just a minute," her sister interrupted, and Betsy could hear the news repeated to Albert and then a crash, as if he'd thrown a Chinese vase or stumbled over the kidney-shaped coffee table.

"Marja!" Betsy shouted. "Listen! I'm going to get out, I'm waiting for the union lawyer . . ."

Despite the fuzziness of the connection, she could hear her father's harsh voice demanding, *"Give me the phone!"* Then, "Where the hell are you?"

To her shame, Betsy discovered that her mouth was dry and her voice had shrunk. "I've been arrested and I'm in the Women's House of Detention, Papa. On Tenth Street in the Village—"

"Good!" he said. "That's exactly where you belong!"

The matron stood by with arms folded, keeping her eyes on the minute hand of the clock.

"I need money for bail. I only have seventy-five cents on me—"

"Well, you'll just have to learn the hard way. Let your precious union bail you out," said her father. "I have nothing more to say."

Marja came back on the line, now in tears. "He's really upset, Betsy—"

"I did what I thought was right," Betsy replied steadily. "I'm not going to change my principles to make Papa happy—because he'll never be happy with anything!"

"He's not letting you back in the house, Betsy. That's what he's saying."

"He's being stupid. He'll forget."

In the heat of it, Betsy was unaware that a tall, impatient young man had pushed the matron aside and was standing right over her, circling a forefinger in an urgent sign to hang up.

"Marja? I have to go—"

The line went dead. The impatient young man had pressed the plunger on the desk phone to cancel the call.

"Come with me, Miss Ferguson," he said.

He put a hand in the air above her shoulder, invisibly guiding her through a set of double doors and out of the booking area. They came to a lobby where globe lamps cast a tired glow on a hectic scene of attorneys set up at makeshift tables, even on the stairs, conferring with women who'd been arrested during the strike.

"My name is Calvin Kusek," the young man was saying. "I'm one of the lawyers for the retail workers union."

"What took you so long?" Betsy cried in desperation. "I've been waiting for hours!"

"Busy night," he said mildly, indicating that she have a seat at an improvised office consisting of two chairs and a briefcase on the floor.

He was practiced and calm, projecting competence. He wore a straw-colored linen suit and had recklessly loosened his tie. His stick-straight glossy brown hair kept falling into his eyes, and he kept sweeping it back with his fingertips in a boyish gesture. There was a sheen of sweat on his face from the steamy night, and he had a lean body that could not get out of high gear. He was several years older than Betsy, used to talking fast and moving fast because his mind was racing ten steps ahead of the opposition. He had a legal pad on his lap and a cheap fountain pen at the ready.

"Tell me what happened that might have led to the arrest. In your own words," he added, brushing back his hair.

"What other words would I use?" Betsy shot back irritably.

He peered alertly into her eyes. "Need a cigarette?"

"Desperately."

He gave her half a pack. "Keep it. When's the last time you ate?" he asked, then dove for the briefcase and came up with two candy bars, one an Oh Henry! and the other a Mounds. Betsy chose the Oh Henry! and Cal said, "Damn!"

Betsy smiled in spite of herself. "Want to trade?"

"No, thanks," he said, unwrapping his. "The game is rigged. I like them both."

"Then it's a no-lose proposition?" she said before she could amend the suggestiveness of the remark.

"We'll see about that," he replied gravely. "In the matter of your arrest, bail has been set at ten dollars."

"I don't have ten dollars."

"Nobody does. The union picks it up. Sign here and you're free to go."

Twenty minutes later, Betsy charged the brass doors and shouldered them open, bursting gratefully onto the avenue of the living. Never mind that she had barely enough for subway fare—there, among jubilant union girls freed from prison, was the young lawyer waiting for her.

"Which way are you going?" he asked, offering a cigarette and lighting it for her.

Betsy inhaled. The smoke was soothing. "I'm afraid I'm not going anywhere."

"The Lex's still running up to the Bronx."

"I'm in kind of a pickle. My dad won't talk to me. He hates unions and hates that I'm part of one."

"Then he's a crumb and I'm glad you hung up on him."

"You're the one who hung up *for* me," she reminded him.

"Stick to your guns," the lawyer advised. "Your dad will come around."

Betsy gave a halfhearted smile, but could no longer hold it in. He saw her eyes were filled with tears.

"Are you all right?" he asked.

She nodded, but a sob escaped her lips. Calvin Kusek whipped out a clean white handkerchief and she took it gratefully.

"I'm sorry," she managed.

"Don't be."

"It was awful in there. Everything was awful."

"It's okay. Take your time. Want to sit down?"

They found a bench near the entrance and shared another cigarette in silence. Intrigued, she glanced more closely at his face in the burned yellow light falling from the prison windows. Despite exhaustion—even disillusionment—from toiling on behalf of desperate people, his penetrating dark eyes maintained a look of confidence—in himself as well as their shared ideals of justice. The combination was hopelessly seductive.

"I can't tell you how good it feels just to breathe the air," said Betsy. "I never really appreciated what freedom means."

"Freedom is worth fighting for," he agreed without irony. "What do you say, Miss Ferguson? It's late and you must be exhausted. Let me put you in a cab."

"That's very nice of you, but I can take the subway to my friend Elaine's. She's a real pally. She got arrested, but I don't know where she went. Her roomies will take me in."

"Which way are you going?"

"I'm taking the six up to Twenty-Eighth Street," she said. "What about you?"

"I can take it down to Chambers and catch the J. I live in Brooklyn. I'd be happy to walk you to the station," he said. "But you better start calling me Cal."

"Betsy."

They shook hands formally.

"Do you have your own place?" Betsy asked, then bit her tongue for the implication of the remark. She couldn't seem to stifle her attraction.

"I live in a one-bedroom apartment with three male cousins, one more of a slob than the next."

"Sounds like fun."

"If you're a beer bottle."

Betsy's laugh was a little too shrill, but he indulged her with a grin. Her thoughts sped like the number six train into darkness. *Probably engaged. He's got to have a girl.* By the time they'd reached Spring Street, her romantic delirium had turned to panic, triggered by the approaching moment of truth at the token booth. She would go uptown and he would go downtown. Would they part with another awkward handshake ... or—*was this crazy?*—a kiss? On the other hand, what if he just said good-bye and walked away forever? They arrived at the entrance to the subway.

"Thanks for everything," she said breathlessly. "It's such a beautiful night. I think I'll walk through Washington Square."

"I'll go with you," he agreed offhandedly.

"Oh, you don't have to. We're already at the station ..."

He shrugged. "I don't mind."

She was so disoriented that she bumped right into him as they crossed the street. They found their way to Washington Square and back down to the subway stop at Bleecker Street, but when they got there Cal said, "Do you feel like walking?" as if they hadn't already covered thirty blocks, and Betsy said, "Are you sure that briefcase's not too heavy?" and that's the way it went all night, at least the way they would describe it later: the story of how they fell in love.

At every subway station they would just keep going, talking nonstop, sharing sly jokes about passersby, solving the problems of the world, as they wandered the quiet, tree-lined streets of the Village, easy in the flow of jazz buffs heading to clubs, homosexuals in couples; past redbrick row houses wrapped in fire escapes, tiny gardens, cul-de-sacs of elegant brownstones with ironwork gates, speculating if that's where the famous writers lived who supported their strike. They stopped at a pay phone so Betsy could tell Elaine she'd been sprung but that things were bad at home. Elaine had been booked at the Midtown South Precinct, and she, too, was out on bail. "Stay at my place as long as you like," she said.

Cal told Betsy the facts of his upbringing. He'd been raised in rural Pennsylvania. His father, Emile Kusek, was a judge, descended from a line of clergymen going back to the eighteenth century. His mother, Annabelle, had been a scholar of French literature and an early feminist. She would have been president of a university, he was certain, except she had died giving birth to him, a tragedy that Betsy deeply understood, having lost her mother not so long ago. Calvin, an only child, was sent to Jesuit schools, which he found compatible enough. When he was a teenager his father remarried, to the widow of a lawyer in town named Mary Schneider, who had children of her own, and her family became his.

"Mary is a nice woman," Cal said dutifully. "She takes good care of my dad."

Betsy felt there was something missing in the way he said it, and wondered if he'd been lonely, growing up without his real mom, and if there had been more than a whiff of small-town scandal around an affair between a widowed judge and the wife of a deceased attorney that further distanced Cal from his family, but said nothing, grateful to live in the big immoral city, where the lights were still on in dive bars and grocery stores, and briefly there was dry thunder and the scent of summer rain that arises when the breeze picks up and miles of asphalt are cooling beneath darkened, fast-moving clouds. A shiver of wind passed through the trees and Cal pointed out their delicate tracery of leaves.

"Those are the famous ailanthus that John Cowper Powys wrote about," he began, but Betsy interrupted him. "I know," she said, and they recited together: *"The ailanthus is my tree. Her buds are jets / Of greenish fire that float upon the air"*—and burst out laughing because they'd each had to memorize the same poem at boarding school and neither could remember the rest.

The artsy tempo of the Village flattened out as they wandered down Prince Street, Broome Street, Grand Street, until they were in the dead-quiet commercial district, mainly of sewing factories, having to avoid the bums sleeping on the bare sidewalk. Signs in warehouse windows said TO LET. A sleepy bootblack emerged from a doorway and tried to brush Cal's shoulders with a whisk broom. Cal got rid of him with a nickel. A street vendor led a horse-drawn wagon home with unsold sacks of beans, and a young prostitute was plucking cigarette butts from the gutter as if they were nuggets of gold.

"Just like the poor things who were stuck behind bars in prison," Betsy murmured, seared by the memory. "I'll never be able to get them out of my mind."

As if he could feel her trembling, Cal offered his arm. Betsy snuggled up gratefully and he tightened his grip.

"Are you this nice to all the girls?" she asked flirtatiously.

He smiled too quickly and gave her a line. "Only the prettiest," he replied, in a tone that left her to wonder if maybe she wasn't really pretty enough and if he had someone else who was. Her hopeful feelings were getting ahead of her.

"Let's get some coffee," he suggested, and there were plenty of places still open—Greek coffee shops, bohemian hangouts, diners, and kosher delis—but none of them was alluring enough to break the rhythm they had found, so they kept on walking, as happens in New York City on a summer night, passing through Little Italy, where the street lamps seemed brighter, and even at this late hour happy groups of young folks and big, lumbering families strolled arm in arm—dressed in hats, coats, and neckties, showing off their babies in big-wheeled carriages. For no reason at all, an operatic tenor stood up from his chair in a sidewalk café and poured his soul into a passionate a capella aria that caused everything on the street to stop—followed by whistles and applause from the entire neighborhood.

Sharing the thrill of the moment, they found that they were holding hands.

"Let's go over to the water," Betsy suggested, which took them to the East River piers, where they could smell the brine and oily gas of fishing boats and great billows of steam continuously rising from the power plant there. Incongruously, seaplanes were tied up beside sailing vessels at the foot of Fulton Street, rocking on their skids.

"This is where they land private planes," Cal said. "Millionaires who live on Long Island and work on Wall Street."

"Is that what you want to be?"

He shook his head. "It sounds conceited, but I believe I was put here for better things—to help people. When I was an undergraduate, I worked for a congressman from a rough neighborhood. I thought it would be the real nitty-gritty stuff, but it was all about drinks with the big boys and keeping track of payoffs. I was a highly educated bagman."

"What about the union job? That's helping people."

"The jury's out on that. I've seen what happened to my buddies from Yale. They got corrupted. They live on the Upper East Side, go to the swankiest parties, but never feel like they have enough. They're exhausted, and yet their slogan is 'I don't have time.' What gets me is the ones who benefit from the marketplace are always the ones in power, not the little guys. They're stuck in it, can't imagine life any other way. I'll bet these big shots take off in their Cubs and bury their heads in the stock report and don't even look out the window at the view."

"That's my father," Betsy said. "All he did was work. Now that he's not working, he takes it out on everyone else."

"Maybe you have to get out of your own life to see what it's all about." Cal looked back at the seaplanes longingly. "I've always wanted to fly. If we do get into this war, I'm going to put in for pilot training."

They walked toward the fishermen's shacks beneath the Brooklyn Bridge.

"Like oysters?" he asked.

"Love them."

"All repressive regimes have the same thing in common," Cal went on. "Frankly, the Wall Street mentality is as bad as the Russians'. They make it impossible to think outside the system. They really want to keep you in fear, those liberators of the masses."

Betsy's palms grew damp and she let go of his hand, afraid that the same argument she heard at the dinner table at home was going to cause the magic of the night to evaporate.

"Then I'm afraid you're not going to like me very much," she said.

Cal gave her a sidelong glance. "What makes you think I like you at all?"

"I'm a member of the party."

She scrutinized the look on his face—disappointed and dismayed.

"I am opposed to Communism," Cal admitted. "But I'm also opposed to denying Communists their constitutional rights."

"Spoken like a true lawyer," she replied defensively.

"It's a dream. It's a con. Communism has never worked, Betsy. You're asking too much of people—to give up their wealth and ambition to some kind of amorphous 'state' that turns out to be corrupt and even murderous? Look at Stalin. Why are you so enamored of it?"

"Are you cross-examining me?" she said lightly.

"Answer the question, miss."

"My friend Elaine came out of an orphanage at age sixteen in the middle of the Depression to a very sad world, Cal. You have the rich on one side and desperately poor working people on the other, and you're never going to bridge that gap, not with capitalism the way it is."

"You're talking about utopia."

"Maybe I am."

"Yes, but utopia is impossible. It goes against human nature. Everyone acts in their own self-interest—"

"Why am I enamored?" Betsy interrupted brusquely. "Because people who believe in Communism are also stronger in character and more committed than anyone else. They sacrifice personal satisfaction to get things done. And I do believe there can be equality and a fairer way to live."

Cal snorted derisively. "The dyed-in-the-wool Communists I've come across are a bunch of egomaniacs, just like their power-hungry pals in Moscow. Dictatorships never hold. We'll beat Hitler, and democracy will spread through Europe. Don't put your money on the wrong horse."

They stood apart, she with arms folded against the midnight chill, Cal with his back turned, facing the river.

"It's okay," he said after a moment. "You made a mistake, but you'll grow out of it."

"Says who?" she fired back.

His condescension took her breath away. She'd gone to jail for her ideals and all he did was talk. At that moment she hated Calvin Kusek. He was as coldhearted, arrogant, and egotistical as the so-called party thugs he was describing, and she kicked herself for ever imagining otherwise.

"You've done so much for me," she managed stiffly. "It's late. Let's just say good night."

They were at a stalemate. Cal didn't answer. But he didn't walk away. He sat down on a block of concrete and looked up at the tower of the Brooklyn Bridge. It seemed very close, just over the oyster houses squatting beneath it.

"The marvelous thing about New York City," he said dreamily, "is that it agrees to let everybody in. There's a kid in my office, came east from Kansas. He's got a light in his eyes. He goes around amazed. *'I ate a blintze! Say, did you know you can see the* Queen Mary*!'* We can laugh at a hick like that, but he's no sap."

"He's in love," Betsy said matter-of-factly, joining him on the concrete block, not because she wanted to, but her feet hurt from all that walking and there was nowhere else to sit.

Cal said, "This is the city we're supposed to inherit."

"I guess."

"I could see it," he decided. "A big apartment on the West Side, close to the park. Raising a family. Knowing all the ins and outs, and in a decade or so, we'd be on top. I could make big money if I wanted to, in corporate law, or some other form of legal robbery. Forget working at Gimbels, you could buy out Tiffany, but so what? We're supposed to be the blood and bone of the city," he said, gazing up at the struts of the bridge. "But what do we stand for?"

It had taken a few moments for Betsy to realize what this perplexing Calvin Kusek meant. He was talking about a future for them, together. It hit her like the hot wind of an onrushing train, as if they had been on separate sides of that subway station, as she'd imagined, but instead of burying himself in a newspaper, he'd looked at her across the tracks with the most beautiful and inviting smile.

The world fell away until there were only their eyes, fastened on each other, first bright, then sleepy with desire. They moved closer, and in the next breath he took her in his arms and their lips met in a first sweet kiss, asking a thousand questions, then closer, harder, hungrier, to ask a thousand more.

The cabin door slammed open and there was her husband, back from the Roys' and smiling.

"Everything's fine with Doris!" Cal announced loudly.

"*Shh!* The baby's sleeping!"

He cringed comically. "Sorry! Whatever you thought she was thinking about unions, there was no mention. Not a ripple. So put it out of your mind."

Betsy noticed he was alone. "So—where is our daughter?"

"She's with Doris and she's having a ball."

"You were supposed to bring her home."

"She didn't want to leave."

"Since when does a four-year-old decide?"

With an effort, she kept her voice low. Cal opened a beer and sat down heavily.

"You had to see it, it was just so cute. Jo is sitting on the kitchen floor with Doris, and they're both washing walnuts. They each have a bucket and Jo is wearing a little apron and she's scrubbing away."

"She's supposed to be at home, in bed."

"Well, they had to finish so they could make walnut bread."

"Walnut bread," Betsy echoed flatly.

"Jo asked if she could sleep over so she could be there first thing in the morning to feed the hens."

"*Jo* did? She's never slept over anywhere by herself."

"Sure she has. At your dad's apartment."

"When she was six months old! This had to be Doris's idea."

"Doris means well."

"I hope they at least have a proper bed for her," Betsy said begrudgingly.

"She'll sleep in Flora Mae's room," Cal said.

"Who is Flora Mae?"

"They lost a child when she was ten. That was years ago."

Betsy stared at her husband. "I'm sorry to hear that. But . . ."

"Honey, you have to adapt."

Betsy was silent. *People here are nice,* she reminded herself, but couldn't get over the ache in her chest where Jo should have been hugging her good night.

"We're part of a community now," Cal insisted.

"Which means we're the lending library of children?"

"Honey, I wouldn't let Jo stay there if I thought anything was screwy."

Never mind good intentions. She wanted to leave Cal to his noble ideals. She wanted to go to the station with Jo and the baby and get on the next train for New York City.

Instead, she would open the can of Vienna sausage and serve supper.

Jo looked up, expecting the neurosurgeon, but the young man who strode into the waiting area of the intensive care unit was not a doctor. He was wearing a dark gray suit with a parka over it and a badge holder on a lanyard with a police ID.

"Miss Kusek? I'm Special Agent Robert Dolan, South Dakota DCI. May I join you?"

She motioned for him to sit. "What is DCI?"

"The division of criminal investigation. We're part of the attorney general's office in Pierre," Agent Dolan explained. "They call us in when local law enforcement needs assistance with major crimes and homicides—"

Major crimes and homicides. Those were words that belonged on a TV show, not in the real world.

"—kind of like the FBI on the state level," he finished as they sat across from each other on the burgundy chairs.

Agent Dolan leaned forward and gazed at her with dull brown eyes. "Condolences for what you're going through," he said.

Jo wanted to trust everything to Agent Dolan, but he looked like he should be pumping gas. He had close-shaved hair and the smooth-brawny face of a high school football player. He shifted uncomfortably in his suit and nervously pulled at the knot of his tie.

"We'll do everything we can to catch the suspect or suspects," he said, as if repeating the words of a training manual. "Typically, the trail goes cold fast, so we need your cooperation in providing information." He took a notebook from his pocket. "I understand you just got in from Portland. What do you do in Portland?"

"I'm a landscape designer," said Jo impatiently. "Just tell me what happened."

Agent Dolan considered, and then gave in to her unflinching stare.

"It looks like a household burglary that turned violent, which in actuality is pretty rare. Your professional burglars are swift. They take the cash and whatever they can sell and leave things tidy. But in this case there were signs that robbery was not the primary motive."

"What kind of signs?"

"The main thing is there was no forcible entry, which could mean Mr. and Mrs. Kusek knew the suspect. Or some random criminal wanted to get in and thought, yeah, it's Christmas Eve. They were expecting dinner guests. It was natural they would open the door." He looked at his notes. "Your brother is an attorney. Does he have any enemies?"

The question snagged her. They'd had plenty of enemies when they were kids, but that was more than twenty years ago.

"Everybody loves Lance," Jo replied. "He's a super dad. I just can't imagine it."

"Did Lance mention a client, maybe, who might have a grudge?"

"Not to me," she answered flatly.

"And his wife, Wendy? Was she the popular type?"

"Yes. They're a great couple."

Jo shut down. Exhaustion settled over her shoulders like a too-big overcoat. All she wanted was to disappear inside. All she cared about was what was happening to Lance and Willie behind the security doors of the ICU, and apparently nobody was going to tell her. Meanwhile, they'd sent a rookie cop and that made her mad.

"Why would they do this?" Upset was rising and it couldn't be stopped. "I mean . . . why so . . . vicious?" she cried. "Why couldn't they just take the damn credit cards?"

Agent Dolan hedged his words. The crime scene investigation was still in progress, but he did owe something to the victims' relative.

"This burglar did not have a style you would call professional," Agent Dolan said.

"Not just neat and tidy?"

Dolan looked somber and shook his head.

"You mean he's a cold-blooded murderer?" Jo suggested with red-enflamed eyes.

"It seems that he—or they—did arrive with some kind of plan in mind. Yes, ma'am. As to why that house and why that family, I couldn't speculate until we have more evidence," Agent Dolan said finally. "Are you married?"

The upset turned to outrage. "What?" said Jo.

Was this guy making a move on her?

"Children?"

"Why are you asking me that?"

"Do you have people you can stay with?" asked Agent Dolan.

"Yes. Sure. I don't know. I haven't thought that far."

"Give me a name and I'll contact them."

"Nelson and Stella Fletcher," Jo spurted instantly. "They're my parents' best friends. Their son is Robbie. I don't even know if they still live here."

"Good," said Agent Dolan, making a note. "I want you to know that you and your brother and nephew are safe here, okay? There are sheriff's deputies posted all over the hospital."

"Great," said Jo. "Do you mind getting a neurosurgeon in here? Nobody's talking to me!"

"Yes, ma'am. I'll get someone."

Agent Dolan left the waiting room. Completely frustrated, Jo turned to the window. The dense white streaming blizzard filled her vision. She put her forehead on the icy glass. Her breath made a circle. Her finger traced two eyes and a nose. The view was limited to a brick wall jutting from the entrance to the hospital. Beside a pathway leading from the portico, a huge black dog, easily over a hundred pounds, was lying on its belly in the snow, possibly a Newfoundland, the kind that rescues people in the Alps. You wanted to kneel down beside him and rest your head in his fur. He had a thick, heavy coat and smallish hanging-down ears. His strong front legs were crossed, his dignified muzzle pointed up, unperturbed by snowflakes falling on his nose. Jo felt she knew that dog and a feeling of deep sadness came over her.

The way she'd heard it from her dad, there was a Lakota Sioux legend about an old woman and a huge black dog. The old woman sits in a cave hidden in the Badlands that nobody has ever found. She's sewing a blanket strip for her buffalo robe using dyed porcupine quills. She's chewed them flat to make them soft and her teeth are worn to stumps. She's been doing this for a thousand years. The black dog is by her side, watching carefully. An earthen pot containing red berry soup hangs over a fire. The soup has been boiling ever since the fire was lit. Since the beginning of time. Whenever the frail old woman gets up and hobbles slowly over to stir the soup, the huge black dog pulls all the porcupine quills out from her blanket strip, so that her work is never finished. They say when the old woman in the cave sews the very last quill and finishes the design, the world will come to an end.

Jo remembered standing near a bookshelf in her father's study when he told her this, and that he'd held in the palm of his hand a Lakota artifact that he'd collected, a sacred medicine circle made of dyed black porcupine quills. He was smoking a pipe. The scent of it now seemed very dear. A man in a red hunting jacket came out of the hospital and the big black dog got to its feet. Why had she not realized that her father loved her very much?

5

"This lamb has to be bottle-fed," Doris was explaining. "Because the mom's an old lady who don't got enough milk."

Over the past few weeks Betsy had been acquiring the skills of a cowman's wife. She learned how to crank out homemade ice cream and to spot a sick calf and give it an injection, when to feed the barnyard animals their crumbly cakes of hay.

"It'll be in your pockets," Doris had warned. "Just so you know."

Betsy mixed up the powdered milk and Doris followed her out of the shed with Whiskey, a red heeler, who lay down and waited calmly outside the pen. Betsy couldn't help but wish that Doris Roy would do the same. She'd softened toward the woman and was grateful for the advice, but was itching to be out from under her control. To have her own garden. And a real working kitchen. She couldn't wait to run their own cattle, make it a business like she'd observed at the Roys'. She and Cal had a lot to learn, but they were ready.

"You have better things to do. I can handle this," Betsy offered. "After all, I did bottle-feed my kids."

Doris laughed. "Truly, but you ain't no mother sheep, far as I can tell," she said, and followed Betsy into the pen.

The animal bottle was big as a football and just as slippery. The nipple was enormous. The baby charged and latched on, almost ripping it out of Betsy's hands. He was named Tiny, a black-and-white little thing with teeny horns, but *whoa* that hungry grip was strong. He tugged so hard that Betsy stumbled and almost lost her grip. Blinded by the dust, and with Doris hollering about this and that and colic and deadly air bubbles, Betsy felt like instead of a feeding session, she and Tiny were combatants in a stadium fighting for their lives.

She was vastly relieved when the men came back in the truck from the grange. Cal was holding Jo's hand and Scotty carried Lance in his arms, which made Betsy smile.

She teased the young cowboy: "Watch out! You might get used to that."

"Lance and me, we're buddies," Scotty said.

"Lance liked the bull!" Jo announced.

Betsy played along. "He did?"

"There was one bull in a field of cows," Cal reported. "And Lance kept pointing at it. Didn't care about the cows, only the bull. I swear he knew the difference."

Scotty held the toddler above his head and shook him so that the boy broke into pink-faced giggles. "He's gonna be a bull rider and Uncle Scotty's gonna teach him."

"Scotty's a professional rodeo rider," Cal told his skeptical wife.

"I'm sure he's very good at it," Betsy said, taking back her son.

By and large the families were getting along. Dutch had taken a liking to Cal because he caught on easily. They worked side by side, ten or eleven hours a day, and it became a habit for them to sit down together after supper with a cup of coffee and a piece of pie, going over the ranch bookwork. Cal showed Dutch how he could manage his accounts better, and after a while he was doing legal work for the Crazy Eights, a fair trade for use of the cabin.

The first Monday of the month rolled around, which meant auction day at the stockyard. Dutch had his eye on some yearlings, and since the town with the sale barn was an hour away, he'd been hell-bent on taking off no later than eight a.m. But when Cal drove down from the cabin, the truck was gone and the empty cow trailer was still parked by the corrals.

It was a dark gray morning with a dusting of frost on the ground, but still warm enough to melt the prints of his boots. Betsy had teased Cal about how sexy he looked in his new western wear, but couldn't stop laughing every time he put on his "John Wayne hat." He took her point. No matter how he angled it or turned the brim this way and that, it just never felt like an honest hat, so he ended up wearing his good old fedora. Better to look like the city slicker he truly was than a pretender. He still missed *The New York Times* and WQXR, and looked forward to the day when they could afford a stereo setup for his collection of classical records. Crossing the chicken yard, he saw the reason for the delay. Scotty was still out there, working on the tractor, which had refused to start since the day before. They'd worked by flashlight into the night checking every possible glitch, but there it was, just the same, a useless green hulk going nowhere in crisscrossing flakes of snow.

"Any luck?" Cal asked.

Scotty shook his head. "How's that tractor book?" he asked. "Keep you up all night?"

Cal heard the sarcasm but let it go. "Oh, it's a page-turner," he agreed.

He'd taken a ribbing last night when he asked Dutch to pull the manual for the 1947 Ford out from under the junk-heaped desk that served as an office in a corner of the barn. Above it, where some men might have hung a girlie calendar, was the 1950 South Dakota professional bull riding tour, where Scotty had circled a dozen events in which he planned to compete.

"I've been starting tractors all my life," Dutch had grumbled. "I think I know how to start a tractor." He tossed Cal the unopened packet that contained the manual. "Knock yourself out."

It was obvious to Cal from studying law that there was a system to everything; all you had to do was crack the code. Here were diagrams and a chapter called "Troubleshooting." *Why fuss around taking out every screw when you already have a road map?* he thought, sitting on the sofa in the cabin to read. After two pages on crankcase ventilation he was dead asleep.

Now he watched Scotty removing bolts from the battery pack under the seat, thick, blackened fingertips oblivious to the cold.

"You said the starter was okay," Cal said.

"It is okay, but Daddy wants me to take it out and get it tested at the garage. Rebuilt, if necessary." Scotty puffed out his cheeks and blew air, the frustrated but respectful son. "So that's what I'm doing instead of training for the Sioux Falls Invitational."

"Where is Dutch?" Cal asked, surveying the empty yard. "He was adamant about not missing that sale."

"He should be back. He had to take the truck. The calves in the south pasture need a bale to eat off, but with this sombitch out of commission, we have to feed 'em by the bucketful."

"Can I do something?"

Scotty paused to wipe his nose on his sleeve. "You could give him a hand with the trailer—unless you want to stop by the library first," Scotty said, cackling.

By the time Dutch returned from feeding the calves and they got the trailer hitched to the truck, it was almost nine in the morning. Scotty removed the starter and took off in Cal's wagon for the garage, cursing the slippery ice. Everyone was antsy except for the cattle dog Whiskey, who lay on her belly, still as stone, watching Dutch's every move with alert amber eyes.

"What's she up to?" asked Cal.

"She figures I'm thinkin' about it," said Dutch.

He climbed into the truck and settled his big frame into the driver's seat. There was a moment of stillness, and then, without any sign from him, the dog hopped inside.

"How did she know?" Cal wondered.

"Read my mind. A good dog is like five good men," Dutch pronounced. "A bad dog is like fifteen bad men."

Cal laughed admiringly. He'd seen how shrewdly Whiskey managed the herd, zipping back and forth to move them through the pens—almost as if the dog and the men had divvied up jobs beforehand, and nothing more needed to be said. He liked these people. He liked the way they treated their animals on an equal basis but, oh boy, he thought, as they drove past the dead tractor, what a lot of punishing work it would take for him and Betsy to keep the balance of nature going on their own place.

Things were always breaking down, which was why the inside of Dutch's pickup was a hardware store on wheels. Stiff pairs of gloves lay in piles. A wooden box held tools for fixing fences. On the console, a tin of oil was stuck inside a coffee cup. A kit was open to a rusty mash-up of screws, bolts, wrenches, old spark plugs, and duct tape. Pens and pliers had dug themselves into the space where the back of the bench seat met the cushions. Over the windshield was a mounted rifle, and in the back bed rode an electric generator, along with rolls of barbed wire and rope, everything finely talcumed with grit.

"Take a look at that for me, will you?" Dutch pulled a newspaper from the mess and shoved it at Cal. "What time are the catalog bulls?"

It was a publication from the sale barn listing the day's auctions.

"Eleven o'clock," said Cal.

Dutch grimaced. "Cutting it close."

He was so big, the tall crown of his cowboy hat brushed the roof of the truck. Later Cal would learn the secret of the right hat was all in the crease, of which there were particular shapes. Dutch wore a cattleman's crease, signature of the gentleman cowboy, the big ranch owner who'd earned his personal style. Dutch liked to move in deliberate ways. He paced himself from house to barn to field, half in thought. He ate slowly and was last at the table, taking his time with coffee and a cigarette. Something would have to be way out of the ordinary to get him as agitated as he seemed now.

"Worried about the tractor?" Cal asked.

The question seemed to surprise the older man.

"The tractor? No, that's something you can fix. But if you miss buying the right bull, you might have to wait a year for the next good one, and I've got a picky customer. Most of my beef is sold to the air force at Ellsworth Air Force Base outside Rapid City," Dutch said, offering a pack of Marlboroughs. He pushed the cigarette lighter into its socket on the dashboard. "The air force is my biggest customer. Ninety percent of my time is spent keeping them happy. They like my beef because it's quality. We run only purebred Red Angus."

The lighter popped out, ready. Dutch maneuvered the coil squarely to the tip of his cigarette without taking his eyes from the road, then handed it to Cal, a move that reminded him of his dad, who had driven a string of Buicks filled with cigarette smoke until the day he died. They both lit up, and the chill inside the cab was eased by the satisfaction of the day's first smoke.

"There'll be some good-looking yearlings for sale today out of a ranch called Lee Brothers," Dutch went on. "I've been watching those Lee Brothers bulls and promised the air force I would get 'em. The fella we deal with at the base, name's Hayley Vance, he'll be at the auction.

I need him there like a hole in the head, but he's an old lady, has to be in the know."

"So you better look smart," said Cal, exhaling.

"I have to *be* smart. There's a dozen guys in line for this contract."

"And I'm guessing they're all your best friends."

Dutch grinned, showing crooked, tobacco-stained teeth. "Son, you just gotta outlive them."

The sky was white as paper and snow outlined the hills. During the night it had made striped patterns on the ridges of the plowed fields, like wales in a swath of olive corduroy. Under soft, overcast skies, Cal found the landscape surprisingly subtle. Not flat and color-less, the way he'd pictured it from back east, but delicate and undu-lant, silver water winding through grassy folds of pale lavenders and gold. He watched a row of black cows follow one another in a per-fect line, daintily lifting their feet from the snow, passing with compo-sure beneath the lyrical branches of the cottonwoods, still skeletal in spring.

The snow turned into driving rain. Instead of slowing down, Dutch plowed ahead through deep eddies of water. The empty trailer rattled behind and the front tires kicked up rocks that ricocheted against the windshield. Cal flinched as a fissure appeared down the right side.

"Oh, hell. That will be costly."

"Not worth fixing," Dutch said matter-of-factly. "Every windshield in South Dakota's got cracks."

Cal now noticed that there were pockmarks and scratches all over the glass.

"Why do it?" he asked impulsively.

"Do what?"

"Live out here. I'm thinking about settling here with the family, and you have to wonder."

"Well, a lot of people don't make it. They come with big dreams, or maybe they're just not suited to the work. A couple of hard winters, and suddenly they can't pay their taxes and the bank takes the ranch. That's why land's so cheap right now. This rain is good, but according to the signs in the *Farmer's Almanac,* we're due for a drought cycle, and that'll wipe out quite a few. Hang on a while, and you can cash in on the failures of others," he said with a sour wink.

"I'd hate to think of it like that."

Curious, Dutch turned to his passenger. "You're not the type to take advantage, I can tell."

"I hope not. My wife and I came west to find a decent way of life and to serve the greater good. I come from a line of clergy. At one time I thought about entering the seminary."

Dutch nodded with approval. "Then you'll find this to your liking. We're a Christian community."

"Well, to profit from another man's suffering would not fit the family tree. I could have stayed a New York lawyer if I wanted that."

Dutch laughed appreciatively. "Why don't you all just keep on in the cabin? Long as you want, till you make up your mind where to be. Then, if you like the lay of the land, I'd be happy to sell you good acreage at a fair price."

"That's very generous," said Cal.

"I got all the ground I need. I don't need to own more ground. I was saving it for Scotty, but Scotty's different. Far from settled."

"I wouldn't want to be the cause of breaking up the family—"

"You are family. I said it, so you are. Scotty don't want it. He's gonna get famous riding bulls. Truthfully, I'm just being selfish. You and Betsy would make good neighbors."

Genuinely pleased, Cal thanked the older man.

"It's a beautiful way of life," Dutch said.

"But hard."

"As long as people are willing to stay, the way of life stays. As far as I'm concerned, we're blessed to have it."

They passed a barn with a huge hand-painted sign on the weathered old boards: FISHY FRIENDS? TURN THEM IN!

"What's that all about?" wondered Cal, imagining it had to do with poaching trout.

"Just a reminder to watch out for Communists."

"Here?"

"Why not?" said Dutch. "They're everywhere."

It was so preposterous that Cal had no reply. The town where they were going was a single intersection where two streets met at a gas station. It had a market and a bank and BADLANDS RANCH RIDES, which persisted only in bleached-out lettering on the side of an empty storefront.

Running into a Russian spy was about as likely as meeting Greta Garbo in the do-it-yourself car wash.

"You buy what Joe McCarthy is selling?" Cal asked.

"He ain't stupid. He knows that carrying on, waving papers, that'll get notice, but look, they haven't listened to us all along, and they're paying attention now."

"Who is?"

Dutch settled his shoulders and re-gripped the wheel.

"The ordinary farmer gets no help from Washington," he said. "You'll see that for yourself, soon enough. McCarthy's the only person with the guts to stand up to big government and put a stop to it."

"To what?"

"To the patriotic values of our country being attacked by enemies within—inside our own State Department, for the love of Christ. The Communists have targeted America for destruction by tearing down our churches and poisoning our way of life. They are *anti-Christian*!" Dutch bellowed, shaking the wheel. "Wall Street and your Washington elites, they're the ones who caused the Great Depression, now look where we are," he said, indicating the vacant storefronts.

"Seems to me that FDR and the New Deal got us through the Depression."

Dutch squinted at the road as if he couldn't stand the sight of Cal. "Don't tell me you're a damn Democrat."

"I am a damn Democrat," Cal replied genially. "Not only that, a liberal damn Democrat. Still family?"

"Might have to take that offer under advisement," Dutch growled, but then turned to Cal and smiled. "Nah, you're all right. You and Scotty, you're my boys. Won us the war."

"Damn straight," said Cal.

Whatever tiny houses made it through the Great Depression had petered out by the edge of town, and pretty quickly they were thrashing through gullies of mud along a string of Quonset huts that housed hardware and plumbing supply stores, until finally the road dead-ended where the grim sky opened to unfenced plain. Livestock pens sprawled to the west, but the rust-colored roof of the sale barn was visible above the slew of dirt-streaked trucks and trailers that told you it was auction day. Dutch cut the engine and pinched the bridge of his nose with fatigue.

"Well, we got a few extra minutes," he said. "Would you care for a coffee?"

Whiskey didn't need to be told to wait in the truck. They made their way around the puddles to the C-A-F-E, spelled out on yellow tiles above a door you couldn't see from the road. You weren't meant to. It was for locals only. Inside, the stuffed head of a long-horned steer presided over an empty hallway. Straight ahead was the entrance to the barn where the animals would be shown. The sales counter was shuttered until auction time.

The Bison Café, as it had been called since creation, was accessed by an unmarked door that opened to a plain wood-paneled room that was considerably warmer in temperature than anyplace Cal had experienced since arriving in South Dakota. The heat was as welcome as the smile they got from the cook, Lucille Thurlow, a cheery if lackluster woman in her fifties, who was setting paper plates of homemade cherry and apple pie on a table, making sure they were evenly spaced and the wedges all pointed the same way. The strings of her apron were loosely tied around an ample waist, and a checkered sleeveless shirt showed squashy arms. Her tannish hair was cut short and her cat-eyed glasses had sparkles.

"How are you today, Dutch?" she asked.

"Oh, they felt sorry for me and let me live."

Lucille laughed. "Tell Doris I'll see her at the 'Pink and Blue' baby shower for Mrs. Ostenberg Sunday afternoon at Legion Hall."

"Will do," said Dutch, immediately flushing every word from his mind. He could tolerate very few female preoccupations. Gals were good and necessary, but he didn't appreciate their meddling. He never approved of the "improvements" made by Shirley Hix, who inherited the whole shebang—the Bison Café and the sale barn—when her husband, Woody Hix, died of leukemia. A good guy, very sad, especially the terrible way he lingered on. Dutch recalled the chili suppers they had right in this room to raise money. Then his widow takes over and does things like putting up those silly curtains made of denim skirts sewn together and the touristy signs—BORN TO RIDE! HAPPY TRAILS! HOWDY!—as if any outsider would dare walk through that door. Couldn't a woman ever leave well enough alone?

Cal followed Dutch to the table in the center of the room, where hefty men who had not removed their heavy jackets and cowboy hats were holding court on folding chairs, chewing on toothpicks along with the day's gossip. Like the water that fed the grasslands, this quiet talk among the patriarchs of old-line families was the life source for local ranchers. Disputes were settled and marriages approved over fat-soaked bacon and farm-fresh eggs, judgments were passed on newcomers, and Christian America vehemently defended.

When Dutch took his place at the head of the table, Cal realized the reason for getting there early was not the bulls, as much as the bull being slung by the regulars of the inner sanctum. The others made room for Cal without comment. There were no introductions. They kept their faces down. And yet Cal felt strangely elated.

He'd stumbled into the center of power. Like the back rooms of New York's Tammany Hall, he recognized this was where real business was conducted—without banks, without middlemen, in cash, and sealed with a handshake. There were rules, a pecking order. He could see by their deference that Dutch Roy was boss. He owned the most land and had that lucrative contract with the air force. The others had to sit on their envy and pick at his crumbs. As for Cal's plan to open a law practice to augment ranching, he would somehow need to convince these insular, hardened people to trust him with their futures, and his friendship with Dutch would help. It would be uphill, but that's what drew him to the challenge. He had a strong feeling that one day he would have a seat at this table. He could be of real service here. He didn't realize it then, but he was already running for public office.

The door opened with a cold draft, and a thin, nervous-looking man without a hat hurried in. He had a pockmarked face and his black hair spiked in all directions from the wet weather. In contrast to his disheveled appearance, he was dressed in a prim, buttoned-up plaid wool coat that looked like something his mother picked out. From the smirks among the insiders, Cal guessed he was the runt of the litter—probably had been all through high school—whose only way to survive was to be the uncomplaining object of their scorn.

"Hey, T.W., you're late," said the one with glasses and pure white hair, thin as spun sugar. His name was Spanky Larson.

"That was me in the blue pickup," T.W. said, sighing and taking a seat. "Skidded out and got stuck in the mud."

"Next time try the brakes," suggested the one they called Charmin'
Charlie. "See if that'll help."

"I got stuck three times!"

The waitress came and laid down plates.

"Why'd I order roast beef?" complained Vaughn Anders, who had
the mustache.

You couldn't miss the mustache.

Vaughn Anders was maybe thirty-five, but he looked like a throwback to the gold rush of the last century. He lived alone in a cabin in the
Black Hills, raising a few cows but mainly hunting for a living, while
attending to his real devotion, which was working his granddaddy's
claim at an abandoned gold mine. He wore several flannel shirts on
top of one another, with an old-fashioned union suit at the skin, and an
impressive, hairy, overgrown handlebar mustache—so huge, it looked
like he'd run into a beaver and it stuck on his face. But the most unsettling thing about Vaughn Anders, Cal would later tell Betsy, was three
nasty-looking knives he wore on his belt. One to throw, one to kill, one
to skin.

"Last thing I've eaten every day for the past four months at every
bull sale is roast beef," Vaughn said grimly. "Why don't they have a pork
chop?"

Charmin' Charlie shrugged. His fleshy cheeks were uncommonly
pink, and his eyebrows grew into bushy gray tips. He had small brown
eyes that were usually downcast or looking sideways for enemies. The
dusty black jacket and black cowboy hat, crimped and sat-upon, added
to his habitual look of woebegone resignation.

"You can't get pork at a bull sale," Charlie chided Vaughn,
straight-faced.

"Hard to get," his sidekick, Spanky, agreed.

"You know beef today is cheaper than chicken?" T.W. announced.

"Is that right, Shirley?" Dutch asked.

"Why would I tell you?" she said with mock offense. "You'll just
complain about my prices."

"Never complain about you," T.W. said, making doe eyes and pulling on her sleeve.

"Get away from me."

Shirley Hix was groomed. Every night she did her hair in rollers and rubbed her hands with cold cream because they were in hot water all day. She wore jeans and boots like everybody else, but tight around the waist, as if she were still *in* those jeans when they got washed and kept them on to dry. She was no less pretty than the high school cheerleader she'd been twenty-five years ago, and well aware of being the only lady there—except for goofy Lucille Thurlow—yet if a man expressed interest, she would smack him down with a stare as mean as a hind kick from a lazy horse.

"What can I get you, Dutch?"

"Coffee and cherry pie."

Shirley looked at Cal. Looked right through him, really.

"For you?"

"Same. Coffee."

"No pie?"

"No, thanks."

Her face screwed up into a hostile stare. "You don't want *any* pie?"

Cal realized his mistake.

"Sure, I'll take some pie. Apple," he added meekly, as she showed him her back.

"I got stuck in the mud three times," T.W. was repeating, as he tucked into his one-dollar roast beef dinner.

Ignored up to now, Cal saw his moment and jumped in. Putting his forearms on the table, he leaned toward T.W. in a friendly way, as if he'd known him all his life.

"I'm right there with you, buddy. We got stuck the first night I got here with my wife and kids. Luckily Randy Sturgis came by and pulled us out."

At this offhand mention of a local, the weathered faces around the table came up and shot skeptical looks at Cal.

Who the hell are you?

"Randy drives a flathead six, far as I know," Charlie pronounced. "What'd you guess is the horsepower on that thing, Spanky?"

"Couldn't pull a mole out of a molehill."

The others chuckled. Cal was unfazed.

"Sorry, gentlemen. I misspoke. Randy didn't pull the wagon out, but he did drive us over to the Roys'. Otherwise, we'd still be there."

"How in hell would you know Randy?" Charlie demanded.

Cal shrugged. "We just met."

There was silence. Dutch took his time putting three sugars in the coffee Shirley had set down. The table was littered with used white mugs, but out of spite, it seemed, she left them there.

"This is Calvin Kusek," Dutch said finally. "He's a big lawyer from New York City, out here for an education about the regular world, and he's getting one, ain't you, son?"

Cal smiled his most priestly smile, full of gentleness and humility. "Yes, sir. Every day."

"Why, he just witnessed his first broke-down tractor."

This sparked laughter and a bevy of suggestions and complaints about the starters on 1947 Ford 8N tractors, until Dutch waved them off.

"I ain't worried, because Cal's gonna find the answer. You know how? *He's reading the manual!*"

Cal took the hooting and laughter good-naturedly. In fact he welcomed it. He sat back and let them poke each other and roll their eyes, urging Dutch to let them know the minute the city boy got the tractor rolling again. *Initiation,* he thought. *That's good.*

"How are you and Dutch related?" T.W. asked shyly, for family was the only way he knew.

"We're not, but almost." Dutch became solemn. "You see, Cal was with Scotty in the service," he continued in a respectful tone. "He's the pilot who flew the plane."

That changed everything. They all stood up at once and there were congratulations all around.

"I flew an old Jenny biplane back in World War I!" Charlie declared, shaking Cal's hand.

"You were on the mission in France?" said Spanky.

"Italy," said Cal.

"Dutch told us all about it. Friendly fire, wasn't it?"

"Scotty tells it better," T.W. interrupted. "How he parachuted down right in the middle of the American army on the beach and told those fellas they was making a terrible mistake and to stop firing at their own planes."

This was news to Cal. It was nine years ago, but he could still recite the coordinates where his paratroopers were deployed, and there was no doubt they'd been inside Italy, well behind enemy lines and nowhere near the beachhead, where Scotty Roy claimed to have jumped and single-handedly warned the Allies to stop shooting their own guys.

"He says he landed with the Americans?" Cal asked, completely perplexed.

Somewhere inside the auction barn a bell was ringing.

"We better go," said Dutch, getting up.

But the ice had been broken.

"So what brings a New York City lawyer to South Dakota?" Spanky asked in a decidedly warmer tone.

Dutch threw some coins on the table. "He wants to be a millionaire rancher," he said.

"If you want to be a millionaire rancher," Charlie suggested drily, "you better start with two million."

6

They left the café and joined the crush in the hallway heading for the auction. Like their animals, the ranchers ambled along in a sociable pack: big-boned, cowboy-hatted, wearing brown or denim work jackets and jeans, boots encrusted with the ubiquitous dried manure of Pennington County. With Cal and Dutch somewhere in the crowd ahead, the regulars were able to regroup and compare notions about the newcomer.

Charlie spoke his mind right off: "What's Dutch doing with that egghead?"

"Just havin' some fun," answered Vaughn Anders, the unsmiling hunter.

"Show some respect. Mr. Kusek is a war hero," Spanky reminded them. "What kind of a name *is* Kusek?"

"Jew?"

"Maybe."

"I wanted to join the army," T.W. remarked. "But they said my eyes ain't good."

Charlie looked skeptical. "Then how come you can shoot a rattlesnake at twenty feet? I seen you do it. What do those signs say over there?"

T.W. stared at the words BUYERS and SELLERS and shrugged.

"Dunno. Can't read 'em."

"He can't read, period," Spanky snorted.

The shutters had been opened and the office was all lit up and buzz-ing with anxious customers. Whatever tension arose from the unfamil-iar task (for cowboys) of filling out paperwork was cheerily handled by a pair of blowsy gals, who knew everyone by name, property, wife, kids, grandparents, and church affiliation. While business was carried on politely enough, you couldn't miss the cutthroat competition among the dozens of buyers entering the arena, strong as the smell of horse piss and sweat.

Very quickly Cal came to appreciate why the men had kept their coats on in the café. Inside the sale barn there was no source of heat. They might as well have been standing around in the freezing weather outside. Instead of outside, though, the crowd of grubby working cow-hands was ensconced in grandeur, and that was the oddest thing: the seating arrangements.

Dutch explained that when Shirley Hix's late husband, Woody, who owned the local feed store, bought the sale barn in 1946, he'd made a deal with a defunct movie theater in Rapid City, which allowed him to outfit the place with old-fashioned tiers of fancy ironwork seats. Cal found it entertaining to watch the rough, tough cattlemen squeeze themselves onto narrow red velvet cushions with barely enough room to cross their timber-like legs, as if they were waiting for a Hollywood double feature, or a fund-raising speech by a well-heeled candidate, when actually what they were looking at was a sawdust pit where live commodities were up for sale—as primitive as it gets—and not that different from the political arena, when he thought about it.

The main event started right on time, with a crash of metal doors as a brown bull with a big white chest and massive horns was chased out of the holding pen. A groundsman waved a white flag to maneu-ver him to the center of the pit, shouting, *"SHHHA-SHHHA!"* while the auctioneer took off at ninety miles an hour in a nasal whine Cal could barely comprehend.

"Goodageyoungbullverygoodyoungthingbidderbidderbidderbidder."

Dutch leaned over to explain. "The trick is to know if they need more pasture time, versus the market price per pound."

Cal could see nothing about the bull to indicate whether it needed more pasture time. It looked like a muscular brown prizefighter in top condition. A straight-faced clerk pointed with both outstretched hands at certain men in the audience who didn't seem to be doing anything, but in less than thirty seconds it was announced that the bull had been sold, and it was shooed out the exit door. Cal was stumped. Along with Whiskey the dog, who knew when to stay and when to follow, the buyers had invisibly communicated with the auctioneer. Was everyone in South Dakota born with mental telepathy?

Cal realized that enterprise here was not carried out with words; you didn't win with an eloquent argument in court, or by making brilliant conversation at the dinner table of a powerful city commissioner. Like the sensitive prairie with its fine-tuned climates of sandy, rocky, grassy, and dry, he'd have to look a lot harder to read the signs. When he really paid attention to the subtleties of this assemblage, he began to notice the dip of a pen over there and a thumb wag down front, signaling the bids. You needed a sharp eye to pick up on the action, but it was there—camouflaged to hide the game from adversaries. The men held crumpled scraps of paper literally close to their chests, on which they scrawled pencil marks to tally up their holdings. In a glassed-in phone booth, a man spoke animatedly with his back toward the arena so nobody could read his lips, Cal assumed. Dutch pointed out that he was a buyer for a big meatpacker in Chicago with thousands of dollars at his disposal.

"That's who I got to compete with," Dutch said. "Aw, hell. Lee Brothers' Red Angus is up next, and Hayley Vance from the air force just walked in. Run interference for me, will you, son? Keep him busy."

Hayley Vance was easy to spot at the open door, exhaling great gusts of steam, wearing a dark blue air force uniform with the chevron of a senior noncommissioned officer, and shamelessly overweight. Relieved to be doing something useful, Cal scrambled down the aisle and introduced himself as a friend of Dutch Roy's, offering his hand.

"Pleased to meet you, Master Sergeant Vance."

Master Sergeant Vance's chapped lips spread in a crinkly grin, enjoying the recognition of his rank, which didn't happen often except by another airman.

"You're air force?" he asked Cal.

"I served with the Eighty-Second."

"Where were you stationed?"

"North Africa. I was a second lieutenant transport pilot."

"What'd you fly?"

"The old reliable C-53."

Master Sergeant Vance agreed. "Could not have won the war without those birds."

His complexion was fair, with the kind of unlucky facial skin that peels off in patches. Although he stood erect with military posture, there was a good-sized belly beneath the wool serge uniform; he had pudgy fingers and the bureaucratic savvy of someone with no talent whose livelihood depended on the laziness of others. As long as he kept the commanding officers distracted from looking too deeply, nobody would notice Hayley Vance. His career could slide through the system like the smooth pour from a can of motor oil. No clunking, and nothing would stick. Case in point: the sweet deal he had going between the air force and the Crazy Eights Ranch, which paid dividends to Hayley Vance in the form of cash bonuses from the owner, Dutch Roy.

"Hang on!" he now exclaimed. "You're *Scotty's* buddy!" and his cheeks flushed at the realization. "You were in the Invasion of Sicily!"

"Along with a lot of other guys," Cal said modestly. "What about you?" he added, to keep the master sergeant occupied while Dutch was making his bid. "I understand you're local."

"I'm an East River boy, but they let me come around."

"What's an East River boy?"

"Other side of the Missouri. You'd think it was Soviet Russia," he added with a grin. "We sure don't need any more of those. But it looks like Senator McCarthy's going to finally flush 'em out into the open."

Even here, in an arena filled with ranchers and the smells of cows and sawdust, people believed the Red Threat was imminent. For the second time that day, Cal was made aware of the deeply held belief that enemy forces were secretly invading the United States.

"Where are you from?" Vance asked with no real interest.

"New York City."

"I imagine that's a rat's nest, but we have them out here, too. Don't you worry, steps have been taken. The base is secure. You'd be amazed how well they blend in. That's how they work to undermine Christian society," Master Sergeant Vance said assuredly. "From the inside. Like termites."

"Well, it sounds like you fellows are keeping us safe."

"My job is easy," Master Sergeant Vance said. "All I do is buy hamburger. Nothing like what you and Scotty had to face overseas. Did that operation get all bitched up or what?" he continued. "Did you ever think you weren't going to make it? Shot down by our own troops. What a way to go, huh?"

"It wasn't pretty."

"Around here everyone is proud of that boy for what he did. Think of it, landing there, after parachuting down under fire, right in the middle of it, the beachhead where our troops are so screwed up they're shooting at our own aircraft, and navy ships are launching bombshells at the American flag, and there's Scotty Roy from Rapid City, South Dakota, he races right up to a U.S. tank and *takes his helmet off*—never mind that he could get his brains blown out—no, he wasn't thinking of himself—he bangs on the side of the tank, yelling for them to stop killing our own guys . . . And you, sir," he continued emotionally, "you flew on, into the night, and did what you had to do. I only wish I'd been there with you, to give it straight to the Krauts and those bastard Wops who sold us out . . . they sold out democracy and everything we stand for . . ."

Passion overtook him and Master Sergeant Vance's eyes filled with tears.

"Jesus," Cal murmured. "Take it easy . . ."

"All I can say is thank you, Lieutenant."

Master Sergeant Vance saluted with a trembling hand, forcing Cal to return the salute, feeling awkward as hell in the middle of all those cowboys with their secret messages sitting on red velvet chairs, as Dutch, victorious and smiling broadly, appeared out of the crowd.

He'd bought the Lee Brothers' Red Angus bulls at a good price, but Master Sergeant Vance wasn't interested in their birth weight or when they had been weaned; he was so wound up, all he wanted to do was retell the story of Scotty Roy's bravery in the presence of his fellow airman, Second Lieutenant Cal Kusek, who'd lived through it. Dutch wasn't sorry to listen to the legendary exploits of his son, but Cal could hardly restrain himself from boiling over at the way everyone believed Scotty's pack of lies.

The rain was holding off when they left the barn, but the ground had become a churning sea of muck as buyers lined up trailers to load up their bulls, and others headed for the exit. They found that Whiskey, instead of lying down and waiting quietly, was snarling and pawing at the glass, frantic to get out of the cab. As soon as Dutch opened the door she leaped out, crouched down, and continued to bark furiously.

"What is it?" Dutch asked the dog.

Cal saw it first. "Did we hit a tree when I wasn't looking?"

The side mirror had been sheared halfway off and was hanging by a twisted metal prong.

"Shit on a shingle!" exclaimed Dutch. His finger traced deep gouges in the paint. "This ain't from no tree," he said.

Dutch told Whiskey to stay and strode through the mud to a knot of cowmen standing in the middle of the parking area, scratching their heads and gesturing angrily as they compared the damage to their vehicles, while Cal examined his shattered reflection in the remaining shards of the mirror frame.

"Dutch is right," Cal told the dog, who hadn't taken her eyes from her master. "Someone smashed the hell out of this on purpose."

"We're not the only ones," Dutch reported after a brief conference with the other victims. "Looks like they went right down the line with a hammer, knockin' off everybody's mirror."

"Why?" asked Cal. "Just for fun?"

"A broken mirror," Dutch was saying ominously. "It says in the *Farmer's Almanac* that means seven years of bad luck. I just paid good money for those bulls," he added grimly. "This ain't what you would call a promising sign."

That night Tyler "Honeybee" Jones didn't make it home for supper, but it hardly mattered, because in the small white bungalow with the metal awnings on Saint Patrick Street in Rapid City, supper was rarely served. Mostly he had to fend for himself. The can opener was his best friend. If his mother, Louise, had been at all interested in what her fourteen-year-old was up to, she could have easily found him where all the boys hung out, at a pool hall and bowling alley called the Hole in the basement of the Buell Building in downtown Rapid City.

The Hole sold only pop, and cussing wasn't allowed, so Honeybee stood outside and smoked with the older guys, watching the girls come out of Donaldson's Department Store across the street. Even in the bitter cold, and long after the girls had been picked up by their glowering fathers, he'd wait until dark so he could be sure that by the time he walked home Louise would be passed out on the sofa from drinking in front of the TV. You had to hand it to her, she still held down her job as secretary to the products manager in the local concrete factory. Her husband, Eddie, had worked there, too. He dropped dead of a heart attack, on the field, while playing catch with Tyler, who witnessed the whole thing. His dad had given him the nickname "Honeybee" at the age of six, for throwing a fastball so hard it stung your glove.

Louise was not a sloppy drunk, but if his timing was off and she was still awake, Honeybee would fall victim to her "speeches"—hours-long tirades while chain-smoking cigarettes, hand on her hip and chin in the air, complaining about aches and pains and incompetent doctors, vicious neighbors, uppity salesgirls, the electric company, either his father's weakness for having left them or his exalted heroism for having served as a mechanic in the war, and back to her usual theme, delivered with smoke streaming from both nostrils like a dragon, that she was "legally obligated to provide food, clothing, and shelter" only until the child turned eighteen, and then he could "do as he damn well pleased." Honeybee had always known his mother's unhappiness was his fault, but since she'd never provided instructions on how he might make things better, he concluded that would be impossible and rejected her as fully as she had rejected him.

The night of the bull sale, Honeybee's timing had been excellent. He saw through the front window that his mother was already knocked out on the sofa. *The Perry Como Chesterfield Show,* still playing on the TV, would cover the sound of his footsteps. Carrying a paper sack heavy with contraband, he opened the door and tiptoed down the hall, avoiding the squeaky spots. Earlier in the day he and his buddies had piled into the back of a pickup and driven through the rain to a bootlegger's spread where they knew they could buy booze, but when they'd passed the sale barn and seen the parking lot was packed because it was auction day, they decided to go back and have a look. Now he entered his room, closed the door, and emptied the sack of half a dozen broken-off car mirrors into a carton in the closet, adding to the pile he'd already stolen around town; no reason, just because he damn well pleased.

. . .

That same night, when the kids were asleep, Betsy found Cal at the kitchen table, reading.

"Want some popcorn?" she asked.

When he ignored her, or didn't hear, she knew he was deep in concentration. After working all day learning the business of cattle ranching, Cal would stay up studying for the South Dakota bar exam, and she was grateful. The sooner he could open a law practice in Rapid City and bring in money, the sooner they could buy their own place and get out of this prehistoric hut. She could think about a nursing job again.

He was out and about, but she was stuck with two young children. She heated water on a wood-burning stove and the toilet was a hole in the ground. With the prairie right up to the door, there was no safe place for kids, and Lance was always getting into cow dung or stinging nettles. She missed the neighborhood playgrounds in New York, where you could strike up a friendship with another young mother over a box of Cracker Jack. She missed her sister and her union friend, Elaine O'Grady. She missed having a telephone.

"When are we going to have our own house, Mama?" Jo would ask.

"Why do you want our own house when it's so nice living here?" Betsy would say, amusing herself with her own humor.

"I want a house with a swing."

And a washing machine, Betsy thought. And privacy. She shook the popcorn pot over the stove.

"Smells great," Cal said.

"To help you study for the bar."

"The bar would be a cinch compared to this." He laughed and spun the book around so she could see. "I'm reading the tractor manual."

"Oh, for heaven's sake, why?"

"The Roys' tractor broke down and it's causing all sorts of havoc."

"Have you tried horsemint tea?" Betsy suggested lightly. "That's Doris's cure for everything. This afternoon Jo had a rash on her arm because I didn't stop her from picking some kind of who-knows-what flower, but don't worry because warm compresses of horsemint tea will fix her right up. Why don't you brew a pot of horsemint tea," she concluded tartly, "and pour it down the tractor?"

Betsy was wearing slippers, an old rayon skirt, two sweaters, and a woolen muffler. In the light of the fire, the pot in one hand, a wooden spoon in the other, she looked irresistibly quaint. Cal got up from the table and stood behind her and massaged her shoulders.

"What's cookin', good lookin'?"

"I thought you were taking the bar exam in July," she said, relaxing under his strong fingers.

"I am."

"Then why waste time on a tractor?"

"Because something's not right, and I'm trying to make it right," he answered tightly.

He didn't want to bring up Scotty's fabrications about his war service. It had gotten under his skin, but it was tricky because Dutch and the rest of the world believed his lies. Cal had to work things out in his own mind first, before he stepped into that hornet's nest.

He sat back at the table. She set the bowl of popcorn down.

"It's cabin fever," he told her. "You need to get out."

Betsy's answer was to take out the Olympia typewriter and compose a letter to her sister. They corresponded almost every week. The Fergusons had a neighbor, Mrs. Zajac, a widow with eyes on Albert, who read the letters to Marja and would write her answers. Betsy set the typewriter on the kitchen table. It had been a gift from her parents when she graduated from the Knox School. The Olympia lived up to its name as the pinnacle of freedom for a sheltered girl. She could write an article. She could apply for a job. Even now its round keys seemed uplifted on their levers, awaiting the touch of her fingers to come alive; but loneliness stilled her thoughts.

There was little comfort here. Comfort was their apartment in the art deco building on the Grand Concourse, morning sun falling across the baby-blue carpeting, of which their mother, Rosslyn, would have approved. She had called herself an interior decorator, although she had no training and had never held that job, and the living room was stuffed with relics of her bourgeois aspirations: Japanese lamps, porcelain figurines of shepherdesses, heavy mirrors, a baby grand piano.

Bright sun from the corner window would be unkind to Marja's ample, big-busted figure, in a simple gray cotton frock with the buttons closed up to the collar, in the discreet way they taught girls to dress at the New York Institute for the Education of the Blind. The hem would fall below the knee, so that the white stockings and manly shoes, chosen for stability, would be awkwardly revealed. Her black hair would be parted on the side, following its natural waves until stopping midair in a crimped mass like an unanswered question.

It pained Betsy to remember her little sister going about looking so matronly. Whenever she passed the Junior World Sportswear at Gimbels, she would assemble imaginary wardrobes for Marja, so she'd fit in better with the sighted world. The doctors said she could see well enough to choose her own clothes, but Marja wasn't ready to leave the cocoon of semi-blindness where she'd been indulged all her life. She held her lids downcast, and had acquired dark, freckled-stained circles underneath her eyes. Her habitual expression was of a faintly humble smile—really just a pose of acquiescence that masked the fury, which sometimes lashed out like lightning, of being trapped in a life of dependence.

While their mother shopped in Manhattan and golfed at the country club, Marja had been raised by live-in nurses. Betsy sat on the floor with the fretful toddler and, as she grew older, made up games they could share. When the neighborhood kids ganged up on "the dumb blind girl" and pounded her with snowballs, it was Betsy who fired back and tackled the boys and stuffed chunks of snow down their necks—her premature height finally an advantage. She was Marja's defender, but failed to be her savior.

"Let's go to the beach this weekend," Betsy would suggest. "Coney Island! Some friends are going from the store."

"Are you mad?"

Marja could sound incredibly pretentious. Betsy thought it was from listening to radio dramas all day.

"Why not?"

"We'll be on the subway for hours," her sister complained.

"So what?"

"It'll be crowded and hot."

"No worse than this apartment," Betsy insisted.

"You go on," Marj would say. "I'll stay with Papa."

. . .

Cal closed the tractor manual and said he was going to bed. Without realizing it, Betsy had begun to type. There was something about the hammering of it, and the bold black letters striking the page, that demanded truthfulness, and she did her best:

Dearest Marj,

Cal and I are finally talking about finding our own place. The Roys have gone out of their way but it's time to move on. I want to get on a horse and ride across land that is *ours.* To fall asleep dead tired from harvesting vegetables from my own garden and to put up preserves and bake a lemon chiffon pie (if I can only master the wrist action). I'm excited about putting down roots—only sad because I miss you and still haven't made any real friends. (Sorry to sound like a spoiled teenager.) When we have our own place you MUST come out here and see it all, dear Marja—everything working together!

Your loving sister, B

7

The first time Betsy met Stella Fletcher, she had ventured downtown alone, pushing Lance in the carriage and holding hands with Jo. There was no indication they had settled in the fastest-growing city in the state. In those early days, the double-wide western streets were still virtually empty. To Betsy's eye they looked surreal, as if you disappeared the crowds from Fifth Avenue, hung a broad blue sky, and put giant fans on every corner. No matter that it was spring; the wind prevailed, sweeping down shining streets that were ruler-straight. Cars passed rarely. The next pedestrian might be a hundred yards away. You could see infinity from every intersection.

It was an innocent and drowsy pace, with none of the battle scars of the wheezing, middle-aged municipalities of the East. According to the enthusiastic 1950 *Rapid City Business Survey,* the current population of 24,310 was projected to grow by half in the next ten years. "Ninety-five percent native born, no foreign element, no Negroes," the *Business Survey* bragged. By the time Jo was in high school, the city called the "Summer Playground of America," whose claim to fame was Mount Rushmore and a dinosaur park, would have shamelessly renamed itself the "New Denver of the West." It would boast forty-four grocery stores, sixty-six restaurants, three drive-in movie theaters, four music stores, a sanatorium for tubercular Indians, two museums, and thirty-five lawyers, including Calvin Kusek.

On that afternoon in late spring, there would have been no cause for Betsy Kusek to feel anything but optimistic as she promenaded her babies down Main Street. She'd dressed the children up, put on a yellow shirtwaist and her spring coat, and tied a scarf around her hair. It was marvelous to be wearing heels and walking on pavement. Returning the smiles of the occasional passersby *("What adorable children!"),* Betsy began to imagine the wispy fragments of her life coming together.

A year from now Lance would be out of diapers and Jo would be in kindergarten. What would Betsy want if she were free? To work as a nurse in the hospital, or maybe for the school system? Do typing for Cal? He'd need the help lawyering as well as running the ranch. All of that was fine, but what Betsy really badly needed was a bosom buddy like Elaine O'Grady back in New York, who worked in the hotsy-totsy Fashonia Dresses department at Gimbels, but was one of the most earthy girls she knew. On lunch break, they'd skip the company cafeteria and take a sandwich to the park, hoping to meet a guy. The guy—snagged or not—inspired hours of analysis of where and with whom they should lose their virginity, swearing to tell each other the minute it happened. The guy was really an excuse for Betsy and Elaine to skate along on their exhilarating new friendship. Betsy missed her terribly. Just then, although the day was fair, a brutal crack of thunder followed by a spit of lightning reverberated in the distance, as if to mock the futility of her thoughts.

Jo flinched. "Mommy, is it going to rain?"

"No, sugar. That's just heat lightning, and it's far away from us." To distract herself as well as the child, Betsy added, "Isn't this a pretty town?"

The turn-of-the-century planners had decided their best bet in drawing people to their newborn city, in a place where the wind comes at you full force no matter what the season, would be the guarantee of permanence. Middle-class stability. A collective fist against the elements. So they built downtown on a squared-off grid, out of bricks made from local clay fired by wood from the Black Hills, installing blocks of Italianate buildings with elegant facades, arched windows, leaded glass, and ornate cornices that were ordered by mail and brought in on trains. Mornings and evenings, when the prairie light was crystal clear, the austere setting gave you faith in the solid, democratic values that built this city.

Betsy was delighted by the variety of modern stores that currently inhabited the shells left by Victorian dreamers fifty years before—beautiful dress shops, Billiam's Fabric, all filled with the cutest notions. Three shoe emporiums on one street! The jewel of the city, the Hotel Alex Johnson, was a grand high-rise with a rooftop garden, as luxurious as any in Manhattan. Around the periphery of downtown there had bloomed beautiful parks and neighborhoods of large, tasteful homes that reminded her of childhood in the suburbs of New York City.

All of that was due to giddy postwar affluence. The Depression had come early to South Dakota, in the 1920s, after the failure of so many farms. That was the shock of it. Until then, those industrious, decent Christian folk who had settled in Rapid City could dupe themselves into believing they *had* achieved the impossible—a durable and lasting way of life—when in fact they had dug down deep in a place of no boundaries. In the cold void above the clouds, above humanity, atmospheric forces would push and shove as they always had, blowing apart and renewing, in an endless, pointless turbulence that froze calves and killed wheat and turned farmland into dust, all of it as careless of human hopes as the late-spring squall that dropped that day out of the blackened sky, pummeling the Kusek family.

In a matter of minutes the temperature dropped by twenty degrees. Large pellets of hail came down hard. Moments ago the thunder was a faraway tease; now it was above them, suddenly colossal, loud enough to make store windows rattle. Betsy pulled the carriage hood down over the baby, scooped up her little girl, and ran. The scarf blew off and tangled around her neck. She kept her head down, her usually agreeable features a grimace of determination. The icy rain was blinding. With one hand Betsy propelled the carriage while with the other arm she carried Jo on her hip. Nothing would make her lose hold of those children.

Assaulted from all directions by capricious wind, she hobbled to the nearest shelter, shaken by how the world had changed in a snap. But for now they were safe in the entryway of the Duhamel Company western wear store.

"That was fun!" said Jo. "Carry me again."

Betsy shook the ice particles from her hair, pocketed the soaking scarf, and arranged another blanket over Lance, who stopped his panicked yowling and gratefully took the bottle. She wiped her cold, wet face and sighed. It was too late to pull Jo away, she'd already seen the toys cannily displayed in the window among grown-up jeans and riding shirts and braided belts. But it wasn't the Happi-Time Camera or the Tweedie Singing Bird that drew the child in a trance right up to the glass.

"I want cowboy boots!" Jo declared.

In her size they were adorable: tooled red leather with white embroidery.

"Cowboy boots are expensive," Betsy said. "First you have to learn to ride," she added, dodging.

"I can ride Pete."

"I know, but Doris has to hold you."

"Doris doesn't hold me. She lets me ride all by myself."

Betsy's stomach tightened. "She does?"

"It's easy. Pete likes me! Look, I'll show you."

Jo grabbed her mother's hand and dragged her toward a coin-operated horse set beneath the awning as an enticement. It was painted bright yellow, yellow as butter, all four legs outstretched in a flying gallop. On the pedestal, RIDE CHAMPION! was written in a lasso that spelled out the letters.

A boy Jo's age was sitting on the mechanical horse. He wore jeans, suspenders, and a flannel shirt. His flax-blond hair was mowed in a scalp-revealing crew cut. Although the horse was still, he was energetically slapping the leather reins against its fiberglass neck. The boy's mother stood nearby. Like Betsy, she seemed to have been caught in the storm, for she wore just a pink cardigan over a skirt and blouse and carried a white straw purse.

"Please," she was saying.

Bending toward her son, she was not the picture of a confident parent, more like a desperate teenager.

"Robbie, please."

"One more ride," the boy insisted.

"I'm out of dimes. Let's go."

"No!"

Robbie's mother spun away as if she'd been slapped. As if the boy's rebuke was the absolute last thing she could bear that moment. Fumbling with her purse, she found a handkerchief and pressed it to her eyes.

"Why is that lady crying?" Jo whispered. "It's just a stupid ride."

"Don't say 'stupid,'" Betsy said. "Excuse me," she continued to the distraught woman, "I've got dimes, if you need one."

"That's very nice of you," the woman said. "But his father's waiting."

She was several years younger than Betsy, with natural strawberry-blond hair that framed an oval face in waves that fell to sloping shoulders that seemed to have sunk under the burdens of life. Her wide, high-flown eyebrows contributed to an open expression that would have been sweet as a high school portrait if her face hadn't been ravaged by some kind of deep-seated unhappiness.

She twisted the handkerchief in her hands. "I'm sorry. This is embarrassing. It's funny but he's not usually like this."

"One of those days," Betsy replied sympathetically.

A dense curtain of cold rain fell on the other side of the awning over the entry, cutting off the street. They were silent, staring at the barrage of water.

Finally Jo tugged on Betsy's coat. "It's my turn."

"You'll just have to wait."

"But he's not even riding—"

"*Hush!* Can you believe this weather?" Betsy said, still trying to console the young woman. "Back east, this is what we call November."

"Are you tourists?"

"We just moved from New York City. What about you?"

"We both grew up in Rapid. My husband went to law school in New Jersey, but now we live in town."

"My husband is a lawyer, too!"

"No kidding. Where are you staying?"

"With the Roys."

"Oh, the Roys. My husband knows them better than I do."

A well-dressed young man was running across the street with an umbrella over his head. He was dark-haired and wearing a business suit, the first time in weeks she'd seen a man in a suit. When he got close Betsy saw he was clean-shaven with bright blue eyes behind wire-rimmed glasses, a striped varsity scarf around his neck. She didn't know which college, but maybe, because the woman had mentioned New Jersey, it was Princeton.

"Stella, what are you doing? Everyone's waiting," he said.

"I can't get him off," said his wife.

The father faced the son. "Robbie, come down off that horse. I'm going to count to three."

"Obey your father," Stella said.

Robbie's lips compressed and the tips of his ears flushed red as if he couldn't decide whether it was to his advantage to stand his ground or give in to remorseful tears.

"Let's go. This little girl is waiting," said the father.

"It's okay," Betsy said.

"No, it's not!" Jo protested.

Despite his frustration, the man bent down and smiled at Jo.

"You're right, young lady, it isn't, and we are going to fix that immediately. Hello," he said, extending his hand to Betsy. "My name is Nelson Fletcher and this is my wife, Stella."

"Stell," said the woman from behind the handkerchief. With her husband in charge, her mood seemed to lift.

Betsy introduced herself and they all shook hands.

"We just have to go across to the bank and sign some papers," Nelson said.

"Go ahead," said Betsy. "I'll watch your son."

Nelson glanced uncertainly at his wife, wondering whether they should trust even a well-dressed stranger.

"They just moved here from back east," Stell explained.

"New York City," Betsy added, for credibility.

"They're staying with the Roys."

Nelson nodded. "Scotty Roy. I knew him in high school."

"Robbie really is a good boy," Stell interjected quickly. "He won't be any trouble."

"Go on," Betsy assured her. "I'll be right here."

"Ten minutes," Nelson promised, as the umbrella flared and they headed into the rain. To the children: "You two get lollipops if you're good. Take turns, got that, Robbie?"

Robbie murmured yes. He'd defeated the enemy. He was not doomed to sit in the boring old bank all day.

Jo and the boy ignored each other as he slid off the horse. She clambered up but her chiffon dress wasn't meant for galloping, so she gathered it above her knees and plunked her bottom on the saddle, feeling the not unpleasant sensation of warm hard plastic through the crotch of her cotton underpants. Betsy put a dime in the slot and Champion moved up and down in smooth oval loops. Jo shot the boy a disparaging look and took up the reins the way Doris had taught her. Like a real cowgirl.

The following morning the sun was shining and the wind brought the scents of anise and mint from the prairie flowers. The Roys were putting in their two-acre vegetable garden and Cal drove down to help. With the tractor out of commission it would be hell to pay, breaking up the rain-compacted soil, but according to the *Farmer's Almanac,* the next two weeks were favorable for planting. As each twenty-four-hour cycle passed, Dutch became more incensed by the problem of the tractor he couldn't solve. After dinner, while Doris served Dutch his coffee and pie and he tried to smoke a cigarette in peace, she would tick off all the vegetables—cucumber, carrots, radish, and beans—she would not be able to pickle if they didn't get seeds in the ground. Finally Dutch had decreed: horsepower.

That morning, when he arrived from the cabin, Cal saw that Scotty was leading two big chestnut workhorses out of the barn. He tied them to the post, went into the tack room, and came back with the heavy leather harnesses to pull a plow that hadn't been used in years. Doris passed with a wave, carrying a bucket of water for the ram. Cal noticed that ranch women don't waste time. They strut fast, their arms are strong and movements efficient, and they're always looking ahead at the next task—or several at the same time.

The ram was kept separate from the ewes. He was excitable, pacing back and forth, distressed that his only companion was a wayward hen. Cal felt like butting someone's head as well, and that person was Scotty Roy, but now was not the time to bring up Scotty's tales of his war escapades. As he walked toward his old air force buddy, boots crunching the dirt still wet from yesterday's downpour, Cal's hands were clenched inside the pockets of his jacket.

"Get the starter fixed?"

"Like I thought, nothin' wrong with it in the first place," Scotty said. "I installed it back in and tried again. No luck. Right now Daddy's on the phone over to the dealer in Pierre. I tell you, it's a head-scratcher, and every day it's costing money."

"Can I try?"

"Have a ball."

Cal climbed into the seat and started moving the gearshifts, trying to get a feel for anything that did not seem right. For one thing, the shifter had a lot more play than any car or truck he'd driven.

"This feels kind of loose."

"Does it now?" Scotty drawled.

Cal started fooling with switches and buttons and the tractor started.

Scotty's jaw dropped. "Do that again."

Cal cut the engine and turned it on. Twice more. Each time it fired up like a dream.

"For God's sake, Kusek, don't mess with the odds. Let it run."

Cal hopped down as the engine rumbled. "It's okay. I think I know where the problem is."

The sound brought Dutch running from the house, where he was so amazed he'd simply hung up the phone on the talkative Ford dealer in Pierre. They gathered around the machine like worshippers at Stonehenge, awed by the mystery.

Dutch said, "What the hell?"

"Got your tractor working," Cal said.

"You did this?"

Cal shrugged. "Beginner's luck."

"What's the trick?"

"Okay, there's a neutral interlock switch that prevents you from starting the engine when the shift levers are out of line," Cal recited from memory of what he'd read in the manual. "It works off the linkage in the transmission."

Dutch and Scotty exchanged dubious looks.

"We're aware of it," said Dutch. "You're talking about a safety feature they put in to prevent accidents. Stops the tractor from starting while it's in gear."

"Right," said Cal, "but if the shift levers are too loose, the safety feature kicks in, preventing the engine from turning over."

"Bullshit," Scotty said, scoffing. "That's way too simple. Come on, us country folk are not as dumb as we look. Believe it or not, I have, on occasion, consulted the almighty manual, too."

The manual had been sealed and unopened when Dutch gave it to him, but Cal kept himself in check. "It's in the footnotes at the bottom of the page," he said stiffly.

"There you go!" Dutch said to Scotty. "I always told you—*read the fine print!*"

He was halfway kidding, but Scotty took it badly.

"I took the starter out, like you said, which was no help. I spent all that time on nothin', and because of that I never got to the post office so I went and missed the cutoff for the rodeo in Deadwood."

"Oh, give it up," said Dutch, irritated. "You ain't never gonna make the finals."

"I won't if I don't compete."

"Not my fault."

"You think bull riding's just a pastime—"

"I never said that."

"It's a professional sport that requires training and commitment—"

"Then stop whining and act like a professional," his father snapped.

"I can't when you got me running errands for a fool."

"Scott," said Dutch, pointing a thick finger, "I told you ever since you were a little boy: I never want to hear you say *'I can't.'*"

The two men faced each other with hips squared and chins out. Cal felt his own blood rise. Everyone was getting way too hot.

"For what it's worth," Cal interrupted, "the problem getting it to start *was* hard to pinpoint. It's one of those maintenance things that people don't pay attention to."

"We pay attention," Scotty said menacingly.

"Just trying to help," Cal replied, jaw tightening.

Dutch clapped him on the shoulder. "You did help, son. Scotty, move them horses back inside and drive the tractor around. Put the harrow on, let's get going."

"Yes, sir."

But Scotty did not take the horses in. When his father was out of earshot, he leaned toward Cal and said, "Hey, Kusek. Stop trying to get between me and my dad."

"Why would I do that?"

"You tell me."

Cal's response was a statement of fact. "I've flown an airplane."

Scotty's eyes bugged out in exaggerated confusion. "*Huh?* What's this about an airplane?"

"What's this cockeyed story you've been telling everyone about how you landed with the Americans and got in the middle of friendly fire?"

"I don't know what you're talking about."

"You know damn well and I'm tired of hearing it."

"What are you trying to do, buddy?"

"Fix a tractor," Cal said over his shoulder. He walked around to the driver's side.

Scotty followed. "Hey, professor, just because you read the foot-pages, you think you know everything—"

"I do know, Scotty," Cal said, facing him. "I was the pilot. I know where the drop zone was, and it was behind enemy lines, a hundred kilometers north of the beachhead."

He was angry, but more than that, he was hurt. It hurt to know the kid he'd admired for his moxie, whose innocence and spirit had convinced him to pick up his family and move to the other side of the country, was a fraud.

"Why'd you have to make something up?" he asked almost sadly. "Everybody over there was a hero."

"What's it to you? Nobody really knows what went on. A lot worse stuff happened that night, believe me."

"It's disrespectful to other soldiers," Cal said gravely. "It's stealing from men who deserve it."

"Stealing what?"

"Honor."

Scotty gave a hollow laugh. But the word hit him and he appeared shaken. "For Christ's sake," he managed.

"Somebody might have landed on the wrong side of hell and warned our boys to stop shooting our troops, but it wasn't you."

"Not your concern," Scotty said, drawing himself up. "You're just mad because you want to be the hero."

Cal watched the other man carefully, calculating his defense if Scotty threw the first punch. "What's my secret plan to be the hero, Scotty?"

"Taking over the ranch. Learnin' all the ins and outs."

"Your father offered to teach me. All I ever asked was to get in out of the rain."

"Then he's drivin' you to the sale barn, introducing you around.

Don't think I don't hear about it. Then him and Mama start talking about selling you the cabin *and* the upper pastures. You're angling for acreage, ain't you? A piece of the pie you got no right to."

Cal's mind went fuzzy. He didn't trust himself. He stalked back to the wagon, where the manual sat on the front seat. He reached through the open window and picked it up.

"Don't need this anymore," he said, throwing it against Scotty's chest.

"Nah," said Scotty, catching it easily. "I guess not, since you've driven so many tractors." He snapped his fingers. "You're the expert."

"Admit it. Just between you and me. Admit it about Italy and I won't bring it up again."

Whiskey had begun to bark her head off, putting a stop to their unfinished business. A car pulled into the driveway and the question went unanswered as the barnyard erupted in bleating and squawks. It was a sky-blue Dodge sedan driven by a young woman—a blonde with a pink scarf tied under her chin. She rolled down the window and waved.

"Hi there!" she said brightly.

"Don't worry. I won't spill your secret," Cal said over the racket.

"Hello?" the woman called again. She took off her sunglasses. "Excuse me. Can I ask you boys a question?"

"Over there you were a big swinging dick," Scotty told Cal. "But here you're green as grass, so just stay out of my way."

8

Up at the cabin, Betsy was washing clothes in the kitchen sink, using a washboard and a chunk of homemade soap. Made the old-fashioned way by boiling water, lye, and fatty scraps saved from the kitchen, the soap did the job but left her hands red and itchy. She would have run barefoot over stones for a box of Ivory Flakes right now—except a sky-blue Dodge sedan was heaving its way up the hill toward the cabin.

Betsy looked out the window as a woman with strawberry-blond hair stepped from the car.

"That's Robbie's mom!" she exclaimed.

"Who's Robbie?" piped Jo.

"The boy on the horse we met yesterday."

"I'm gonna hide!"

Jo climbed into the crib with Lance and pulled the blanket over their heads.

Betsy met Stell Fletcher at the front door.

"Hello! Good to see you again."

"I just stopped by the main house and your handsome husband said you were here. I won't stay long," Stell said, taking off her scarf.

"Come inside and meet the mess! What do you think?" Betsy asked, sweeping a hand over the woodstove, kerosene lamps, worn curtains that didn't block the daylight, cots they slept on, suitcases they locked because of the mice.

Stell said, "Let me guess. No phone, no electricity except maybe a cranky old generator that never works when you need it?"

Betsy nodded.

"Well, at least you don't have to vacuum."

Betsy laughed. "Hey, would you like some coffee? I just spent fifteen minutes getting a damn fire going."

She spooned some instant into the only two mugs that came with the cabin and they sat at the zinc-covered kitchen table. Stell put down two Ball jars filled with dark red jam.

"These are for you. Homemade wild plum preserves. I wanted to thank you for watching Robbie," Stell said.

Betsy smiled with delight and held the jars to her chest. "You made this?"

"I'll show you where the wild plums grow. Way out in the prairie, a place they call, well, the 'Spooky Place,' because everything's burned black from a fire. Robbie loves to pick—we'll take the kids there."

"Jo will love that."

"Robbie's really a sweet boy. It's just that things have been rough. My mother died recently, and he was close to Grandma."

"Oh, dear. I'm so sorry."

"I must have looked a nut, crying my eyes out on Main Street."

"Hey, no, not at all. I lost my mother, too," Betsy said earnestly. "More than ten years ago, but she's still with me every day."

Stell nodded. "Sorry, dear."

"When did your mom pass?"

"On the fifteenth. It's funny but it was very sudden."

"Geez, that's hard."

Stell's eyes grew teary. "You were really nice to me yesterday," she said, touching Betsy's hand.

Betsy's eyes also welled, but the feeling was too poignant and she snuffed it with a polite smile. "So what kind of law does your husband practice?"

"General law, I guess you'd call it—but half the time he's out in the hinterlands, trying to organize the party."

"The Republican Party?" Betsy ventured cautiously.

"Democratic," Stell said almost apologetically. "We're very much the minority in South Dakota."

"Well, now you've got two more."

Stell slapped the table. "Democrats? I'll tell you, it's an uphill battle. If we had any hills."

Jo popped her head out of the crib, shouting, "Surprise!"

"Oh, no!" exclaimed Stell theatrically. "You scared me!"

"Look! Papa's coming!" said Jo, climbing out and dashing for the door. Lance pulled himself up on the rails and stood tenuously.

"I do have children," Betsy admitted. "I just don't always know where they are."

"They're beautiful," Stell said.

"Spontaneity," Betsy advised slyly. "In the car."

"Really?"

"Works every time."

They were giggling together when Cal came through the front door holding Jo's hand.

"I see you found Betsy," he told their visitor.

"Good directions," Stell replied. "Nice place you have here."

"We're camping out," Cal replied. "This is temporary."

Betsy knew something was up. He'd forgotten his hello kiss and didn't seem interested in chatting. Normally a new person would spark his curiosity.

"They're Democrats!" Betsy announced.

"What do you know?" Cal said.

"And Stella's husband is also an attorney."

"I look forward to meeting him. Where's his office?" he asked politely.

"Rapid City. Right now he's trying to sell my mother's property. That's what we were doing at the bank, when we ran into Betsy. It was my grandmother's ranch, that's what's so sad. The ranch my mother grew up on. It's been in the family three generations, but we just can't afford the taxes. I hate to give it up, but we have to sell. Nelson's not optimistic about finding a buyer. There's a lot of stuff for sale right now."

Cal was at the sink washing his hands. "I don't know if Betsy told you, but we're looking for our own place."

Betsy was shocked. She'd thought that was months or years away. "We are?"

Cal rinsed off the foam from his wife's homemade soap and, with it, dependence on the Roys. He hadn't wanted things to end that way, but the flare-up with Scotty made it clear that it was time to move on—forward or back, he wasn't sure which—but one way or another they could not go on living in the borrowed cabin.

"If it's copacetic with your husband, I think we'd like to see the property."

"Never hurts to look," Stell Fletcher agreed.

Cal and Betsy left the kids with Stell for the day and, following her directions written on the back of a grocery bill, drove thirty miles southeast, along roads with no names and landmarks like "large oak tree." They passed it several times before realizing the nondescript white farmhouse was the old Fletcher place. On paper, the property included two barns, four good-sized cattle pens, and smaller pens for farm animals, and a horse corral, henhouse, and tack shack. But when they got there, both were disappointed. It was a shambles, and as far as resale value was concerned, the house, mail order from Sears half a century ago, had been built too close to the road.

But they'd come all this way, so they pulled over. Betsy got out of the wagon first and walked around the house ahead of Cal, following a path of stepping-stones matted with overgrown chickweed. The backyard had become a field of weeds two feet high—quack grass, clumps of foxtail, thistle, and dandelion. She sat down on the porch steps. An umbrella clothesline, nudged by the wind, was turning slowly with spokes outspread like a skeleton carousel.

Cal followed, inspecting the foundations of the house. He pulled on the handles of the cellar doors.

"I'm not going down there," Betsy warned.

"Stuck anyway," he said, and left it to sit beside her. They watched the grasshoppers and dragonflies rise and fall in the silky grass, and after a while Cal said, "Well, what do you think?"

"It needs a lot of work." She sighed. "I don't know."

"Don't know what?"

Her pale white skin had taken on some color but still was clear and fair, no lines yet from weather and wind, smooth and trusting. She turned to her husband, squinting in the sun that outlined his broadened-out shoulders and the shape of his fedora, cocked just so, leaving his face in shadow.

"Harder than we thought it would be, isn't it?" she said.

"Do you want to go back?" Cal asked.

Betsy shook her head and stood. "We should go inside, so we can at least say to the Fletchers that we looked."

She took a few steps before she realized that Cal was still reclining on the porch, leaning back on his elbows, long legs crossed.

"What is it?" she asked, half teasing, wondering if his languorous pose on the warm planks was an invitation to climb on board right there in the midst of the wild meadow.

"I meant," said Cal, "do you want to go back east?"

The question was a surprise. "But why?"

"I've received a new job offer. From a very good firm in Manhattan."

"When did this happen?"

"The letter came two weeks ago, forwarded to the Crazy Eights." He pulled an envelope from the back pocket of his well-worn jeans. "I've been mulling it over."

"You have?" Betsy stared at him, eyes flashing. "Were you ever going to tell me?"

"Figured I might," he said, drawling like the natives.

"Oh, stop!" she cried, striding back and snatching the letter. "What am I supposed to think?"

"A man presents an opportunity, and I'm considering it," Cal said, his own tone rising.

"Who is the man?"

"John V. Lindsay."

"Who the hell is John V. Lindsay?" Betsy retorted.

"I have no idea!" Cal shot back. "He's the one who signed the letter. The firm is top-notch, and the client is the meatpackers' union—right up my alley. The reason this kid, Lindsay, thought of me is that he also graduated from Yale Law School—"

Betsy interrupted with uncharacteristic sharpness. "That's nice. So?"

"So, that's not all. There's a double whammy. Read the letter."

I checked around and saw that you have a sterling reputation representing Gimbels Local 2, as well as Berle, Berle, and Brunner, but what caught my attention is an uncanny coincidence. Not only are you and I both Yalies, but we each served in the navy during the Allied Invasion of Sicily. This makes us men of good taste and courage. I'd like to swap war stories over drinks, but more than that, I'd like you to consider joining us here at Webster and Sheffield . . .

Cal said, "You see why this caught my attention?"

"No, I don't. Why are we here, Cal?" she asked, letting her arms drop. "Why did we come all this way?"

"Look, I haven't made a decision—"

"Thank you very much!" She turned away. "Since when are you deciding our lives from up high?" she said, flinging the words over her shoulder as she rounded the house.

Cal stopped her before she could get back into the station wagon.

"Why are you so hot over this?"

"Are you backing out on me and the kids?"

Cal looked astonished. "Of course not. I thought you'd be pleased."

"It's a vote of confidence for you, of course . . . I just didn't think we were looking back."

"Who knows if South Dakota will work out?" Cal reasoned.

"We haven't really given it a shot," Betsy said.

She was close to tears without understanding it. Neither did her husband. All he could do was put his hands on her shoulders and offer something, any little thing, just to make peace.

"Let's take a look inside before we decide anything," he offered.

As Betsy turned the key in the lock on the peeling, half-rotted door of the farmhouse, she wondered what it was that had sprung up like a dirt devil to cause this rift with Cal. It wasn't the job, she realized, but that her husband had been holding back a secret. It brought up painful memories of the same thing that had happened in New York, shortly after they'd first met. He'd confessed that he'd been having an affair with a woman in his office named Frieda. He'd said it was over and didn't mean a thing, but she'd trusted this man without question and in an instant it had all been shattered. They'd almost broken up because of it. Now he had been keeping something from her once again, just when she had to face one of the biggest decisions of her life.

The night she was released from jail, and Betsy and Cal walked all over New York City in the blissful delirium of new love, they'd said good night in a swoon of expectation that was buoyed over the next few weeks with breathless phone calls and hasty meetings over lunch and drinks, as they began to weave the strands of their lives together. But soon enough, Betsy noticed a disturbing pattern. Her new beau's free time did not seem to include anything after six p.m., and rarely on weekends. No dinners, no clubs, no Sunday afternoon walks in the park. Betsy was still bunking with Elaine and her roommates, who, in pajama-clad midnight consultations, came to the conclusion that Calvin Kusek was not a serious prospect, but a married man looking for a fling.

"This is not normal," Elaine warned.

Despite the bowel-churning possibility of losing him forever, Betsy ironed her black linen sheath dress, pinned a spray of violets on the collar, and decided to wait for Cal, unannounced, in the lobby of his office building. He spotted her right away, standing against the brown-freckled marble wall, her face pale and drawn in the glow from the lighted office directory, and when he saw her, his delight seemed genuine.

"Why, hello!" He kissed her cheek. "What a nice surprise!"

Despite her rehearsals and determination to appear unconcerned, Betsy couldn't stop herself.

"I have to talk to you," she said right away.

"Is something wrong?"

"Are you really single?" she asked frankly.

"That's a funny question."

"I'm serious."

He looked bemused. "Am I single? Why do you ask? What is this, some kind of a cockamamie proposal?"

"Don't flatter yourself," she answered, but couldn't stop the smile that was softening her face.

"Cross my heart and hope to die," he pledged, exaggerating a frown.

"I'm a confirmed, single bachelor! Now that we've cleared that up, can we please go somewhere and get a drink?"

"Why not dinner?"

"Sure, if you like."

"Uh-huh. Well. That would be a new one," Betsy commented sarcastically.

"What do you mean?"

"We never go out to dinner," she protested, not moving from the safety of the wall. "Or see each other over the weekends."

Cal didn't seem to be listening. "I'm just thinking ... How about that Italian place?" he suggested. "We could sit at the bar."

"Are you seeing someone?" Betsy blurted out.

He must have been listening, because without hesitation he answered truthfully: "Yes."

"Yes?!" she cried. *"What are you telling me?"*

"Calm down. Her name is Frieda. She works at the firm."

Betsy's eyes narrowed. "Ain't that ducky?" she said.

"She's a nice girl—"

"I'm so glad."

"—but it's over."

"Since when?" said Betsy.

"Since yesterday," said Cal.

"You mean to stand there and say that with a straight face?" Betsy said. "Talk about a surprise!" she added acidly, and headed for the revolving brass doors.

He followed, and when they were both out on the street, he made her stop in the crossway of evening crowds.

"I swear, I was just going to tell you," he said.

"When?"

"It's over. I promise. I'd never lie to you."

"But it *is* a lie, when you don't say anything, all this time, letting me think one way when it's actually the other."

"It's the same. Except different. I'm not usually this tongue-tied, it's all your fault," Cal said, trying an appealing grin. "It just took a while to get everything straight with Frieda. Honey, I owed her that. Look, I'll tell you anything you want to know."

"Is she still working there?"

"Yes, of course. But she knows that between us it's kaput."

Betsy was torn between forgetting it and murdering both of them. "So you'll still see her every day."

"It doesn't matter," Cal insisted. Then, with the best intentions in the world, he earnestly took both her hands and said exactly the wrong thing: "I need you, Betsy. You can help me get over her."

After that, Betsy refused to see Calvin Kusek or answer his phone calls. Her father had relented and she slunk back to the Bronx like a wounded animal. The Gimbels strike was settled on September 12, 1941. The union won a forty-hour week and two dollars a week raise. She went back to her old job at the store. Betsy and her comrades had changed the standing of retail workers forever.

But along the way, Betsy had become disillusioned with the revolution. At Young Communist League meetings, the big talkers were all in the same clique, imposing rules and ridiculing weaker members. Earlier that year Hitler had invaded Russia and nearly brought the country down, until Stalin regained his iron grip. Human nature was brutal and not going to change. If you wanted to help humanity, Betsy decided, the best way to do it was person-to-person.

She quit the party, but continued to work the soup line at headquarters down on Twelfth Street near Union Square. A month passed. On a clear fall day, she was ladling watered-down minestrone into bowls held by the needy, many of them men dressed in coats and ties, when a taxi pulled up and double-parked, blocking traffic. Drivers honked and yelled as the cabbie got out, unlocking the trunk for a well-dressed male passenger who looked incongruous in this shabby neighborhood.

Someone was calling her name.

It was Calvin Kusek who had climbed out of the cab, and he was engaged in lifting from the trunk a cardboard carton so enormous he could hardly get his arms around it. As Betsy stared, he staggered to a donations table piled with Carnation evaporated milk and a mountain of carrots with the tops still on, and shoved everything aside to deposit the box, which was packed to the brim with poppy seed Kaiser rolls.

"For the unemployed."

"Thank you for your contribution," Betsy said primly.

"It wasn't easy to find you," Cal replied, dabbing his forehead with a handkerchief. "They said you'd quit."

"I did, but I still do this."

Smartly, Cal refrained from congratulating Betsy on seeing the light about Communism.

"You look nice," he said instead.

"Get out of here. I look like your great-aunt Ethel."

Like the other volunteers, Betsy was wearing a long white apron over her dress, and her blond curls had been squashed into a very unbecoming black hairnet.

"So," said Cal, smacking his palms together, "are we finished now?"

"Finished with what?"

"The worst thirty-two—no, thirty-three—days of my life?"

"Maybe."

"We never did get those oysters," he reminded her slyly.

In response, she handed him a ladle. He pushed the lock of shiny brown hair that always fell across his noble forehead aside and joined her, offering rolls and soup to the destitute shuffling by the scruffy six-story brick structure that held the offices of the *Daily Worker,* as well as the radical Yiddish paper *Freiheit.* On that mild October day, the lofty blue sky seemed to bless the intentions of anyone who chose to labor beneath it in order to fashion a more just human world, and yet Cal sensed unhappiness lingering over Betsy.

"No more pretending," he promised. "Not about anything. I mean it."

She stiffened. "You're the one who was seeing someone on the side."

"I was stupid. But I came clean, didn't I?"

"Not until I practically had to ambush you—"

He set the ladle down with a finality that scared her.

"I refuse to fight."

"I don't want to fight, either," Betsy said with a catch in her throat.

"You have no idea how hard it is for me to abide beneath that sign on the building that says 'Vote Communist,' but that doesn't change—"

Betsy stopped him with a deep and passionate kiss.

"You're right." Her smile was glowing. "Doesn't change a thing. Let's get married."

As they walked out the front door of the old Fletcher farmhouse and locked it behind them, Cal asked what Betsy thought. Inside, the place was scarcely better than the Roys' cabin. Every inch needed to be stripped out and replaced. There were no indoor toilets, and mold in the bedrooms had eaten the walls down to the studs. There were water stains on the ceilings where the roof leaked. The skunky odor that pervaded the rooms was even more dreadful outside.

Betsy shrugged. "It's the best we can afford. What's that funny smell?"

"Probably the septic tank," said Cal. "Needs to be replaced."

"Oh, joy."

They picked their way across the rotted porch boards and through the empty front yard toward the barn.

"Chickens!" Cal pointed to the hard-packed dirt, then counted off imaginary livestock in the large pole pens with swinging gates between them: "Cows, cows, cows, cows, horses, horses, training ring."

The barns were in better shape. Beside the largest was a tack room and smaller pens for sheep and goats, and across the way a Quonset hut that housed a workshop.

"The house is secondary," Cal remarked.

"That's for sure," Betsy said.

"The rest is pretty much ready to go."

They followed a path behind the farthest pen, where they found a creek. Two deer hopped away into the thick foliage, flicking their white tails. Cal and Betsy crossed the stream and climbed a short trail up a ridge, and then they saw a staggering view of the top of the world. The farmstead was below them and rolling open pasture dotted with cottonwoods lay ahead. They could own a piece of this magnificent country. It would be there for Jo and Lance.

Betsy turned to him with a look in her eyes that said she'd made up her mind.

"It's fantastic," Cal agreed.

She grinned mischievously. "What will the Roys say?"

He gave her a hug.

"Good-bye, New York!" Cal shouted to the sky. "Forget the law offices of Webster and Sheffield. I'd trade anything for this."

"Even Chinese restaurants?" Betsy said.

They laughed and kissed, and the wind was as mild as that warm fall day when they'd stood together, working the soup line at the utilitarian brick party building, which now seemed like a page out of a children's book, she had been that naive. How dark and convoluted those idealized youthful arguments had been, compared to the bright simplicity of living off the land. In a marriage, whether you know it or not, you are always making the choice to stay, Betsy thought. Nine years, two children, and twenty-five hundred miles later, she was on the brink of choosing a new life with the same good man. She was falling in love all over again, and she felt it all with a full heart.

"It's everything we hoped for," Betsy said.

On the way to the truck, across the windblown yard they'd already claimed, they reminisced a bit about New York, reciting the addresses where they'd lived, naming all their favorite haunts, and recollecting times they'd shared with other young couples who used to matter so much in their lives, but who were gone now, just memories. Betsy felt lucky. It was so easy to emphasize the wrong things.

Jo was on the pay phone in the hall when the male nurse came to get her. She'd been talking to her boyfriend in Portland. As a firefighter and EMT, he'd seen every kind of medical trauma, but he didn't have enough information about Lance and Willie to help Jo. Instead he assured her she was doing as much as possible and spoke encouragingly about their friends who had formed a prayer circle. He was taking an emergency leave from the fire department and would be in Rapid City the following night.

"Before you leave, can you fax the plans for the waterfront park to my office?" Jo asked. "They're in a file on my desk."

"It's Christmas, nobody's working."

"I know, but next week we have a meeting with the city, and I might still be out here."

"Sure," said Warren. "Of course. I'll do that."

"Thanks, sweetheart. Hang on—the nurse is here."

"Go," said Warren. "Call me back. I love you."

"Love you, too."

The nurse said, "Miss Kusek? There's someone to see you."

Jo hung up and turned around. A middle-aged man with short gray hair was watching her. His face was rounded at the chin, and behind the tinted aviator glasses his eyes were puffy and tired. He wore chinos, hiking boots, and a big orange waterproof jacket with a hood.

"Robbie?"

She froze. It was surreal. There was Warren on the phone and her high school boyfriend standing right in front of her, world-weary and aged.

Their eyes met and Robbie Fletcher's face contorted with tears. Arms outstretched, he came forward and they embraced. Jo clung to him and let herself cry for the first time since leaving Portland.

"I'm so sorry about Wendy," he murmured in her ear.

She nodded silently, clutching the downy folds of his jacket.

"How are Lance and Willie?" he asked.

"Unstable," she said, not letting go. "They're doing tests."

"Oh, God."

"I know."

After a while they both began to breathe again and broke apart.

"How are you?" she asked, wiping her eyes. "It's been way too long."

"I'm fine. Everyone's fine. Not important."

"How'd you get in here?"

"Used my creds." He pulled a press pass from his pocket.

"From the *Rapid City Journal*?" Jo asked. "Lance told me you're a reporter. He sees your byline all the time." She stepped back warily. "Are you here to write a story?"

Robbie shook his head. "No, not at all. That would be a conflict, and besides, I'd much rather be here as your friend than a journalist. If that's okay."

"Of course it's okay. I'm so glad to see you." Jo guided him to a seat beside her in a burgundy chair. "Do you see much of Lance?"

"Not on a regular basis. We run into each other in town."

"How are your parents?" Jo asked.

"They moved to Arizona."

"Really? What are they doing in Arizona?"

"Oh, my dad's writing a book. Mom's doing her thing." Robbie leaned forward, adding urgently, "They're on their way here. They're sick about it, Jo. Everybody is."

Jo's back stiffened. "Really? Someone tried to kill the dirty Reds," she said mockingly. "Rid the town of Communist spies. I thought there'd be dancing in the streets."

"This has nothing to do with that."

"How do you know?"

"It's a robbery that went horribly wrong."

"That's what they're telling us."

"Don't go paranoid on me," Robbie said half jokingly.

"Why not? Everyone else is."

"Let's be logical. The Cold War is over, for all intents and purposes. The Red Scare is history. Your dad's trial was way back in 1963. You and Lance were kids at the time. Someone would have to hold a pretty crazy grudge to take it out on his son two decades later."

The nurse interrupted. "Miss Kusek? You can see your brother now."

Jo stood uncertainly. Robbie assured her that he'd wait.

In a slow nightmare waltz, she followed the nurse through the security doors. Inside, the unit was larger than she expected. It was a regional hospital prepared for a catastrophe and there were many beds. After the low-key waiting room, the lights seemed excruciatingly bright and the temperature was freezing; nurses were wearing sweaters and seemed to glide along in an orderly, positive way. Everything spoke efficiency. Jo made sure not to look at the other patients. She was frightened of what she might see, especially when they got to Lance's bed, but the tubes had been cleaned up and the only bad shock was the enormous bandage around his head. His eyes were closed and his face very pale from loss of blood, but there was no respirator. He was breathing on his own.

"Just for a few minutes," came the nurse's voice. "It's all right. You can hold his hand."

Jo hadn't held her brother's hand since they were little children. It felt almost indecent to be touching the inert, clammy skin.

"Lance? I'm here," she said. "It's Jo."

Another nurse brushed past, explaining that she had to check his vitals. She thumbed his eyelids back and Jo reluctantly noticed that the pupils were huge and black. A moment later the neurosurgeon joined her. All she was capable of taking in was that his name was Dr. Pataki. He had coffee-colored skin and black wavy hair and wore green scrubs.

"You want to know how your loved one is doing," he said.

Jo nodded.

"Your brother's condition is grave."

"But look—he's breathing!" Jo said. "Before they said he was on a ventilator and now he's breathing on his own."

"Yes, that's true. Respiration will keep going because the back of the brain has not been affected," the doctor explained gently.

"Why are his pupils black?"

"The pupils are dilated. They do not change according to the light. They both came in that way. The boy, too. He's still being assessed."

"What about Lance?"

"We're monitoring him carefully. You should understand that if the heart rate slows, the breath will need to be artificially enhanced."

"You mean put him back on a respirator?"

Dr. Pataki nodded.

She had to ask again and again, like a child or someone going out of her mind. "And then what?"

"Wait and see. Give nature a chance."

When Jo came out of the ICU, Robbie Fletcher was waiting for her, a question in his eyes.

TWO

HOPE

9

What is time? How long does a butterfly live?

Jo looked at her new glow-in-the-dark Cinderella watch and saw that it was four o'clock. Her mama had come to wake her even though it was still night.

"Rise and shine, children!" she'd called. "Today is branding day!"

The second hand passed serenely over Cinderella's blue dress. Jo watched it carefully. Was this what they meant by time? When you wound up the screw, did the little wheels inside, which she'd seen in old-fashioned clocks, did they manufacture time? Was it the watch that produced seconds, minutes, and hours, the way the big wheels in the community mill could grind wheat kernels into different kinds of flour? But that meant time itself had to be made of something. The problem was, the minute you thought of it, it would disappear; for example, she couldn't remember her fifth birthday last year, when she'd gotten her red cowboy boots because she could walk, trot, and lope on Pete. Maybe time was invisible, like air—or maybe there was no such thing at all. Now that it was fall, dozens of monarch butterflies had appeared, clustered in the cottonwood trees near the creek. They huddled very close together, like brown clumps of autumn leaves. Jo asked why they came, and Mama said, "Because it's time."

Jo could read now, and always went to bed with a library book close by so she could climb into those big black curious letters that made words that had a story inside. This book had a yellow cover and was about a school for cats. Jo had just opened the first page when the overhead light went on with glaring whiteness. One, two, three blankets were stripped away, exposing her body to frigid air.

"Let's go. Pajamas off!" Mama said, a lot less cheerfully. She tugged on the sleeve of Jo's flannel nightgown as if she were trying to pull her arm off.

"I can do it myself!" Jo cried.

"Then do it. They'll be here in half an hour," Mama said, and left the room.

Through the doorway Jo could see that all the lights were on in the house. There was noise—the radio—and the smell of sweet dough baking. She forgot about the book, eager to be part of everything. Jo had the top bunk because she was oldest. The ceiling was flat and cold, and so were the walls. They didn't have big wood logs like their old house. She kept her clothes with her because it was too cold to climb up and down in order to change. She pulled on an undershirt and jeans and closed the snaps on the paisley cowgirl shirt she'd chosen the night before, and scrambled down the ladder. Despite the glaring light and her mother trampling in, her brother was still asleep, lying on his stomach, so Jo pulled his covers off and pajama bottoms down and began slapping his bare bottom like the hindquarters of a horse.

"Get moving, you!"

He kicked out, wildly yelling, "Stop it!"

"Get up, dopey!" Jo let the waistband snap. "Don't you know it's a special day?"

Two years had passed since Betsy and Cal, using all their savings, had bought the four-hundred-acre Lucky Clover Ranch that had been owned by Stell Fletcher's mother. The six-room Queen Anne–style home that had been shipped out on a train in pieces from Sears was renovated top to bottom, starting with indoor plumbing and hot water. With just their four hands and the occasional hired man, the work was hard enough to undermine anybody's pioneer spirit—but not theirs.

"Baby steps," Cal kept reminding Betsy.

In retrospect, they should have just taken the whole thing down and started over, but once they'd proudly told Doris and Dutch Roy that they'd found a new place and were moving on, the offer of welcome to the Crazy Eights Ranch was reeled in as fast as a rotting walleye, dead from one of those fish kills for which nobody knows the cause. From that time on, everything about the relationship between the Kuseks and the Roys began to stink. The young family moved out of the cabin and onto the dilapidated property as fast as possible, rather than withstand the cold wind of resentment coming from their former benefactors.

Each of them had reasons to feel offended. Dutch, because he'd expected Cal would be the son he could be proud of—as well as a fine attorney whom he'd planned to make executor of his will—instead of his real heir, Scotty, who cared more about riding bulls than keeping up the family legacy.

For his part, Scotty knew that Cal was tight with his dad, but what he envied was that Cal had the freedom to get out from under his father's thumb, which pressed harder each day against that hollow spot at the bottom of the windpipe where a person breathes, as if by threatening to cut him off, Scotty would wake up and die right, give up his dream of following the bull riding circuit—Jackson, Las Vegas, Myrtle Springs, Cheyenne—and spend the rest of his life riding a hay mow in his own backyard. Cal had been his commanding officer, and Scotty still held him in respect because of that. Despite their disagreements, deep down he longed for Cal to see him as a worthy friend.

But when it came to retribution, it was Doris Roy who held the sharpest knife, because the departure of the Kuseks caused her the deepest wound. Like it says in the Bible, *"Paul laid a bundle of sticks on the fire and a viper came out of the heat and bit him on the hand."* When her husband told her that despite his offer of giving them land and a place in the family, the Kuseks had bought their own property—from the liberal Democrat Fletchers of all people—she felt poisonous fury seep into her soul. It caused her to shake and her heart to beat strangely. Her vanity had been assaulted. Her generosity had been rebuffed, which alerted all the memories of all the slights she'd ever suffered as a teenager, the humiliation of coming from illiterate, dirt-poor Pentecostals and not finishing sixth grade because she had to help her parents on their dirt-poor claim, driving the pickup when she was fourteen, Dad pitching hay off the back. The whole thing caused such a state of distraught indignation that she'd written a half-crazed letter to Betsy Kusek, accusing her of "takeing my recipies" and "recking our home." She'd skipped the housewarming party at the Lucky Clover Ranch, but would not miss, Dutch insisted, the couple's first branding.

Over Doris's objections—because this was business—he'd sold Cal Kusek a hundred cows and a Lee Brothers bull at a good price, and now he favored a look at the calves. Besides, helping a neighbor was a Christian duty that went beyond social graces. With this, Doris had no argument. She'd always thought of herself as a charitable person. If the Roys didn't show up, there'd be talk. A black mark would go against them, and rightly so.

It was the first branding of the first group of calves that had been born on Kusek property—an exciting ritual that would mark their true ownership, as well as acceptance into the ranching community, and Betsy was under a lot of pressure to pull it off. Cal had a crew of men to round up the cattle, but Betsy was single-handedly responsible for creating a hospitable atmosphere and making sure everything went ahead right on time. That included minding the children and preparing a parade of meals from scratch, although she did cheat on the home-made biscuits, which she still hadn't mastered.

They'd worked out a schedule: 4:30 a.m. first breakfast, 5:00 a.m. saddle up, 5:30 a.m. move the cows in from the south pasture to the pens. By nine they'd be separating out the calves, and then women bearing covered plates would start arriving for a potluck lunch, after which more folks would arrive for the traditional social hour—which could last all afternoon—of coffee, cookies, and homemade ice cream.

Getting seventy-three calves vaccinated and branded and back to their mothers by the end of the day was serious business, but there was a sweet part to it, and that was the partnership that had developed between Betsy and Cal. Two years of physical labor had honed their temperaments as well as their bodies. They ate less and grew stronger. Work and sleep went by the sun. They learned patience with things that were beyond their control. The clothesline now held eight pairs of Levi's Saddleman jeans in different sizes and washes, all hanging upside down with the pockets turned out to dry. Although Cal had passed the South Dakota bar, he dressed only in work clothes now, and his long Scandinavian Polish face was sunburned and deeply fissured. However, he still struck the figure of the stubborn individualist. He wore a fedora as often as a cowboy hat, and disdained the hand-rolled cigarette for a White Briar pipe: the contemplative rancher.

Both Kuseks had become easy in the saddle and good with hammer and nails. There were no jobs, really, either one couldn't perform. They'd achieved a kind of domestic democracy, a triumph of having moved west: it was possible to live the life of their idealistic vision. But social justice was still a prime concern. The 1952 election was less than a month away, and while everyone was predicting Dwight D. Eisenhower to win by a landslide, the Kuseks were unapologetic in their support of Democratic presidential nominee Adlai Stevenson.

Cal had written a series of letters to the editor of the *Rapid City Journal* attacking the lies of Richard M. Nixon, Republican candidate for vice president, and his cohort in character assassination, Senator Joseph McCarthy, calling them "a threat to our civil liberties," which made him famous—at least in the eyes of two Democratic friends in town, Nelson Fletcher (whom they'd nicknamed "Fletch") and Avery Saugstad, M.D., dedicated general practitioner, former county coroner, and current representative from Pennington County in the state legislature, whom everybody called Doc Avery.

Fletch had invited Cal to join his law firm, and Betsy sometimes filled in at Doc Avery's office. Together, Fletch and Doc Avery had become the center of the Kuseks' lives in South Dakota. Their professional practices and personal connections opened doors for the new couple—so when Betsy would enter the home of a housebound patient, she'd be welcomed into the family. She also saw some amazing things, like an eighty-one-year-old widow confined to a wheelchair who continued to mine her dead husband's claim, using a soup spoon and a strainer to pan inch by inch for gold. The doctor himself was a country original—a scrawny, white-haired old bird with slumping shoulders who sang in a barbershop quartet and also found time to raise llamas as a hobby. But his true love was medicine, which he practiced with superhuman devotion. His patients came first, which his wife, Maryanne, understood. Their only sadness in life was that they had no children.

Every morning Cal and Betsy parted with a kiss, but on branding day they were too preoccupied. The kitchen was steamy and Betsy's face was flushed from the heat of the oven as she took out batch after batch of Ballard's Oven-Ready Biscuits, the kind that come in a can. The dining room table was piled with dishes they'd put out the night before. Jo took an apron from the hook and tied the strings twice around her waist with a bow in front, just like her mom's. The stiff canvas came down to her ankles.

"Fry up some bacon," Betsy told her.

"All of it?"

"Yes, and while it's cooking, start cracking eggs."

She pushed a big ceramic bowl Jo's way. There were four cartons already on the blue-checked countertop. Jo stepped up on her special stool and opened the first one. The eggs were not just white but also pale shades of lavender and lightly speckled brown. Every day she collected them in a red wire basket, rinsed them under running water, gently scrubbing off the gunk, and then set them in a dish rack to dry. Afterward she'd disinfect the sink with Lysol. They were her eggs, harvested from hens that Papa said were her project, so she could learn how to manage money. She'd already bought two new chicks with her first quarter. Jo was proud and careful as she cracked each egg cleanly with a knife and spilled it into the big mixing bowl.

Betsy glanced at the clock and wiped her forehead with the back of a wrist.

"Holy smokes, look at the time. They'll be here any minute."

"When is Robbie coming? And Uncle Scotty? When are they coming, Mommy? When?"

"I don't know, honey."

There had been several misfortunes at the Crazy Eights since the Kuseks left. The blizzard of 1951 had upended the Roys' windmill. The ponds had shrunk by half when the drought set in, which also destroyed natural forage areas. Hungry livestock broke through the fences and ate off chokecherry bushes, sending them into convulsions. Their lips turned ghastly blue and they died. The Roys lost twenty-six sheep and ten mother cows. Then there was an infestation of grasshoppers that stripped their garden in one day. It was as if they were being punished by the plagues.

And then the worst happened. Dutch had an accident. Several weeks ago he'd been driving the tractor on the main road in the middle of the day when he was hit by a car driven by a traveling salesman selling vacuum cleaners. The guy was speeding while at the same time being serviced by a skirt from Potato Creek in exchange for a bottle of carpet cleaner, but on the other hand, Dutch had refused to install warning lights on the back of the tractor—even though it was the law—insisting that farmers have the right of way and the government wasn't going to tell him what to do. He was tossed off the seat, traveled twenty feet in the air, and landed on his back smack-dab on the centerline of the asphalt, lucky to have shattered only his pelvis. Recovery was slow and questionable. Neighbors were still helping to fill in with chores at the Crazy Eights.

Whether the Roys showed up or not, Betsy's cooking would be judged. In haste, she showed Jo the instructions in *The Good Housekeeping Cookbook*. The print was stained and crusty flour had gathered in the cracks between the pages.

"When you finish the eggs, I want you to make these chocolate spice cookies. They need to be in the oven by six."

Jo looked at the kitchen clock on the wall. Although it was just a plain white clock in the shape of a teapot, it was in charge of everything that happened in the house, and now that she could also read time, she knew everything the same as grown-ups and why things had to get done when they did. The clock said four twenty, and already headlights had begun to show in the dark beyond the window. She started cracking faster, not even stopping to pick out the tiny bits of shell.

Pretty soon a lot of men were standing around the dining room eating bacon, scrambled eggs, biscuits, and thick toast with lots of butter, and drinking mugs of instant coffee. Even though he wasn't wearing his uniform, she knew the state trooper, Randy Sturgis, who had rescued them from the mud. He was very tall, but he bent down to shake her hand, and smiled and called her "miss." The others were nice except for the horrible man with the knives. His clothes were dirty and his beard so big and black you couldn't see his eyes. He looked like an evil monster. When he turned her way, Jo ran into the kitchen.

Lance had dressed himself and put on his straw cowboy hat. He stood on the orange chair in the kitchen, looking out for Scotty Roy's truck. When he saw it he ran to the front door. The rifts that had grown and mended between the families did not include the children, and nothing had changed an early attachment Lance had formed with Uncle Scotty.

Lance had inherited his parents' lean, athletic bodies, but unlike his outspoken sister, his disposition was quiet and floaty; you never really knew what was on his mind, unless he had homed in on something, and then he would chase after it until he had it in his teeth—the same disposition as his "uncle." From the time well-meaning older people began to ask that anesthetizing question, *"What do you want to be when you grow up?"* Lance would answer with blazing certainty, "A bull rider, like Scotty Roy."

"Morning, sprout," Scotty said, knocking off his cowboy hat.

Lance scooped it up and squared off, feet planted, hands on hips, fierce as a scowling bobcat. "You said you would teach me."

"I will."

"Today!"

"Gotta help your folks out today," Scotty said, sidestepping the boy.

Lance blocked his path. He barely came up to the man's belt. "We have to start sometime!"

He cocked his head, looking at Scotty with a stare that was both pleading and bold. Scotty didn't mind someone wanting his company that much, even if it was a four-year-old.

"Next time you're out at the ranch, me and you will pick out the meanest, nastiest sheep and we'll see what you can do. Sound good?"

"Yes, sir!"

Riding a sheep was the way you started out. Then you went to calves and steers and finally bulls. Lance felt like he'd just won the Youth Rodeo World Finals. He rushed back and forth, importantly doing his job of putting glasses on the table.

The Fletchers got to come in through the back kitchen door. Robbie's family was special because his dad worked with their dad. First Stell shouldered inside, carrying a cardboard box, followed by her husband with six-year-old Robbie asleep on his shoulder.

"Have you seen this?" Fletch asked, waving a copy of the *Rapid City Journal* over the boy's head. "Hot off the press this morning. Cal's latest letter to the editor."

"Cal's inside. Show it to him. Robbie can lie down in the bunkroom if he wants," Betsy added.

Miraculously, Robbie woke up. "I don't want to sleep in the bunkroom!" he said, wiggling out of his dad's arms.

Instantly, Jo was tired of washing the mixing bowl.

"Do I have to keep doing this?" she whined.

"I'll help," Robbie said, and picked up the towel to dry.

Since their first encounter on the mechanical horse outside the Duhamel Company store, Jo and Robbie had become pals. She was in kindergarten and he was in first grade, and they had decided to get married, so washing and drying dishes together was normal.

"Can we go now?" Jo asked when they were done.

The tiny kitchen was hot and overcrowded, and Betsy had forgotten which task she was about to do next. She felt this exotic day getting off to a wobbly start, like a lopsided flying saucer heading off to parts unknown.

"Go!" she said, and the kids ran off.

Stell pulled an ice cream maker from the cardboard carton. "I hardly use this anymore, since we moved to town and Snow's Ice Cream is right down the street."

Hand-turned ice cream, like handmade soap, was one of the devotions countrywomen expected of themselves as well as one another. Store-bought was frivolous. Doing anything the hard way gave it higher value; doing it the easy way might even be taken as an insult. Betsy certainly wanted to avoid that, but had no patience for endless cranking, hence a supply of Breyers chocolate and vanilla in the freezer.

"Is Doris coming?" Stell asked.

"I doubt it. Dutch is barely walking."

Stell had put on an apron and started putting things away. "If Doris does show up, she better behave."

Betsy smiled, relieved to have an ally in the fray. Although they'd heard each other's secrets and desires a hundred times, Betsy and Stell couldn't seem to get enough of each other. Anything was a lot more fun with the other gal around. There were certain intimate things only *she* would understand, and it was a real plus that both their husbands and their kids got along. The families shared Sunday suppers and cocktails-and-bridge nights that ended with the grown-ups smashed, listening with boozy absorption to records from Cal's collection of classical music that he spun with gusto on the brand-new Magnavox console, which they'd apparently acquired instead of a kitchen. The four of them had found safe harbor in the land of anti-intellectuals, where everything was tinged with ironclad religious beliefs, even the daily stock report that was coming across the kitchen radio:

"Overnight U.S. stock futures trading changed little from Friday's closes. By the grace of our Lord, Jesus Christ, trade was moderate to active on good demand in Kansas and Nebraska," said a smooth-voiced man.

"Good God," said Betsy. "Is that Thaddeus Haynes?"

"Did you know he's up for state legislature?"

"Haynes isn't that bright. Kind of a nincompoop."

"So is Joe McCarthy," Stell said. "But people listen to him."

Haynes had moved on from the stock report. *"Are you worried about the Communist plot for the ultimate takeover of America?"* he was saying. *"Do you know they have plans in place to liquidate thirty million people?"*

Stell made a shocked face, mugging indignation. "Gee, I didn't know that!"

"Nobody told *me!*"

"Right now," Haynes went on, *"liberals and socialists are secretly working with Moscow to destroy our freedoms. Join like-minded patriots at one of my exciting study groups and get the facts. We'll send, absolutely free, all the information you need to spot a Communist and turn him in. Let me remind you the election's coming up. If you want to fight Communism, vote Republican—"*

"Get out of my kitchen!" Betsy said, and clicked the radio off.

Two Australian sheepdogs, Lois and Bandit, waited outside the barn while the men were saddling up. Lois, named for Superman's girlfriend on TV, was a blue merle with bright blue eyes, and her brother, Bandit, was tricolored with dark eyes receded in a mask of black and gray. Cal had bought them from a trainer in Wyoming and was pleased. They were intelligent ranch dogs who immediately took a dislike to Master Sergeant Hayley Vance riding up in his air force jeep, barking to save the day, until Cal gave them the word and they quit. The entrance of the air force official was embellished by a swirl of dust from the parched barnyard.

"They trust you with that thing?" Cal joked of the jeep.

Master Sergeant Vance grinned. "One of the perks," he said, swinging out.

It was the first time Cal had seen Hayley Vance out of uniform.

He had come ready to work like the rest of them—Fletch, Scotty Roy, Randy Sturgis, Vaughn Anders and Spanky Larson from the Bison Café—attired in leather chaps, assorted woolen vests, and buckskin jackets, as it was before dawn and near freezing. Their well-worn boots and dusty cowboy hats had seen good service, molded over time to fit their preferences.

A couple of lamps in the barn provided the only light. Trailers in which the others had brought their horses were parked haphazardly. Cal had his favorite paint, Jesse, saddled up, and ready for Master Sergeant Vance was a handsome bay gelding named Junior, who stood sixteen hands high.

"What is he?" Master Sergeant Vance asked, respectful of his size. "Draft?"

"Draft–quarter horse mix." Its muscles quivered as Cal ran a soothing hand along its shoulder. "Don't worry, Hayley, he's a gentle giant. Didn't want you to get hurt."

"Appreciate that," said Vance, hoisting his weight into the saddle.

"Although at times he *can* get fresh."

"Nothin' old Hayley ain't been warned about before," Scotty shouted. His horse was spinning in restless circles.

"Only about a thousand times," added Spanky, cleaning his glasses on his dusty shirt.

"His legend precedes him," Fletch agreed, which the others found a hilarious proposition.

In fact the huge, well-apportioned animal greatly improved the slumped profile of the bureaucrat who was usually bound to his desk.

They sorted into single file and started out slowly around the barn, Lois and Bandit following. You could still see streaks of fireflies over the creek. In the dark everything was alive. You could feel the pine trees breathing in the gloom. There was a fresh, moist wind and the constant calls of roosters and cicadas. Dawn broke, colorless and quiet. Sound stopped. The wind fingered the tops of the trees, and the tender sky of the new day was like a pale blue piece of onionskin paper, fragile and empty.

Fletch trotted up next to Cal, who was wearing his fedora.

"Your latest letter defending Adlai Stevenson was the best thing you've written."

"Every day we get closer to the election, I get madder than hell at the Democratic Party for not coming out guns blazing against McCarthy and his partner in slime, Richard Nixon."

"You're not the only one," Fletch assured him. "Doc Avery called this morning raving his head off about what you said. He thinks you're a natural politician."

"That's flattering."

"He's mentioned you to Verna Bismark, Democratic state chair."

"What for?"

"I know you have political ambitions, Cal."

"But I'm an outsider here."

"It's the West, my friend. Everybody came from somewhere else. It's open territory. We need someone like you to energize the Democratic Party. Think about it."

Cal had been thinking about it and listening to people talk about what mattered around here. Honesty. Family. Independence. Land. They wanted to be left alone to follow God's plan, but when they did need help, they expected it from a government that upheld their way of life. Without being too "egocentric" about it, Cal was coming to the idea that when they had the ranch going, he might be ready to get back into the mix of things. He'd been captain of the debate team at Yale and the competitive juices were stirring. Sometimes talent just won't let you be.

The men rode on, following a shortcut to the pasture along a chalky path beside a river so overflowing they were covered with spray and so loud they had to shout above the rapids. Then the forest opened up to a sun-drenched meadow called Bottlebrush Creek, where the trail mingled with bunchgrass until it disappeared, becoming nothing more than a forgotten direction in the wild plain. A vista opened out of the trees, and they were met by a warm, tranquil breeze that escorted them over rich slopes of wheatgrass high as the horses' bellies, then down through lowland gulches choked with greasewood, where they sighted cattle drinking from a stream.

The rhythmic shuffle of hooves brought them steadily closer to the center of a widening bowl where the herd was scattered, shrunk by distance to brown grubs in the tawny grass. They stopped to take in the breadth of the valley, ridges of pine and the blue-gray mountains behind.

"This was once a Lakota village that was burned to the ground by

Custer," Cal told the party. "They have photographs of the ones who survived in the Hotel Alex Johnson. Little kids wrapped in blankets, big sad eyes. Miles of corpses of dead buffalo."

"That's what happens when you've got demagogues and bullies," Fletch said meaningfully. "Slaughter of the innocent."

Scotty pulled a flask from his saddlebag and passed it around.

"The meek *do not* inherit the earth," Master Sergeant Vance commented.

"What does that mean?" Cal asked.

"You gotta be out front and way ahead." He shrugged. "You know what you got here, don't you? Water. Lots and lots of water, while the rest of the county's dying of thirst."

"The grass at our place is this high," Scotty said worriedly, pinching two inches of air between thumb and forefinger.

Master Sergeant Vance smiled amiably at Cal. "You got real lucky when you bought this place, Lieutenant."

Custer's men would have recognized the lone column of westerners moving across the grassland accompanied by cow dogs, horses plodding dreamlike under heavy saddles and coiled lariats, eyes drooping, sometimes sighing deeply from their chests or sprinting to get up a rise. Fletch's gelding wore a bridle with turquoise and silver studs on the brow band. Vaughn had worked hand-tooled crucifixes on the flaps of his saddle. After several tries, Master Sergeant Vance got his big horse into a trot. Tipping and bouncing, he caught up with Cal, and for a while they rode side by side ahead of the others.

"I want you to listen, because I see it coming plain as day," Master Sergeant Vance began. "This drought cycle is going to put a lot of folks out of business. Over the next few years it'll happen because it's nature's way. Slowly and surely, ranches will fail, but not yours, for two reasons. You've got water, and you're smart about management. In my job, I have to look ahead to the next generation of calves, understand? I want to make you a proposition. I'm offering you a contract to supply the Ellsworth Air Force Base with beef."

"Along with Dutch Roy?"

"I wouldn't just let him go. I'd keep him on another year."

"Hold it, Hayley. I don't know about that. Scotty and I served together. He brought us out here. Dutch opened his home to us."

"I understand." Master Sergeant Vance nodded sympathetically.

"But the Crazy Eights Ranch ain't gonna make it," he said with finality. "They do not have a rich enough water source. It's a sad fact of life, but somebody else will profit from their hardship. Might as well be you."

Cal shook his head. "I can't take away a friend's livelihood."

"Any one of these nice Christian boys would steal food off your table if they had to."

"I appreciate it, but I can't live like that."

"I'm not sure you understand." Master Sergeant Vance sounded deeply peeved. "I'm willing to bet on your future. That's a hell of a vote of faith. Try borrowing off the future from the Cottonwood National Bank!"

"If the time comes when Dutch can no longer meet your needs, I'd be more than happy to supply the air force. Until that happens, I'm indebted for the offer, but that's not why we came here. I'll take my chances. Okay? No hard feelings?"

Cal offered his hand across the trail between them, but Master Sergeant Vance was too unsteady in the saddle or too furious to shake, so Cal scooched his horse forward and it exploded into a gallop, eager to finally go to work, and then the rest broke the line, scattering to gather up the cows that were sheltered under trees or had wandered half a mile away. The men and horses instinctively knew how to spread out and work together, coming up from behind the animals to urge them toward the center.

The cows were not surprised. They picked up their heads and quickly trotted along, mothers and babies side by side, long-horned bulls standing where they were. Then it was an adrenaline-charged game to anticipate one another's moves as the men and dogs, without signals, without speech—riding high on pure confidence—caused the herd to converge and funnel through a pass that would take it over flatland and back to the Lucky Clover Ranch. In an hour they'd gotten all the cows ahead of them and they were looking at a horde of red-and-white-spotted hindquarters running for home.

A small crowd had gathered at the corrals waiting for their return. Trucks and cars had nosed into every available space around the house—in the driveways and halfway up the road. It was a big to-do, as big as waiting for the freight train from Chicago to arrive. And then the spectators were rewarded. The herd came pouring down the hill at a heart-stopping rate, into the holding area where Randy Sturgis and Vaughn Anders were already dismounted and on the ground, yelling, *"Move on! Hahhh-hahhh!"* waving their arms so the two-thousand-pound animals would siphon off into the correct pens. Children perched on the red iron rails and cheered, hoping to see the cattle crash into each other, or miss the gate and get loose and run all over hell, leaning over and swishing branches to help things along, until they were yanked away by grown-ups. A cloud of brown dust stood over everything.

Jo stood at the very top of the gate and waved, calling, "Papa!"

Cal, riding the paint Jesse in the midst of the pandemonium, called back. "Get down from there!"

Jo squinted. Her father was a high-up shape in the sun.

"I want to ride with you!"

"Get off," he yelled. "It's dangerous."

Spectators had clambered to the roof of the tack room to watch the cows and calves being separated, but Jo had a better idea. She wanted to help. She and Cal rode double all the time and she wanted to do that now, in the roundup. It was her dad and their ranch, which put her above the other kids. If she dropped down inside the corral, he could ride by and scoop her up like he always did.

"Papa! Look! I'm coming!"

She waited for her moment and jumped. Her boots touched the ground at the same time the gate opened and a red cow and her baby stampeded past. Onlookers began to scream warnings. Cal saw his little girl standing still in a crush of confused, bawling cattle and felt a lightning stroke of fear like none other. He signaled to Jesse, and the horse showed his breeding, nimbly cutting in and out of charging bodies and flashing hooves. Cal bent over and hoisted Jo into the saddle while the crowd sighed with relief.

Cal did not have time to scold her, nor the disposition.

"Never do that again," he said, breathing hotly in his daughter's ear.

Worse than the reprimand was the humiliation of being lifted away from her father and handed over the fence into the arms of strangers who berated Jo with disapproval. She ran across the yard, up the steps, and through the front door, vengefully letting it bang.

Her mother and Robbie's mother were laughing in the kitchen. They didn't hear. Ladies were setting the pans of food they had brought on the table so that their contributions would be more conspicuous, even if it meant moving others' out of the way. Nobody noticed Jo. She felt invisible in the room with heavy brown furniture inherited from old Mrs. Fletcher—the towering cabinet with glass doors she must never open, gray photographs on the wall of "ancestors" she didn't know. Tears of shame stung her eyes, and she felt that same empty thump in her chest as when she'd woken up that first morning in the cabin and Papa was gone. Why didn't he want her riding proudly in the saddle with him? Why did he kick her off in front of everybody? Now she saw that her father had left the pouch with his tobacco, pipe, and cigarette lighter made of transparent yellow stone on the sideboard. When nobody was looking, she took her father's lighter and put it in her pocket.

Doris Roy squeezed her platter of corn fritters next to Joanie Ostenberg's Indian meat loaf and realized that in her haste to get Dutch settled before she left the house, she'd forgotten maple syrup. Lance was standing by, perusing the offerings on tiptoe.

"Does your mama keep maple syrup?"

Lance nodded. "Yes, ma'am. For pancakes."

"Can you show me?"

Lance took her hand and led her to the kitchen.

When he pushed the door open, Betsy and Stell froze. They were caught in the middle of a heinous act: spooning store-bought Breyers ice cream into the ice cream maker.

"Ice cream!" Lance yelped. "Can I turn it?"

"Don't look like it needs turning," Doris observed icily.

He climbed on the stool and reached for a jar. "Here's the maple syrup, Mrs. Roy."

Doris spied the trays of chocolate spice cookies.

"Did you make those?" she asked Lance.

He shook his head. "My sister did."

"Aren't you an honest scout!" she declared, deliberately not looking at Betsy.

Betsy struggled to find something to say. Stell was behind her, an incriminating scoop dripping from her hand, the picture of two does caught in the headlights.

"Let's go put this syrup next to the corn fritters, shall we?" Doris said.

"Thanks for coming," Betsy managed. "Give our best to Dutch."

"I surely will." To the boy: "Lance! Whatever happened to your hair?"

"My mom cut it."

"Next time tell your mom to take you to the barber."

At this remark, Stell shot a *Do you believe the nerve?* stare at Betsy, who returned the look with such exaggerated sarcasm that she expected Doris Roy to turn around and slap her, but instead Doris headed for the door—pausing to cast a superior look around the disordered kitchen.

"Good luck," she said enigmatically, and left.

"Same to you," Stell replied under her breath.

Betsy let out a huge, humiliated sigh and put a hand to her chest. "I've never been so mortified!"

"Don't worry. Nobody will know."

"Until she tells the world that I'm a phony."

"I think you have a bigger problem, pally." Stell had pulled the ugly orange curtains aside and was looking through the window.

Betsy was at the end of her rope. She'd been on her feet for—she couldn't remember how many hours—and there were still lunch and the social hour to get through. She hadn't been out of the kitchen since dawn and could only pray that nothing had gone horribly wrong at the roundup, nobody'd been thrown or trampled to death.

"Please, don't tell me!" Betsy begged.

"I think you'd better know," said Stell. "There's an elephant in your front yard."

Thaddeus Haynes had it figured to the minute. He knew how these things worked. There was always that short break after the roundup when everyone was hungry and tired and in need of refreshment. That was your opportunity. The whole neighborhood would be there. You arrived unannounced and didn't stay long because folks had to get back to their homes for evening chores. Surprise was important, especially if they were Democrats. Better, truth be told, because here was a chance to win new converts. Everybody loved Dino the elephant.

Haynes had heard about Calvin Kusek. People liked him even though he was a newcomer and an East Coast intellectual. He had a nice manner, people said, and was the kind of person likely to settle an argument rather than start one. Dutch Roy spoke his praises, although he was disappointed when Kusek moved to his own place, but who could blame a young man on the rise? The wife was supposed to be pretty, which helped, because Haynes considered himself a ladies' man who understood the feminine mind. He got dozens of letters from women proposing marriage, just from hearing his soothing voice on the radio.

They each believed he was talking to her alone, from some kind of palace on high, when the whole setup amounted to a microphone on a table in a rented room in a hotel. But that would change when everyone got television. It was around the corner—God's gift for spreading the gospel—and Thaddeus Haynes intended to fulfill His word by owning a TV station one day.

In the meantime, he was doing his best. He drove a polished aqua-green Cadillac convertible with balloons and signs that said VOTE FOR HAYNES!, followed by wranglers in a truck similarly festooned, pulling a trailer that held a baby elephant he'd borrowed from friends at the Omaha zoo. To avoid being charged with trespass, they were always careful to stay on the public road, which they did at the Kusek property, across the way from the modest farmhouse.

Wearing a three-piece suit with a flower in the lapel and a sincere look of humility, Thaddeus Haynes was conspicuous among the cowhands and families who had taken their lunch plates outside and were standing around, or sitting on a couple of logs that bordered the sparsely planted backyard. Haynes was carrying a big pink Mrs. Ellen's bakery box and his pockets were stuffed with leaflets promoting the Republican Party. He introduced himself, handed out flyers, and politely asked for the lady of the house, working quickly because he never knew how long he would have before some drunk spooked the elephant. Meanwhile the wranglers had unloaded the beast and led it by heavy shackles to the top of the driveway. Soon the backyard emptied as the visitors came around front, drawn to the novelty of a creature from Africa in the middle of wheat fields. The elephant flapped its ears and made low chirping sounds. Its wise eyes rolled back and forth as people crowded around to touch the creases in its hairless skin, and children begged for a ride.

Cal, Betsy, Fletch, and Stell were simply astonished.

"What do we do?" Betsy wondered.

"Don't get into a debate," Fletch warned as they reluctantly stepped forward to meet their uninvited guests.

Cal introduced himself. "How are you, Mr. Haynes?"

"I am blessed!" he proclaimed.

The man with the smooth radio voice had a rounded belly and a big square head. The forehead was high, blond hair rising up in a girlish pompadour. The nose was large and fleshy; the eyes deeply hooded with swollen dark circles underneath, which belied his serene disposition. This was a troubled man who didn't sleep at night. The lips were wide and sensual, but the mouth was in a perpetual sneer, as if he had superior knowledge of everyone's secrets.

"Say, I don't mean to bust up the party," Haynes said, offering his hand. "But with the election just around the corner, I thought I'd come by. Thaddeus Haynes, radio host of *The Hour of Truth* and running for the state legislature on the Republican ticket. Ever listen to my show?"

"Whenever I want to hear the hog report," Betsy replied sweetly.

"I understand you just moved here."

"Two years ago."

"Why, you don't look like newcomers at all! You really fixed this place up. I'd love to stay but I have another appointment. Here's a little housewarming present."

Haynes offered the box of doughnuts covered with gaily colored sprinkles.

"Hope I'm not ruining anybody's appetite!"

"Of course not," said Betsy, who had no intention of putting Republican doughnuts on her table. She set the box down on a tree stump.

"May I ask how you folks are planning to vote?" Haynes asked jovially.

All four answered Democratic.

"You don't favor Eisenhower? The greatest war commander of all time?"

"I like Ike," said Cal. "I detest Nixon."

"But the man's a visionary," Haynes replied. "He saw right away that Communists were infiltrating the government at the highest levels."

Betsy couldn't stop herself. "You mean the Alger Hiss case? It's still not been proven he's a spy."

Haynes cocked his great head at the woman who had spoken up so sharply and was about to reply when the Australian shepherds, Lois and Bandit, came out of nowhere, seemingly possessed by the devil, barking and charging through the crowd at the elephant. The wranglers took out their pistols and shouted, "Call off your dogs!" while Cal, Vaughn, Betsy, and Scotty lunged for them and grabbed them each by the collar, practically having to wrestle their squirming eighty-pound bodies into the tack room, where they kept flinging themselves madly against the door.

"Time to go," Haynes said, and smiled.

He was not perturbed; he knew the majority in the crowd saw things his way. The wranglers had given balloons to the kids and the women had VOTE REPUBLICAN shopping bags, so they were in the pocket. He'd learned that if you can't convince them in thirty seconds, you might as well move on. So he turned to the Fletchers and Kuseks and said, "God be with you," signaling his boys to pack up.

Minutes after the circus left came the far-off sound of motorcycles— a pack of three young hoods led by red-haired Tyler "Honeybee" Jones. The young thief, who had gotten his start in crime by stealing mirrors off cars, was now a high school dropout stealing cars off the street. He skidded his motorcycle to a throbbing stop in front of the Kusek farmhouse, raising as much dust as possible.

"Which way's the elephant?" Honeybee shouted over the hopped-up engines spitting noise like strings of firecrackers. In the pens the cows jammed together and horses whinnied nervously.

"Get out of here, you're spooking my stock!" Cal shouted back.

Honeybee and friends took off, throwing sprays of dirt and pachyderm dung. The adults shook their heads, hoping the elephant would break loose and stomp all over those punks, who were known to raise havoc in town.

The visitors regrouped around the corrals. Two branding irons had been heating in a rusty old pipe with a propane flame blowing through, getting ready for a ceremonial moment Betsy and Cal had been looking forward to for a long time. They were about to brand their first Lucky Clover–born calf. Jo and Lance couldn't be found, so their parents went ahead.

Scotty was on horseback in the calf pen. He maneuvered a bit, scrutinized, then, fast as a frog tonguing a fly, his lariat lashed out, caught a little red calf around the hind legs and heeled it into the chute.

Cal sat down in the soft dirt holding the calf's hind legs. Betsy was on the front end, pinning his shoulders and head down with her knee. They pulled in opposite directions, exposing a white underbelly. The rest of his body was covered with baby-soft fur. He was calm. His clear, trusting eyes looked around curiously.

Randy Sturgis squatted beside them with the syringe.

"Pin his arm back," he said, inserting the needle in the fleshy underside. The vaccination drew a drop of blood.

Then Spanky Larson gave them the branding iron.

"You two ready?" he asked. "I never seen it done like this, but you asked for it, so now both of you put your hands on—and smile! Just like cutting a wedding cake!"

Cal gripped the end, Betsy put her hand over his, and together they pressed the tip of the scalding-hot iron down. The animal flinched. There was smoke and the faint smell of burning meat. When they took it off, the hair had been burned away, leaving a shiny LC.

"Is he okay?" Betsy asked anxiously.

"That's just oil in the skin," Randy assured her.

They released the calf. He instantly sprang up on his feet and ran down the chute to be reunited with his mother.

"See?" Spanky said. "It didn't bother him none."

Betsy and Cal looked at each other and saw all the way back to the first time they met; the street in Greenwich Village lined with ailanthus trees, the walk along the harbor, and the hopeful cross-country journey that followed. Kneeling in the dust in South Dakota, they were drawn into that same first kiss.

It was done. It was theirs.

Jo had taken Lance and Robbie to her secret place, inside the henhouse. She showed them her father's lighter and Robbie showed the cigarettes he'd snitched. After a few tries they got one lit. Puffing wasn't really that hard. They sat on a bale of hay while the chickens pecked around them.

"What in hell are you all up to?"

They froze. It was Doris Roy, framed by the light of the doorway.

"I thought I smelled smoke! You three little dickens aiming to burn this place down?"

"Maybe yes," said Jo defiantly.

"Well, not today, young lady. Give me that."

She confiscated the pack and shook a finger at the children. "You're in big trouble," she warned them, and squeezed out the door.

There was silence except for the quiet fussing of the hens. Jo drew up her legs, resting one cheek on her knees.

"Papa's going to kill us," Lance said.

Robbie said, "Maybe she won't tell."

"She'll tell," Jo said solemnly.

"Anyway, there's going to be a nuclear war," Robbie went on.

"Who says?" asked Lance.

"Everybody. Us against Russia."

Robbie removed a purloined cigarette from his pocket and fished the lighter from where Jo had stashed it. He took a puff and made a sweeping gesture. "So it doesn't matter what we do," he said grandly, flicking ashes on the hay-strewn floor.

10

Two years later, by late winter of 1954, anybody would have told you the Kuseks were valued members of the community. The two children were just normal ranch kids—took the bus to school, raised bunnies at 4-H Club, competed in junior rodeo. Eight-year-old Jo was a fearless little barrel racer, and her brother, Lance, turning six, was already riding calves. The dad, Calvin Kusek, was a partner in longtime resident Nelson Fletcher's law firm, situated in downtown Rapid City.

Kusek was considered smart, but not a smart-ass. An honest and decent fellow, most agreed, even though he was a Democrat and never joined a church. He was a patient listener and did well by his clients, getting them out of jail or a miserable marriage, protecting their water rights, and settling wills. Rumor said he was biding time, that he had political ambitions, which was not surprising in such a good-looking, strong-minded man. The mom, Betsy, was an educated woman, but still down-to-earth, and a licensed visiting nurse who helped out with Dr. Avery Saugstad's patients—and if Doc Avery gave the okay, there was no better endorsement in town.

One of Doc Avery's patients, Mrs. Jolene Johnston, age forty-nine, was in a particularly bad way. She'd come down with severe stomach pains that turned out to be a bowel obstruction that needed emergency surgery. The surgeons removed the blockage, closed her up, and sent her home—along with a bacterial infection she'd picked up in the hospital.

Jolene and her husband, Allen, owned the A&J market on Route 24. They had no children and were each other's rock—married seventeen years, working in the store together twelve hours a day, steadfast as Mount Rushmore. Allen was easygoing and took care of the customers out front, while Jolene, nervous and shy, kept to the back office and hid inside her accounting books.

When she came home from the hospital, Jolene started acting strange, even for her. She shouted at the customers using curse words, or she'd look blank and ask, *"Where am I?"* She refused to eat because she believed Allen was poisoning her. By the time Doc Avery was called to their living quarters above the store, Jolene had gone delirious and was running a fever of 105. Deadly sepsis had invaded the abdominal cavity as well as the brain. Jolene was rushed to the hospital and a second surgery was performed to repair the unhealed wound, which would need constant care in order to mend properly.

Allen couldn't do it. He was under emotional strain from running the store and worrying about his wife. Besides, he had his own health problems and suffered from diabetes. Doc Avery wanted Betsy Kusek to visit the couple twice a day, morning and night, to check on them both. They went together the first time so he could give her the treatment plan, which was fine with Betsy, who enjoyed home visits when Doc Avery came along.

His buoyant personality matched his royal-blue 1948 Chevy truck with grillework that shone like grandma's silver. In town he drove slowly enough so kids could jump on the running boards for a ride, but out on the road he let the souped-up engine roar. He claimed to need a fast car for zipping back and forth to the state capital of Pierre, where he had twice been elected to the legislature, but at heart he was still the teenager with a rebel streak, who once threw a tire over the post office flagpole.

Folks liked the fact that he'd come back home after medical school to marry his high school sweetheart, Maryanne Welch, a former drum majorette, of whom he affectionately boasted, "She can still toss those hips." While Betsy cared for his patients, Cal served alongside the doctor on local committees, eager to soak up his wisdom.

"Cal knows how to stand his ground," Doc Avery told Betsy as they headed out to Route 24. "Someone takes a shot at him, he doesn't flinch.

He's not a screamer, but he won't back down, and I say good for him. He's a smart cookie and he'll go far, as long as—hold on, what's this?"

Inspirational organ music was swelling out of the radio, announcing the start of Thaddeus Haynes's *The Hour of Truth.* Doc Avery turned it up in time to hear Haynes crowing over the fact that Joseph McCarthy had been able to get an army dentist named Irving Peress discharged from the military for refusing to answer loyalty questions, calling his commandant, General Ralph Zwicker, "unfit to wear a uniform."

"Barbarians," Doc Avery muttered. He was so angry his hands trembled on the wheel.

"Can't they see McCarthy is a menace?" Betsy said, exasperated.

"They think he's standing up for something."

"All he's standing for is fear and intimidation."

"But he's our only hope against Russia, don't you see? Spies are everywhere! Root 'em out! He's not stupid—he knows the more outrageous his behavior, the bigger the headline. He takes a swing at a newsman, and everybody cheers! He's protecting America from the liberal press! They like his bluster and he puts on a good show."

"I hate to say it, but McCarthy's not stirring up anything that isn't already there," Betsy said, watching unplowed fields pass and registering that they were awfully dry.

Doc Avery was shaking his head, wisps of long white hair flying on the window breeze. "I didn't think the country could get any more right wing. I thought I'd seen it all when the Rosenbergs were convicted. I always thought that Julius was a spy for Russia and that he did steal atomic secrets, but the wife, Ethel, she's innocent. She didn't know anything about it, but—you watch—she'll be executed along with her husband. That's how they do it," he went on with a contemptuous shrug. "*Guilt by association.* If you ever had a radical *thought* or cohabited with someone who did—God have mercy if you *married* one—they label you a 'fellow traveler' with the Communist Party. *'Fellow traveler.'* What in hell does that mean? You put on a rucksack and march along the forest green, whistling the Russian national anthem?"

Betsy had fallen silent. She hadn't felt unease creeping up like this since the House Un-American Activities Committee tried to force screenwriters to testify about their supposed ties with the Communist Party, to name those very "fellow travelers." When many refused, on the grounds it would violate their right to privacy, the heads of the studios got together at the Waldorf Astoria hotel and came out with a statement declaring they would not hire any writer, actor, or director "associated" with Communism, or who refused to testify before the committee. Many stood behind the Fifth Amendment for protection from self-incrimination, which only infuriated the interrogators, who simply threw them in jail.

Betsy's friend, Elaine O'Grady, had been present at the Waldorf Astoria that bleak November day in 1947. She'd stood outside in pouring rain along with a crowd of activists, waiting for news of whom the studio bosses had decided to sacrifice to the anti-Communist fever gripping the nation so they could go on making films with the blessing of the government. Elaine had a personal connection to one of the accused. At a party for the left-wing magazine *New Masses,* she'd met a successful screenwriter named Alvah Bessie, who refused to answer McCarthy's inquisitors. As a result, he was about to be labeled a "Red Fascist," sentenced to prison, and blacklisted in the movie business, his career over.

When Alvah Bessie's name was read that windswept New York day as one of the convicted Hollywood Ten, Elaine went to a phone booth and called Betsy in tears. Betsy listened, dumbstruck and terrified that such a hateful witch hunt could take place openly in America—broadcast live on television!—and that she, or anyone who'd signed up with the party, even on a whim, even to pass out soup to the poor, might be next. The icy rain cut sideways as Elaine left the phone booth, huddled beneath an umbrella that was doing nothing to protect her, while at home in the Bronx, Betsy hung up with the unsettling knowledge that even ordinary people were not safe.

The windshield of the Chevy truck was divided by a metal strut, and Betsy shrank even farther on her side, as if to escape the stomach-churning foreboding that arose from the doctor's outburst. She'd quit the party so long ago the fact of her membership rarely came to mind, but when it did, she was haunted by the possibility of discovery, still: a refugee in her own country.

She shook herself. *But no.* Not now, not here. As a precaution, nobody in Rapid City knew her past—not even her maiden name. She and Cal agreed to not say a word about her former association to anyone, not even Stell and Nelson Fletcher, their closest friends. As they pulled up at the A&J, Betsy had to remind herself there was no better place on earth to keep a buried secret than the open plains of South Dakota.

The A&J market took up the bottom half of a two-story white clapboard building with a peaked roof. There was a gas pump out front and a post office inside. The porch was deserted except for a lady from the Lakota Sioux tribe, who was sitting on a pile of bags of flour and holding a baby. Her hair was cropped short, western-style, and she wore a faded cotton dress with bows on the sleeves, thick woolen stockings, and lace-up shoes. The moment she saw Doc Avery, she smiled, climbed down, came over, and shyly held out her hand. In her dusty brown palm was a small black circle.

The baby grabbed his finger while Doc Avery spoke to the mother in the Sioux language. Her name was Makawee. She was insisting on something, and he was arguing, and Betsy listened with fascination. At last he bowed his head and accepted the offering, a small open hoop wrapped in porcupine quills that had been flattened and dyed black. It was divided into quarters—the four directions—by two crossbars that met in the middle like intersecting roads.

"What is that?" Betsy asked curiously.

"A medicine wheel," Doc Avery replied.

"Because you're a doctor?"

He chuckled. "No, just a humble being compared to this. The Lakota Sioux call it the Sun Dance Circle. It means the furthest limits of the world that man can know."

"And why would you deserve such a thing?"

He shrugged. "Her baby was sick and then he got better, but it had nothing to do with me. Yup!" he said, pocketing the charm. "Today is a good day to die."

"What do you mean?" Betsy said, alarmed. "Is Jolene Johnston going to die?"

Doc Avery laughed. "No, no, that's something the Sioux warriors say when they ride into battle. *Hoka hey!*"

"Marvelous. So we're going to have a battle?"

"Jolene can be difficult," Doc Avery admitted. "I might call on your feminine wiles."

The moment the screen door of the market banged shut behind her, the fresh produce in damp wood boxes and the sugary smell of home-baked pies triggered the grocery list always ticking in Betsy's mind. *What do we need?* She scanned the immaculate shelves of Campbell's soup, Brillo, Rinso, Duz, Wheaties, Kix, Raisin Bran, and Quaker Oats. On the hardware side, there were lanterns, matches, tin plates, dishes, brooms, and heavy canvas gloves—but her eyes slid back to the pies on the counter, only one apple crumble left, the family favorite. *I should grab that for the kids*, Betsy thought, like a panther protecting her young, but chided herself. *You're not here to shop!*

Allen Johnston was weighing out a string of hot dogs on the scale for Makawee's husband, a middle-aged Lakota man named Tatonga. The A&J also served as a free bank for members of the local tribe, and Tatonga, attired in a cowboy hat, button-down shirt, and a tie with a tie clip, covered head to toe with prairie dust, was withdrawing money from his account. His savings were kept in a cigar box with his name on it, stored inside the Johnstons' safe.

"I hope Mrs. Johnston gets better soon," Tatonga said, taking out a few bills before closing the box and handing it back.

"Appreciate the thought," Allen replied.

All the world needs is a little more trust, Betsy decided, as the Indian left with a tip of the hat and the hot dogs wrapped in paper under his arm.

"How are you, Allen?" Doc Avery asked.

The storekeeper replied with a shrug and a sigh. "I'm all right, but she's still got pain."

Allen had large ears, fleshy cheeks, a bulbous nose, and thin lips in a tired smirk that said, *What can I do?* He wore hand-knit pullover vests that never seemed to have come out right—stretched at the armholes and hanging loose. The skin lay in thick folds on his neck. Without his wife around, he looked even more like an abandoned hound.

"You got to cure her," he pleaded.

"That's why Nurse Betsy's here," the doctor replied cheerfully.

"I'll take very good care of her," Betsy assured him, but following Doc Avery through the back of the store and up the stairs to the living quarters, she had a feeling this would not be an easy case. When she watched Doc Avery examine the patient, what he'd told her outside was confirmed.

The incision looked healthy, but Jolene Johnston had a morbid fear of being touched. Doc Avery seemed spooked already. He reached out slowly with soft words and quivering fingertips, but she flinched away, begging him to stop torturing her. Upset with his failure to calm the patient, he stuck his hands in his pockets.

"You try," he told Betsy.

"Hoka hey!" she murmured.

Jolene was ordinary looking, except for the way she could braid her thick black hair into a wondrous crown that circled twice around her head. All she needed was a wreath to look like a woodland fairy creature. Betsy wondered what Jolene had endured that had created her misery and strange obsessions, or if she simply was possessed, the way she screamed bloody murder at Betsy with eyes rolled back.

But the wound had to be cleaned. At night Betsy would apply a gauze pad soaked in hydrogen peroxide and iodine, and in the morning she would peel it away, tearing off a layer of dead skin along with the dry bandage. It was painful, and Betsy took to giving her patient a stiff shot of cough syrup with codeine so they could both get through it. The real treatment, though, was patience.

Inspired by Doc Avery's commitment to his clients, Betsy Kusek drove out to the A&J twice a day, no matter how much she needed to be home at the Lucky Clover Ranch, telling the family they would have to pitch in. When she finished with Jolene, Betsy would go downstairs to help Allen with the store. She swept the floor and stocked the shelves, chatted with customers. Keeping things going was part of the treatment. His hangdog look grew brighter, and little by little, layer by layer, new pink skin had begun to grow, healing Jolene's wound as it should, from the inside out.

Their bedroom was barren except for a handmade dulcimer hanging on the wall. When Betsy asked Jolene to teach her to play, the woman looked down and shook her head. So the nurse went about her business, but singing now, whenever she would give Jolene a bath or gently brush her hair. Betsy's guess was right. Music soothed her wild and unsettled soul.

"You're bringing her back to life," said the grateful husband.

A month passed before Jolene Johnston was strong enough to go back to the accounting books. Betsy knew the time was coming when she trudged upstairs one morning to hear the crystal sound of dulcimer strings. Jolene was sitting in a rocking chair and playing the old folk song "Will the Circle Be Unbroken." She'd given up the phantasmal braided crown and let her waist-length hair fall loose like her Appalachian forbears', and sang in a coarse and reedy voice that came by way of rutted axle marks and hoofprints along the trails that brought those women west. Betsy sat on the floor at her feet. Looking up, she noticed for the first time that the sound holes in the walnut instrument, from which the clear-struck notes rang out, were shaped like hearts.

11

"Can I borrow your husband?" Verna Bismark asked.

Betsy Kusek could hardly say no. The woman standing on her porch was president of the state Democratic Party. She was big and well proportioned all around, dressed in a seersucker suit and heels, an unapologetic bosom thrust into your face. She spoke with the deep, husky voice of a lifelong smoker and carried a cigarette like a gun, always ready, always smoldering, even at rest between two fingers at her side. The way she looked at you, it was a challenge.

"If you can find him, you can keep him," Betsy joked.

Verna Bismark looked at her watch. It was getting dark. She'd driven from her home in Cottonwood, an hour away.

"Cal knows we're on a tight schedule, right?"

Betsy nodded. "He said you two have to be somewhere, but it's all very mysterious. Should I be worried, Verna?"

Betsy was teasing, sort of. As fired up as he'd been about Stevenson when he lost to Eisenhower and Nixon by a landslide, Cal had stepped back, deciding to concentrate on the law practice with Fletch, building up the ranch, and learning the political ropes by volunteering to take on the day-to-day business of community affairs. Over the past two years he'd joined the Young Democrats and served with Doc Avery at the County Board of Education, the Cattlemen's Association, and the Rural Electric Association, where he'd been introduced to the out-spoken Mrs. Bismark. She and her husband owned the Cottonwood National Bank, one of the biggest lenders in the county, which meant even Republicans had to listen to her.

Although she was in her forties, Verna Bismark had the smooth skin of a country girl, whose squared cheekbones flowed pleasingly toward a wide, flawless chin. Her narrow lips were painted coral pink and sensual, despite their determined expression. Her eyes were deli-cately hooded beneath light brows, as unruly as when she had been a teenager. She considered plucked eyebrows to be trashy. She wore her thick blond hair poufed up with two spit curls shellacked to her cheeks—armed for battle in a man's world.

While Betsy stood in the doorway, barefoot, wearing mud-stained work overalls.

"Sorry for the way I look," she said. "I'm trying to get everything done before *See It Now*."

"I love that show. What's on tonight?"

"Edward R. Murrow is going to go after McCarthy for accusing the Signal Corps of subversive activity."

"Good for them."

"They've been showing clips of the dirty things McCarthy's said. When you put them all together, he is truly out of his mind. He calls the Fifth Amendment 'a shield for the guilty'? What a switch-up! And that officer in the air force who was falsely accused and wrongly dis-charged? They proved him innocent, but McCarthy ruined his life."

Verna clicked her tongue in disgust. "Going after the armed ser-vices is a big mistake on his part."

Betsy nodded. "You bet. They say the Senate's finally investigating *him*."

"I always knew he'd get his comeuppance."

Cal joined them on the porch with his hair still wet from the shower. Whatever this was about, he seemed to think it was important enough to put on a fresh shirt and the reliable tweed jacket.

"Let's go, mister," Verna said in a familiar way, taking a sharp pull off the cigarette and turning to spit smoke into the wind.

"Where is she taking you?" Betsy murmured.

Cal gave a shrug. The sun was setting and she couldn't read his eyes.

"No idea," he said, and hurried up behind Verna Bismark, who was halfway to her car, a white Cadillac that had been standing in the driveway, door open, motor running.

At the same time, Thaddeus Haynes was sitting down at the audio console to begin the evening broadcast of *The Hour of Truth*. Two years ago, with the help of sprinkled doughnuts, Dino the elephant, and a nationwide Republican landslide, he had won his seat in the state legislature, which had given him ground to lead the charge against the Red Threat. Following the example of Joe McCarthy, Haynes set up a fact-finding "committee" with himself as chairman, using the power of the legislature to investigate citizens whom he, personally, suspected of un-American activities, such as history professors and homosexuals. That his tactics were identical to the tyranny employed by the KGB in the USSR was a dark irony that flew as high over his head as a turkey vulture.

Haynes realized early on that the fight against Communism was a salable commodity. People—whom he saw as either "very good" or "the radical element"—fell for stories of the secret enemy within, and Haynes knew all about that. He had always been a watcher. He made his living by slipping through the cracks. He liked cameras. He liked the power of the hidden observer, which led to a lifelong practice of drilling holes in motel walls and public restrooms, allegedly to collect evidence of narcotics transactions and other indiscretions that he would share with the police, who came to value Haynes as an off-the-record source. He saw nothing wrong with dropping a wire to listen in on an attorney's office. In his younger years he did these things even though he was not a cop—a great disappointment, but he'd failed the physical twice. He was nothing more than an amateur with a four-by-five Speed Graphic camera, which allowed him to pass himself off as a freelance journalist. He knew a guy who sold police equipment, which gave him the ability to spy on anyone, making him "a friend" of the Rapid City Vice Squad and the FBI, which in those days ran extremely loose operations when it came to acquiring evidence.

Haynes had an elevated opinion of himself, one that put him above the daily grind. He believed that by shortcutting the law, he was helping to improve the quality of police work. Because he had a special gift of "knowing" who was crooked and who was not, he quickly became frustrated with helping out on small-town capers. Wiring up pimps and whores, or bugging the faucet in a hotel sink to listen in on the Chinese opium trade coming down from Seattle, had become beneath his talents. He needed a bigger adversary, one that would put him in a good spot with newspaper editors and provide a steady income to support his wife and four children on the farm they'd bought along the Cheyenne River, God's country.

Haynes was looking for the big story and found it in Detroit during the sit-down strikes against the automotive industry in the 1930s. For several years he traveled east, keeping his expenses down by selling cars that he drove back and forth between Chicago, Milwaukee, and Rapid City; using his "credentials" to get deals at motels; eating cafeteria food, sometimes only a baked apple for dinner. The decisive moment in Haynes's career came when he was photographing an assembly line in the Chevrolet plant and union thugs broke in, shouting, "We're on strike, stop working and sit down!" carrying sticks, beating anyone who refused. The attackers—working on behalf of the "liberal apparatus"—grabbed Haynes's precious Speed Graphic camera, held him down, and, in front of scores of silent workers, smashed his one and only source of income to pieces.

He was nothing.

And any doubts he might have had that the infiltrators were from the Communist Party were put to rest that night as he lay awake in yet another sordid hotel room, agonized with humiliation, flicking bedbugs, and remembering the nights he'd stayed up listening to Father Coughlin on his transistor radio deliver sermons of hate with thrilling, mellifluous cadences that found their mark inside the empty ear canals of Thaddeus Haynes:

"Oh, how this Sacred Scripture has become perverted . . . My friends, the outworn creed of capitalism is done for. The clarion call of Communism has been sounded . . . They are both rotten! But it is not necessary to suffer any longer the slings and arrows of modern capitalism any more than it is to surrender our rights to life, to liberty, and to the cherished bonds of family to Communism . . . The apostles of Lenin and Trotsky bid us forsake all rights to private ownership and ask us to surrender our liberty for that mess of pottage labeled 'prosperity,' while it summons us

to worship at the altar where a dictator of flesh and blood is enthroned as our god and the citizens are branded as his slaves . . ."

And: "Somebody must be blamed!"

Soothed by the memory of the amorphous, unfathomable jumble of words, helpless Haynes, the wounded warrior brought low, heard only one message: Father Coughlin had preached against Communism, and he had thirty million listeners every week.

The studio clock said 6:58 p.m. "Two minutes to air!" Thaddeus Haynes announced.

The studio audience came to attention. The Red Threat was still Haynes's beat, the radio his bludgeon, although compared with the success of other demagogues, on a vastly smaller scale. It wasn't a studio; it was an empty ballroom in the Hotel Alex Johnson, one wall covered by a Technicolor mural of the Badlands. It wasn't an audio console; it was a card table with a standing microphone and a lavender chair with white enameled legs that had been carried in from the ladies' lounge. It wasn't a clock; it was a Timex watch worn by the host. And it wasn't even a studio audience, but a collection of true believers from a "study group" led by Haynes at the American Legion post, thrilled to be part of a real live broadcast, waiting in respectful silence and trying not to squeak their folding chairs.

As his fingers hovered over the on switch, Haynes's expression was as grave as if he were at the controls of a bomber cruising over a sleepy village, vested with avenging power in the name of democracy. He wore a dark pin-striped suit that contrasted with his youthful wavy blond hair. His eyes, deeply set beneath a protruding brow, were empty of emotion, and a cockeyed tilt to the head made you wonder if his mind was somewhere else entirely. But when he spoke, his voice was deeply resonant and supremely confident, and the fifteen or so assembled could be relied upon to applaud on cue. Over the radio it would all sound so much bigger.

"This is Thaddeus Haynes speaking. I am blessed to visit with you again, as I do each week at this time, from our modern studios in Rapid City."

Applause.

"As a proud Republican, I get a lot of mail from patriots saying, 'Keep up the fight!'"

Applause.

"But there was one letter in today's mail that touched my heart. It's from a young mother, Mrs. Eleanor McGreedy of Spearfish, South Dakota, who writes, *'Recently you said on the radio that the Soviet Union is sowing the seeds of its own destruction. If that's true, why do we have to fight Russia?'* This dear lady does not understand the nature of Communism, even though it's right at her own front door."

Thaddeus Haynes took a painful pause and shook his head. The studio audience clucked sympathetically.

"My friends, something very bad is going on. The Soviet Union is planning to invade the United States. They hate us and they want to destroy us. They believe that we are a divided and weakened nation, ripe for the picking. As you and I sit in our comfortable living rooms with our loved ones close, the Soviet army is building up forces to come across Siberia to Alaska and down through the Pacific Northwest. Something dangerous is taking place right under our noses!"

Outside the ballroom, Honeybee Jones was sauntering down the hallway on the lookout for ghosts. They said the Hotel Alex Johnson was haunted by the "Lady in White" who'd jumped out of an eighth-floor window. Honeybee had his fingers crossed just in case. He'd been angelic-looking as a seven-year-old filching pencils from the teacher's desk, and a lumpy fourteen-year-old swiping car mirrors, but after adolescence his features settled into a permanent screw-you sneer, set off by a stiff mile-high pompadour of carrot-red hair.

In the deserted hotel corridor, he crouched down low and sprang up high just to see if he could knock a stuffed bison head off the wall. He clipped the thing, but it was mounted pretty solid, which went right along with the run of sore luck he was having. On his prowls through the hotel he could usually pinch a tourist or two. All the rooms he'd tried were locked, but just ahead of him a voice was coming from the ballroom. Something was going on.

Honeybee cracked the door. They were ladies, mostly, listening to a lecture by some big shot. He eased inside and sat down.

"Has mass ignorance invaded our town? We don't *really* know what's going on, do we?" Haynes intoned.

The people in the audience shook their heads obediently.

"They could be right here among us—those losers who joined the

Communist Party because they're *afraid* that democracy might win, and that's the last thing these cowardly Reds want. But fear makes people do stupid things," Haynes was going on. "And I can tell you, all it takes is one *whiff*—one little *seed* carried by a member of the Communist Party—to s-p-r-e-a-d the poison," he said, raising his arms like a preacher. "Sucking out all the Christian godliness that's in you and replacing it with *pinkeye.* But we're smarter than that, aren't we?"

The audience murmured, "Yes," and "Right you are!"

"Friends," Haynes said, building steam, "you know what I'm talking about: a disease of mind control that threatens the very survival of the white race. It's a fight to the death—*us against them!*"

When everyone stood to give a fevered ovation, Honeybee noticed that right in front of him was a row of ninnies dumb enough to put their pocketbooks on the floor. He ducked down and skillfully removed a wallet from a purse under the nearest seat. At the same moment, Haynes was coming down the aisle with a donation plate.

"My wallet!" screamed the lady in front of Honeybee. "Someone stole my wallet!"

She turned around, face-to-face with the grubby teenager.

"Tyler! I know it's you. You did it! Give me back my money!"

All her friends started squawking and half the room was turning around to gape like monkeys.

"He's a juvenile delinquent!" the woman declared.

"Shut up! What are you talking about?" said Honeybee, surreptitiously letting the wallet drop to the floor.

Haynes was there and he saw it.

"Look, madame!" Haynes said, pointing to the billfold. "There's your property. It's all a mistake."

The woman turned scarlet with embarrassment. "I am so sorry. I thought this young man—"

Haynes patted her shoulder. "I understand," he said magnanimously. "Even so, we must forgive one another, as God in Christ forgave us. Right, son?"

Honeybee stared at his benefactor and had a conversion experience. No one had ever let him off the hook for anything.

"Yes, sir," he managed.

The woman put two dollars of guilt money on the plate, and Honeybee Jones silently pledged loyalty to Thaddeus Haynes for the rest of his life.

On a clear night, *The Hour of Truth* could be heard a hundred miles in each direction—by housewives and barkeeps, gas station attendants and traveling salesmen and grandpas in rocking chairs—but tonight, despite the cloudless sky deepening to a flawless violet over the Black Hills, the voice of Thaddeus Haynes did not break through the stunned silence that prevailed inside the cream leather interior of Verna Bismark's white Cadillac heading north from the Lucky Clover Ranch.

"Doc Avery is dead?" Cal repeated, dumbfounded.

Verna lit another cigarette. "It happened today."

Cal stared straight ahead. "Where are we?" he wondered vaguely.

"Iron Mountain Road."

"Where was Avery?" Cal said, still trying to get his bearings at this shocking turn of events.

"He was home," Verna answered.

"Was it a heart attack?"

Verna's coral lips twitched up tight. Cal turned to her, demanding, "Verna? What happened?"

A little after eight that morning, Avery Saugstad, M.D., was found by his wife, Maryanne, lying in a doorway between the kitchen and the hall. He was dressed for a workday in a plaid shirt, brown pants, and brown shoes. His belt was buckled and shirt tucked in tight. He was lying on his side, half turned onto the right hip, so that his right arm was lying beneath him, bent at the elbow and reaching out, the hand facing upward, his sensitive doctor's fingers languorously open in poetic surrender. The left arm had fallen across his torso, making the body look strangely relaxed, as if he were just turning over in bed. The black medical bag stood beside a metal lunch box near the wall, as if he'd been on his way out but changed his mind. A .36 Colt pistol had fallen on the floor beside him. Ever the scientist, he'd used a hand mirror from the bathroom to aim precisely through the mouth at the autonomic nervous center at the base of the head, which controls the heart and lungs. The skull was shattered, the avulsed brain preserved in a lake of blood.

"He shot himself," Verna said.

They were ascending forests of ponderosa pine, riding the curves of a scenic byway that led through small square tunnels cut out of the granite to sharp curvy views of the mountains fading in the dusk. On a hairpin turn you could see Mount Rushmore and the bizarrely human faces of Washington, Jefferson, Roosevelt, and Lincoln staring out of the green natural surroundings.

Cal felt numb, as if he'd left his real self back on the porch with Betsy, in the sunset light, when everything had been normal.

"I've already talked to the governor," Verna said.

"Why?"

"He's calling a special election to fill Avery's seat."

"I mean, what about Avery? What on earth made him do it?"

Verna's eyes were fixed ahead and gleaming in the headlights of an oncoming car. "He had Parkinson's disease. He was trying to hide it, but he was already having tremors and knew it would get so bad he couldn't work. Maryanne said he hadn't been sleeping lately and fell into a deep depression. My uncle had the same thing. I know you can live with it, but Avery couldn't live without being able to practice medicine. If he couldn't be a doctor . . . I guess," she said, her voice cracking, "he just couldn't be."

Cal squeezed his eyes shut and pinched the bridge of his nose. "He was a great doctor but also so much more than that."

"He was too damn hard on himself. I spoke to Avery just yesterday," she said, almost helplessly. "Everything was fine. We were planning to meet in Pierre next Wednesday for the Toastmasters Club dinner." She swiped at angry tears.

Cal let out a long breath. "Where are we going?"

"We're meeting Nelson Fletcher. He was seeing a client in Hill City so we thought this would be halfway."

They pulled into the parking lot of the Mount Rushmore National Memorial. The long spring evening had not quite let go. A wide dappled fan of pink cloud still held in the western sky. A light blue Dodge sedan was coming their way. It parked and Fletch got out.

"What is this all about?" Cal wondered.

"It's a powwow," Verna answered grimly.

"Sad day," Fletch said, joining them.

Verna lit a cigarette. "I'm so mad at Avery! What was he thinking, taking his life?"

They sat on a bench at the rim of the observation area where a few tourists were lingering in the dusk. There was no view. There was nothing to see. The giant faces of the presidents were shrouded in darkness. They watched the dim ghost of a mountain sheep climb the rocks and disappear into a crevasse.

"Cal, we felt it was urgent to have our ducks in order before this gets out," Fletch began. His round glasses picked up a glint of light from the parking lot. "The governor is calling a special election and Bill O'Connor's likely to run. He's the guy who owns the Dodge dealership in Hot Springs."

"I know who Bill O'Connor is," Cal allowed.

"We have to act fast," Fletch insisted. "The filing date is coming up in fifteen days. We want to get your name on the ballot."

"Are you sure you're talking to the right guy?" Cal asked with surprise.

"We can't afford to lose a Democratic seat," Fletch said. "Bill O'Connor's weak."

"No backbone," Verna agreed. "No position. He inherited the dealership from his daddy, which alienates farmers who are fighting just to make ends meet. They need someone who speaks for them."

"It's what you and I have talked about," Fletch said. "A chance to turn things around, energize the party."

"I'm sorry, but this is still a complete shock." Cal ran a hand through the lock of hair that fell boyishly over his forehead.

"It's a shock to all of us," Fletch demurred.

"I mean—Avery Saugstad, rest in peace—but this is way too soon for me to jump in."

"Won't be easy. You have to start now and hit the road hard," Verna said in that dusky voice.

"I've never run for office."

Verna shrugged. "Doesn't worry me."

Cal was staggering under many emotions pulling on him at once. "First of all, it's calving season," he said. "I can't just leave."

Verna squinted at him in a very practical way. "How many of your girls have already calved?"

"Maybe half."

"Wait as long as you can, let Betsy handle the rest. She can do it."

"Yes, yes, of course she can, but I'm supposed to cover—how big is the district?"

"Five thousand eight hundred square miles," Fletch said.

In the basement of the visitor center, switches were thrown. Those outside on the deck heard a deep scraping sound like the squeaky closing of metal doors. Electricity sizzled, small popping explosions echoed off the mountain, and then all at once, all four faces of the greatest American presidents came to life under glaring white floodlights.

The three stared in wonder.

Verna's hand came to her chest. "Gets me every time," she said emotionally.

What did the noble presidents see, gazing off in all directions? Did they comprehend their own mortality? Did they regret the world they'd left behind? Silence was all they gave you. Pure chalk-white silence.

Nelson Fletcher nudged his friend. "We want to put your face up there, Kusek," he said, teasing.

Cal grimaced. "Why ruin a nice work of art?"

"This isn't some petty local race." Verna turned to him. "This is about the future of the United States. And it's not just about winning the election but, as your friend Adlai Stevenson says, *how* it is won. Do we cave to bullies, or fight for our personal freedoms?"

"We have a one-party monopoly in this state," Cal said. "That's the problem."

"The problem is hate. Hate that scares people into hating more. Look at that bigot, Thaddeus Haynes."

Fletch shrugged Haynes off. "Small potatoes."

Verna shook her head. "I disagree. He's popular. He's a radio personality. He won his seat the first time out and he knows how to rabble-rouse. No, it would be a mistake to underestimate Haynes. He'll be Cal's opponent in 1960."

Cal chuckled. "Holy moly, who is talking about 1960? That's six years from now."

"It's when you'll be ready to run for the U.S. Senate," Fletch said with a smile.

Cal blushed with humility. "You guys are way ahead of me."

Verna took a check out of her purse and gave it to Cal. "For the campaign. Go out and wake up the Democratic Party. And when the going gets tough, remember those faces up there and what is possible in a free country."

Cal stared at the check. It was for two hundred dollars. He was awfully moved. "You're taking a crazy risk," he said.

This drew a small, unwilling smile from the banker lady. "That's my job," she told him. "To invest in the futures of the up-and-comers. If you're afraid of risk, you end up walking in circles, like a half-dead mule. My dad had a mule that he used to turn the mill. He'd take the thing out of the barn and hitch him up. That animal walked in circles my whole life, until I shot him."

Cal and Fletch recoiled in shock.

"You shot your father's mule?" Cal said.

Verna's shoulders lifted in a neutral shrug. "I couldn't take it anymore."

Cal looked at Fletch in cautious silence.

"I'm guessing, Cal, that's not something you would do?" Verna asked.

"No. I don't think so. I would not shoot an animal that was trapped, with no way to escape, just because I felt like it." Cal smiled wryly. "Does that disqualify me from politics?"

"I promise you: the other side wouldn't hesitate."

When the children were asleep, Cal and Betsy closed the door to their bedroom and sat in silence on the edge of the bed.

After a while Cal spoke quietly. "Verna and Fletch make it sound like nothing, but I can't just pick up and run in his place."

"Nobody can take his place," Betsy agreed. "His patients will be devastated. I should have seen the signs when he asked me to change Jolene Johnston's bandage."

"Why is that?" asked Cal.

"He couldn't manage it. I thought it was just old age, but he must have been mortified. It's just too awful."

Everything unanswered finally gave way to grief. They clung together forcefully and sobbed; the only reassurance they could find in this unknowable world was in the warm, living body of the other.

Cal removed the small black medicine wheel from his pocket. "He gave me this."

Betsy gasped. "You're fooling, aren't you?" She touched the shiny porcupine quills wrapped around the hoop. "He got that from a Lakota woman. I was there. It's a charm. It represents the world—the universe!"

"It's the way he gave it to me that's troubling," said Cal.

"When was this?"

"Last Monday. No, Tuesday. That's the last time I saw him. Tuesday, just before lunch. I came out of the office and he was walking down Saint Charles Street. I said, 'Let's get a bite at the Daisy Dell,' but he said he was busy. He was distracted, but that's nothing new. Then he starts to go, turns around, comes back, and says, 'Oh, hey, look—I've got something for you.' He had this in the palm of his hand." Cal paused. "Now that I think of it, his hand was pretty wobbly. I went after him, but he didn't want to stop and chat, so I just said, 'Hey, thanks,' and watched him cross the street. Like an idiot."

Betsy hadn't moved. She was staring it, mesmerized by the simple power of the circle and the two crossed lines.

"It means the center of the earth. You're always at the center whenever you pray."

Cal's fingers closed around the tiny wheel. "He said he wanted me to have it. As if he knew. As if he was already planning it. He said, '*If you accept your death, then you can be dangerous.*' It just came out of nowhere. He was smiling. I thought he was just being coy."

Betsy's eyes rose up to meet Cal's. "We could not have known. Right?"

Cal had no answer. He laid back on his pillow and she on hers. They loosely held each other's hand and listened to the wind circling the house, smashing against it, coming back and hitting it again.

She rolled on top of him. "How long will you be gone?"

"Gone where?"

"On the campaign trail."

"Do you really want this?" he asked.

"I want it for you."

"We both have to want it, because if this works out, it could be just the beginning."

"I know that."

"Tell me the truth."

"Yes. I'm all for it," Betsy said. "It's your calling."

"My calling," he reflected.

"I just have to know one thing."

"What?"

"That you'll come back to me and the kids."

He held her eyes. "I'll always come back for you."

She nodded, taking it in. "You'll be running for both of us. I still believe in fighting the good fight, and I'll support you—"

"Okay."

"—but on one condition. No matter if you win, we're going to stay here. On the ranch. With the kids. I don't want to move back to a city. I don't want to live in god-awful Pierre."

Cal agreed vigorously. "Neither do I! This is our home. Something's bothering you, though."

"You'll be back and forth. I'm worried you'll be gone a lot—"

"I'll get an airplane."

"Funny."

"I do know how to fly," he reminded her.

"Yes, well, in a month of Sundays," she said, pretending to ignore the way he was running his fingertips through her hair. "Because this is where my heart is. I love the way we're living now, the kids at this age, and we've just started to make a go. I've even decided that I like cows."

Cal smiled. He cherished that sense of irony that still surfaced now and then. He raised his lips and kissed her. His work-strong arms were tight around her and she rested for a while with her cheek against his chest. She could feel the pulsing of his heart and pushed away the thought that one day it would stop. The wind changed pitch again. It was nameless. It was always there. While he was gone, she would be alone with just the land and the wind. They unbuttoned their clothes and she seized on him. She opened herself to him, and a gentle feeling of trust grew to closeness so overwhelming that she found herself in mystifying tears.

12

"Which one's the mom?" Lance whispered.

"That one, looking right at you," said Jo.

They were squatting outside the pen, peering at a newborn calf, fifteen minutes old, motionless as a wet ball of dirt.

"Should we get Mama?"

"We can't. She's working at the hospital today," Jo said.

"I wish Papa was here," fussed Lance. "What if it ain't born right?"

"Don't say 'ain't.'"

"What about the belly button?"

"I know how," Jo assured him in her grown-up voice. "We'll do it together."

They linked pinkies to prove it.

During calving season, which was just about over, Jo had been called upon to help in all kinds of situations, like when they had to be pulled out using human hands, or sometimes with chains around their legs to get a better grip. She knew how to iodine the navel to prevent infection, and that when you saw the head it would be okay, but if it came out backward, rump first, that was an emergency and you better call the vet.

"Go on, lady," Lance urged the cow.

"Shhh! Don't spook her!"

They crouched behind the lowest plank in the fence and watched with big eyes, spellbound, as the little thing lay helpless in the sun. The light buckskin mother stood a few yards away, rubbing her nose on her foreleg and acting as if nothing had happened. You'd never know a seventy-pound animal had just passed out of her body except for a red string of goop trailing from her rear. On the ground, they could see a little head and eyes looking glassily out of its sack.

"She's got to lick that off or it'll die," Lance said, urgently grabbing Jo's arm.

"No, look!" said Jo. "She's going ahead."

The cow had strolled over and begun to lick the baby. It was so weak it got pushed to the ground. Little by little she licked the membrane from the nose so it could breathe, then kept exposing the hide in widening spots. It would have a good red coat. After several collapses, the baby got up and found its balance on tiny, fairy-like hooves. It tried to get through the mom's hind legs, then stumbled blindly around to her chest. She stood patiently, turned her head, and gave the newborn a push. Then a holler.

"She's telling him it's right there!" Jo said breathlessly.

They waited. Horses neighed to each other in nearby pens. Lois and Bandit, the Australian shepherds, were lying near the house, waiting for orders. The baby was shivering and awfully thin. Flies swarmed around the children, and Jo clutched the jar of iodine as they watched tensely for the moment when the cow would be absorbed with the new baby and least likely to charge. It was still poking under her belly, looking for the teats with pieces of hay stuck to its mouth, while the mother cleaned its butt.

"Now!" whispered Jo, and they both ducked under the fence.

Armed with a stick, Lance took up a position in front of the cow to threaten her if she thought about getting mean, while Jo used an iodine-soaked rag to clean the nub of the baby's umbilical cord, which had snapped off during birth.

"Roger!" she called, echoing their favorite radio show.

"Over and out!" replied Lance.

They scrambled back to safety. Finally the baby got turned toward the bright pink udders, which Jo prayed were flowing with milk. When at last it began to suckle, Jo and Lance stood triumphantly, brushing dirt

155

from their overalls. They felt important to have made it through the crisis because, as their parents said, every healthy calf meant *"money in the bank."*

"Papa will be proud."

"What should we call him?" wondered Jo.

"Ruby!" said Lance. "Look, he's already strong. We can show him at 4-H."

"I bet he's good enough to be a breeding animal," Jo declared. "We could start our own herd."

"And win the state fair!"

They shook on it, which turned into a thumb-wrestle, a tug-of-war, and then Lance sprawling in the dirt. Jo sprinted away before he could get her back.

Lance was big enough to drive the tractor, so he got on board, fired it up, and went around to the vegetable garden, where they still had an acre to disc harrow. Every Saturday he'd show up at Crazy Eights and hang around until Uncle Scotty had a couple of minutes to give him a pointer about calf riding. Scotty had advised him to find a flat-backed horse and ride bareback, in order to build his muscles, so after doing his chores in the garden, Lance would take the big gelding, Junior, into the round pen to painfully stretch his legs over its broad back; anything for Uncle Scotty's approval.

Jo picked up the bucket where she'd set it when the birth pulled her away from chores. She entered the cattle pen and latched the gate behind her, quietly pouring water into the trough. The sun was hot on the top of her head. Her reflection was dark and elongated. She didn't look in mirrors much and hardly recognized the cocky eight-year-old who'd learned independence from barrel racing and raising animals, and was bristling with confidence and still immune to boys; who was sturdy and tall like her parents, with a short spring haircut that she hated. Behind her the new mother let out a deep bellow and lifted her nose to the wind. The baby had fallen again and she lay down beside it, peacefully soothing it with her tongue.

A breeze came to Jo with a fresh, grassy smell. She looked toward the house and her gaze found the empty spot where they usually parked the station wagon. Her father had taken it to go on a trip by himself, which was very unusual. He had to go before they moved the last batch of moms and babies to the spring pasture up on Bottlebrush Creek with the rest of the herd. Nobody had explained to the children why he was leaving or when he would return. She'd seen her parents kissing good-bye in the kitchen. Dad picked up the hem of Mama's skirt and Jo could see the backs of her legs and her white nylon panties. He put his hands over both cheeks of her mother's behind and spread his big fingers out, and Jo turned away, stricken with a terrible feeling, like unhappiness on the inside that could never come out.

It always made her feel better to be out with the cows with fresh air in her face, ankle-deep in good, fertile muck. Unconcerned, the cattle roved around her in their knowing way. There were so many of them. Bawling constantly, they sounded like the revved-up motors of a thousand cars and tractors and trucks all at once, but Jo barely noticed. To her the blanket of sound meant comfort, away from troubling thoughts. The big, gentle animals pushed toward the trough. She stepped back so they could drink.

Cal Kusek had taken Verna Bismark's advice and written to the chairmen of the Democratic clubs in his district, saying he was running for state legislature and would be stopping by their townships. Only one replied. *"Come if you really want to,"* he'd written, *"but we don't recommend it."*

That's because being a Democrat in South Dakota meant putting up with a daily dose of isolation and ridicule. You had to have a strong stomach and an iron-fisted mind, which Cal Kusek found strangely reassuring. One committed individual was better than a dozen undecideds. In the far-flung steppes of his district there would be little competition for the seat vacated by the sudden death of Dr. Avery Saugstad, as his only opponent, Bill O'Connor, counting on a low turnout, wouldn't bother to leave smug harbor among fat-cat friends in Hot Springs. Like the first pioneers, Cal saw open territory ready to be claimed.

The distances were grueling, the population small and scattered. Fletch explained that if he did win, it would be by a very slight margin, but he'd be building a following, brick by brick, for the next run. Having delayed his start as long as he could because of calving season, Cal now had less than a month to turn strangers into friends before the special election.

He left the ranch and drove straight on hot dogs and coffee toward his first stop on the map, the town of Ardmore. Passing the otherworldly formations of the Badlands, he was awed to think it was wind and water and time that had sandblasted the hills into such fantastic buttes and waves. As he drove on, the landscape changed to dark green hills spotted with ponderosa pine. On the radio there were preachers and country music. Inside Cal's head, the steady beat of calls to wake up voters played like themes—*we are the party of the people . . . politics is not just for the privileged . . . what I stand for . . . agriculture . . . schools . . . rights of landowners . . . freedom of speech . . . not our goal to annihilate the opposition . . . democracy, what it really means . . . in your hands*—shifting with the curves in the road, each new vista another idea, another turn in a driving belief in justice and change that was thrumming in his veins like tires on the road of ambition, so that after this, his very first day of campaign travel, Cal rolled into the town of Ardmore with certain knowledge that he had found his true calling as a politician . . . which was paradoxical, since there was nothing and nobody there.

There was a *sign* for Ardmore. A metal sign, punctuated by bullet holes, on a mesa rimmed by jagged hills and clear blue sky, all by itself except for a tiny, weathered gray shack leaning so far over it was comical. The whole thing was comical, Cal had to admit, getting out of the station wagon and relieving himself on a patch of thistle. A couple of feet beyond, he spotted a prairie dog, standing up on its burrow, staring straight at him. Then he realized there were dozens of burrows spread out across the plain, and scores of prairie dogs, darting here and there and yipping at each other. Cal couldn't help it, he laughed out loud. At their all-too-human antics. At himself, and the fact that he'd driven way out to hell and gone to arrive at a prairie dog town.

"Not many registered voters!" he told the wind.

The crack of a rifle made all his muscles flinch. A bullet whistled past his cheek. He ducked. Three more shots in rapid succession. The prairie dogs disappeared underground and the sound of a wheezing motor became present behind him. Turning cautiously, he found himself looking down the barrel of a .22 resting against the open window of an ancient, rusted-out red pickup in the hands of a fourteen-year-old boy.

"I think you got a few," Cal said.

The boy shrugged. He didn't bother to get out and collect the corpses. Ranchers had been fighting prairie dogs for a hundred years—in this war, there would always be more bodies. He was twisted toward the window, one bare foot up on the seat so he could prop the rifle on his knee. His flushed cheeks were coated with powdery dirt—everything about him was coated with powdery dirt. He had ruler-straight yellow corn silk hair, a simple, angelic face, and transparent eyelashes so thick they were like thorns—a beautiful creature, born to dust storms and broiling sun. From the driver's side came the sharp odors of adolescent sweat and gasoline leaking from somewhere.

Cal told him the name of the Democratic chairman he had come to see.

"That's my granddad," said the boy.

"Which way is town?"

"He don't live in town."

"How do I get there?"

The boy's pale eyes flicked from Cal to the station wagon.

"You can follow me, I guess."

"Thanks," said Cal, and offered his hand through the window.

The boy shook it uncertainly. Cal took a deep breath and addressed his first potential voter:

"My name is Calvin Kusek," he announced. "And I'm running for state legislature."

Jo paid attention. Her mother had stopped peeling beets and turned up the radio. Jo recognized the low, mesmerizing voice of the man who came on during breakfast and sometimes on a religious program that Mama would instantly turn off.

"I thought you hated that guy," Jo said.

"He's giving the weather," Betsy replied shortly.

"Friends, this is a spring storm that could be historic," Thaddeus Haynes was reporting. "Yep, the word over the wires is '*his*toric.' They're predicting heavy rain and snow for the Black Hills and high winds with gusts up to sixty miles per hour. There's a 'no travel' notice in effect from Sturgis to the Wyoming state line . . ."

"Is Dad in Wyoming?" Jo asked anxiously, trying to remember her maps.

"No, dear, he's on his way south," Betsy assured her. "He's going in a different direction. He's fine."

"There are reports of pea-sized hail already moving in from the west," Thaddeus Haynes went on. He sounded serious. "A bunch of storms—"

They lost power and everything went dead: the radio, the lights, the telephone. With a sigh the whole house shut down, instantly seeming to become ice cold, absorbing the dull daylight so there was now no difference between the roiling outside and the safety of the rooms within.

Betsy peered through the window. "We'd better get the hay inside."

The beets stayed put in the sink, leaving the white enamel streaked bloodred. Outside the temperature was falling and dark thunderheads were building fast. Jo got the chickens in the henhouse and moved the sheep and goats to their pens, while Lance and Betsy forked hay into the truck, then unloaded it in the barn. They got two stacks in before the rain came pelting down.

Thunder and lightning broke above them.

"Best we can do for now," Betsy said, as they secured the barn door and headed for the house.

"The man on the radio said it's going to snow," Jo said. She was always reminding her parents about important things.

Betsy glanced at the sky. "This'll pass. I don't believe anything that lying blowhard, right-wing egomaniac Thaddeus Haynes says. Bet you a nickel all we get is rain."

Lance turned his freckled face up and water spilled from the brim of his cowboy hat. "You really don't like him do you, Mama?"

"I don't appreciate it when people puff themselves up and try to scare other people so they'll look like big men."

"You don't like him because his elephant made poopy in our front yard!" Lance shouted with glee, and ran madly through the mud, stomping puddles.

The generator wouldn't start, so for supper they had Wheaties and milk. Betsy put the children to bed while it was still daylight, excited by the prospect of a night alone without any means to do useful work. She owed a letter to her sister, Marja. By flashlight she located the typewriter in the closet.

Like many things from childhood, the machine seemed so small out here in the prairie; her life in New York far away. Six weeks ago Marja had written to say their father had died of a heart attack while taking a nap. "He was in his chair with the blanket pulled up," she wrote. "I tried but he didn't move." Albert Ferguson was already buried, she said. It was too late to come home.

Betsy's heart had broken open, and she begged Marja to move out west, but her sister refused to leave the city. "I'm doing fine," Marja wrote. "Mrs. Zajac has been a great help, and everyone at the institute has been kind." As their correspondence had quickened, Betsy rediscovered a compatible soul. Distance seemed to bring them closer: more trusting, more willing to confess, and this Betsy did in her letters typed on the Olympia—how secretly alone she felt because nobody in South Dakota really understood her except her one real friend, Stella Fletcher. The other gals thought she was too tall, too thin, too bossy. Somehow, too fancy. Betsy was aware when she was not included in private occasions, like the bridal fitting for Joanie Ostenberg's youngest daughter. "Out here they say alfalfa and cows grow slow. Maybe it's the same with people," she wrote drily. Marja answered that Betsy was too good a person for people not to adore. "Stick it out," she wrote. "The cows will come home!"

But tonight, by the light of a kerosene lamp, Betsy had good news. Her fingers hit the keys, excited to tell Marja about Cal's first run for the legislature. How proud she was that he'd been asked and said yes, that he wanted to do something right for the county. Despite the hardships, they'd fallen in love with this way of life and wanted to preserve it. She wished only that Marja could see her niece and nephew! They were growing up just fine into such responsible—

Betsy had to stop. It had become too cold to type. Gale-force wind was battering the farmhouse with such strength she expected it to come right through the walls, blow the lamp over, and start a fire. Now the tumult had quieted, but Betsy knew the storm wasn't over. She could tell by the drop in air pressure that something more was coming their way.

As if by the extraordinary ESP that binds mother and daughter, Jo had heard her thoughts, and was already standing in the shadows of the doorway with a blanket clutched over her nightgown.

"Mama," she said gravely, "it's snowing. We have to get the calves."

Alarmed, Betsy looked outside. "Put newspaper down," she said quickly.

"I'll go with you," Jo insisted.

"No," said Betsy, pulling on her boots and taking the heavy duster from its hook near the door. She'd heard horrific stories of children being lost in blizzards and frozen to death just yards from the house. "You and Lance build up the fire. Get hot water going."

There were four calves in the pen that were less than three weeks old and needed to be brought inside. The others were strong enough to stay with their mothers. Jo and Betsy understood, in terms of monetary value, that Ruby, the little red one whose birth the children had witnessed, and whom they claimed for their own, would be the least worth rescuing.

Jo was pleading and her eyes filled with tears. "Please, Mama! Please get Ruby. He's small right now but Lance and I are going to raise him special."

"Honey, I'll try."

Betsy opened the door to a blast of arctic air and wet, heavy curtains of snow blowing sideways. She gripped the icy banister with fur-lined leather gloves, but the tips of her fingers were already frozen and she slipped down both steps into a foot of powder. The woolen scarf whipped off her face. Instantly her mouth and eyes and nose sprang with water that turned to ice. Senses completely disoriented, she probed for the right side up of the world. The wind knocked her with a punch and she tumbled down again, afraid of being buried in the drifts that marched capriciously across the yard, changing shape, exuding snow-smoke, lost to her children, until she was able to turn herself around, toward the pens, the flashlight good for just a few inches in the menacing dark.

Holding on to the fence as the wind tried to pry her away, she moved hand over hand to the gate, hammering with a rock to get the frozen latch open. The cows were huddled close together. She ran the light over their shining eyes. Was it right to pull the calves from the sheltering bodies? She wished she had a lifetime of experience to know. Instead she sensed Jo watching anxiously from the window and that was enough to cause her to shout against the wind and shoulder between the heavy bodies of the cows to find their babies. A few minutes later Betsy kicked the front door open with Ruby limp in her arms. His ears and tail were frozen solid. They put him in the bathtub, which Lance was filling with warm water.

"Don't use soap or the mother won't recognize the smell and take him back," Betsy warned, pulling off her hat in the stifling heat of the bathroom.

"Oh, Mama, thank you," Jo cried.

A quick embrace, then Betsy went to save the other calves.

The following morning, a hundred miles away, dawn was tender and the day looked fine when Cal left the home of the Democratic chairman of Fall River County in Ardmore. He'd turned out to be a Norwegian-born, potbellied piano teacher in his seventies. Stored inside his barn was a full-sized, hand-carved carousel. Truth be told, he said, he'd given up on politics. All he cared about was finishing the carousel before he died, that's it. Cal couldn't argue with the sentiment, especially since the next registered Democrat was thirty-five miles away. The visit was over the night he arrived, except for a hamburger supper and a camp bed.

"Don't give up," said the wife when he got into the station wagon that morning. A former schoolteacher, she could still command. "You'll find it livelier at the restaurant in town. Everyone and his brother goes to breakfast."

She was frail, and her face was wrinkled into folds of flesh so loose it looked like she was wearing the skin of an animal over hers and it was likely to slip off. She said Cal reminded her of a man named George McGovern, son of a Methodist preacher—which made him top drawer, in her view—executive something or other with the Democratic Party, who'd once passed this way. He had a trick: for each supporter that you meet, write down the name and pertinent information on an index card.

"I thought that was smart," she said.

She reached into her apron pocket and gave Cal a dollar. He blushed with joy.

"My first campaign contribution!" he said, and kissed her gnarly cheek.

Cal took the dollar and her advice. Between the towns of Rumford and Edgemont, he ate breakfast three times. In spots like the Bison Café back home, you could usually find a coterie of farmers willing to listen to your spiel if you kept it short and sprang for a round of joe. The combination of Yale-educated aristocrat and down-to-earth cattle rancher was something they'd never seen before, and they were intrigued, at least by his moxie. As for the message, he'd gotten it down to just two words: *politics matters.*

"What goes on in the statehouse determines your farm income and your profits," Cal would say, handing out his flyers, "the education of your kids, what your taxes will cost, whether or not we drop another atomic bomb. Politics depends on you, pure and simple. Who votes and who shirks it off, and I think that's the way it should be. I believe in the good judgment of good folks like you."

He continued to wind north through tiny hamlets and unincorporated towns, stopping people on the street, visiting a bowling alley, sale barn, Rotary Club, and veterans' home, dropping in on a backyard rodeo, a body shop, a garden club meeting, even a ladies' riding club that did square dancing on horseback, painstakingly keeping up the index cards he'd bought in a drugstore. He checked in at a motor court and placed a long-distance call to the Lucky Clover Ranch. When the operator said the line was busy, Cal didn't put anything by it. He was just too beat.

He lay in bed and stared at the news. The local CBS station was reporting that as a result of Edward R. Murrow's news show, *See It Now,* along with a damning series of articles in the *Washington Post,* Senate hearings had begun to investigate Joe McCarthy's inflammatory statements and false accusations against members of the U.S. Army. The end of his reign of terror was in sight.

The second night of his campaign, Calvin Kusek slept very well.

13

It was dead cold in the room. The only sound was the shrill whistling of the wind, or two strands of wind, intertwining in a mournful duet. In the chill light of morning, Jo inched across the top bunk and pulled the shade aside to find the window frosted over and fringed by icicles hanging off the roof. The spring blizzard had been faster and bigger than anyone predicted. It left more than six feet on the ground and drifts that had been whipped into smooth white curves so high you couldn't see the mailbox. The world was frozen in place, as if the spring season had been rolled back to January.

Downstairs it looked like a Christmas nativity. There were four live calves in the living room blinking their big eyes and looking bewildered. Little Ruby was lying in a cardboard box near the fireplace. Jo went and warmed up a bottle to feed him.

"One hundred twenty-four plus one hundred thirty-five equals two hundred fifty-nine. Right, Mama?" said Lance.

"Right," came a faint response.

Betsy had no idea what 124 plus 135 equaled. She was lying on the couch with an arm over her eyes, an aching, limp sack of bones after carrying the calves from the corral to the house through the blizzard.

"One hundred thirty-five minus one hundred twenty-four equals eleven." Lance paused. *"Mama!"*

"What?"

"You're not playing the game!"

The game was to solve math problems using the numbers of the yellow ear tags on the calves, but all Betsy could think about was a scalding-hot bath.

Jo, kneeling by the little calf, said, "He's taking the milk, Mama."

"Wonderful."

Jo stroked the soft reddish hide and scratched the white star on Ruby's forehead, knowing that she shouldn't feel the way she did, but this one was different, she was falling in love. It was Lance's job to change the newspapers, which he did while grandly holding his nose. By some internal command, Betsy roused herself from the couch and made cornbread in the iron skillet over a cooking fire the way they did in Camp Fire Girls, dumping a can of beans on top, which they all declared to be the very best breakfast they'd ever had.

Then there was no hope for it. They'd have to attack the snow. They suited up and trooped into the garage, where the winter gear had already been stored away.

"I wish Dad were here," Lance said, heaving a man-sized shovel over his shoulder. "This is going to be a bitch."

"A *what*?" Betsy exclaimed.

"He said we have to dig a ditch," Jo snorted. She and her brother were laughing so hard, another minute and they'd have to unzip everything and run inside to pee.

Beneath the half-sun and grumbling clouds, the three Kuseks shoveled and shoveled in powder up to their waists. As it melted and refroze, the snow became granular and heavy, but by midday they had dug a path to the barn and corrals like a medieval passageway with steep walls. When Betsy went inside to get an aspirin for an irksome backache, she discovered the calves were chewing up an armchair, and they were returned to their moms, except for Ruby, who was still too weak. In the afternoon the sun came out and the temperature edged past freezing. They were able to put out the hay they'd shrewdly stored in the barn for the sheep, goats, and cattle, and to collect a basketful of eggs. The phone lines and electricity were still down, so there was nothing to do until nightfall except keep on cleaning out snow so the ground could dry.

The following morning the weather held and Betsy judged the snowfall in the hills would be soft enough to break trail, so they could check on the herd in the spring pasture at Bottlebrush Creek. She rode a mare named Misty and the children saddled up Sprite, a small chestnut mare with a blond mane and tail and outstanding confirmation who was Jo's favorite, and Lance's black quarter horse, Tex, and they rode behind the barn to the path Cal, Fletch, Randy, Hayley Vance, and the others had followed on that first branding day, but now the trees were bare and blue shadows crisscrossed the untouched snow, sharp as cutout silhouettes. Budding twigs were sheathed with ice that shattered when the crowns of their cowboy hats brushed the lowest branches, raining cold drops down their necks. Beneath a blanket of ice covering the creek, rills of running water worked to bring it down, to open up the crystalline surface to the sun; in a few weeks, the quiet pools would turn algae green and full of life.

The cooped-up horses bucked and tossed their heads, desperate to run. Their breath showed in the stillness of the woods, turning magical when microscopic bits of ice would float in sparking veils across the bright arrows of sunlight that shot between the trees. It would be a slow incline upstream until Betsy and the children reached the upper pasture, but already they were high enough above the creek to be able to look down at the rapids where the rushing ice melt from the higher elevations overflowed the banks in shoals of dark gray mud, and that's where they saw their first dead cow.

The trail the dead cow had taken from the pasture was visible in broken snow. They pulled the wool mufflers over their mouths and squinted at the icefall to see where the barbed wire fence was broken and she'd stumbled down the slope to rocks near the creek. The wind picked up sharply.

"I'll take care of the fence," Betsy told the children. Scanning the field, she saw small dark bunches of cattle in the distance. "They're probably pocketed up near the draw. Go up and take a look. Stay together and do not go farther than the road."

"Okay, Mama. Don't worry," Jo said, cross-reining to turn around. "We'll come back for you."

Betsy smiled and touched the brim of her cowboy hat in acknowledgment. It was the byword of the Kusek family, what they always told each other when they split up in open country. *"I'll always come back for you"* was a lesson Betsy and Cal had instilled early on. You looked out for your partners and they looked out for you. You wanted to move cattle, but nothing mattered more than everyone getting home safely. Betsy had become more even-tempered: graceful, no-nonsense, and present, with little thought to hurrying. She'd learned to be quietly watchful like the dogs. Now she watched her half-grown children riding off, their horses kicking up snow, with satisfaction and pride.

She dismounted and removed the tools from the saddlebag. She put on her soft gloves. Starting at the top wire, she hooked the broken pieces to the stretcher. While others complained about fixing fences, on good days she liked being out there by herself, watching the snow slip off the pine boughs and the eagles ride the thermals in the sky. White-tailed deer eyeing her from the woods. This was not a good day. Looking down, she could see more dead cows in the creek bed.

The children rode toward the herd in the distance. The closer they got, the more they could see that everything was a mess. The snow was all churned up. Turkey vultures were sitting in the trees like hungry priests. They could tell from the different-colored ear tags that these cows were all mixed up from neighboring ranches. They'd gotten lost and drifted over the fences that were covered with snow.

At the edge of the field they saw two pickups hitched with trailers.

"Maybe those guys know something about it," Jo said.

The road was open and three men were busy loading cows into the trailers. Two were older with weathered, rough, unshaven faces. Their winter dusters were black with filth and their boots all worn down, which didn't make them different from any other cowboys, except by the manner in which they were handling the cattle, shouting and cracking bull whips. Like they didn't know them and didn't care. When you knew your herd, you could tell the girls apart: who was gentle or likely to charge; who had trouble nursing and needed to be coaxed. Each and every cow was *money in the bank* and you wouldn't hustle them so fast up a narrow ramp, like these guys were doing, making their hearts speed up and their eyes roll in fear, risking a broken leg or one of them bolting altogether.

Also their dogs were mean. They were just black junkyard mutts who sat in the trucks barking their heads off. They weren't smart working dogs like Lois and Bandit. Something was definitely wrong. Then Jo knew.

"Those are ours," she told Lance in a low voice.

"Which?"

"The Red Angus. See? The rest are Charolais and Herefords. They're all mixed up together. Those guys are stealing our cows."

"Hell!" said Lance, taking advantage of being hundreds of yards from their mother to curse out loud. "They can't do that. Let's get 'em."

The children rode closer.

"Hey!" called Jo. "What do you think you're doing?"

The two older cowboys didn't give them a glance, but went about the business of locking the trailer doors behind the load. The youngest of the gang was Honeybee Jones, who'd been called upon with a knock at the door at three that morning to serve as a hand rounding up the livestock that had surely strayed in this kind of storm. For legit ranchers, the snow would turn out to be a sorrowful disaster. For Honeybee and his cohorts, it was an opportunity, like open purses at a radio show, to get the cows on the train to Chicago before anyone counted them missing.

Honeybee walked right up to Jo and Lance and smiled. Except he wasn't really smiling. His puffed-out cheeks were covered with reddish-blond fuzz. His eyes were small and close-set. He looked familiar—like a nasty woodchuck set to bite.

"What are you two doing way up here alone?" he asked in a phony nice voice.

"We're not alone. Our mama's right over there," said Jo.

Honeybee nodded. All he could see was a white field that stretched to the hills and no traces of another human being.

"Uh-huh," he said doubtfully.

"Get out of here," Jo said. "This is our property."

"I'm collecting my cows."

"They're not yours, they're other people's. And those are from the Lucky Clover Ranch. They're ours."

"Is that so?"

"You bet. We run Red Angus."

"They're all branded up," Lance added defiantly.

"Sorry, our mistake."

"Give them back," said Jo.

"No can do."

"You're stealing!"

Honeybee laughed. "*Stealing?* Naw. What's your name, honey?"

Jo had the advantage of being on Sprite, higher up. She gave the man her most mean and nasty glare, memorizing his evil features.

The others were impatiently smoking cigarettes. The doors were locked and the motors running, spewing vapor. Jo could see the trailers shifting with their weight as the cows poked at the window slits. She saw a red head with a yellow ear tag and her heart swelled up with anguish as if one of her family was being dragged away.

"See that one?" She pointed. "She's definitely ours!"

"Forget what you seen," Honeybee said coldly. "You ain't seen nothing."

"Yes, I did."

"Ain't you the little smarty pants?"

One of the others was calling him to get in the truck, but Honeybee grabbed the bridle of Lance's horse, pulled the animal toward him, and in one sweep of the other arm grabbed Lance's jacket and jerked the boy off the saddle, threw him to the ground, and pinned him down on his stomach with a heavy knee in his back.

"Stop it!" shrieked Jo.

Honeybee whipped out a rope and in three seconds had the boy's arms and legs tied up like a rodeo calf. His kicking and flailing meant nothing, nor the piercing wail for help that his mother was too far away to hear.

Honeybee slung the struggling boy over his shoulder.

Jo yelled, "Put him down!"

"He's coming with us, straight to the slaughterhouse," Honeybee said, carrying Lance toward the trucks. "Nobody'll know where he disappeared to when he's nothing but bones."

Jo kicked Sprite and galloped full speed at Honeybee in an attempt to run him over, but he spun around and raised his arms, yelling, "*Haaaa!*" The horse spooked and Jo flew off, barely escaping Sprite's pounding hooves.

"Leave my brother alone!" she screamed on the ground, feebly throwing snow.

One of the other cowboys opened the truck door impatiently and yelled an obscenity. Honeybee let go of Lance and simply dropped him face-first.

"Keep your mouth shut, little girl. Say one word and I will come back for you, I promise you that. You and your brother and your ma and dad. I know where you live. The Lucky Clover Ranch, ain't that it?" he said in a petrifying growl, popping his eyes.

Terrified, vision blurred by snot and tears, Jo knelt beside Lance, whose blood stained the snow, desperately working to loosen the ropes before Honeybee came back with a shotgun, but he was already in the truck and the rustlers had driven off, leaving behind the couple of dozen cows they couldn't fit.

Betsy had mended the fence and ridden halfway across the plain when she met her children riding the other way to meet her. Their faces were shiny red and they were sniffling from the cold.

"What took you so long?" she asked.

"It's a whole big jumble over there," Jo replied staunchly. "It looks like a bunch of cows came over the fences and they all ended up together. There's some of ours and some of the neighbors', all mixed up."

"When the weather clears we'll sort them out," Betsy said. She noticed that her son had a swollen nose and the beginning of a black eye. "What happened to you?"

"Snowball fight," Jo answered quickly.

"I fell off," Lance mumbled.

Betsy leaned over to grab Lance's face and inspect his teeth.

"No permanent damage," she pronounced, then turned toward the gate. "Looks like tire tracks. Someone's been up here."

"We didn't see anyone," said Jo.

"The road is open," Betsy said. "Let's go home."

14

Cal pulled in late that night, but Betsy was in her bathrobe and already downstairs by the time he'd slipped through the kitchen door and put the suitcase down. They hugged with desperation and relief. Her body was soft and smelled of homemade soap, while he felt like a trooper from a far-off war, stiff and sore, whose clothes should be burned.

"Is everyone okay?" he asked. "The kids?"

She nodded. "But it was bad, Cal. We lost at least five cows that I could count up at Bottlebrush Creek, maybe more."

"What the hell happened?"

"We had a wicked rain. I think it was the rain that killed them."

She started to shake. He took her hands. They were icy cold.

"Come here," he said, sitting her down at the kitchen table.

"We got three inches in a couple of hours," she went on. "I've never seen rain like that, so hard and fast. There was mud this thick in the yard. They say the wind got up to seventy miles an hour. It sounded like the house was coming down. Then, around three in the morning, it turned into a blizzard. You couldn't see a thing. I got the calves that were still in the corral and brought them inside—"

"Jesus, Betsy, you should not have done that! You should not go out in a storm like that alone. What is wrong with you?"

"I had to, or we would have lost all that money."

"Where was I?" Cal said bitterly. "Out dreaming somewhere."

"Look, nobody thought it would move that fast—"

"I could kick myself for not being here. And for what?"

"We both agreed that you should run," she reminded him gently. "What's the matter?" she asked, seeing his deep disappointment.

He gave an exhausted shrug. "We've already lost."

"The election? Why do you say that?"

"The storm took us out. I didn't make it halfway across the county before I had to turn around."

"There's still time before the special election—"

"No, there's not. It was a great idea to grab Doc Avery's seat, but it wasn't meant to be."

"Don't say that."

"I can't take off until we're all dug out, and who knows what we'll find when the snow melts? Half the fences will be down." He stared at his wife, straight and true. "I never want you and the kids to be alone like that."

"We did all right."

"What happened to the calves?"

"Chilled to the bone, but they made it, at least the ones down here. We toweled them off and put them by the fire. The red newborn had to go in a warm bath. His poor little ears and tail were frozen solid. Jo and Lance are quite attached because they birthed him by themselves. They've decided to raise him."

"That'll be good for them."

Betsy nodded but tears sprang from her eyes. "When I think of how those cows died, I just can't bear it! Soaking wet and so cold . . . They went to the low spots, along the creek beds, to try to get away from the wind, and I'm afraid what happened was they got stuck in the mud from the rain. They must have been so tired and just wanted to rest. The snow came down so wet and heavy, it buried them where they'd taken shelter, trying to protect their babies."

Cal's eyes filmed over in sympathy. "It's nature. Honey, there's nothing you or I could have done, even if I'd been here," he added regretfully.

"I don't know," Betsy said, not an answer but a statement of despair.

She got up and leaned against the sink, wiping her glistening cheeks with her fingertips. Cal took the bourbon from the cabinet and flipped the cap off a bottle of Coke.

"I had to mend the fence at Bottlebrush Creek. The children found a bunch of cattle running loose near the road," Betsy told him. "Some of the neighbors' as well as ours."

"So there are survivors."

"Oh, yes. And Lance fell off Tex," she added. "He's got a shiner but he's okay."

Cal was surprised. "Lance is good on Tex. And Tex doesn't usually spook."

"Somebody threw a snowball."

"Oh, I see. Somebody named Jo?" Cal suggested.

He smiled. He loved his daughter's tough, can-do spirit, pleased they'd raised the kind of girl who wouldn't kowtow to boys, not that he'd ever let one near her. He already had suspicions about eight-year-old Robbie Fletcher.

He cracked some ice into glasses and they downed a couple of sweetly burning drinks before going upstairs with every intention of an urgent reunion. But it wasn't right. During trying times they'd always found that making love put things in order. They'd clung to each other when Betsy got the letter about her father's death. When Adlai Stevenson was defeated they got so drunk on cheap red wine they ended up on the floor. Maybe they had underestimated how deeply they had come to cherish their animals and the rangeland that they farmed, because the loss was as grievous as death in the family, and with the breadth of devastation still unknown, it would have been sacrilegious to dance on the ruins.

In the morning, as if the world had changed its frivolous mind and given them another chance, the temperature shot up to fifty degrees. Cal got the generator going and there were chocolate chip pancakes for breakfast, but despite their favorite treat the kids were withdrawn, and when he drove them to school there was silence in the backseat, not even squabbling. He had to probe like a lawyer to get anything out of them concerning the way things went while he was away.

"How'd your new baby calf do in the storm?" he asked Jo.

"Fine," said Jo.

About the fall off Tex, Lance's reply was equally noncommittal.

"I'm fine."

"Dad, he's *fine,*" Jo snapped, hoping to hear no more questions about what happened at Bottlebrush Creek.

Jo and Lance were terrified that the cattle rustler would come back and murder them all. They didn't know he was a small-time punk named Honeybee Jones—they believed he was a criminal escaped from prison, like the bad guys on the TV show *The Lineup*. He knew they lived on the Lucky Clover Ranch, so why not climb through the window and stuff a pillow over their faces *"To keep your mouths shut!"* In whispers in their bunks at night, they kept each other in cold fright about the petrifying possibilities, arguing whether they should tell their parents or just lie low, hoping he had left the country and escaped to Mexico. Meanwhile, they knew where Dad kept the shotgun.

Cal had been right about what lay beneath the snow. As the sun grew stronger and the heavy banks began to melt, people were awakening to a ghastly nightmare. Pennington County had become a mass graveyard. Over spotty phone lines, among clusters of ranch wives who gathered in markets and on street corners in town, friends and strangers alike leaned in close and listened to the stories told in soft, shocked voices as word spread that hundreds, perhaps thousands, of cattle had died in the storm. And it was calving season, the worst possible time, because calves were the future of a ranch. Cowmen were going to lose their livelihood, that much was certain. The only question was how many.

With no sign of outside help, anger focused on the government, feeding the age-old loathing of ranchers toward authority. Cal had already picked up that sentiment from the talk he'd heard through the open windows of the pickups that had gathered at the school bus stop, and then by witnessing the extent of the catastrophe himself as it began to unfold across the region with gruesome regularity.

Every couple of hundred yards along the road there were dead and frozen cattle lying in ditches, on their backs, on their sides, here and there a surreal hoof sticking straight up out of the snow. His stomach lurched watching two cowboys on horses tentatively make their way across the patchy fields, not knowing what they would find on the other side of the downed fence lines, where disoriented animals had stumbled blindly in the blizzard, fallen into the trenches, and died of exposure.

Trooper Randy Sturgis's car was stopped on the side of the road alongside a black pickup with souvenir state decals plastered all over the windows that Cal recognized as belonging to Spanky Larson. Cal pulled over, took out the shovel he always carried with the rest of the gear, and slid down the embankment to where Randy and Spanky were clearing snow from three black bellies protruding from a white grave. Down in the gully the wind was colder than up on the road, shadowed by bare cottonwood trees whose leaves and branches lost in the storm lay in whirlwind patterns on the sparkling crust of ice.

"These can't be yours, Spanky," Cal said, knowing Spanky's property was twenty miles away.

Spanky shook his head. "No, they ain't, but I'll tell you, it's a mixed blessing."

They were digging out around the heads in order to cut the ear tags off and return them to the owners so they could claim their losses— a grim service duty everyone in the county had spontaneously taken on, along with feeding and doctoring whatever stray cattle ended up on their property until they could be claimed.

"Your heart's in your mouth until you see it ain't yours, which is a relief, but then you feel just awful for the fella who's lost his girl. The guilt alone's enough to bring you to your knees," Spanky said.

"We're seeing cows miles away from where they should be," Randy Sturgis commented grimly. "Found sixty head stuck in a steep bend in the creek. They must have stumbled over the bank and into the water, and either succumbed to the cold or got buried in the snowfall and suffocated. And if that ain't bad enough, a ring of thieves is out there, rounding up the ones that got lost."

"Cattle and rustlers go together like dogs and fleas," Spanky commented. "Where there's one, there's the other."

Cal dug deep, watching the tip of his spade slice into the bluish snow so he didn't have to see that fifty-six-year-old, white-haired Spanky Larson had stopped to take off his bandanna and wipe tears from his eyes.

"I've never seen anything like this," Spanky said when he'd composed himself.

When they were done Cal followed Randy Sturgis and Spanky Larson to the Bison Café, where the trooper solemnly gave the three ear tags they'd clipped to a third-generation cowman in his forties named Tim Ehrlich, who closed work-blackened fingers around the tags, which represented several thousand dollars in losses. His tablemates murmured condolences. Tim turned a stubbled and sleepless face toward the officer, staring hard with frank blue eyes.

"Thank you, Randy. This means a lot. Where'd you find 'em?"

Randy described the spot on the highway. "They drifted an awful long way from your place."

Tim Ehrlich nodded blankly. "These were yearling heifers," he said. "Hand-raised. You got to wonder what the good Lord had in mind," he added sadly, and even the most righteous churchgoers among them kept their eyes on their coffee cups.

The volume of talk in the Bison Café had risen to a kind of hysteria, like the meal after a funeral when propriety gives way to garrulous inhibition. During the crisis, the usual pecking order had been suspended. Men roamed freely among the tables and squeezed into crowded booths, cheeks of broken blood vessels to jowls of too much flesh. Horror stories were repeated to every newcomer in full detail. Cowboy hats stayed on.

The café owner, Shirley Hix, delivered heavy plates of chicken fried steak and mashed potatoes with self-importance, a rag wagging from the tight back pocket of her jeans like a suggestive tail. The calamity had not distracted her from putting on lipstick and fluffing up her chiffon hairdo, as she considered herself to be the center of the café, which was essentially the center of town. Baggy-armed Lucille Thurlow's apple and cherry pies were disappearing as fast as craggy ranchers could stand to wait while she arranged the paper plates with wedges lined up facing north. She was known to screech like a cat if you messed up the order.

Poor Charmin' Charlie had lost thirty pounds to cancer. His face was white as flour and his bald head flopped over to the side on a weakened neck. Nobody wanted to leave him out, and Cal was one of those who gathered around his wheelchair, along with T.W. with his buttoned-up jacket and unkempt hair, Spanky Larson, and Vaughn Anders, who'd come down from the hills to help out.

"Got a drink?" Charlie croaked.

T.W. giggled. His pockmarked face made him look like a goofy teenager. "Charlie sure ain't lost his sense of humor," T.W. said, jerking a thumb toward the dying man.

Vaughn Anders pulled a flask from his overalls and poured his home-brewed moonshine into Charlie's cup.

"Cure ya or kill ya," Vaughn said.

Charlie raised a trembling hand in thanks.

Spanky asked, "Will someone help that man to his reward?"

Cal volunteered to bring the cup to Charlie's grateful lips. Randy Sturgis came over to join them, pulling up a chair. He spread his legs and slapped his knees in frustration.

"I thought I'd heard the worst of it, but this is unbelievable," Randy Sturgis said.

They all leaned forward with anticipation.

"Dutch Roy lost half his herd."

Cal felt a double contraction in his chest like a one-two punch. He knew he would always remember where he was when he heard that the Roy family dynasty had come to an end and a new world was opening up. With just a few words everything had changed, like when he'd heard the news that Pearl Harbor was bombed.

"Got any more of that hootch?" Spanky Larson mumbled.

Vaughn Anders poured it, then looked out over the room; his eyes focused nowhere, like he'd gone into a trance, fiddling with the handle on one of the three knives on his belt.

"Roys were way too quick to bring 'em to spring pasture," Randy Sturgis surmised.

"Were they?" echoed Cal with wonder.

It was a miracle that he hadn't done the same—moved his own herd from the protection of the hills at Bottlebrush Creek to the open grasslands, where they, too, would have perished in the storm. If the opportunity to go after the legislative seat hadn't popped up just then, and he hadn't had to hit the road, he, too, would have made the move. He was as stunned as he'd been in the vacant town of Ardmore, when the kid shooting at prairie dogs just missed Cal's head. The second time he'd dodged a bullet. And he had to ask: What was the good Lord saving *him* for?

"I never considered it a sound idea to switch up pastures before Easter," Vaughn Anders was saying. "Wait until Easter, my granddaddy used to say."

Again Charlie tried to speak. "Al-ma-nac," he wheezed.

This time Spanky helped him out. "You're saying they should've checked the weather in the *Farmer's Almanac*?"

Charlie nodded.

"Got one right here." Randy Sturgis whipped the small dun-colored pamphlet from his jacket pocket. "Let's see what it says about the month of April," and he read:

The days lengthen and the cold strengthens.
False signs of spring.
Tornadoes West and you keep on your fur-lined vest.
Rains ice cubes!

Randy finished in a tone of chilling irony, like the last lines of a ghost story. The others looked at one another with raised eyebrows and in awed silence of the prophetic warning come to life.

"What advice does it say about dead cows?" Vaughn Anders wondered.

Randy closed the *Almanac*. "Bury 'em before disease sets in and spreads."

"Haul 'em to Chicago for rendering," Spanky Larson said.

"And who's gonna do that?"

"The government!" T.W. piped up cheerfully, like the smartest kid in class.

The others snickered and made remarks like "You know how long that'll take?" and "Nobody in Washington cares to pick up the phone."

"Someone's got to fix this," T.W. insisted.

Cal didn't realize how intently he'd been listening until two ideas banged together like railway cars coupling in his head. A lot had been lost, but not the election. He could still get on that train.

"Would you vote for the man who got those dead cows buried?"

"Who, you?" drawled Vaughn Anders. "You gonna pile a couple hundred dead cows in your brand-new pickup?"

The others laughed.

"Would you vote for a Democrat if I did?"

"Sure I'd vote for you," T.W. said. "Hell, I'd vote for you anyway."

Vaughn Anders snorted. "I never knew you was a damn Democrat."

"I don't vote for the party," Spanky announced. "I vote for the man."

Charlie's dry, puckered mouth formed the soundless words: "Me, too."

"It's a deal," said Cal. "Now give me your vote."

All fired up, he went table to table, proposing the same—*Give me your vote and I'll clean up this mess*—moving fast, shaking hands, and giving condolences for lost stock. Faces began to look more open and eyes grew bright. By the time Cal reached the door, talk was buzzing, people were all riled up. He'd left these battered men with hope.

And then he was alone with what he'd promised. He stood outside the café in the empty hallway of the auction barn. The bulletin boards had sprouted notices of fund-raisers to help the community. The halls—usually jammed with bidders—were hushed, shutters pulled down over the registration counter, and the doors chained shut to the pit where a week ago bulls were spinning and kicking the old stall boards until they splintered, and buyers played cutthroat competition while the auctioneer droned on. Now there were no bulls to sell and no cash to buy them.

Times were ominous and Cal's plan was just as dire. He picked up the receiver of the pay phone and kept dumping change into the slot as the operator required, until a male voice answered lazily, "Ellsworth Air Force Base, Master Sergeant Vance."

"I have a person-to-person call for Master Sergeant Hayley Vance," the operator announced.

"Who wants to talk to him?"

"Who's calling, please?" came the operator's voice.

The stuffed head of the long-horned steer stared across the empty halls of the auction barn as it had for decades, a mute prince of death crowned with useless horns.

Cal Kusek repeated his name to the operator.

When Cal had phoned Master Sergeant Hayley Vance from the hallway outside the Bison Café and that flat Missouri voice intoned, "*Hel*lo, Cal. This is a *ter*rible day," with the sincerity of a snake oil salesman, Cal knew that what he was asking for would come with a price. Vance liked to go on about Cal's war record as if they were comrades in arms, but having the rank of master sergeant hardly made him a soldier; he was a broker who took a cut of every deal involving a government contract.

It wasn't hard to fathom the scam he had going. Vance lived larger than even his chief commanding officer. Vance was a member of the snootiest country club in town, where he golfed with judges and the owner of a uranium mine that happened to be on national forest land. His wife had been elected to the board of the Sioux Indian Museum as well as the Theater Guild Palace, and his daughters, not the prettiest, were always voted Range Day queens. He'd made a career out of seeming to be a lackadaisical good ol' boy from across the river, but drove a bargain and enjoyed the kill, protected as he was by a big wooden desk in a compound surrounded by barbed wire and a tangle of regulations that only he could bend at will.

"We've got dead cows to bury and we need the equipment to do it," Cal told him from the pay phone outside the café.

"I've seen the carnage. Turns your stomach."

"Nobody knows how big this is going to be, but as it is, carcasses are out in the open and lying in water supplies. We're talking in the hundreds that have to be disposed of now."

Master Sergeant Vance considered. "You'll need trucks."

"A lot of trucks," Cal agreed.

"Bulldozers and cranes, I would guess."

"That's correct," said Cal. "As a concerned citizen and Democratic candidate, I'm asking for the air force to step in and help clean up the mess."

There was a pause on the other end.

"I sympathize, I truly do," Vance said with a sigh, "but all our resources are committed."

"Committed where?"

"The Oahe Dam, upriver from Pierre. They needed heavy earth movers, and the air force sent what we had on base."

"Bring them back," said Cal.

Vance chuckled. "Can't just do that!"

"This is an emergency in the backyard of Ellsworth Air Force Base. Local people need help—*local people*," he emphasized, "are hurting. It's a golden opportunity for the government to do something right. Get them on your side."

"I like what you're saying, Cal, but I'm the low man on the totem pole. You really should be talking to the chief master sergeant. The Oahe Dam, that's a big deal. You're talking about the army engineers and the Missouri River authority—"

Cal interrupted sharply. "Hayley, I'm willing to sell you my beef."

"What makes you think I need your beef?"

"Dutch Roy is out of business. The storm hit him hard."

"I told you, didn't I? On your first roundup, that place where Custer killed the Indians."

"I remember," Cal said quietly.

"I told you Dutch was headed for trouble. I made you an offer, but you turned me down."

"Yes, I did."

Hayley was silent, reshuffling his cards. "How'd you all do in the storm?"

"We got lucky."

"Are you ready to reconsider?" Hayley probed.

"Yes."

"Forgive me if I'm doubtful. You're such a man of principle."

Cal felt like one of his own cows on the gambrel hook. He traded doomed looks with the stuffed steer head. "I want something in exchange, Hayley."

"Money."

"Manpower. What will it take to turn those air force trucks around and use them to dispose of all these carcasses? Just tell me what you want."

Master Sergeant Vance cleared his throat with a note of disbelief. "You told me straight up you'd never betray a friend. Dutch will say you stabbed him in the back."

"Maybe he'll say we saved the business. The rest of us won't survive if the blowflies get started or who knows what other disease. You need beef, I need trucks."

Cal forced himself to wait through the silence on the other side of the line. He could feel that SOB enjoying this. Finally Master Sergeant Vance spoke.

"You know, after the dust settles, the price of beef will go way up. You'll get a lot more if you wait."

"This won't wait."

"From where I'm standing, I can't wait, either. I've got to get the burger on the bun no matter what the market says."

"You're going to lowball me, I feel it coming," Cal said.

"As you say, for the common good. I admire your sense of civic duty, sir."

The price Master Sergeant Vance offered was way below market, plus he would require the same off-the-record "administrative fee" he'd received every month from Dutch Roy. Cal hung up the phone feeling sick and excited at the same time. The following day, the air force ordered a convoy of earth-moving equipment to leave the Oahe Dam flood control project on the Missouri River and head west, in order to provide emergency assistance to storm-struck Pennington County.

Doris Roy was upset about losing her eyebrows. They'd all but disappeared, just about the same time she'd lost desire for her husband. She'd wondered: If she penciled them in, would her lust come back to life? Then he'd gotten himself into that foolish tractor accident and come out of the hospital a bent old man, so without anyone putting too fine a point on it, that part of their lives together had fluttered to a close. She leaned toward the oval mirror on the dressing table, not at all fond of the way her face was turning into her grandmother's, and carefully removed the tiny pink foam rollers that left neat waves in her fine platinum dyed hair, which was showing up these days more in the brush than on her head. She sprayed the sides with stuff that smelled like paint thinner, so the curls would stay put peeking out underneath the brim of her hat. Let the rest of her hair do whatever. Don't matter what don't show.

Dutch was waiting at the landing, resting his weight with both hands on a cane. Despite the curve in his back from the injury, he was still an imposing figure, still a big man, over six feet, wearing his cowboy hat with the cattleman's crease, a fresh white shirt with a silver bolo tie, a plaid vest with his father's gold watch chain, and pressed trousers. Freshly shaved that morning. His facial expression, like his wife's, remained stalwart.

Arm in arm, the Roys made their way carefully down the stairs and out the front door, where their son, Scotty, in clean clothes and his hair plastered down, was waiting to drive them to the lake, all of them looking as sober as if they were going to a funeral in a church about to be demolished.

Now the air force was coming to save what was left of the day. The artificial lake had originally been dug to provide water for the cattle, but it was filled with their carcasses, floating like half-sunk battleships, russet humps in the cold blue surface still marked by ice floes. The first vehicle in the cortege was Master Sergeant Hayley Vance's jeep, followed by a bus carrying air force cadets to do the heavy work, then a bulldozer, trucks, and a crane. All the vehicles flew American flags.

The ground had dried out, all right, and the cloud raised by the rattling caravan laid a blanket of dust over the new growth of weeds by the side of the road that a few days before had been buried in snow. Master Sergeant Vance expressed his condolences to Dutch and Scotty while his boys positioned the equipment. As usual, Dutch got right to the point.

"Who'd you get to replace my contract?" he asked.

"Cal Kusek jumped into the gap," Master Sergeant Vance replied.

Scotty was shocked and angered. "Cal did?"

"He's a smart cattleman. Learned from you, Dutch."

"Don't sweet-talk me, Hayley. I paid for that contract. Is he paying you, too?"

"He's giving me a fair price."

"Sure he is. He's one slick East Coast lawyer."

"You understand, Dutch. I have a base to feed and superiors to answer to. I wanted to show you the respect of coming here first so I could tell you the facts, face-to-face, because that's what your family deserves."

"I appreciate it, but this is temporary. We'll get back on our feet."

"Sure, Dutch."

"Don't write us off, son. We're up to the job, you ought to know that by now."

"Look, I wish it could have been a different way."

"It will be."

Master Sergeant Vance gave a vague salute and went to supervise the dredging. Caught in the jaws of the crane around her belly, the first cow came out of the water, whole, unblemished, limp, and glistening with water and somehow beautiful, like a bashful Madonna, with her head hanging down in gentle repose.

"Don't believe what Vance is telling us," Dutch said. "This didn't just happen by itself. Cal sold us out."

"He saw an opportunity," Scotty agreed bitterly.

"After taking him in, he hits us when we're down," Dutch replied, not listening. "Don't worry. I won't forget."

The jaws opened and the cow was dumped in the truck to be taken to a communal burial pit being dug by the air force near the hills. Then the crane swerved back for another. This went on all morning. Doris Roy stayed in the pickup.

They came in gratitude for the air force burial convoy, which had stopped at each of their ranches and farms and done their saddest, dirtiest work. Nothing like this had ever happened before, but neither had the government responded so effectively. In taking action, Cal had broken the paralysis of grief and created an uplifted sense of community. Not only did he cut through the bureaucracy, but proved he was a man who, in their day-to-day dealings, showed nothing but good temperament, self-confidence, honesty, and humility. If there were such a thing as a good politician, he might just be Calvin Kusek. The weather had stabilized, and even the flow of blood in their bodies felt like the quickening of spring. The feeling was festive. Somebody brought a trombone.

It was the day of the special election against Bill O'Connell, and Kusek supporters had come to help get out the vote. They had put bridge tables covered with red, white, and blue on the sidewalk in front of the Hotel Alex Johnson on Main Street. They had clipboards so you could register, people to take you to the polls, and free cookies, hot dogs, and lemonade, paid for by Verna Bismark, who arrived with her family and a dozen stalwart Democratic Party members from Cottonwood. Surprisingly present were the parents of Jo and Lance's school friends, along with 4-H members and Camp Fire Girls—a small but enthusiastic army that spread out to canvass the downtown shops and businesses to "Vote for Kusek!"

"We're all pulling together!" Cal smiled, selling raffle tickets by the dozen to raise money for families stricken by the storm.

"Vote for my dad!" shouted Lance and Jo, giving away cookies.

"Vote for my husband!" Betsy said, handing out recipe cards for her Western Hamburger Sauté.

At precisely noon, the rally climaxed with a parade of the air force convoy through downtown Rapid City on its way back to Oahe Dam. By then the streets were lined with cheering shoppers and office workers. A polished jeep carrying Master Sergeant Vance stopped in front of Cal and they ceremonially shook hands. The *Rapid City Journal* ran a story that evening calling Cal Kusek a "visionary politician" and comparing him with another prairie lawyer, Abraham Lincoln.

After the polls closed, Stell, Fletch, and Robbie drove out to the Lucky Clover Ranch. Win or lose, at least they'd be in good company. They gathered in the living room. The wives set out canapés and Cal mixed a pitcher of martinis. He put a classical station on the radio, but everyone protested it was too depressing, so he switched to KPIX, which was playing big band music, putting everyone in a rebellious, sexy mood.

"I wish we were all in a wonderful jazz club in the Village right now," Betsy said nostalgically, curling up on the couch next to her husband.

"Do you miss New York?" Stell asked.

"When I think about it, yes, terribly. My sister, Marja, still lives there. I keep hoping she'll come out for a visit."

"My family never visits. *His* parents stay forever. They think we're running a hotel," complained Stell. *"Heavy drinkers,"* she mouthed to Betsy.

Fletch raised his martini glass. "I'm going to bet Cal Kusek takes the race by a mile!" and they all started knocking wood on everything within reach.

The women went to the kitchen to check on the food and came back holding fresh drinks.

"Dinner'll take a while," Betsy said.

Stell sat on Fletch's lap. "We forgot to turn on the oven," she confessed.

"You two are easy dates," Fletch said, giving her a squeeze.

"When are we going to hear something?" Stell demanded.

Cal looked at his watch. "I hope soon. Verna said she'd call."

"Sit tight, it's going to be good news," Fletch said.

"Shh! Don't jinx it!" Stell cried, pulling his ears.

"What have you boys been talking about?" Betsy asked.

"Your husband regaled me with political intrigue. Did you tell Betsy about the fund-raiser?"

Cal rolled his eyes and smirked. "Thanks, old buddy."

"What fund-raiser?" Betsy asked.

"When he was on the road, some grizzled old guy in some grizzled

old town hands Cal Kusek a fistful of cash—for the campaign—a donation, you follow me? How'd he get it? Runs a whorehouse."

Betsy stared at Cal. "You took money from prostitutes?" she said
with mock outrage.

"Yes, dear, but it's better than them taking money from me!"

Even through their raucous laughter they could hear their children
screaming. The jokes stopped. They put their drinks down and pulled
on shoes.

"Where are they?"

"I don't know."

"Did they take the horses—?"

As they scrambled outside the phone began to ring. For a moment
there was confusion—should someone answer it?—but the young,
shrill cries were urgent so they kept on going, breaking up to search
the yard, the barn, the henhouse, and the corrals, and that's where they
found the two boys, Robbie and Lance, standing outside the rails and Jo
on the ground inside, kneeling beside a motionless calf.

"Ruby's dead," Lance said solemnly.

Cal climbed in with the cows and squatted beside Jo, who was sobbing brokenheartedly. The calf was lying on its side. The mother had
already mourned it and abandoned the corpse.

"Leave me alone," Jo cried.

"I'm sorry, Jo," Cal said.

"He shot Ruby and nobody stopped him."

"Now come on, Jo. Nobody shot Ruby," Cal said.

"He said he'd come back for us."

Lance's fingers tightened in his mother's hand.

"Do you know what your sister is talking about?" Betsy asked.

The boy's lips twisted in wretched indecision but he shook his
head. They'd made a blood pact not to say a whisper about the rustler.

"How could anyone get in here, anyway?" Robbie asked. "With the
dogs and all—"

Stell told him to hush.

The phone inside the house began to ring again.

"I'll go," said Fletch.

"While you're there, turn off the oven," whispered Stell as Fletch
took off toward the lighted porch.

"What are you talking about, Jo?" Cal asked gently.

"I can't tell you," said Jo.

Betsy squeezed her young son's hand. "What is going on, Lance? You can tell us, nobody will be mad."

After a moment his mother's reassurance overcame his fear, and he confessed. "We saw them stealing cattle," Lance said.

Jo burst into fresh tears. "They told us not to tell or they'd kill every-body on the ranch. You and Mama and all the animals," she said, throwing her arms around her father's neck.

He crouched there with his little girl and held her tight.

"Who were they?" he asked.

"Cowboys!" she snapped, a dead giveaway that she was hiding what she knew.

"Why didn't you tell us?" Betsy asked Lance.

"We were scared," he said.

"Nobody's going to hurt anybody," his mother promised.

"Don't tell. Don't tell the police!" Jo wailed.

In the faint light coming from the house, the adults exchanged looks of outrage and determination. But the first thing was to calm the children.

"I want to show you something, honey," Cal told Jo. "Nobody's going to harm you or your brother, and this is why. You don't have to be afraid. Look at Ruby. See? There's not a mark on him. They might have been bad guys, but they didn't shoot this calf."

His concerned face was close to his daughter's; her cheeks were bright pink and her clear blue eyes shiny as stones in a creek washed over by endless waves of transparent tears. Cal's heart broke with hers as he examined the carcass. Its neck was blackened and covered with blue-green flies.

"Honey, look—he died of natural causes. Those are called blow-flies. They lay eggs and the eggs are called screwworms. If there's a wound anywhere on the animal, those worms get in there and cause big trouble."

He spared her the fact that the worms survived by eating the living flesh of the host.

"I don't want to see," said Jo.

"That's fine, honey. Just know that nobody's going to hurt you. They didn't kill this calf."

He gently helped her to her feet and turned her toward her mother's embrace. What the girl didn't see wouldn't cause nightmares and self-recrimination. He could tell from the maggots that the infestation had started around the navel, probably not cleaned properly at birth. Jo and Lance had been so proud of attending to the newborn.

He climbed out of the corral after his daughter.

"Please don't put him in that big pit with all the cows," she begged.

"We have to, honey, so the disease doesn't spread." Then he told Betsy, "We have to call the vet. Right now."

She nodded, worried. "I know."

"Why do *you* get to decide everything?" Jo protested. "He's just another animal—money in the bank to you. I want to bury him special, not in the pit!"

"I'll take care of it—" Cal began.

"You say you'll take care of things, but you never do!"

The screen door slammed. Fletch was walking toward them from the house with a big smile on his face.

"That was Verna on the phone. Congratulations. You won, Cal. You won the election by a hundred fifty-seven votes! Hurry up, we have to get back to town—your supporters are gathering at the hotel."

The adults hugged, their mood softened by the children's sorrow.

"Your daddy is a state representative!" Stell told Jo.

"Who cares?" said Jo. "I hate it here."

She ran ahead, with Robbie and Lance close behind.

The others paused on the lawn in the paradox of twilight. Cal took his wallet from the pocket of his jeans and from a certain fold removed a one-dollar bill and waved it back and forth.

"This was my first campaign contribution! It was given to me by the wife of the Democratic chairman in the thriving metropolis of Ardmore, South Dakota. She had to be ninety. Sharp as a tack. Her husband was building a carousel."

"You are out of your mind!" Fletch said, laughing.

"It was his life's work, dammit! Piece by piece, just like this campaign. I'm going to frame this dollar and put it on the wall of my office in Washington, D.C."

"Listen to him!" said Stell. *"Washington!"*

"Why *not*?"

"Come on," Betsy said. "We have to call the vet."

. . .

That week the theme of Thaddeus Haynes's sermon on *The Hour of Truth* was pestilence.

"There's pestilence in this land," he intoned into the microphone set up on the card table in the hotel ballroom. "I refer not to the tragic loss of cattle that all of us have borne, but the most dread disease of our time—*totalitarianism!* Don't be fooled! These are the exact circumstances that Communists exploit when good people are looking for answers to their suffering. *Be on your guard!* This is a criminal band of immoralists trained to penetrate the hearts and minds of citizens at this time of despair.

"Friends, we must stand together against the gods of absolute power. We must be alert to their smear words and crooked shenanigans. We must seek out these strange and twisted personalities and expose their true intentions. *Narrow is the gate and straight is the way of eternal life.* You have a precious soul, and that soul will be judged only by God. What are you doing for your soul today? We pray for the people of Russia who bend their heads to Stalin, because *we bend our knees to God!*"

Times were bad and the ballroom was filled to capacity. They'd had to bring in more folding chairs. The people of Pennington County were reeling from a barrage of plagues that had evaporated the water from their land and buried their animals in snow, cursed them with deadly flies and whipped their houses with winds surely sent by the devil. In those unnatural and mysterious times, conditions had ripened for Thaddeus Haynes and his kind.

"So!" said Jo. "You're married!"

Robbie blushed. It was endearing that at the age of forty he could still blush.

"I'm married to Sherry Ingles. You might not remember. She was two years behind you."

"I know Sherry. She was in homeroom with Lance."

"That's right," said Robbie.

They were alone in the hospital cafeteria, a depressing place at any time, but especially the day after Christmas, with dime-store decorations taped to the cinder block and smelling of stale pea soup. Sipping their coffees, they smiled awkwardly and looked away, searching for something to talk about that wasn't upsetting.

"What are you doing in Portland these days?" Robbie asked.

"I'm a landscape designer. I'm with a company that does work for the city."

"Like landscaping city hall?"

"No, just the opposite. Our goal is more open space. There's a district in Portland called the Pearl that right now is a bunch of warehouses and abandoned old railroad yards, but we're going to redevelop it into three parks, all connected by a waterway. The district will still have historic character, with cobbled streets and the original loading docks, and there'll be retail shops and housing and all that, but what's really exciting is that the waterway will sustain wildlife and become an urban refuge for birds and, well, all kinds of animals. That's the part I'm involved in, and I love it."

Robbie looked unimpressed. "I'm not surprised."

"Really? I was. That I landed there."

"Come on, you grow up in the wide-open spaces of the prairie, and now your job is to make a big park in the middle of a city? Pretty darn clear to me.

You couldn't get out of this place fast enough, but you ended up taking it with you."

Jo laughed, rephrasing the old saying: "Home is the place you can never leave, no matter how hard you try."

"Tell me about it," Robbie said, and sighed.

His eyes shifted to the big-screen TV in the cafeteria, where an attractive woman with long black hair and bangs was doing a newsbreak. In silence, because the sound was off.

"Know who that is?"

Jo glanced over.

"Oh my God!" she squealed, and put her hands over her mouth. "Is that Irene Nassiter?"

Robbie nodded complacently. "That's Irene. I used to date her," he added. "After you left."

"She's cute," said Jo.

"She's a cokehead."

"Are you kidding? She looks so midwestern."

Robbie's eyes were back on Jo. "You look good," he said.

"Me? I'm a mess."

He paused. They were two people who could still speak to each other from the heart.

"What would have happened if it never happened?" he asked.

"You mean the trial?"

"Everything. Would you have stayed here?"

"No, hon. No, I would not."

Now it was her turn to expect an honest answer.

"Are you happy?" she wanted to know.

Robbie Fletcher grimaced. Shrugged.

"What can I say, it's the freaking *Rapid City Journal.* I'm still chasing stories about the ghost in the Alex Johnson, doing front-page exposés on weather."

"What about Sherry?"

"She's a real estate agent, but she works for a big company. She could get a job in Denver."

"Is that the plan? Denver?" Jo waited. "Maybe *The Denver Post*? It's a good paper."

Robbie didn't answer. His eyes went to the TV screen and back. "I had such a crush on you," he said.

Jo was touched. He'd left for college when she was still in high school, but they'd been a hot item at the time.

"Speaking of the prairie, remember the Spooky Place?" she ventured.

He smiled depravedly. "I certainly do!"

"Look at you, you're turning red!" Jo said.

"Look at you."

They finally let go and laughed together, comforted by the tender feelings that arose.

"No, it's good," he said, meaning his marriage. "It's really good."

"Me, too," she hastened to add.

"I'm happy for you."

"You were my first," she told him. "There will never be another."

"The road not taken, I guess." He grinned sheepishly. "I'm trying not to look too mournful here."

"You're not."

The news had switched to a live shot. A seedy-looking middle-aged man with a beard, baseball cap, filthy parka, and shorts despite the cold, was being interviewed in front of a run-down house.

"Remember him?" Robbie asked.

"Who is it?"

"Tyler Jones. Local lowlife drug dealer. We used to call him Honeybee."

Just seeing her tormentor—even without sound—caused a chemical reaction in Jo's body. She had a flashback of Honeybee pulling Lance off his horse and dragging him through the snow. Fear spread from her gut to her fingertips. She felt sick.

"He did it!" she cried. "He always had a vendetta against us!"

"Tyler Jones?"

"He went to prison."

"I remember."

"I'm the one who told on him. Lance and I caught him stealing cattle and I picked him out of a lineup."

"You think he broke into Lance and Wendy's house?"

"He's crazy!"

Robbie considered. "It doesn't look like he's a suspect."

"How do you know?"

"No cops in the picture. He's not under arrest, see? It's just the camera crew and he's just talking—"

"Listen to me." Jo gripped his arm. "Honeybee said—he actually said this—he said he would come back for us. If he's not a suspect, he should be."

Robbie's journalist instincts took over.

"I'll talk to my sources and find out what's going on," he said. "Will you be okay?"

"Honestly? I'm scared to death of that guy."

"Hang on. I'll find a deputy to stay with you," Robbie said, and got up and ran for the lobby.

THREE

HATE

Cal guided the Piper Apache in a wide circle over the Lucky Clover Ranch. The pretty white plane with the yellow stripe was the former air force pilot's pride and joy, and also a necessity. Just as Fletch had predicted, Cal had been elected to the state legislature three times, and was now running for the U.S. Senate. The plane extended his reach beyond Pennington County to every part of the state, giving him an important edge over his opponent, Thaddeus Haynes.

The Kuseks were prospering. After a decade of hard labor, Cal and Betsy had mastered the art of cattle ranching. They were a working family now. Jo was a freshman in high school and Lance a seventh grader, capable of making up for their parents' absence when Dad was at campaign headquarters in Pierre and Mom making her rounds as a visiting nurse or working the ELECT KUSEK storefront office in town. Their success had added luster to the household. People wanted to do business, donate money, be sociable, serve beside Cal and his wife on committees—anything to get into the good graces of a man on the rise.

Cal was generous in giving rides in the Piper Apache to folks in need, but today his passengers were special cargo. Betsy's sister, Marja, and her new husband, Dr. Leon Winter, were stopping for a visit on their honeymoon to San Francisco. They'd taken the train from New York City to Sioux Falls, where Cal had met them at the airport. It was not only their first trip out west, but also the first time for both in the air. Bucking the prairie wind in a light airplane was an alarming introduction. Marja gripped the fine, slender fingers of her surgeon husband's hand—the eye surgeon who had restored her sight—while he sat rigidly in the seat, afraid to look out the window. They passed over forests turned red, destroyed by beetles that had infested the dying trees.

"You can see the effects of the drought," Cal shouted over the twin engines.

On the approach to the ranch, Cal pointed out their farmhouse, pens, corrals, barns, ponds, and pastures. As the wings dipped toward each landmark, Leon kept his eyes on the sick bag and lips pursed shut. His lips were his most alluring attribute—at odds with his pompous medical authority—Cupid's bow–shaped, distinctly carved as the curves on a violin. His aunts always said those lips were wasted on a boy. At a plump fifty-five, he wore a dark, groomed mustache that suggested a thoughtful nature and complemented his prominent cheeks—well rounded by a taste for red wines and moldy cheeses. His salt-and-pepper hair was combed back in long, self-conscious waves, shining with Cussons Imperial Leather Brilliantine. He owned a wardrobe of Savile Row silk bow ties.

Dr. Leon Winter was more than a rococo ophthalmologist. He was also a businessman who understood that just one wonderful Dr. Winter would never do, were he to create the kind of wealth he'd glimpsed while operating on some of the richest people in New York City. He would never own a Park Avenue apartment one eyeball at a time, and so, taking a cue from Nedick's hot dog stands, he opened a chain of Winter Eye Institutes in Harlem, Queens, Staten Island, and, eventually, the Upper East Side of Manhattan, where life-sized cutouts of himself wearing a white lab coat and stethoscope were the closest a lower-class patient in the outer boroughs would ever get to the real flesh-and-blood founder. He hired cheap refugee doctors who'd been displaced by the war, and took out subway ads. Sandwiched between Heinz spaghetti (*"Another 57 household help—cooked and ready to serve!"*) and Knickerbocker beer (*"Less filling . . . more delicious, too!"*) were posters for the Winter Eye Institute (*"You can see today and take your time to pay!"*).

Dr. Winter's expertise was cataract surgery. He met Marja Ferguson when she was teaching music at the Institute for the Education of the Blind. She had performed Debussy's *Two Arabesques* at a recital at the school, and Leon, also a devotee of romantic French piano, found the tableau of the innocent figure alone on the bench in a dusty hall, drenched in music so much bigger than she, and yet restraining it under firm but delicate control, achingly erotic.

Afterward he introduced himself and took her hands in his. Their first touch was electric. The sensitivity of the surgeon's fingertips and the knowingness of the blind pianist's converged with a sexual heat unknown to either of them before.

"What a remarkable interpretation," he told her. He could say no more. His voice had gone hoarse. He managed to ask about the condition of her blindness, and the ensuing encounter in a deserted rehearsal room led to a successful surgery, performed by his own moistly gloved fingers, and, afterward, several ecstatic shopping trips to Saks, during which Dr. Winter waited on a tuffet outside the dressing room for Marja to emerge in costumes of his choosing. She blossomed, unknowingly taking on the appetites of her acquisitive mother, Rosslyn, while undergoing a Pygmalion-like transformation from a poor, unprepossessing spinster to the wife of the surgeon who had saved her sight: a walking, stylish advertisement on his arm. From his point of view, the difference between their ages was all the more reason to rush into marriage. Marja had cared for her father until the end; Leon, whose Cupid's bow lips would often fall into a pout of self-pity, expected the same devotion from his relatively young and nubile wife.

Cal had barely announced they were about to land when the Piper Apache began a harrowing plunge toward the airstrip the Kuseks had added to the property. Marja and Leon screamed as treetops rushed at them, his hand crushing hers in panic, mesmerized for some very long seconds by the swirl of colors about to swallow them whole. They hit the ground and bounced along to a jerking halt, stunned at the shock of finding themselves still breathing. Cal climbed out of the cockpit and opened the cabin door, letting in a flood of light and green-smelling humidity.

"Everyone all right back there?" he called.

"Perfectly fine," Leon answered, mopping his forehead with a handkerchief.

Cal helped them climb out of the plane, which had landed in a former wheat field on the Lucky Clover Ranch. The drought had pretty much wiped that crop out of western South Dakota, and the city shoes of the visitors were immediately covered with the colorless powder that had replaced the fertile topsoil. Marja had never lost her keen awareness of every new sensation: heated drafts of dry air, the howl of the engines winding down, a deafening chorus of insects, scores of which seemed to be landing all over her skin.

She was almost as disoriented as when Leon had removed the bandages, and she'd sat in the chair blinking uncomprehendingly. Bright shapes assaulted her brain, which had no way to sort them out. Before, the world had looked like waves through frosted glass; afterward, she had been awakened to an unbearable overload on her senses, and for months took refuge behind dark glasses and the steadying presence of the doctor and his staff. Little by little, the flat world acquired three dimensions. The ground no longer seemed impossibly far away, nor the sky a glowing ceiling just above her head.

So after a decade apart, it was literally with fresh eyes that Marja gazed upon her sister, when they reached the back of the house on the path that led from the landing strip. The screen door opened and Betsy came running out into a tight embrace that almost knocked them both off their feet. She smelled of things Marja could barely identify—horse sweat, worn leather, pungent herbs. Her body was unfamiliar, too; no longer curvy, soft, and yielding, it had turned sinewy and scarecrow thin. She seemed to have grown taller. She looked like a stranger who oddly had Betsy's same features, but windswept and sharpened somehow. Her skin was browned and deeply wrinkled. Did she always have such hooded eyes? Her hair was several sun-streaked shades of blond, still in short messy curls.

Betsy, too, was shocked by her sister's transformation.

"You look just like Mama!" she blurted out, staring at a contented-looking matron with dark wavy hair, wearing lipstick and a pastel blue travel suit, whose portly husband was heaving a set of "his" matched luggage while Cal followed with a second set of "hers." She noticed her brother-in-law's gold alligator wristwatch, which must have cost as much as the airplane.

Betsy gripped Marja's shoulders and looked deeply into her sister's eyes. "Can you really see?"

"I can see," Marja affirmed, smiling. "It's a miracle, thanks to Leon."

Betsy whispered, "Are you in love?"

Marja replied with a coquettish shrug. "I'm in love! So is he."

"He better be!" Betsy declared with a mock frown, leading her forward. A dizzyingly sweet fragrance hit from scores of purple blossoms bursting from a shrub near the back door. "Isn't it wonderful? You're just in time for lilacs!"

Behind them the men had paused because Leon was having a sneezing fit. By the end of it he'd counted fourteen sneezes in a row.

"Hay fever?" Cal suggested.

Leon nodded while swabbing his eyes with the handkerchief and furiously blowing his nose.

"Sorry, old man," said Cal. "That's rough out here."

"First you almost crash the plane, and now I'm being attacked by allergens," Leon gasped. "You're going to kill me!"

He was trying to be funny to hide his irritation.

"Wait until we get you on a horse," Cal promised.

Leon shook his head in protest. They would never get him on a horse, and he wasn't pleased about the filthy chickens leaving their droppings all over the yard. Now Marja was pointing with distress at a large reptilian head followed by a thick body with brown markings that was making a sluggish appearance from the woodpile.

"Good God!" she cried.

"Are you okay with snakes?" Betsy asked lightly, as if this were an everyday occurrence. "I know, not my favorite, either. We have a mice problem. He's looking for mice."

"As long as he's not poisonous," Marja said.

"No, he's harmless."

"What is it?" Leon asked suspiciously.

"Just a garter snake," said Betsy.

"Won't kill you," Cal added smoothly.

But Leon was annoyed with everything about the Kuseks. Marja had told him all about her sister and her husband, and frankly, they sounded on the freethinking side, living off the land and all that nonsense. So what if Kusek did have a law degree from Yale? These liberals really believed they owned the moral high ground. His sainted brother-in-law had *"thrown it all away"* to come out here to this deserted hellhole and *"serve the people."* Well, Dr. Leon Winter served people, too. He owned clinics in bad neighborhoods. He himself performed eight surgeries a week—sometimes ten—and often pro bono. Or whatever insurance would pay. Now he was ravenous and sweating like a pig from dragging around all this damn luggage Marja had brought only to impress her sister, who didn't seem to give a damn—and he'd had enough of the stink of superiority coming off Cal Kusek like chicken dung, if that's what it was, that gooey crap he'd almost stepped in.

"Will someone please open the door?" Leon growled.

His brother-in-law obliged and the men shouldered inside.

"I've never seen lilacs that weren't in a vase," Marja said, touching the petals in wonder.

Betsy gave her sister's waist a happy squeeze. "I knew you'd love it here!"

The simple farmhouse had seen improvements over the past few years. Marja and Leon were shown to a guest room furnished with a four-poster bed done up with a frilly pink canopy. The Kuseks had built a sleeping porch and updated the kitchen so that it was no longer a hodgepodge of mismatched wooden cabinets inherited from Stell Fletcher's mother, but a modern raft of Formica counters, a new refrigerator, a stove with a stainless steel exhaust hood, yellow linoleum floor tiles, and a breakfast nook—everything clean and sleek as the Piper Apache.

Cal grabbed a meat loaf sandwich. He had to turn around and fly back to Pierre for a nine a.m. appointment with the FBI the following day, another meeting in the glacial process of clearing his run for Senate.

"What are they going to ask you?" Betsy wanted to know.

He shrugged. "When you run for federal office you have to undergo 'special scrutiny.' Basically it's a security clearance. Nothing to worry about. There won't be any red flags."

"Will they ask about me?"

Cal was surprised by the question. "Why would they? You mean the party? That's old news. McCarthy was finished six years ago, and besides, you quit."

"I know it and you know it, but do they know it?"

"Sure they do. You talked to the bureau when we left New York, and they gave you the all clear."

"I can't help it. I still think the FBI is scary. I guess it's from the union days."

"I'm a public servant. We're all on the same side now," Cal reminded her. "I'm more worried about how you and your sister are getting along."

"Fine!" said Betsy brightly. "What do you think of Dr. Winter?"

"To be charitable? A lot of hot air."

"I'm trying to give him the benefit of the doubt," Betsy agreed staunchly.

Cal packed an overnight and took off. While Betsy was assembling dinner—steaks from their cattle, vegetables from the garden—Marja came into the kitchen holding two pink pillowcases.

"Leon says these smell funny."

Betsy was putting the potatoes in the oven.

"I washed them before I put them on the bed."

"He gets fussy about this kind of thing."

"I'll wash them again," Betsy said, sticking to her vow of tolerance.

"Sorry if it's any trouble."

"No, I've got a load waiting anyway," Betsy said, heading to the laundry room.

Marja followed. "Your own washer-dryer—I'm green with jealousy!" she cooed. "Remember in the apartment on the Grand Concourse, how we'd have to go down to the basement and put coins in the machines?"

"What a pain that was," Betsy agreed. "Does Leon remind you of Dad?"

"Leon? No, why?"

"Oh, I don't know . . . physical resemblance," Betsy said, backing off the comparison to their father's dominating personality.

"What time do the kids get home?" asked Marja.

"They have after-school activities," Betsy said evasively. "They take the last bus."

She closed the lid and the machine began its comforting routine. Betsy was not prepared to tell her sister about Jo. She'd never had children, so it was hard to know how Marja would react to the news that her adorable, precocious niece had turned into a troublemaker. She'd been cited twice for truancy, as well as a stunt when the girls from the team stood on the boys' shoulders and wrapped all the swings in the playground around the top pole. Like Betsy, Jo played basketball, which, in a sports-mad school, allowed her to get away with more than most, but three further unexplained absences and the school would be obliged by law to alert the state attorney's office; bad news for the Kusek campaign.

The brightest in her class, Jo was failing two courses because she was "bored." Today she was finishing a week of after-school detention as punishment, but instead of doing her homework, she was reading the sexy parts in *The Basic Writings of Sigmund Freud*, which she'd gotten from the library. Her loyal brother, Lance, hung around until they let her out, so she wouldn't have to ride the bus in the company of the true morons who were also in detention, which meant their chores were late, bedtimes late, and they were dead tired in the morning, when the whole thing started again.

And yet when Betsy heard the dogs bark and knew the kids were home, she forgave everything in a flood of love, relieved that they were safely back, as if there was a finite amount of times they'd make it through that door in one piece and they'd just punched another ticket. Watching them storm the kitchen like a pair of starving coyotes— slamming cabinets, attacking the refrigerator, grabbing this and that, dutifully hugging Aunt Marja with their mouths full of pickles and bologna—Betsy had a feeling, from the way they avoided looking at her directly, that something was wrong . . . and she was right.

"This is for you," Jo said, handing Betsy a folded note.

"What is it?"

"You're supposed to see the principal."

Mother and daughter stared at each other. The air went dead between them.

Silence.

Marja said, "I think I'll go lie down."

"No, stick around," Betsy said, claiming her sister as an ally. She wanted a sympathetic witness. "I thought today was the last day of detention."

"It was!" cried Jo indignantly. "And they made us watch this horror movie, *Communism on the Map*. Did you know Communists are every-where? They're poisoning our food and taking over the world!"

"I saw it, too. They showed it in our science class," said Lance. "They've already invaded Latin America. They're worse than the devil—

pure evil—and they don't care about anybody. Is it true they're going to march up through Texas?"

"They showed that movie *in school*?" Betsy cried, upset. "That's pure right-wing propaganda. That's outrageous! I'll certainly talk to the principal about that!"

"Don't, Mom," said Jo. "Just don't."

Betsy took a breath and read the note. "It says you're suspended from school." She took another breath. "Why is that?"

Jo considered her options. It would be a lot worse coming from their crummy principal, Mr. Emry.

"Okay," Jo began, "don't be mad, but me and Robbie—"

"Robbie and I," Betsy cut in, losing patience.

"Robbie and I were throwing firecrackers out the bus window—"

Together, Marja and Betsy exclaimed, *"You were what?"*

"The bus driver is about seventy-five years old," Lance put in, devouring an apple.

"Robbie got kicked off the bus and had to walk eighteen miles home."

"What the hell were you two up to?!" Betsy yelled.

"They were tiny, this big, from a penny pack. I'd light it and Robbie would throw it, but *one time* the wind blew the firecracker back inside the bus and it went off under the driver's seat."

Lance spit chewed apple all over the floor and collapsed laughing. He just couldn't hear it often enough and it cracked him up every time.

"A *firecracker*? On a school bus?" Betsy exclaimed. "Have you lost your mind?"

"Robbie's suspended, too," said Jo, while Lance snorted derisively in the background.

"Does his mother know?"

Jo shrugged contemptuously. "Depends if he gives her the note or tears it up."

"Jo, your father is running for the U.S. Senate."

"I know that, Mother. I take American government."

"Don't be fresh."

Jo didn't answer. Now she was holding back tears. Marja looked away.

"Everyone in town will find out about this."

"I thought you don't care what other people think."

"We are family. Everybody here counts. Your behavior is damaging to your father's reputation. We are staking our lives on this election."

"Maybe there's something more to life than *politics*. He doesn't care about us. He's never here anyway."

Jo stalked out the back door and gangly Lance followed.

Marja patted her sister's arm.

"Jo and I are having a bad time," Betsy admitted miserably. "I don't know what came over me."

"It's her age."

Leon shuffled into the kitchen wearing bed slippers and Betsy almost took his head off.

"I'm washing the pillowcases!" she snapped before he could complain. So much for tolerance.

Leon was unperturbed. He'd taken a catnap and was looking refreshed. His shirt was casually open at the neck, and he was carrying a double-barreled cylindrical leather case, from which he removed two bottles: one gin and the other vermouth.

"I think I'll make a martini," he said.

"Go right ahead," Betsy said.

"Do you have ice?"

"We live in America," she retorted. "Make me one, too."

The Winters did not sleep well. For one thing, the cat fell on Leon's head. In the litany of instructions about showers and toilets, nobody had thought to warn them that the cat liked to perch on the top of the bathroom door. When Leon got up to urinate and closed the door in a midnight trance, a yowling, shrieking furry mass of claws dropped out of nowhere like a nightmare that had been stalking him all his life. The guest room wasn't safe, either. Moths of every size and color had come to rest inside the pink canopy above the bed and, worse, flap helplessly in the spiderwebs in the corners that Betsy's vacuum cleaner had evidently missed. The loud jungle noises of cicadas and the strange night calls of cattle kept them wakeful and on edge, along with vaguely itchy things on their feet.

Marja and Leon were not the only ones to spend a fitful night. The two FBI agents assigned to shadow Betsy Kusek, a.k.a. Coline Ferguson, had taken turns sleeping in the backseat of their unmarked car, which was hidden in the deepest shadows fifty feet from the turnoff to the Lucky Clover Ranch. But they were alert and on the ready the next morning when they observed Mrs. Kusek leaving the property at 8:09. She was driving a white station wagon and heading toward Rapid City. They followed at the prescribed distance.

16

Leon's snoring reverberated throughout the house. It seemed impossible such thunderous noise could be produced by the relatively small oral cavity of a human being. Honestly, Jo thought, Uncle Leon was worse than her dad.

Aunt Marja was alone in the kitchen, drinking coffee and smoking a cigarette, when Jo came in from gathering eggs.

"How can you stand it?" Jo asked.

"I'll show you," Marja said.

She reached into the pocket of her housecoat, took out two cotton balls, and stuck them in her ears, bugging out her eyes like Lucille Ball when she's fed up with Desi Arnaz.

Jo laughed. "That's not fair! Why doesn't *he* do something?"

"What can he do? Unless we slept in separate rooms, and you don't want that."

"Why not? I'd rather sleep in a tree."

Marja tapped the cigarette ash into the saucer. "It doesn't make for good communication."

"I'm never getting married," Jo mumbled.

"Did you and your mother make up?"

Jo shrugged. "I don't know."

"Where is she?"

"At her friend Stell's—Robbie's mom—so they can complain about their awful children. Want some breakfast?"

"Sure. I'll take some toast, if you're making. Can I help?"

Jo shook her head. "You're the guest."

Marja smiled, hearing the echo of her sister's voice. The problem was Jo and Betsy were too much alike—both hardheaded.

"I thought I'd never get married, either," Marja confided. "The first time the words 'my husband' came out of my mouth, I couldn't believe it was me saying them."

"I'll bet."

"He can be fussy and snore like a sailor, but Leon's a good man. In my position, I'm lucky to have him."

"What do you mean, your position?"

"Leon is a famous surgeon and quite well-off. We have a beautiful apartment on Park Avenue. He could have had anyone—although I'm thinking in particular of a certain nurse with a good figure, about nineteen years old," she said, squishing the cigarette butt in the cup.

Jo snickered supportively.

"Not many successful men want to marry a blind spinster."

Jo sat down at the table with two plates of toasted homemade cinnamon raisin bread spread with country butter.

"Oh my!" said Marja, biting down. "This is even better than the Automat!"

"Then why did he marry you?" Jo asked. "Was it because he felt sorry for you?"

Her niece's candor was a shock, but also touching in a way. After all, she was fourteen years old, hungry to know about the outside world, the adult world, and whom else could she ask but her New York aunt?

"You really want to know why we got married?" Marja asked.

Jo nodded. She had such earnest, clear blue eyes. For a moment Marja hesitated to broach such innocence, but she was drawn by the opportunity to confess a long-held secret to someone who, she guessed, wouldn't judge her.

"All right, I'll tell you, but in total confidence. *I* seduced *him*."

Marja affirmed Jo's astonished look.

"You thought the opposite?" she suggested. "That he might have taken advantage? Well, it wasn't that way. I have a body. I'm a woman, too. Oh, God, don't say anything to your mother. I'm not telling you to ever be like me—"

Jo promised and crossed her heart.

"We were alone in a rehearsal room. It was after a concert at the institute, where I was teaching music. A student concert, really, but I played some Debussy. There were refreshments in the lobby and it was open house—parents and students roaming everywhere, going into classrooms and what have you. I just locked the door and took off all my clothes. We'd known each other five minutes!"

Jo gasped and covered her mouth and then burst out laughing. They whooped and giggled like two grown women.

"You did that?" Jo sputtered.

"I just fell into it, like the music. The moment his hand touched mine I knew he was the one. I think it knocked him off his feet, my boldness . . . and then he came back for more," she added suggestively, getting up to put the plates in the sink.

Jo watched dreamily, intoxicated by this amazing story. That's not the way they told it, the girls who'd gone all the way—according to legend it was always a struggle, and we all knew there were terrible consequences. Her own experience of boys was ducking gropes and ignoring gooses on the staircase in school, or, in their cars, putting off excruciating pleas of "blue balls." Jo refused out of pure, blind self-defense. The only boy who wasn't repulsive was Robbie Fletcher, but he was more a friend. Her aunt's frank description spun her sideways. She had never been given such a vivid picture of what freedom really meant as being able to take off all your clothes whenever you felt like it. As far as she could tell, that didn't happen—at least not willingly—to girls in South Dakota.

"Sometimes, honey, you have to take the plunge," Marja remarked.

Then it just came out of Jo's mouth: "I want to live with you and Uncle Leon."

"No, you don't," Marja reminded her. "He snores."

Jo laughed. "See? You're a lot more fun than my mom."

"The Wicked Witch of the West would be more fun right now. She loves you very much, Jo. This, too, shall pass."

Jo shook her head defiantly. The route of escape was clear and she was fixed on it. "*None* of my friends get along with their parents. If I didn't have to finish high school, I'd be gone! She wouldn't care. She'd be glad to get rid of me."

Encouraged by the belief that she was getting through to her niece, Marja decided to impart another bit of truth: "Now, listen. When your mother left to come out west, I was pleased for her. She was married and, luckily for her, getting out of the Bronx. But my feelings were hurt, too, because I couldn't leave because I had to take care of Dad, and not only that, but you and Lance were babies, and I would miss you growing up. To add insult to injury, I love my sister. But still, we weathered the storm and kept in touch, and here we are. You see, Jo, you can love someone but be mad at them at the same time."

Jo didn't seem to hear a word. "You have a big apartment, right?" she said, her imagination going full pitch. "Park Avenue, you said. I could sleep on the couch."

Marja sighed indulgently. "And where would you go to school?"

"They have schools in New York. It would be so much better!"

Leon came into the kitchen wearing loafers, pressed slacks, and a button-down shirt, ready for another day at the office rather than on a cattle ranch. Before he could say hello, Jo was like a bouncing ball, springing the news on him about their so-called plans. She even made him bacon and eggs to show what a help she could be. Marja remained quietly stunned by this turn of events: Betsy's daughter had asked to live with her! Along with being awfully flattered came guilty triumph over her more outgoing sister, who'd never seemed to stumble while going after what she wanted. Recounting Betsy's move out west had stirred resentment in Marja, always pitied and left behind in darkness to put up with their punishing father. Leon had brought her into the light; circumstances had taken her here. Now she was ready to take her rightful place in the family in the role of cherished aunt.

Surprisingly, the proposition of Jo moving in with them appealed to Leon's generous side. Perhaps he, too, was looking for a way to break the genteel routine of married life by having someone young, fresh, and pretty for company. In his practice, he would often play the fool for younger patients, give them balloons and make them laugh. He liked being the big cheese and he liked showing off. He and Marja could well afford to be extravagant. He pictured traipsing down Fifth Avenue with Jo, awestruck; trips to Europe, just the three of them.

"I think it's a swell idea," he said, patting Jo on the head. "Everyone should live in New York City at least once in their life. We'll take you to the philharmonic and the theater. The Museum of Natural History!"

"Darling, I think she has natural history right here," Marja said playfully. She was very pleased.

Betsy was in a better mood when she left Stell Fletcher's house that morning. Stell had such a sunny outlook. She didn't believe that Robbie and Jo being suspended for a week was cause to commit hara-kiri.

"Anyways," she said, "suspension is *so stupid*. Robbie's lying on the sofa watching TV. You call that punishment?"

By the time they'd finished coffee and the last of Stell's famous blueberry crumb cake, both moms agreed that Jo and Robbie would simply bore themselves to death at home and never pull another prank like throwing firecrackers off a bus.

Betsy had felt so unburdened after yakking it up with Stell that she'd allowed herself a few frivolous stops on the way home, feeling generous toward her guests and recalcitrant daughter. No sooner had she made it through the back door, overloaded with shopping bags, than she was surrounded by Marja, Leon, and Jo, all insisting that it was a done deal for Jo to move to New York.

"She doesn't necessarily have to live with us," Marja explained. "She could go to an academy. What about your alma mater, the Knox School? Leon and I would be happy to cover the costs."

"What's the hurry?" Betsy asked mildly. "She'll be away at college soon enough."

"Please, Mom? I want to go!" begged Jo.

Betsy shook her hands at them as if shooing bees. "What brought this on all of a sudden?"

"What's she going to do here?" Leon asked. "Marry a farmer? Really, Betsy, she's much too bright."

Still buoyant, Betsy refused to take the conspirators seriously. She wrinkled her nose and told her daughter, "Your father and I would miss you too much!"

"What if I came home for Christmas?" offered Jo, watching critically as her mother unpacked things she didn't usually buy: chocolate pudding mix, graham crackers, whipping cream. "Are we making a cake?" she asked sardonically.

"I thought, since you're home—"

"Mom! It's not like I'm in third grade and we're having a bake sale!" Jo snapped. "Can we please talk seriously about my future?"

Betsy felt embarrassed and angry with herself for having given in to the impulse to do something nice. She should have let Jo suffer her penance. Maybe then the kid would be grateful for all the times when she *was* in third grade—and fourth and fifth—and *did* stay home with a fever while Betsy cared for her and amused her until she was mended and out the door. A cold objectivity overcame Betsy and she started to think maybe it *would* be a good idea to let her go. Maybe Marja and Leon knew a better way to raise a teenager. She was about to say so when Lois and Bandit began to bark and someone knocked sharply on the door.

Betsy left the groceries, strode across the living room, and opened it. A young man dressed in a dark suit and wearing a fedora was waiting on the doorstep. Behind him a black late-model sedan was pulled up next to the station wagon, covered with dust as if it had been driven a long way.

"Good morning, ma'am. I'm Special Agent Wentworth with the FBI, and this is Special Agent Breyer." A second man, also wearing a dark suit, had joined him.

They'd followed her to Stell Fletcher's house in North Rapid and waited. They'd followed her to J.C. Penney and the Piggly Wiggly grocery, and then along rural roads for some thirty miles to the turnoff for the Lucky Clover Ranch, parking in the same out-of-the-way spot where they'd spent the night on surveillance. Before risking an approach, Agent Breyer had stalked through the woods with a pair of binoculars to confirm the station wagon was still parked at the house and there were no other visitors. The subject wasn't going anywhere.

"Are you Mrs. Kusek?"

"Yes."

"Do you also go by the name Coline Ferguson?"

Betsy was taken aback. "Not since I was a child."

"Is your husband Calvin Kusek?"

She stared at the two somber men in dark gray suits and her world kaleidoscoped into a thousand pieces. "Oh my God, did he crash the plane?"

"Your husband?"

"Tell me he's all right!" she pleaded. "He's meeting with the FBI in Pierre. He flies a plane. Did something happen?"

Agent Wentworth looked questioningly at his partner. "We haven't heard about an airplane crash, have we?"

The other shook his head. "No, ma'am. I'm sure he's fine. That's not why we're here. We want to talk to you about the election."

Betsy shook her head to dispel the nightmarish shock.

"Is this a poll?" she asked, recovering her sense of humor. "Because if it is, I'm voting for my husband."

They laughed politely. Both were tall, in excellent physical condition, wearing cheap suits and thin ties, awfully young to be FBI. Wentworth looked like a strawberry-blond farm boy and Breyer—a dark-haired, serious type—out of the industrial cities of the east, she assumed. He had a rough beard and hadn't shaved recently, which made him look as hard as any criminal.

"What's this all about?" Betsy asked.

"Very simple and straightforward, ma'am. Your husband is running for the U.S. Senate, and it's our job to make sure his relatives and close associates don't pose a security threat."

"This is certainly a surprise."

"Just a standard background check," said Agent Breyer.

"Why didn't my husband tell me?"

"Likely he didn't know. May we come in, ma'am?"

Betsy backed away. She hadn't realized that the others had gathered at the kitchen door and were watching apprehensively.

"Mom," Jo whispered, "how come you never told me your real name is Coline?"

"She's always been Betsy," Marja said, covering quickly.

The agents wiped their shoes and removed their hats.

"You must be Jo," said Agent Wentworth. He went out of his way to shake her hand.

Jo stared. He was older and handsome as a movie star. "Hi."

"Where's your brother, Lance?"

Betsy's back stiffened, protective of her children.

"Lance is in school," Jo answered obediently.

"And why are you at home?" Agent Wentworth asked kindly.

Betsy moved her daughter aside. "She doesn't have to talk to you."

"That's all right," said Agent Wentworth.

For once Jo didn't argue, instinctively on guard against these cold, strange men who were making her mother upset, although she was pretending not to be. Leon didn't wait to be summoned. He was a red-blooded patriot! He came forward and introduced himself forthrightly: "Dr. Leon Winter, ophthalmologist, New York City."

"What's your relationship to Mrs. Kusek, Dr. Winter?" Agent Wentworth asked.

"I'm her brother-in-law. This is my wife, Marja. She's Betsy's sister."

Agent Breyer had produced a notebook and was writing things down.

"We need to talk to your sister-in-law alone," Agent Wentworth said.

Leon was eager to accommodate. "Don't worry about us. We'll just skedaddle."

Betsy gave him the keys to the wagon. "You can get an ice cream at the A&J market near the turnpike."

Jo looked worried. "Are you sure, Mom?"

"Yes, dear. It's fine."

"We'll take good care of her," Marja said, touching her sister's arm in a way that said, *Be careful.*

When they were gone, Betsy asked if she could offer them something.

"A glass of water would be much appreciated," Agent Breyer said.

"Where'd you come in from?"

"Pierre."

"That's quite a drive."

"Not unusual, not for us."

Betsy came back from the kitchen with two glasses. "You could have flown in with my husband," she said blithely, feeling the old hostility toward their authority rise.

When they'd settled in the living room armchairs, Agent Breyer turned to a fresh page in his notebook and asked Betsy if she was ready to get started.

"Fire away."

Agent Wentworth took over the questioning. "Do you believe in the Christian spirit?"

Betsy was immediately thrown off. "If you mean by 'the Christian spirit' loving-kindness toward all living creatures, as well as your fellow man, then, yes, I do believe in it. I was raised Presbyterian—is that what you're getting at?"

"Thank you, ma'am, you've answered the question. Are you a member of a labor union?"

Betsy stood and went to the window. The station wagon was just disappearing down the road.

"I hope they know where they're going."

She was stalling for time, running the traps in their questions through her head. *What did they know? How did they know?* She hadn't thought of it for years, but in a blink she was back walking the picket line in front of Gimbels department store, on the edge of incendiary violence by scabs and cops. Worst of all was the fear of Hoover's FBI, the hidden enemy with unlimited power.

"It's all right, Mrs. Kusek, no need to be nervous. We're just looking for information. There are no right or wrong answers."

"Oh, I'm not nervous," Betsy said, sitting back down. She realized that the groceries were still not put away. "It's just a little unexpected to be thinking about these things, going back into the past all of a sudden."

She clasped her damp hands together.

"Take your time," Agent Wentworth said. "Surely you remember if you joined a labor union?"

"Yes, I did," she said, showing her teeth. "Gimbels Local 2. It's come back to me now, clear as a bell."

Lance was waiting at the airstrip for his father's plane to land. He'd taken Lois and Bandit for company, but they were tired of fetching sticks, so they all three sat on the ground. It was evening and the bugs were biting. Once in a while one of the dogs would jump up to catch a mosquito, but they always missed. Lance was starving. When he'd gotten home from school the FBI was there. They'd stayed a long time and supper was late.

He heard the drone of propellers first, then caught a flash of setting sun off the white body of the Piper Apache as it descended from the rose-colored sky. It seemed forever before his dad was on the ground and walking toward him, still wearing his dark blue Pierre business suit, carrying his overnight and briefcase. He was surprised to see Lance waiting.

"Hey, partner. How are you?"

"The FBI was here, Dad."

"What the hell for?" Cal asked, alarmed.

"They wanted to talk to Mom. They showed me their guns! Guess what kind?"

"I don't know."

"Thirty-eight specials with a four-inch barrel."

"Did they ask you questions?"

"No, just Mom. And by the way, Jo's moving to New York."

"Is that right?" asked Cal.

"She's going to live with Aunt Marja and Uncle Leon."

"Since when?"

"They decided."

"Who?"

Lance shrugged. "Everyone, I guess. Uncle Scotty said I could ride Beethoven," he said. "Are you listening, Dad? Beethoven is a *bull*. He's a big white Holstein with a lot of kick. It's hard even for Uncle Scotty to stay on him. He said if I go eight seconds on two practice steers, he'll let me try. He's my first uncut bull, Dad!"

Cal was thinking about trouble ahead in the house. This was not the time to get into the argument he always had with Lance about bull riding, possibly the most dangerous sport in the world. You'd think the cowboys who showed up in wheelchairs at the rodeo would convince him otherwise, but Lance was twelve years old and invincible, and not likely to grow out of it by the time they entered the back door, so Cal, feeling like a lousy father and promising himself to do better, took the short way out.

"I'm proud of you, son."

17

They walked back from the airstrip to find Leon in the backyard looking at a newspaper. By habit he'd folded the paper into four longitudinal sections, the way you'd read it on a crowded subway car. Occasionally he rubbed his mustache with amusement or laughed out loud, pausing to take a measured sip from an icy martini he would then fastidiously replace on the flat arm of the weathered Adirondack chair.

"Howdy, stranger!" Leon called when Cal appeared with Lance.

A citronella candle to ward off the wasps that had come with the warmer weather had been placed by Betsy nearby. Cal scanned the eaves of the sleeping porch for nests. Just between the plane and the house he'd seen half a dozen odd jobs that needed doing for which, running for Senate, he didn't have time.

"Hello, Leon."

"We've had quite an interesting day," Leon said cheerfully. "Starting off with a visit from the FBI!"

"I heard. What were they doing here?"

"I couldn't tell you. They didn't want us around so we went out to the A&J store, but they didn't have *The New York Times.* All they had was the local paper, which is filled with fascinating stuff, like Hank is putting on a new roof, and Maude is visiting her mother who lives in Idaho. I tell you, everything you need to know is all right here," he said mockingly, rattling the pages.

"How long did they stay? The FBI."

"Oh, they left when we got back from the store. This is funny, though. I asked the sourpuss behind the counter how to get back on Route 24 and she says, 'I don't pay attention to road numbers.' *Don't pay attention to road numbers?* How does that broad get through life?"

Cal's mind was absorbed by the puzzling behavior of the FBI. Although he'd prepped for a cross-examination, his interview in Pierre had been innocuous: puffball questions about his background as an attorney from a bored agent who was close to retirement and just going down the list. A couple of ringers about his patriotic ideals, but those were no surprise, and he answered easily. There'd been no hint that they were talking to Betsy at the same time, or reference to the interview she'd had in New York.

"I've got to get out of these clothes," Cal said abruptly, following Lance into the house.

Leon heaved out of the chair, picking up the cocktail glass.

"I could use a fresh one. How about you, my boy?" he said, addressing his nephew.

"No, thanks," Lance replied shortly.

"Loosen up, I'm only kidding," his uncle said, tweaking his shoulder.

Cal was surprised that Marja was the one working at the stove. The kitchen was filled with the smells of onion, peppers, chili powder, and ground beef, which he recognized as Betsy's special Western Hamburger Sauté. Jo was setting the table.

"Where's your mom?" Cal asked.

"She's lying down."

"Is she sick?"

"Your wife is having a nervous breakdown," Leon announced almost jovially as he entered the kitchen. "I told her all she needed was a drink, but she refused my medical advice."

He opened the fridge and took out a mason jar filled with gin and a couple of kisses of vermouth.

"Can I get you one, Captain?"

Cal ignored the offer. "Would this have anything to do with the government agents being here?"

"All she said was that she wanted to rest," Marja told him. She had a wooden spoon in one hand and a glass in the other. Cal realized she, too, was tipsy. "We saw two deer with the cutest little white tails!" she squealed.

"Dad," said Jo, tugging his sleeve, "I'm moving to New York."

"I did hear a rumor, but I don't think I have the whole picture."

"Why can't I?" Jo asked, immediately hostile. "Aunt Marja and Uncle Leon think it's a marvelous idea."

"Just hold your horses. We'll talk about it as a family."

"What is this, the state legislature? Both houses have to agree?"

"Don't be such a smarty-pants. I'm going to check on your mother," he said, and carried his bags upstairs.

Leon patted Jo on the head for the second time that day, a gesture she was coming to dislike, as it made her feel like a puppy.

"Your father will come around. He'll see the wisdom of it," Leon assured her. He sniffed at the pan. "Don't you get tired of beef every night? When you come to New York, we'll take you to City Island for a lobster dinner," he promised.

Jo shot a superior look at Lance, who was rummaging through the cookie drawer. "Too bad for you, baby face."

"Big deal," he mocked. "While you're gone, I'm gonna ride Sprite."

Jo's expression turned to anguish and she flushed red. "No, you're not!"

"I'm gonna run Sprite into the ground and never brush her or anything!" Lance taunted, becoming a gorilla, scratching his armpits and jumping up and down.

Furious, Jo socked him repeatedly. He socked her back and tried to pull her hair while she kicked his shins.

Marja cried out, "Le-on!"

Before Leon could rally, Lance gave everyone a big wet raspberry and stalked out, leaving a fart behind for good luck.

The hamburger sauté was more than done, but nobody was ready to eat. Marja and Leon took their drinks and settled in the living room, empty minds humming along in pleasant oblivion. Jo turned off the stove and joined them, sitting cross-legged on the floor. In the contrary emotions that pushed and pulled her teenage heart away from and to her parents, she still longed for the reassurance of a trusted adult who would always be on her side. Marja had opened that door, confessing her secrets as a confidante and equal, or so it seemed, which was enough for Jo to shift her allegiance with lightning speed to the new guardians of her future, who, after a couple of cocktails, were more than willing to take her into their boozy refuge.

"Why was my mom so upset before?" Jo asked. "Why'd she just stop making supper like that and go upstairs?"

"No reason to be upset if there's nothing to hide," Leon droned.

"What would she have to hide?"

Aunt Marja took off her shoes and stretched her legs out on an ottoman. "I'm sure your mother would rather the FBI didn't know about the party."

"What party?" Jo asked with a smirk. She was trying to picture her mother drunk. Her parents sometimes did get loaded with the Fletchers.

"It's political," Aunt Marja explained.

"What party?" Jo repeated, realizing she must have meant Democratic or Republican.

"The Communist Party."

That was out of left field. "Oh."

"Your mother was a member for a while."

Leon blinked. His Cupid's bow lips formed a downward frown. "That's not the way she makes it appear."

"For a while," said Marja with an impatient sigh. "A short while. She was very young."

"I'm not sure I like that," Leon said.

"None of your beeswax," his wife replied breezily.

"What's the big deal?" asked Jo, looking up from the floor at her aunt.

"A long time ago your mom joined the Communist Party. That's all."

"That's all?"

"Then she quit. She didn't like it, so she quit."

"Communists?" Jo was puzzled. "Like in that movie?"

"Just forget it. Over and done."

A small whirlwind was building inside Leon. Lies! Betrayal! Communist spies in his own family! When it broke he was almost shouting. "No wonder the FBI was here! She's un-American and they know it! Now they'll suspect all of us!"

"Oh, stop. It was nothing like that. You have no idea what Betsy went through. They were all striking against Gimbels department store and she got arrested—for no reason. Cal is the one who got her out of jail."

"He's a Red, too?"

"For God's sake," Marja said. "Calm down, Lee. You're making a mountain out of a molehill."

Up in the bedroom, Betsy was lying on top of the red-and-blue Navajo blanket, hands clasped on her stomach, wondering if she was doomed to live and die in a room where the pattern on the curtains was cowboys and long-horned steers. The new, modern kitchen could have fit in a smart home in a cul-de-sac in suburban Maryland, but their boudoir still had plywood walls, a barrel for a nightstand, a bed frame standing two feet off the floor carved with Texas stars and lassos.

A decade ago the rope motif seemed thrillingly rugged, but at the moment she'd succumbed to Jo's rebellion and Leon's disdain, and was weary to the soul of all things western. The jumbled-up farmhouse reflected the unfinished business of their lives. What were the chances that the kids would grow up, inherit the place, and want to remain cattle ranchers? Or were they a soon-to-be senator's family, bound for Washington, D.C.—home at last, back to the sophistication of the East Coast? Everything depended on the outcome of this election.

"How'd it go in the capital?" she asked when Cal came upstairs.

"Good news. I'm first in the polls among Democratic candidates. The Republicans are split, with Thaddeus Haynes trailing the incumbent by eighteen points."

Betsy got up on an elbow and smoothed her hair. "That's terrific! Verna and Fletch must be pleased."

" 'There's a new wind blowing in the South Dakota Democratic Party!' That's what they're saying in the latest ads. Everyone is all revved up. Big plans for rallies and TV ads."

"South Dakota Democrats are *happy*? That's historic."

He sat on the edge of the bed. "We're out to make history, baby!"

"If anyone can do it, you can," Betsy said, smiling and stroking his cheek.

"Before I was hopeful. Now I'm optimistic. We're going to build a strong grassroots base and go after the missile program."

"Missiles?"

"Eisenhower's announced a nuclear deterrence scheme using Minuteman missiles. They're going to headquarter part of the operation at

Ellsworth Air Force Base. Eventually we'll have more bombs than the Russians."

"South Dakota is going to attack Russia?"

"Could be."

"Are you kidding?"

"They're going to build a missile field with nuclear ICBMs. They call it mutually assured destruction—the idea is to avoid nuclear war by threatening nuclear war. It's nuts, but the Russians have them, so we need them, too, I guess," he added.

"Where are the missiles going?" Betsy asked.

"On private land."

"Whose private land?"

"Well, a rancher can sell them two acres or the government can just take it, on the basis of national security. Then they come in and dig a big hole and build a concrete silo. But that's not the end of it. Military personnel will be living in those silos twenty-four hours a day, seven days a week, with their fingers on the button."

"You mean we'll each have our own nuclear bomb station?" Betsy said, laughing incredulously.

"Not if I can help it, and I think a lot of ranchers are going to agree with me. I'm making it the centerpiece of my campaign. It'll appeal to their independent spirit—keep the government out of our business and off our land."

"Did you know that the FBI came by to clear me for security because you're running?"

"Lance said. But they never told me anything up in Pierre."

Betsy lay back on the pillows. "I bet they planned it that way. Both of us at the same time, so we couldn't talk."

"They're not that smart."

"Should we be worried?" Betsy wondered.

"What about?"

"I don't trust the government," she said simply.

"Baby, we have nothing to hide."

Betsy nodded but tears had escaped her eyes.

"Hey, did those bastards rough you up in any way?"

"No, no. I don't know what's wrong with me! They couldn't have been more polite."

"Did they ask you about the party?"

Betsy shook her head. "It never came up," she said emphatically.

"If it ever does come up, I want you to tell the truth. You were, you did, and then you left, just like lots of other idealistic kids at the time. But it sounds like they don't know," Cal mused.

"They can't know, unless someone ratted me out," said Betsy. "But why would they after all this time?"

"Put it out of your mind."

"All right, darling," she said, still distressed.

Cal looked closely at his wife. "What's really bothering you?"

"Leon." She sighed. "It makes me sick the way he ingratiated himself to the FBI. You should have seen that big phony. When Lance came home from school he sidled up to them and asked if they'd like to show his nephew their guns. I wasn't particularly happy about Lance handling a police revolver, but never mind. Then Leon walked them to their car like they were all old buddies. 'Got a long trip back? Well, great to meet you, keep up the good work!' Like a goddamn Nazi collaborator."

"Whoa! That's saying something!"

"I love my sister, but he drives me crazy," Betsy admitted. "He's so rigid, and so far right, I don't know how Marja stands it. He actually said Rapid City's a good place to live because there aren't any Negroes and Jews. I told him, 'You're cozying up with the enemy.' He says, 'What are you talking about? The FBI is there to defend our Constitution,' or some malarkey, and I said, 'They are not our friend. They are no friend of the labor movement and J. Edgar Hoover was a henchman for Joe McCarthy's witch hunts,' at which point he accused me of becoming hysterical, which I was not, I was quite calm. I only left the kitchen because I was about to cut his heart out with a potato peeler."

Cal chuckled. "How much longer are they planning to stay?"

"Another week." Betsy rolled her eyes at the same moment they heard angry voices from downstairs. "Or maybe less."

When Cal and Betsy came down to the living room, Leon was standing in front of the fireplace, flushed in the face, drink in hand, in the midst of an argument.

"You never told me your sister was a Communist!"

Marja was so angry she could hardly pull her shoes back on. "Are you going to divorce me now or what?" she said.

"You hid her past! It was a deliberate lie!"

"It was years ago!"

"You know how I feel about these things," said Leon.

"I sure do now," said Marja, standing up. "And it's quite a revelation."

"Please don't fight about me," Betsy told them.

Jo was huddled on the couch. Betsy sat down and gently put an arm around her, but the girl pulled away.

"Well," said Leon, "if it isn't the Red queen."

"How much have you had to drink?" Cal asked.

"What do you care?"

"Watch how you talk to my wife," he warned.

"It doesn't matter what Leon says," Marja declared dramatically from the middle of the room. "I was there. I lived through it. Our father threw her out of the house because of her principles. When she got out of jail, she had no place to go."

Jo turned big, troubled eyes toward her mother. "Where did you go?" she whispered.

"I was fine," Betsy assured her. "I stayed with friends from the union."

"I hope you're not turning out to be like my father," Marja told her husband.

"Don't be absurd," Leon said.

"He was a monster. He got between us," Marja said, voice breaking. She turned to Betsy. "He turned me against you. I never wanted you to leave New York."

"I never wanted to leave you with him."

"I'm sorry," said Marja.

"I'm sorry, too."

Betsy stood and held her sister in a hard embrace.

"It's all because she had ideals," Marja sniffled. "I should have stood by her."

"Mom?" asked Jo in a small voice. "Are you really a Communist?"

"Not anymore, and it wasn't what you think. Not like what that movie said, or the McCarthy hearings on TV."

"What was it, then?"

"More of a social club. We had dances," Betsy said, almost desperately. "You went there to meet men. There was the charitable side, that's why I joined. It was the Depression, you know. We worked in soup kitchens. We helped the poor. We weren't trying to bring down society—it was just the opposite. We wanted fair wages for working people. We believed in a better world, that's why."

"Don't listen to that bologna," Leon told Jo. "Your mother took a secret oath pledging to defend the Soviet Union."

"I did not!" Betsy spat.

Jo shut her eyes and clenched her fists. "Stop it! Why is everybody going crazy?"

"Leave her alone," said Marja. "She's an innocent child."

"She needs to know the truth. That's what they do in the Communist Party," Leon insisted. "They pledge allegiance to Moscow. It's a fact."

"I never took any kind of oath and I don't know anyone who did," Betsy replied heatedly.

Jo looked questioningly at Cal. "Did she, Dad?"

Leon shot Cal a challenging look, calculated to trigger a tirade, but Cal put on the brakes. It was Leon's indifference to the torment he was causing Jo, by pitting the girl against her parents, that made Cal pull back and do everything in his power to stay rational and calm everyone down.

"No, honey, your mother did not. She just decided that she'd had enough," Cal said, then turned to his brother-in-law. "Nobody's hiding anything, Leon. The FBI didn't even ask. You're making this into something it's not. And by the way, if they do ask, we'll tell the truth. Yes, she joined, but it was a youthful mistake."

"Yes, but it's better for everyone if it never comes up," Marja added nervously.

"Because people are sheep," Betsy said. "Frightened little lambs."

Jo said, "I don't understand. They showed a movie in school that said Russians are horrible, filthy people. How could you be like them?"

"I'm not like them," Betsy said. "That movie is propaganda. It isn't true."

"You mean the school is lying?"

"Can you please explain this to her?" Betsy asked Cal, finally exhausted.

"People lie when they have something to gain," Cal said. "The Red Scare was the result of politicians wanting power. Fear is very powerful. It makes people build missiles and start wars."

"Why?"

"Because you can make a lot of money from missiles and wars. This is exactly the mind-set that your mother and I wanted to get away from back east, and I'm going to fight to the finish to stop it from happening here."

Leon sat down next to poor Jo, placing her squarely between himself and her mother: between New York and freedom, and the prison of home. Then he spoke quietly, as if for her ears only. "It's all very well to have high ideals, but what about the consequences? You see, now that the FBI was here, and they know who I am, they also know that I'm associated with a Communist. Okay, let's give her the benefit of the doubt—a former Communist. What if my colleagues in New York find out? The hospital? My patients? Your parents' noble principles could affect my livelihood."

Jo looked at her father questioningly, and Cal could barely restrain himself from grabbing the ophthalmologist by the throat.

"Everything comes down to what's best for Leon," he said harshly. "What are you so afraid of that your colleagues will find out? Could it be that you're such a coward that you have to put a little girl between you and a fair fight?"

Leon stood. "We're leaving right now," he told Marja. "Find out when the first train leaves for San Francisco."

"Find out yourself," said Marja.

Jo was looking back and forth between the adults. Her eyes were wild with disbelief. "Does this mean I can't go to New York?" she cried.

Just like that her future was shattered.

"We'll talk about it later—" Betsy began.

Sobbing, Jo flew off the couch and slammed the door to her room. They could hear desolate crying all night. In the morning, when Marja and Leon were loading their bags into the station wagon, her inflamed cheeks were still wet with streaks of grief.

Taking pity on her niece, Marja ushered Jo around the side of the house and held her against her bosom until the very last moment before they had to depart.

"Why can't I come with you?" Jo moaned.

"I have to go with my husband now."

"Why can't I come, too? He doesn't like me because of Mom?"

"Of course he likes you. He loves you. You're a lovely girl. None of this has anything to do with you. You'll visit very soon, I promise."

"I hate it here. I'll run away!"

"And I'll put you right back on the train," Marja replied affectionately. "Stay and help your parents. They love you very much."

"I can't go to New York!" Jo raged. "I'm stuck here because of something that happened before I was born!"

"That's usually the way it is," Marja said, releasing her. "You'll have your chance. Come on now, be a big girl. Let me go and catch the train."

Jo couldn't bring herself to watch the station wagon pull out, taking away the one person who understood her. She couldn't bear to see her mother's strained and angry face at the wheel. She turned around and went into the house and called Robbie Fletcher.

"Meet me at the Spooky Place," she said.

"What's the matter?"

"Everything."

She got on Sprite and rode bareback through the yard, across the stream, and toward the pasture. Instead of taking the trail up to Bottlebrush Creek, she took the dirt road going east. A quarter of a mile from the farmstead it widened to bald clay flats, and she came to the marker, an old tire with a block of salt inside for the cattle. Ahead of her the view was nothing but sameness: russet-colored grass along a wire fence she'd fixed a hundred times; the prairie should have been green this time of year. The wide-open sky, well, right now it was pretty plain, dark blue fading to turquoise along the bottom, a row of high-up clouds with tails like commas. She reviewed the things in her life— school, friends, parents, the ranch—and decided there were only three she would have missed with all her heart if she'd left for New York: Lance, Robbie, and Sprite. Tears stung her eyes at just the thought of leaving her horse, and she bent all the way down to hug Sprite's neck, whispering words of remorse against her taut muscles.

They walked on. An hour passed. A great blue heron lifted out of the creek bed. She was almost at the Spooky Place. You knew you were close when your horse was stepping over a mishmash of tire tracks embedded in hardened clay, the imprints of generations of kids showing off. Weekend nights you could see bonfires, hear the radios from a dozen cars, but during the day it was deserted and back to nature, although there might be someone ditching school who went out there to not be found.

Lightning strikes had burned the shallow canyon black, felling trees at odd angles and leveling the brush from a gravelly flat rumored to be an old Lakota burial ground. Everything about the Spooky Place said demise. Life was in suspension here, while death sat down and lit a cigarette. Greenish puddles showed what was left of the creek, dormant under a trash pile of bleached branches. Deformed trunks of cottonwoods struggled through, putting out spiky twigs. There were no frogs and dragonflies, no clusters of monarch butterflies stopping to rest on their migration, as there had been when Jo was younger.

They came to a halt in a patch of shade, chilled by a cool wind, the only two living, warm-blooded beings in this boneyard of dreams. Or were they? A truck was parked near the fire pit but it wasn't Robbie Fletcher's. As she walked Sprite around, Jo saw a boy she knew from school, Brad Angerhoffer, sitting on the tailgate drinking from a pint.

They said hi and Jo dismounted. He was hunting antelope, he said, and asked if she'd seen any. She said no. Better anyway to wait until dusk and this seemed like a good place. He was outfitted for the day: Southern Comfort and a six-pack. She took a pull from the bottle and joined him in the truck bed, sitting on the cooler. She'd known Brad forever. His mom worked in the office at the high school, which was Brad Angerhoffer's only claim to fame, besides the fact that he wore thick glasses. He wasn't good-looking or particularly bright, but on the surface not a bad guy, either, and therefore invisible in the hordes that filled the lunchroom, hiding his shyness in a coterie of other clumsy boys that the popular girls might generously label "immature."

Brad was pleased to have Jo Kusek to himself in the Spooky Place, even if she did say she was waiting for Robbie Fletcher. She played basketball and her brother was a bull rider, which made her socially untouchable, aside from the fact that her father was a mucky-muck in the government. But Fletcher was taking a long time and Jo Kusek was getting drunk, even crying. She was sad because her aunt was going home. Brad offered comfort. He managed to get three grubby fingers around her shoulder and ease her resistant body toward his one inch before princely Robbie Fletcher pulled up in his Ford, kicking up a talcum cloud.

Jo sprang off the tailgate and into his arms, and Brad could do nothing but watch. Robbie waved hello and Brad tossed him a beer in a manly way, then they all ended up leaning against a log under a half-wasted locust tree.

"What's the big emergency?" asked Robbie.

"My life is ruined because my mother is a Communist!"

Brad chortled. "Is that a joke?"

"No! I'm so mad!" Jo said, pounding a fist against her own knee.

"What are you talking about?" asked Robbie.

"I was supposed to leave this stink hole and go and live with my aunt and uncle in New York, but when it all came out everyone starting yelling at each other and they left."

"But being a Communist," Brad said with awe. "Geez, that's really serious, you're supposed to turn people in for that."

"She can't turn in her own mother, dumb-dumb," Robbie said.

"You can't tell anyone!" Jo told Brad fiercely.

"I won't," Brad swore.

They sat in silence except for out-cursing one another at the swarming gnats. Jo leaned her head on Robbie's shoulder while Brad drew circles in the dirt.

"Let's run away," said Jo.

Robbie stroked her hair. "Sure thing."

"Let's drive to San Francisco. We could stay with my aunt and uncle at their hotel."

Brad said, "Your relatives must be rich."

"Kind of. Yeah, I think so."

Brad had an idea. "Let's kill them and take their money!"

"You are such a nitwit," Robbie said.

Jo smiled. She could feel Robbie's hip press against hers. They understood each other. Both wanted Goofy to go.

"Then Jo could do whatever she wants," Brad said.

Jo shivered. "Ugh, don't talk that way. Did you hear about that robbery where a whole family was murdered?"

"When was this?" asked Robbie.

The wind shook the dead drooping branches of the locust tree, and the Spooky Place seemed a lot spookier.

"A year ago. It happened in Kansas. All four of them were shot to death in their own house."

Just sitting next to Jo made Brad so horny, all he could do was jump up and grab her by the shoulders and growl, "Boom! Boom! Boom!"

Jo rolled her eyes and Robbie stood up, peeved.

"What the hell are you doing, Angerhoffer?" he said, giving him a shove.

"Nothing."

"How about you take a hike?"

"Me?"

"Yeah, you. Go to the store and get some more beer."

Brad's eyes were on the ground. "Okay," he said, defeated. "I get it. Sure."

They waited until they heard the engine turn and the passing crunch of tires.

"He's not really coming back, is he?" said Jo.

"If he does, it's his own damn fault for being stupid."

Robbie took a blanket out of his truck.

"I can't stay long," said Jo. "I have to ride Sprite all the way home."

"We'll make do." Robbie smiled, spreading the blanket on the ground.

They were lying down facing each other, lost in each other's eyes. They'd made out with their clothes on, but this time was different. *Aunt Marja said,* Jo thought, unbuttoning her shirt, *sometimes you have to take the plunge.*

18

The principal's office was a busy place where the opposing worlds of high school society—students and teachers, parents and staff—collided in a high-windowed room painted cheerful aqua, with a long polished oak worktop that kept the privileged in and the public out. Only honor students and parent volunteers were allowed behind the consecrated counter, which held banks of drawers containing file cards with sensitive information and, holy of holies, the microphone for the PA system that, if commandeered, could send disruptive messages through the loudspeakers into every classroom. As parent adviser to the yearbook, Betsy Kusek was one of the favored few who had access to the inner office. While others milled around waiting for Mrs. Kay Angerhoffer, the school secretary, to attend to their needs, Betsy would lift the hinged panel in the worktop and breeze right through. Until today.

Kay Angerhoffer, private secretary to the principal, Robert T. Emry, blocked her entry with a smile.

"Hello, Betsy. Can I help you?"

"Hello, Kay. I have an appointment to see Mr. Emry."

"I'll tell him you're here."

"And I have three more sponsors for the yearbook." Betsy opened her purse and removed the forms with checks attached. "Isn't that wonderful?"

"Excellent!" Kay Angerhoffer agreed.

She was tall and thin and wore glasses like her son, a young-looking forty-five. She had on a sheer white blouse with a polka dot scarf at the neck, and a maroon skirt with a matching jacket tucked at the waist. Nylons and heels. She was always businesslike, but kind to the students, and with two of her own—Brad and his younger brother—at the school, Betsy thought of her not as an employee, but another overtaxed and sympathetic mom.

"How's your husband's campaign going?" Kay Angerhoffer asked.

"He's getting a lot of support, it's very exciting," Betsy said.

She was trying to lift the panel on the counter, but it seemed to be locked from the other side.

"Do you mind opening this?" she asked.

"Why don't you have a seat on the bench?" Kay Angerhoffer offered.

"These pledges have to go in the file."

"I'll take them," the secretary said nicely. "We're kind of crowded back here today."

It didn't look crowded to Betsy, but she didn't think much of it. She sat down on the bench in the public area, next to a student who was being sent home because she was sick. The girl was listless and her cheeks were flushed. Betsy automatically eyed the distance to the nearest wastebasket, but was more preoccupied with what the principal might have in store for Jo. He had a reputation as a harsh taskmaster; on the drive out from the ranch she had tried to face the real possibility that after all her high jinks, her daughter could finally be expelled. Stell thought that was nuts—even Mr. Emry would never go that far—but Betsy had already decided if it came to that, she would call her sister, Marja, and beg her to let Jo go to school in New York.

The bell rang and the tide changed. The hall was filled with raucous students, some flowing into the office along with teachers checking their mailboxes. The sick girl's mother came to pick her up—a young farm wife carrying a baby with a toddler in tow. Betsy watched the second hand on the big white clock go around. Thirty-five minutes later, Kay Angerhoffer lifted the entry panel in the counter and invited her inside.

Robert T. Emry had been principal of the high school since the new building opened in 1948. He was a self-sufficient bachelor and his private office reflected mental austerity. Mr. Emry liked things to be in tidy twos. He sat behind a dark walnut desk upon which there was nothing but a double-deck tray and two telephones. There were two wooden chairs for visitors and a large radiator beneath two bare windows. He had a high, deeply furrowed forehead with a narrow hairline winnowed by age so it resembled an archipelago of white hair brushed back to infinity. He was the kind of person who would never show you the back of his head.

Betsy smoothed the peach-colored nylon tea dress she'd worn for the occasion beneath her thighs and sat primly. Mr. Emry sat straight as a flagpole, forearms inside a pressed glen plaid jacket on the scrupulously empty desk, and hands resting in perfect symmetry on either edge of a single sheet of paper. His gaze was flat, his posture tense with the seeming strain of holding back on some terrible threat. Betsy was uneasy, wondering how she could feel so overpowered by a scrawny, bookish man behind a desk, until it came to her that the feeling was the same as when she'd been arrested and held in custody by the New York City police—afraid, immobilized, and stifled by authority . . . but the comparison was so improbable that she dismissed it out of hand.

When Mr. Emry finally spoke it was, astoundingly, not at all what Betsy was prepared for. Instead of giving her a stern talking-to about her out-of-control child failing classes and throwing firecrackers from a bus, possibly blowing her fingers off, or causing the driver to crash and kill everyone in a fiery inferno . . . instead of scolding Betsy about her failure as a parent . . . Mr. Emry was deferential. He agreed that suspension at home was not an ideal way of disciplining children and asked what punishment *Betsy* considered would fit the crime. When she came up blank, the principal had a suggestion: Robbie Fletcher and Jo Kusek would wash the windows of the school buses every day for the rest of the term.

Betsy almost clapped her hands with joy. The sentence was so much lighter than she'd anticipated that she actually thanked him and picked up her purse for a swift exit. But Mr. Emry remained seated, with the same unreadable stare through the two circles of the transparent frames of his glasses, further hiding his features behind a mask of blandness.

"Is something wrong, Mrs. Kusek?" he asked.

"Not at all! I think what you've said is very fair."

"You look troubled in some way."

"Do I?"

"Well, maybe it's me. Something's come up and I'd like your opinion. You're one of our most trusted parents. Do you mind if I pick your brain?"

"Not at all." Flattered, she settled back in the chair.

"We've been showing a movie in school called *Communism on the Map*—"

"My kids told me."

"Good! Then you're in a position to help! My question is how the message about the Russian threat is being received. I'm wondering if it's too strong for children." He lifted one hand in a gesture of openness. "Feel free to speak in confidence."

He waited with such indulgence that Betsy quickly concluded that not only was her answer truly important to him, but that everything had changed—Jo had been punished and pardoned, and she no longer had to worry or be ashamed. She and the principal were back on equal footing. So eager was she to regain her status as a "trusted parent" that she ignored the cautionary warning she had sensed coming in. He was keen to know her opinion; why not be truthful?

"That movie has been on my mind as well, Mr. Emry."

His shoulders shifted slightly. "In what way, Mrs. Kusek?"

"I don't think a piece of propaganda should be shown in schools."

"Go on."

"Not everyone agrees the Russians are infiltrating the country with spy rings and such, or that there *is* such a thing as absolute evil. People are people, but from what I understand, the movie makes the Russians into despicable enemies. It stirs up prejudice and hate, like what Hitler did to the Jews."

"You don't think Communism is evil?"

Betsy wet her lips and gathered her thoughts, eager to use the opportunity to speak her mind. "I don't believe public schools are the place for extremism of any kind," she said boldly. "Our kids have no choice but to sit at their desks and watch this thing and be terrified of a nuclear disaster—is that fair? Is that democratic? In my thinking, the rigid and prejudiced views of the Far Right are more of a threat to our liberties than some far-fetched Communist invasion that has no basis in fact."

Mr. Emry responded with a tight smile. "Duly noted!" He stood and shook her hand across the desk. "Thank you for coming in, Mrs. Kusek. We look forward to seeing Jo back at school."

"So do I!" Betsy said merrily.

Going out, she and Kay Angerhoffer commiserated briefly about a retirement party planned for a beloved science teacher, and said a cordial good-bye.

When she was certain, by watching out the window, that Betsy Kusek had driven off campus, Kay Angerhoffer knocked, entered Mr. Emry's office, and closed the door. He held up a finger signaling her to be silent, then pulled out a drawer in the massive desk, where a tape recorder installed by FBI special agents Wentworth and Breyer on a tip from Brad Angerhoffer's mother, Kay, had been secretly documenting the interview with Betsy Kusek. He punched the stop button and the double reels halted.

She could hardly contain herself. "Well, Mr. Emry?"

"Well, Kay, it turns out that what your son Brad told you is absolutely true."

She looked stricken. "Really? I was hoping he was mistaken about what Betsy's daughter told him."

"No doubt in my mind. Betsy Kusek is a Communist sympathizer."

Kay Angerhoffer's hand went to her throat. "How can you tell?"

"She gave herself away. They always do. Ducking questions. Twisting the truth." He sighed regretfully and tapped the tape recorder. "It's all right here. Thank God we were warned and kept her away from the school files."

"You don't think it's contagious, do you?" Kay wondered.

"We're going to put a stop to it right now."

Kay fingered her polka dot scarf with worry. "What should we do?"

"We have to turn her in. It's our civic duty," he replied stoically. "In the meantime, it's incumbent on us not to spread rumors or involve her child, so not a word—not even to your son. They're the innocents in this Cold War. Just let me take care of it."

"Yes, Mr. Emry."

"I feel sorry for the daughter," he mused. "No wonder she's turned out to be a little rebel. She knows something's not right in that house."

"I feel terrible. Betsy's such a nice woman, it's hard to believe."

"She's been trained to appear that way. In any case, this is not for us to judge. Get me an outside wire, will you?"

Kay Angerhoffer hurried from the room and Mr. Emry sat down in his fortress. He felt suffocated by responsibility. He'd never had to face anything this big. He looked at the chair where Betsy Kusek had sat as if she'd left a stain. The phone on the right was buzzing. His hand shook as he lifted the office receiver and asked the outside operator to connect him to FBI headquarters in Pierre.

19

Cal was in that state of mind where you can drive twenty miles and get to where you're going without a clue of how you got there. All he saw—without seeing it at all—was the dirt road barreling ahead of him until it turned at the signposts for the Crazy Eights Ranch, then the big house swung past and the barn came up on the right. He cut the engine in a swirl of dust, and fought to get his bearings in a familiar setting now grown strange.

He hadn't come by the Roys' in a while, and found the place looking tatty and run-down. The American flag still flew on a white pole in the driveway, and he wondered if it was true, what he'd heard, that Dutch had lowered it the day Joe McCarthy died. A pile of fallen antlers, bleached into stone, had been thrown into a disused fire pit in the front yard, and masonry was shedding off the cement silo. Before the drought, the silo would have held a winter's worth of wheat. Now they used it to burn garbage.

There had been no answer at the front door, but the trucks were there so Cal headed down toward the pens, first sighting Lance, who was perched on a rail overlooking the ring where he trained with Scotty.

"Hi, Dad!" he called cheerfully. "What're you doing here?"

Cal waved. "Dutch around?"

"He's at the pond."

Cal squinted toward the flat horizon, figuring Dutch must have taken a horse. He was about to get back into the wagon and drive up there, when Scotty Roy came out of the barn carrying two buckets of water, which he set near the pen that held the white bull.

The two men came toward each other and met halfway.

"How's it going?" Scotty asked.

"I've got bad news," Cal said. "Charlie Hauser is dead."

Scotty took a long deep sigh and shook his head. "I'm real sorry to hear that. He was having a hard time of it, though."

"He passed about an hour ago. Betsy was working at the hospital. She heard it was peaceful."

"That's a blessing."

"I stopped by to tell your dad. I thought he should hear it in person and not over the phone."

"Kind of you," Scotty said, and his eyes were full of appreciation for the fact that he wouldn't have to be the one to break the news to Dutch that a friend he'd known for sixty years was gone. "We're losing the old-timers way too fast," he added.

Cal turned toward the house. He'd acquired the cowboy habit of hooking his thumbs in his belt loops, the better to philosophically tug up his jeans. "Time is speeding up, that's for sure. I remember the first night we drove up here, with Randy Sturgis, in the pouring rain," he said.

"I remember opening the door and there was my old war buddy. Shockeroo!"

"Kind of was."

"A wife and two babies? Who woulda thought, Kusek?"

"After the invasion, I didn't know if you were dead or alive."

Lance had hopped off the fence and scrambled to the small rise where they were standing.

"What're you all talking about?" he asked breathlessly.

"Just swapping war stories," Scotty said, faking a punch at the boy's chest so that Lance brought up his arms in defense.

Cal was still thinking about the black storm that night. "You realize how long it's been? Since we first came to South Dakota?"

Scotty nodded and shifted around to take in the whole property. "Every ten years you see the world in a whole different light," he observed. "I guess you've decided to switch gears."

"How do you mean?"

"Running for the U.S. Senate! My folks can't stop talking about it."

"What're they saying?"

"They don't favor more government, so they don't know why you'd choose to waste your time in Washington, D.C."

Cal laughed. "I see some talks with Dutch coming up."

"He don't like the United Nations. He thinks we should get out of there. According to him, the United Nations is a Communist plot."

"Where's he getting all this?"

"He and Mama joined the John Birch Society."

"Hey, Dad—" Lance interrupted impatiently.

"The Birchers? The most ultraconservative right-wing bigots in America? Oh my Lord, say it ain't so—" Cal began, but Lance was insistent.

"Hey, Dad! I'm gonna get on Beethoven."

Cal left off his indignation and glanced distractedly at the pen that held the white bull. A black patch around one eye made him look like a sixteen-hundred-pound murderous pirate.

"Is that Beethoven?"

Lance nodded eagerly.

"He's really rank!" the boy said with excitement. "He's not like a practice bull."

Cal turned to Scotty. "That true?"

Scotty shrugged. "He's your three-year-old bucking bull. Don't know yet. Has potential, though. Fast out of the chute and a mean spinner."

"He's not flat," Lance put in, echoing the words he'd heard men use to talk about a bull who kicks or doesn't. This one was bred to kick and never stop.

"No, he ain't flat," Scotty agreed. "But the key is attitude, not heredity. If the bull's got heart. If he wants to work. You'll get an argument about that from a lot of breeders, but I'm right."

Cal chuckled. "Course you're right."

"Not always," Scotty answered, squinting off with an impenetrable stare.

"You know this crazy loon once jumped off of a railroad car?" Cal told Lance.

Lance stared in wonder. "You really did that? Jumped off a train?"

"It was parked in the desert going nowhere," Scotty said. "The thing ain't budged in a hundred years."

Cal's scrupulousness got the better of him. "Sure it did," he objected, like a fussy professor. "That was the train that brought in the troops."

"Okay, you tell the story, Mister Stick Up Your Butt," Scotty replied.

Lance blushed scarlet and collapsed in giggles. Nobody talked to his dad that way except his old army buddy, which made him want to join the service even more than ride bulls.

"Was this before you bailed out of the plane, Uncle Scotty?" he asked.

Scotty nodded. "We were waiting around doing nothing, so why not do something stupid?"

"Yeah, but then you saved the American soldiers on the beach," Lance prompted, perhaps wondering why all of a sudden his father and Scotty were looking like they were peeved at each other and the story stopped.

"Dad?" Lance said urgently. *"Come on!"*

"Come on what?"

He raised his head toward his father. He would soon be of equal height. In the shadow of the cowboy hat, the boy's smooth face was radiant with longing to prove that he, too, had the heart of a hero, like his dad and Scotty during World War II. They didn't have to tell him; he knew it by heart: how his dad piloted the lumbering transport plane through pitch dark and crazy wind, how Uncle Scotty fearlessly plunged into space, falling through a barrage of shells coming from our own navy ships and landing on the beach to warn the other soldiers of the colossal mistake.

Every impulse in his body was craving that same test of fire, but there were no guns, just Beethoven, right now doing nothing but standing in the ring whipping his horns back and forth at flies, so the cascade of heavy white flesh hanging loose beneath his jaw swung like a pendulum. Bull snot shot across the pen like silver bullets, indicating the kind of power that neck might have, should it rapidly twist like a ratchet to throw you off his spiny back so he could lean down and gore your brains out.

"Dad! You have to watch me ride," Lance said boldly.

Cal was stunned by the command in his clear young eyes and the firmness of his stance in the dust. Sensing the need coming off his son, Cal didn't hesitate. "Better get geared up," he said.

Lance sprinted off as if the answer had already been ordained—it had just taken a while—as the two men walked toward the enclosures, along the way sending panic through a herd of spotted quail-like birds scooting across the yard, all following in the same direction.

"This dry weather caused a plague of grasshoppers on us, just about destroyed the garden," Scotty explained. "The old people kept saying we should get guinea hens, so we got sixty or seventy. They'll eat a hundred grasshoppers a day each."

"Make a difference?"

"Sure they do. It's funny the way they hunt—they go in a pack like you see in the safari movies. They're pretty good at working together. I've seen them terrorize a bobcat. They make a rattling sound when they all come at you at once. That bobcat took off."

Cal smiled. "He was thinking, *That's not the way things are supposed to work.*"

"No, they ain't," said Scotty, looking troubled again.

Cal, too, was searching for something that wasn't apparent. For a while both were silent.

"Dad should be coming down soon," Scotty said vaguely. "The blizzard of '54 cost us half our stock and we still ain't made it back. I wish he'd give it up. It's pathetic."

Dutch was stubbornly trying to piece his business together, every day going up to the pond where the air force boys had pulled his dead cows out from the ice floes.

"He goes up there hoping to preserve the water," Scotty said. "But all that's left got covered in blue algae. He thinks he's going to build a fence to keep the cattle from drinking. I keep telling him we got two choices: haul water or sell off the rest of the livestock. He won't do neither. He just stays angry. They hardly go off the property anymore except to Bircher meetings. There's a secret book they won't show me. Just as well. I know it's about Negro- and Commie-hating."

"Keep away from it, Scotty. It's hate. It's just plain poison, like that algae on your pond."

"I don't care for politics," Scotty Roy agreed. "That's their deal. I just want to get on with it, make some money. You know, bull riding has a life limit."

As they got to the ring, Cal considered what kind of future lay ahead for Scotty on eight hundred acres of burned-out grassland, and a larger feeling of despair came over him. He regretted the fate of the Crazy Eights Ranch and tried for the hundredth time to toss aside the guilt he felt about stealing Dutch's contract. Not stealing, really, but benefiting from another's bad fortune. At the same time, Charmin' Charlie's death was becoming real. When Cal was a stranger at the Bison Café, Charmin' Charlie put on a show of giving him a hard time, which Cal appreciated. Like the good-hearted kid on the baseball field, Charlie tossed the ball to the newcomer, inviting him into the game. Even when he was very sick, sucking oxygen through a tube, Charlie let Cal know he was still on his side. With Charlie gone, a marker had been laid.

Lance came out of the barn wearing his cowboy hat, chaps, spurs, and riding gloves, working his bull rope to soften it up.

Scotty said, "Ready to have some fun?"

"Yes, sir," said Lance, heading for the maze of chutes that led to the ring.

"I appreciate you watching out for Lance," Cal said. "Teaching him the right way."

"He's a good kid."

"Are you really going to let him on that animal?"

"Don't think we can stop him, do you?"

Cal lowered his eyes as the same strange feeling of separation in time came over him. He realized the Invasion of Italy had happened almost twenty years ago, and however Scotty Roy wanted to exaggerate his part, he'd risked his life to defend his country. After Cal called him on it, it had lain between them all these years. Maybe it was Charlie, or hopeless love for his boy, and for all the sons of unbending men, but Cal was flooded with the warmth of forgiveness.

"You know how you said years go by and things look different?" Cal ventured at last. "Well, whatever's happened between us, I'm sorry for it."

Scotty's reply was ready, as if he'd been waiting for it. "No need to apologize. I'll tell you something else," Scotty said, as if he hadn't been the one who'd started it. "I was PO'ed at the time, but you were right to turn down that land deal that my father offered and get your own place. I thought you were ungrateful, but to be truthful, I was jealous because you got out."

"It's hard to work for someone else, especially your own father."

"He's all right, just getting old. Will you do something for me now?" Scotty asked. "Will you pray with us?"

Cal followed Scotty and Lance into the ring. They all knew the ritual. They got Beethoven into the chute, and worked the ropes, passing one beneath his hindquarters and another with a bell on it below his belly—as if he needed encouragement to kick, which he'd already started to do, massive hind legs striking the wooden planks so hard the apparatus shook all the way down the line.

The bull secured, Cal, Scotty, and Lance went back into the ring. Unlike a competition, there was no one there to watch them except the sky as they took off their hats, knelt in the dirt, bent their heads, and placed their hands on one another's shoulders in the brotherly bond of cowboys.

"Heavenly Father," they recited, *"thank you, O Lord, for the many blessings You have given us. We ask that You be with us today in this rodeo arena, just like in the arena of life, and that You bestow Your protection on both bull and rider, and keep us safe in Your loving arms. Amen."*

Cal couldn't tell if the lump in his throat was because he'd never heard his son recite anything with such sincerity, or because some bottled-up part of himself was scared to death of what might happen when the 115-pound youngster got on an untamed animal filled with testosterone that weighed as much as a car, with nothing to hold on to but one hand on a rope, one fall away from paralysis or death. He desperately wanted to pull his boy away from danger, but at the same time realized that he had no place in what came next. It struck him that in his son's world, he had become a bystander.

Lance climbed into the chute and settled on the back of the bull, and there was Scotty right beside him, making sure all the ropes would hold. His face tight with concentration, Lance gave the nod, and it was up to his father, waiting in the ring, to pull steadily on the rope so the gate would open smoothly, with no collisions inside the chute.

Cal performed his part and the white bull jumped out with fast, explosive kicks—wild to get that wolf or coyote off his back where its teeth could shred his muscles and bring him down. Lance held on, his free arm snapping wildly, and Cal's eyes blurred to see the scrawny body tossed into the air over and over, coming down hard on the bull's spine. With every loft he caught his breath—would this be when they lost their son? Would this? The animal let loose, enraged, pivoting on his forelegs in a dizzying tornado of revolutions, until Lance flipped off like a stuffed doll and landed facedown in the dirt, while the bull kept spinning, enormous hooves coming down with the force of a dropped ton of steel, missing the boy by inches as he tried to roll away. *Where is Lance?* Cal lost him in the dust. *Was he stuck on the horns?* Scotty darted out in front, waving his arms to get the bull's attention, and Cal was shouting, *"Go-go-go,"* pulling at the gate. Beethoven saw the opening and trotted indignantly into the chute, still kicking up his hind legs, and there was Lance on top of the fence, red-cheeked, victorious.

20

"Charlie Hauser's mom and dad were homesteaders who came up from Colorado on a pair of saddle horses in 1891. Charmin' Charlie liked to say it takes someone special to love the prairie—and someone *loco* to live here."

The mourners chuckled warmly.

"Charlie was a decorated airman who flew in World War I," the reverend went on. "When he came back he married a local gal, Mary Clawson, who has since passed away. He loved to tell the story of how he almost lost his wife—not because of another woman, but because of a tractor!

"One day Charlie decided his youngest were ready to drive the Harvester—at the ripe old age of three and four. He put one on the pedal and the other steering. When Mary came out and saw her babies careening nonstop across the yard, she just about divorced him there and then. But Charlie didn't see the problem. He'd told the kids, 'When you get to the fence, just turn the key!'"

The congregation broke out in laughter and Cal's hand tightened around Betsy's. They were gathered at the Pine Lawn Memorial Park, out on Mount Rushmore Road, a few days after Charmin' Charlie Hauser lost his battle with cancer at the age of sixty-three. He was remembered as easygoing and dependable, a good soul who never asked for much except to go along, and so he had a lot of friends. There were the cardsharps from the senior center where he played pitch and rummy, Bison Café morning regulars Vaughn Anders and T.W., as well as the couple's six children—all of whom had gone to college—and their clans.

Affection for the man was reason enough to attend, but it was hard to ignore the fact that a funeral for a long-timer like Charlie would bring everyone in for miles, a pot of gold for a candidate. When Cal and Betsy arrived, there were plenty of cars in the parking lot. Randy Sturgis's maroon Plymouth was there, along with Spanky Anderson's truck with decals from his trips covering the windows. They recognized Dutch Roy's pickup and the jeep driven by Master Sergeant Hayley Vance, who was paying his respects to an air force veteran. Just as they joined the line to enter the stone chapel, Thaddeus Haynes pulled up in his aqua-green Cadillac convertible, signs proclaiming VOTE REPUBLICAN— VOTE HAYNES unabashedly displayed.

He got out carrying his usual pink Mrs. Ellen's bakery box as if it were the sacrament. Betsy and Cal maintained their composure, chatting with people in front of them, while Haynes worked the line toward the door, balancing the box on his fingertips like a waiter, while shaking with the other hand like a maître d', humbly acknowledging the recognition that came with his new status. *The Hour of Truth* was televised, now that 78 percent of households in Pennington County owned a TV, and Thaddeus Haynes had become a "personality"—a big boost to his chances of beating Calvin Kusek in the race for U.S. Senate.

Inevitably the two came face-to-face and Haynes's pompous smile switched to appropriate mournfulness. The competitors greeted each other stiffly. Standing side by side showed up their differences: Cal, with the features of an eighteenth-century aristocrat, body leaned-out from physical work, wearing a charcoal-gray Continental suit he could still fit into from his days as a New York attorney. Haynes, carrying thirty pounds around the belly, was dressed in a brown corduroy sport jacket, flannel slacks, a tan pinchecked shirt, and a maize-yellow acetate tie with a duck in flight. He inclined his head with insincere sincerity; beneath the hard square brow, half-mad eyes were ringed by lines of emotional exhaustion. You wondered if in private moments, in a hotel room in a strange city, say, this seemingly self-possessed, single-minded demigod broke down in inconsolable tears.

After they'd exchanged regrets about Charlie Hauser, the Republican hopeful said, "God be with you," and pushed his way into the chapel, slipping into a seat up front with the family, where the whole church would have its eyes on him.

The service ended with a reading from Ecclesiastes and the hymn *"The King of Love My Shepherd Is"* played on an electric keyboard. The congregation stood. The front doors were opened, flooding the wood-paneled chapel with bright daylight. The coffin was carried out. The pastry box Haynes had placed on a chest in the foyer was causing some confusion—is it proper to grab a doughnut on the way to a grave site?

In normal years, the congregants would have been greeted by the pleasant sound of a waterfall that flowed behind the chapel while they paused in the shade of the pines before interment. But the brook had vanished, along with the dragonflies that had served to distract children from the business at hand; mosses had curled into tiny fists and turned brown, and all you heard was screaming crows.

Today the assembly was forced to leave the shade for a sun-parched field, where wilted floral arrangements marked the graves. *"Neither death, nor life, nor things present, nor things to come, nor anything else in creation will separate them from the love of God,"* the reverend had said, but hope turned to weary resignation when they faced the eye-searing vista of scorched earth. Here we go again, they thought, no break from the punishing heat.

Dutch Roy walked toward the newly dug grave, each thud of his cane harsher than the last. His uneven gait slowed him down, which made him angry, and when Doris wasn't around—like today, visiting a cousin up in Spearfish—he was free to show it, pounding the tip of the walking stick into the dried turf. He never fully recovered from the accident that broke his pelvis and gave him pain at night, nor from the betrayal by his two boys—Scotty, the natural son, who wanted them to sell out so he could go and ride the rodeo circuit, and Cal Kusek, the perfect son, who'd refused the offer—from Dutch's heart—to be partners on the family ranch. He could see Cal and Betsy in the crowd, young and confident, like those other Democratic elites, John and Jackie Kennedy, all flash and dash.

"I'm surprised he brought his wife," said an evangelical voice beside him.

Thaddeus Haynes offered his arm, but Dutch pulled away irritably, snapping, "Leave me alone. No one's putting me in a box just yet."

"Still," Haynes continued smoothly, "mighty bold to bring her on a sacred day like this."

"Who are you talking about?" asked Dutch.

"Betsy Kusek."

"What about her?"

"First off, Betsy Kusek isn't her real name."

Dutch halted with both hands pressed on the silver top of the walking stick, peering down at Haynes, who noticed that the old man's skin had gone flaky and he'd missed shaving off a patch of white stubble on his chin. Still, he stood like a timeworn monument in the sun, even taller in his cowboy hat and wearing his best funeral clothes.

"She was born Coline Ferguson," Haynes explained. "Changed her name to Betsy."

"So what?"

"Suspicious, don't you think?"

"Nope."

"Well, it is, according to my friends in the FBI."

"All right, I'll play along. What do your friends in the FBI say?" Dutch said mockingly.

"That Coline Ferguson changed her name to Betsy in order to sound more American."

Dutch looked doubtful. "Now you've got me scratching my head," he said. "Of course she's American. What's the point of that?"

"When a gal has questionable associations, she doesn't want to stand out."

The old rancher guffawed. "Well, she's married to Kusek, no hiding that association!"

"Didn't you two have a falling-out?" Haynes prodded. "Wasn't it over a contract with the air force base?"

"Yes, well, Kusek just was quicker on the draw."

"Let's call a spade a spade, Dutch. Cal Kusek stomped you when you were down. After you opened your hand to him."

Dutch's gaze met the other's sharply. "What are you up to, Thaddeus?"

"Tell me this: How's your herd doing?"

"Just about back to where we were."

"I'm going to share something that might be of use, but it stays between us."

Dutch squinted uncertainly in the shade of his hat. "Okay."

"Back in New York, Kusek's wife was a member of the Communist Party."

"What?"

"True."

"How'd you find that out?"

"Someone had a suspicion and called the FBI. I've got friends at the bureau. They let me know right away."

"I'll be damned," said Dutch, amazed.

"She left New York, changed her name, and here she is. An avowed Communist spy living among us."

"Ah, come on, that don't make sense. Why send a spy to the middle of nowhere? Why not someplace that matters, like Sioux Falls?"

"Think about it. They've been planning this. Kusek, say he wins, becomes a U.S. senator. They move to Washington, D.C. Now his wife's in the perfect position to pollute the government with Communist ideals."

"Maybe Cal don't know what his wife is up to," Dutch ventured.

Haynes shrugged. "Maybe, at best, he fell for a she-devil. But the way I look at it, someone with good intentions doesn't steal a contract out from under a friend. And you've been a good friend, Dutch."

Dutch wasn't convinced. He considered himself a fine judge of character, and looking back at the greenhorn who showed up on his doorstep, a young father drenched to the bone with his kids, who worked with the Roys side by side . . . as hurt and angry as he'd been . . . Nope. As deeply as his anti-Communist convictions as a Bircher went, Dutch still couldn't see Cal Kusek as a fellow traveler.

But Haynes pressed the point. "He grabbed that contract because he needs the money."

"Everybody needs money—"

"But for immoral purposes. To raise money for his campaign. So he can get to Washington. Don't you see? That's why they're here in out-of-the-way Rapid City. It's all part of their evil plan to further the interests of the Soviet Union from inside our own government."

Dutch didn't answer. He was still trying to make sense of it.

"We need to stop him, right now," Haynes insisted. "Are you with me?"

"What exactly are you asking for?"

"We get Hayley Vance on our side. Then we get you that contract back."

"How? Is Vance in on this?"

"He will be, when he realizes he's got a traitor on his payroll. It's up to us to expose Calvin Kusek and Coline Ferguson for what they are. If you don't believe me, consider this," he said, thinking fast to come up with an irrefutable argument: "Kusek won't say the Pledge of Allegiance."

"What?"

Haynes whispered, *"He refuses to pledge the American flag."*

They had reached the grave site and stood among the assembled in the brutal sun. Dutch looked carefully over at Cal, whose head was bowed, as the reverend consecrated the burial. Could a decorated airman be a traitor? Maybe he was captured and brainwashed during the war. The logic of Thaddeus Haynes's pronouncements squeezed around his head like a tight hatband. There seemed to be no escaping them.

"In the midst of life we are in death. Of whom may we seek for succor?"

Dutch Roy's mind drifted from the reverend's words. He hadn't told Thaddeus Haynes the truth about his herd. It was not up to speed, not by a long shot. He had no cows ready for market. But he did know where he could get beef from Wyoming to put a deal together to supply the base, with a nice cut for him as broker, and with that, he could buy new stock, reclaim his losses . . . He looked across the grave at Master Sergeant Hayley Vance in his blue dress uniform with the gloves and the epaulets, and decided he wouldn't lose anything by talking to the man.

"In sure and certain hope of the resurrection to eternal life through our Lord, Jesus Christ, we commend to Almighty God our brother Charles; and we commit his body to the ground; earth to earth, ashes to ashes, dust to dust. The Lord bless him and keep him, the Lord make his face to shine upon him . . . and give him peace. Amen."

Dutch shuddered. One by one the mourners threw dirt on the coffin, way down in that grave. His eye caught Thaddeus Haynes's and a look passed among the three of them: Dutch, Haynes, and Vance. Dutch couldn't help thinking he was helping to bury his hoped-for son, Cal, along with poor old Charlie.

21

When Brad Angerhoffer sauntered up to the table where the girls' basketball team ate lunch, everything went into slow motion. At least Jo would remember it that way, the shock of what he would do next freezing her intelligence so every detail crystalized: his smeary glasses. Magnified eyes. The crimson flame of a shirtsleeve as he raised his arm to strike. A strangely contemplative expression on his skinny donkey face as it fixed on hers, acknowledging with a smirk that he knew exactly what he was doing. One swipe and he would change Jo Kusek's destiny forever. Pretty. Rich. Going out with Robbie Fletcher. No longer. Fletcher wouldn't stand the sight of her once he knew. Like Brad himself, she would become an outcast, and they would live together in a world of hell.

"Bastard!" he called her.

Jo was hungering for that first bite of a pork roast sandwich she'd brought from home, on soft white bread with mayonnaise and sweet pickle. Her mouth was open and trusting as a baby's, when Brad slapped the sandwich right out of her hand—sideways, a perfect hit—so it flew apart and scattered over the metal lunch tray like pieces of a plane wreck.

There was a shrill gasp from the players on the girls' basketball team. Nobody dared intrude into their elite clubhouse during the lunch period, a private safety zone, off-limits for anyone but athletes, far above the pushing and shoving, bullying and profanity that went on among the lower classes. Team tables were fortresses. Breaching one could bring instant martyrdom, and Brad Angerhoffer wasn't that brave. *What is he trying to do?*

Jo shook her head in disbelief. "Is that a joke?"

"Not as much as you," Brad Angerhoffer said. "Bastard."

The players clicked their tongues and grimaced in astonishment. Jo stared hard at her attacker, willing him to remember that just a few days ago they'd been friends and drinking buddies in the Spooky Place, talking loose and fast. Now he was behaving like a jerk.

Not only that, but there were kids behind him, Jo noticed, emerging like faces out of a jungle; a group of boys, maybe three or four, enough to send alarms racing through her body. Nobody would back up Brad Angerhoffer, for two reasons: one, his mom worked at the school, and two, he was a doofus with a stupid name. But somehow he'd assembled an army and become a person she didn't know.

Jo got to her feet and kicked her chair away, ready to fight. "What did you call me?"

"Everyone knows your parents ain't married," he drawled. "That makes you a bastard."

"What in hell are you talking about?" Jo retorted.

"Commie bastard," one of the boys put in, to clarify.

"Your mom and dad are just pretending," Brad Angerhoffer went on. "They're really Russian spies."

"You're an idiot," Jo snapped, but her heart was pounding. Faces in the background were beginning to blur.

"Does your dad really fly his plane to meet the Russians?" said another boy.

"Sure," Jo scoffed. "And Martians, too."

Murmurs of an impending brawl rippled across the adjoining tables. People were standing and turning around, making room for the action about to explode.

"Then what does he have that airstrip for?" taunted Brad Angerhoffer.

"He's in the state legislature, dummy. Do you even know where the capital of South Dakota is?"

The bell rang. Jo gathered her books.

"Hey, you forgot this."

One of the boys snatched the remains of the sandwich and mashed Jo's face with it. Her teammates rallied, yelling and throwing things at the attackers. A carton sailed through the air, leaving a white arc of milk. Everyone could see Jo Kusek standing there, smeared with garbage. The whole school was laughing. She saw Robbie Fletcher coming to her defense, but she was too mortified, she turned and fled, bursting through the double doors of the lunchroom into the hallway and up the stairs to the nurse's office, which was empty. There was a sink and a paper towel dispenser above. In its metal surface she saw her shamed and reddened face and broke into tears. Turning on the faucets, she sobbed uncontrollably into handfuls of cold water, refusing to say what had happened when the nurse came back.

Jo stayed in the nurse's office all day, reading *Alas, Babylon,* a science fiction novel about the end of the world during a nuclear holocaust. The school secretary, Kay Angerhoffer, peeked in at one point, and asked the nurse to come into the hall. It was clear to Jo what was going on: she'd be punished for starting a food fight while Kay Angerhoffer's son, that piece-of-dirt traitor, would walk away scot-free. But nobody said a word to Jo. When dismissal rang, she was told to go home. She worried about getting on the bus, but nothing bad happened.

The phone started ringing as soon as she walked through the door. She hesitated to pick it up but it was Robbie.

"I'm going to kill Angerhoffer!" he shouted.

"Don't sweat it," said Jo, relieved to hear his voice.

"Candy-ass piece of shit!"

"Are you hearing this crap about your parents, too? Like suddenly we're all Russian spies?"

"No! I don't have a goddamn clue," Robbie said.

"Me, either. It's like from out of nowhere."

"I'm not telling them. My dad'll go ape and sue everyone."

"No, don't. They already think you and me are bad influences."

Robbie laughed suggestively. "What they don't know . . ."

"Shut up! How am I supposed to go to school?" Jo whimpered.

"Forget about it."

"Easy for you to say. Everybody hates me now."

"Come on," Robbie insisted. "You're one of *the* most popular girls."

"Will you sit with me at lunch?"

"Of course, babe," Robbie said. "Nobody's going to touch you."

That day Lance had a short schedule, and Scotty picked him up from school early so they could train for a rodeo the following weekend. After supper, Jo retreated to the room with the bunk beds they still shared. She was writing an anguished description of the day's events in her diary when she heard Lance's spurs clinking along the wooden floor. He'd be dead tired, like he always was coming back from the practice pen, and Jo decided not to tell him about the fight in the lunchroom. But he already knew.

She tried to brush it off. "Just a bunch of stupid boys," she said.

"Not what I heard. I heard folks are saying rank things about Mom and Dad. Like they ain't even married? What in hell kind of crazy talk is that?"

"Of course they're really married," Jo said with a heavy sigh. "The rumors aren't true."

"Then why's everybody saying it?"

"They're ignoramuses."

"Something ain't right."

"Will you stop saying *'ain't'*?!" Jo shouted. "You sound like *them*!"

He certainly looked like them, in his worn boots, thick jeans, and flannel shirt, a big belt buckle and beat-up hat, everything encrusted in crud. In a flash of sympathy, Jo saw that her brother belonged to this place much more than she. His mind wasn't lost in imaginary worlds. He didn't read books for fun, like Jo and her dad. In ways he was more like their mom, of a practical, down-to-earth nature, which, luckily for the two of them, she thought, kept things simple. Lance's idol wasn't exactly Sigmund Freud; it was Scotty Roy. He didn't care to discuss anything deep—all he wanted in life was to stay on the back of a bull for eight seconds.

"Don't you get scared when you ride?" Jo asked.

"Mainly I'm scared I'm going to screw up," said Lance.

"Not like you might get hurt for life or maybe killed?"

"I'm ready to die," her brother said quite simply. "Any time. Scotty says you have to make your peace with it. You have to be that free in order to get on top of a wild animal."

"If you ask me that's a bunch of bull, excuse the expression," Jo said. "Nobody wants to die."

But Lance had something else on his mind. He held up a noose made of clothesline.

"I hope you didn't make that," Jo said, alarmed.

"Found it in my desk."

He toggled it back and forth. She watched, hypnotized, as Lance twirled the noose around and around on his finger.

"Was it in your desk at homeroom?" Jo asked, thinking that would narrow down who did it.

He shook his head gloomily. He'd thought of that, too. "Uh-uh. Math."

"What period?"

"Oh, who gives a rat's ass?" Lance said. "We ain't never gonna find 'em."

"We should tell Dad."

"Oh, sure. That's a great idea. He'd go straight to the principal and then it's all over the school and we're dead. That's why they hate us in the first place, because of Dad's almighty causes. He doesn't care. All he wants is to go to Washington, the rest of us can hang."

Lance let the noose spin off his hand and fly against the wall.

"It's not his fault," Jo said, defending her father. "It's really because of something Mom did."

"What's she got to do with it?"

Jo patted the red wool blanket that covered Lance's lower bed. "Come 'ere, pookie face," she said, reaching back to first or second grade.

So they sat side by side, under the protection of the upper bunk, scooched against the wall with their knees pulled up, like overgrown kids in a pretend fort, and Jo told her brother how Aunt Marja had spilled the beans about Mom. It was all because of one little mistake their mother made back in the day, and even though she quit the party a long time ago, people still thought it was some kind of unpatriotic sin you could never get over.

"Nobody ever told me anything about it," Lance said.

"No reason to, except for this coming up now."

"So what?"

"So nothing."

Lance stuck a pillow behind his head. Dog-tired, he leaned against the wall. His neck was tight as a screw. The crooked ring finger on his right hand was throbbing where he'd broken it before. Scotty had been unimpressed. *"You got nine fingers left,"* he'd said. Scotty was big on "the foundations," teaching Lance to squeeze his knees and turn his feet out at the same time in order to grip the sides of the bull. That afternoon they'd practiced this tortuous position on a barrel until his hips were screaming and then some, but the pain was a small part of the long-term deal he'd signed on for. Glory.

Except the thing about bull riding is it always ends with being tossed. No way around it, even after a championship ride you're going to end up in the dirt, and that's where Lance was lying now, filthy and banged up, a couple of raw scratches from today, grime in his hair and under his nails, a twelve-year-old doing his best to hold on, even though the world of Mom and Dad as he knew it was quaking beneath him. Sad, bewildered eyes peered out from the shape of a man in the shadow of his childhood bed.

Jo had thought the harassment would stop after the lunchroom thing, but it only got worse. "Accidental" shoves in the hallway. Pulling her hair. Tugging on her clothes. Degrading new nicknames every day: "Jo Blows." "Jo Stalin." A heckling swarm would follow her across the yard like a cloud of blowflies, feasting on her wounds. Robbie and his buddies formed a shield around her, but they couldn't be everywhere and kept getting into fights—none reported so nothing stopped. The principal, Mr. Emry, turned his back, and many teachers did the same so as not to be seen as "sympathizers."

In the coming weeks, Jo would be constantly afraid. She had bruises. After basketball practice in the locker room one day, she couldn't find her regular clothes. She asked the other players, but nobody had seen them. She panicked, afraid she'd have to ride the bus in her uniform—the ultimate humiliation—until finally she found her stuff dumped in the trash. When she worked up the nerve to tell the coach, she was told: "Everyone goes through it. Girls can be vicious." That was the ultimate. Even her teammates had turned.

For Betsy, at first the rebuffs were hard to pin down. Then they became a pattern. A face turned away. A forced smile instead of the customary chatty conversation. Betsy wondered what she'd done to offend the ranch wives, who were usually so easygoing. Was it because she was campaigning for Cal, a stand-up Democrat? Was it her outspokenness at PTA meetings? You never knew. Tiny things could snag people's ire, like the barbs on the devil's claw weed, and they'd stick to your shoe for eternity. Even after all this time out west, with kids in the schools and her dedication to a dozen community organizations over the years, she understood that she was still on the outside of certain longtime female circles . . . But never in a million years would she have thought she'd be labeled the enemy.

It was Thursday and she'd made a run to the A&J market near the turnpike to pick up a dozen of the homemade tamales they had each week, delivered by a Mexican lady, Mrs. Sanchez. A few years ago this barren crossroads had been the center of a farm community, but so many ranches had gone bust that all that remained was a water tank, a bank, and the A&J, whose claim to fame was still their nickel ice cream cones at the take-out window. Upstate the dams were low because of the drought, which made the cost of electricity skyrocket, so the lonely store was kept in the half-dark. Only the freezers and refrigerated sections buzzed with cold white light, and they'd given up on produce except for a few bananas. People were buying just canned goods and necessities.

Jolene had always been an antisocial recluse, but when her husband, Allen, died of complications from diabetes, she was forced to work out front, which did nothing to improve her hospitality. Customers were favoring the new big supermarkets anyway; you could feel the A&J winding down to oblivion. Her mass of coal-black hair had turned yellow white, but she still wore it in a woven crown like her West Virginia grandmama, along with cotton aprons depicting soldiers from the Civil War. On cold mornings she'd pull on one of the lumpy oversized vests she'd knitted for her dead husband, which never fit him anyway.

Jolene Johnston was occupied with checking trays of pig's feet, kidneys, liver, tripe, strings of hot dogs, and sallow, previously frozen fish fillets next to a stale bucket of macaroni, and therefore refused to acknowledge Betsy Kusek, even though she was the only customer in the store.

"Good morning, Jolene," Betsy said nicely. "Do you have any tamales?"

"Give me a minute!" she replied irritably.

"Sure thing."

Jolene turned her back to cut a block of yellow cheese on the machine. She did this very slowly, one slice at a time, before carefully placing a huge pile inside the display.

"I don't see the tamales," Betsy said, losing patience.

"That's right."

"Usually Mrs. Sanchez brings them on Thursday mornings."

Jolene didn't answer.

"Is Mrs. Sanchez okay?"

The woman's stony expression didn't change. "I reckon," she allowed.

"So . . . do you have any?"

"Why don't you go back to Moscow?" Jolene shot back.

"What are you talking about?"

"Ever since you got here this place went downhill."

Betsy was dumbfounded. She'd once nursed this woman back to health, faithfully showing up twice a day to change her stinking bandages.

"This *place*?" she managed to say. "You mean *this flytrap* you call a market? And the prices you charge?"

"I'm talking about the wrath of the Lord."

Betsy's heart began to race. "Never mind the tamales," she said, closing her pocketbook.

"Nobody can replace Doc Avery," Jolene spat between thin, trembling lips. "Everybody knows you killed him!"

She'd gotten it only partly right. The rumors were everywhere. People said that Betsy shot the doctor with his own pistol and *made it look like suicide,* so that her husband, Calvin Kusek, could run for office and take his place. They said it was part of a conspiracy to penetrate the U.S. government and that Betsy had been trained in Moscow to kill whoever got in the way. If you wanted proof, they said, it was because Betsy Kusek was the one who found the body and then told his wife. Of course, there was no proof to any of it, but that didn't matter.

"Good-bye," said Betsy, and headed for the door.

"We are punished because we allowed the devil in our midst!" Jolene shouted after her. "We've had no rain, and terrible storms out of season. We've had worms and flies, and fruit ripening before its time. You've brought the plagues upon us! The times are full of signs and wonders. Dirty Reds! Go back where you came from or face the consequences. We don't want your kind."

Livid, Betsy turned back to face her attacker. "I was born in New York City." She pointed a finger in the woman's face. "As far as I know it's still part of the United States, and in a free country, we don't tolerate hate-mongering and intimidation, so *you* button it up, or face the consequences when I call the health department on your lousy store."

Jolene folded her arms, looking smug as a bug in a rug. "Why doesn't your husband, Mr. Calvin Kusek, salute the American flag?"

"He fought in the air force! Of course he salutes the American flag!"

"He refuses to say the Pledge of Allegiance."

Betsy was speechless. The woman glared with the burning eyes of the righteous.

Betsy said, "That's crazy."

"It's well known," she replied, unmoved.

Betsy left. In the car she was shaking so hard she could scarcely keep to the road. When she got home the phone was ringing. It was Stell.

"Hello, Betsy. How are you?"

"I'm having the worst possible day." There was a pause on the other end. "Stell? What is it?"

"Look," said her friend, "I wasn't going to tell you—"

"Tell me!"

"I thought you might be upset—"

"What's wrong?" Betsy asked, alarmed. Was it her children? Somebody hurt?

"There's a tape going around—"

"What kind of tape?"

"I don't know, I swear I haven't heard it. But people are saying it's incriminating."

"About what?"

"About you being . . . un-American."

"Is this something on the radio?"

"No, it's in private hands."

"*Private hands?* What does that mean?" Betsy was chilled at the phrase. It sounded like a euphemism for the Gestapo.

"The tape is being passed around in people's homes. They're playing it in their living rooms."

"That's sickening," Betsy said quietly.

"I know."

Phone in hand, Betsy began to pace. "That must be how these lies are spreading. That loony Jolene Johnston at the A&J said right to my face that Cal refuses to say the Pledge of Allegiance!"

She couldn't repeat the murder accusation; it was just too sick.

"That's wild," Stell agreed.

"Cal is such a patriot," Betsy went on frantically. "If the Pledge of Allegiance didn't exist, he'd have written it himself. We have to get the tape and find out who's doing this."

"The person didn't actually have it, they only heard about it."

"Oh, for Christ's sake, Stell, don't beat around the bush! *The person!* Who is it?"

"Hon, really, I don't know. I heard two gals talking in Becky's hair salon downtown on Fourth Street. I've never seen them before, I have no idea who they were. Be careful," she said, "your phone may be bugged."

"That's ridiculous—" Betsy began, but the line went dead.

22

The Bar C Rodeo was a backyard operation hosted by a family out in Belle Fourche, near the Wyoming border—not on the championship circuit, nothing to get wired up about, but the kind of thing that happened every weekend during the season somewhere on the plains, meant for young riders to hone their skills and, after the sun goes down, for dads to trade stories over hard liquor in the barn.

Lance didn't talk much on the way. Scotty figured he was preparing psychologically, and that was good. The boy's mood had been up and down, but competition would sharpen his focus. Scotty had hope for his apprentice. Lance had the mental fortitude to block the fear. He didn't flinch riding Beethoven. Today he'd be on a steer—smaller, less aggressive. If he drew a good animal, he could win.

They drove in Scotty's truck a good hour and a half to Route 34 at St. Onge, then fifteen miles out of town to Rural Road E, left on Road L, and left again at the Y, past the family home in a stand of cottonwoods, to a field next to a Quonset hut that had become a parking lot for trailers and pickups. Four light poles stood against a leaden sky stippled with clouds that might mean rain; the air was muggy and grasshoppers abundant in the golden stubble.

There was a set of metal bleachers, plus some rusty chutes with hard-to-move gates, which Scotty warned would agitate the steers when they were confined there waiting for the buzzer. Walking toward the registration table, they checked out the competition. Peering beneath a small sea of cowboy hats, they were able to pick out familiar faces in Lance's age group. Younger boys and girls were practicing their roping skills with intense concentration with loose dogs and toddlers under-foot. The rancher's wife and daughters sold pancakes and bacon on paper plates for a dollar. You got either coffee or Coke. The nasal prairie twang of the announcer's voice came over the loudspeaker, and every-body gathered at the arena for opening ceremonies, where a ten-year-old cowgirl with flying braids loped through the gates on a tawny mustang, waving an American flag. The setting was humble but the flag was historic.

"Folks, this is the real, true flag that was proudly carried by our boys of the Thirty-Fourth Infantry Division, the National Guard from South Dakota, during the assault on Anzio beach on March twenty-fifth, 1944. God bless our troops!" the announcer shouted over whistles and cheers. "God bless America!"

The cowgirl stood in the saddle and galloped around the ring, lifting the flag up high. Hats came off and tears burned in red, wind-scorched eyes. The national anthem played on the tin-can audio system, and before it was over, a great crest of cheers rose from the crowd in anticipation of the competitions ahead, devotion to country as well as to winning braided together in the western soul.

Lance and Scotty waited through the mutton-busting contest, calf roping, barrel racing, and a pony parade, until the young bull riders' events were called. By then it was high noon and the sun was pound-ing like a hammer on an iron peg. Lance went into his pre-ride ritual of putting on his leather chaps and riding glove and working the bar of resin into the bull rope.

They called his name. There was the heady, unstable, adrenaline-driven pandemonium of the chute. He'd drawn a good young steer, an aggressive tan-and-red mutt named Hullabaloo, who came in butting his head against the boards so his horns caught and he had to be backed out again. Lance got on and gripped the rope in his riding hand, got his hip area down so he was balanced in the safety zone. He squeezed his thighs and turned out his feet. It seemed like a hundred guys were yelling at him at once: rodeo cowboys standing on the chute, making sure the flank rope passed cleanly underneath the steer's belly; Scotty shouting in his face.

"He's gonna drop his head and spin. Watch his nose to see which way! Use your spurs. You need this score!"

"Yes, sir!"

"It's between you and this bull, that's all it's about."

"Yes, sir!"

"You dominated on Beethoven. You can ride this guy all day. Are you ready?"

"Yes, sir!"

"Show 'em who's boss!"

Lance gave the nod and they let him fly. The chute opened and Hullabaloo came out twisting to the right. Lance stayed with him on the first jump. The rope around his riding hand went taut and tightened. It should have been a sign he had control, but his high-strung nerves received a different message. The rope was a noose. His tormenters at school would unseat him. They were jeering and they wanted him to fail. *Fail! Fail! Fail!* At the same time Scotty's voice was in his head, shouting, *Keep your body forward. Don't lean back. When life throws you around, keep your balance!* Instead of the concentration that came so easily in practice, the boy's mind went into a fog. After less than two seconds, Lance slid off-center and hit the ground. The buzzer sounded. No score.

The steer continued to buck and twist violently. Two bullfighters dressed like clowns chased it back into the pen while Lance got to his feet and jogged out of the ring. Scotty was waiting with a puzzled frown.

"Hey. You want to explain that?" he asked quietly.

Lance didn't answer. Scotty followed through the crowd.

"You had him. You just let go."

Lance kept walking with his head down. "Leave me alone," he said.

Scotty grabbed his shoulder. "What is wrong with you?"

Then he saw that Lance was crying.

"Are you hurt?"

Lance shook his head.

"What are you, a baby? He got you. He won. So what? You got two more rounds on two different steers. Let's check 'em out right now. The more we know about 'em the better we're gonna beat 'em."

Lance swiped a sleeve across his dirt- and tear-stained cheek. "I don't want to ride."

"Sorry, pal. You're registered for two more rounds. Cowboy up."
Lance shook his head.

"Everyone gets scared, that's normal—"

"No, sir. I'm not scared. I want to go home."

"What have I always told you, since you were four years old? What do we call it?" He waited.

"The beautiful place," Lance mumbled.

"Right. The beautiful place. The center of gravity. So you came up against something bigger and stronger than you. What do you do?"

"Find my balance," Lance replied in a tortured voice.

"All right then."

Scotty was satisfied. He felt tenderness for the young man and put an arm around his shoulders, but Lance pulled away.

"Can we just go?" he said.

His coach frowned. "I never made you for a quitter."

"Think what you want."

"You can wait in the truck until I'm good and ready," Scotty told him, tossing the keys. "Have a ball."

Scotty took his time. He drank a few beers and watched the junior bull riding competition to the very end. It finished in the semi-dark, since two of the spotlights had shorted out because of bugs. The winner was a show-off who knelt in the dirt and thanked God and tossed his hat to the meager crowd. He walked away to ecstatic hugs from his family and twelve dollars in cash. With Lance's skill, he could have easily placed in the top three. Scotty let him stew in his juices all the way home, hoping his protégé might see fit to explain his behavior when they pulled into the driveway of the Lucky Clover Ranch.

"If it's a girl, you can tell me," Scotty said. "I won't say nothing to your folks."

"Wish it was." The boy drew a sleeve across his nose.

"Well, that's a relief," said his coach, lightening up. "A broken heart, I cannot fix."

"You can't fix it," Lance agreed, opening the door. "Nobody can."

"Wait a minute!" Scotty leaned across the seat. "What are you telling me? Is it serious? Somebody sick at home?"

"Yeah," said Lance, jumping out. "The whole freaking world."

He grabbed his gear and slammed the door. Scotty's tolerance was gone. He jammed the truck in reverse, backed out hard, and burned rubber when he hit asphalt.

It was past ten p.m. when Scotty pulled into the Crazy Eights Ranch. The lights were shining in the big windows of the main house and a dozen cars and trucks were parked outside, which could only mean another meeting of the John Birch Society. Scotty sneaked in through the kitchen. It was funny, he thought, how his father, the great individualist who hated the government and would "fight to the death" to defend personal liberties, was first to join the crowd. The older, weather-beaten white faces in their living room were the same gang that approved of Senator Joe McCarthy's anti-Communist crusade—they'd just moved over to the Birchers. The familiar voices, the coffee urn and potluck dessert table loaded with cobblers and fruit pies, because that was the season, were standard issue. But the message was not.

The message was sometimes hard to grasp. Thoroughly beat in body and soul from the long, disappointing day, Scotty rummaged through the refrigerator, giving half an ear to the speech he'd heard a dozen times, the one Dutch gave to newcomers, because it always grabbed them, about the secret code on the dollar bill.

First he'd tell everyone to take a buck out of their wallet, make a joke that this was not a *donation* but a *revelation,* and then call their attention to the pyramid with an eye on top on the reverse side of George Washington. The eye was put there on that dollar bill by *President Franklin Roosevelt,* Dutch would announce to hisses and boos for the New Deal Democrat, as a signal to the other leaders in a top secret society, a conspiracy that went back to 1778, that the time had come for the "New World Order," or, translated, the Communist takeover of the world. He could prove it by the Latin words inscribed on a scroll near the pyramid, *novus ordo seclorum,* which nobody understood, but it sent delicious scary shivers down their spines. This clandestine Commie scheme to destroy democracy and the American way of life was what the John Birch Society was fighting against, they were told, a conspiracy that nobody could pin down, but somehow it could kill you.

Scotty's attention wavered as he dug into a cold bowl of leftover spaghetti, until Lucille Thurlow, the cook from the Bison Café, came into the kitchen with a pile of used plates, grabbed his wrist, and whispered, "Come on in, you got to listen to this," and Scotty realized he was hearing a familiar voice talking over the stereo loudspeakers.

He followed Lucille into the grand living room. His parents were sitting there comfortably along with about twenty other people whom Scotty had known all his life. Nobody spoke. They nodded or just raised a hand to him in silent greeting. Seeing Scotty, the dogs stirred and began to whine.

"Quiet down," Dutch told them.

It seemed his parents were getting smaller every time he saw them, sometimes even on the same day. Now they made two fragile figures beneath the steep pitch of the timbered ceiling, Doris squeezed between three ladies on the butterscotch plaid sofa, and Dutch's big frame, thinner after the accident, in the brown leather recliner. His father gripped his cane as if he might be called to get up and fix the fire, except there was no fire, the room was dead cold, and everyone there was strangely rapt, as if he'd walked in on some kind of mass hypnosis routine.

With the dogs settled, Scotty realized other voices were echoing in the vast room, speaking through the stereo system, and that the glittering reels on the Wollensak tape recorder were turning slowly.

Scotty leaned over and whispered in his father's ear, "What is this, Pops?"

"It's a recording of Betsy Kusek."

"Who's she talking to?"

"The FBI," said Dutch.

Hushed to silence by the crowd, Scotty stood behind his parents and listened. It didn't seem real. It sounded like something on the radio. But that was Lance's mom, Betsy Kusek, it was really her, and she was talking to an official-sounding man about why she'd joined the Communist Party.

"How'd you get this?" Scotty wanted to know.

"Wolf Harrington," Dutch replied softly. "Still going strong at ninety-eight. We were over for his birthday. He played it and passed it on," Dutch explained. "We thought to let the members know—"

"Stop interrupting!" Doris said impatiently. "I want to hear!"

. . .

There wasn't much to take. The belt buckles he'd won in competitions. His bull rope, custom made. His competition gear. A couple of suitcases, mostly filled with jeans. He'd told his folks that he was going to the rodeo in Silver Springs, Texas. He didn't say that he was never coming back, not even to himself, but he'd known it—deep in that place where you *know*—by how easy it was to pluck out stuff from here and there and throw it in the truck, as if he'd been thinking all this time without thinking about it—how and when he'd finally leave.

It hurt. The hardest part was forcing himself to say good-bye to the dogs, with their questioning, abandoned looks—they knew exactly what was going on—and the trusting horses. He stopped by every stall and fed each one an apple, offering it from an open hand. Let them remember him that way. And he'd remember their patient eyes and individual goodness. Even the bad-tempered mares, they did their jobs.

It was barely daylight when Scotty Roy left his parents' home. The summer morning was in full glory by the time he arrived at Lucky Clover Ranch. Cal came out of the barn wearing overalls, surprised to see the truck idling in his yard. He went over, as Scotty seemed to have no intention of getting out.

Cal leaned in the open window. "Where are you off to?"

"Texas."

"Got a rodeo?"

"I'll find me one."

"Come on inside, have some coffee."

"Gotta hit the road," said Scotty.

He handed over a flat white box. Cal opened it. Inside was a reel of tape.

"Where did you get this?" asked Cal.

"Not important."

Cal looked at it for some time. Finally he said, "If this is what I think it is, why are you giving it to me?"

"Because I know it ain't true," Scotty replied. "Someone's out to get you. It's a plain raw deal."

"We heard rumors about something going around," Cal told him.

"It's ugly, but you should hear it."

"Thank you, Scotty. I can't tell you . . . this means a lot."

"Mainly I'm worried about Lance. All of it coming back on him."

"What does it have to do with Lance?"

Scotty told Cal how the boy had quit the ride.

"He probably won't tell you, but he is deeply troubled about something. Might have to do with what's on that tape."

Cal could feel his knees go weak and a surge of rage through his body that anyone should be hurting his son.

"You ought to know—your kid's got heart," said Scotty, and put the truck in gear.

Cal slapped the roof good-bye. "Good luck in Texas."

Scotty grinned. "Or wherever is the beautiful place."

"Give a shout when you're back."

Cal held the box in both hands like an offering received and watched his friend depart with a wave. It was the last time Scotty would see Cal Kusek alive.

23

The law offices of Fletcher and Kusek were situated on the fourth floor of a downtown frontier-style building dating back to 1884. Sometime in the 1930s, it had been wrapped in an art deco stone facing with fluted columns and geometric patterns in an attempt to cover its rough-and-tumble origins with rural notions of sophistication. It was eight o'clock on a weekday night when Betsy found herself staring through the large double-hung window, watching couples headed for the movies and single men drifting in and out of bars along the placid streets of Rapid City. It was possible that she'd never hated anything in her life as much as she hated that view.

Across the street was the Duhamel Company store, where the Kuseks and Fletchers had first met on a thundery afternoon when the children fought over rides on Champion, the mechanical horse—who was still there, although the price of his hay had gone up to a quarter—and Jo had fallen in love with a pair of red cowboy boots in the window. Betsy, too, had been enchanted by everything western, but now the paltry lights and stern, ruler-straight avenues seemed anything but romantic, rather a reflection, it seemed to her, of the small minds that had conceived them, and the narrow lives that were lived along monotonous blocks of grim red brick, corridors for the empty wind.

Betsy had reason to feel sick to her stomach. She was listening to a recording of her own voice, created in stealth and manipulated to say things she'd never said, a clumsy concoction of lies put together by one of those average citizens down there: some ordinary Joe who loved his children and went to church and cast his vote for president. That was the nauseating part—how matter-of-fact the accuser sounded, even warm and folksy. The others also hearing this tape for the first time— Stell, Cal, Fletch, and Verna Bismark—were quietly stunned. They'd gathered in the law office because it was the safest place they could think of. At this hour the rest of the building would be empty. The tape was maybe a minute long but seemed a lifetime:

INTERVIEWER: *Feel free to speak in confidence. We want to know if you agree that Communism is not the threat it's made out to be. There are parts of socialism and Marxism that make a lot of sense.*

BETSY: *I think what you've said is very fair.*

INTERVIEWER: *How did you find out about the Communist threat?*

BETSY: *My kids told me.*

INTERVIEWER: *You can be honest. The real truth is you were acquainted with the Soviet philosophy long before you had children, weren't you, Mrs. Kusek? And in fact, you were a sworn member of the Communist Party. And secretly changed your name from Coline Ferguson. How do you defend that?*

BETSY: *People are people.*

INTERVIEWER: *Sounds like a pretty weak defense to me, but let's go on. Isn't it Moscow's aim to bring down the United States government, starting with our children?*

BETSY: *Public schools are the place.*

INTERVIEWER: *You think so? Well, that's frightening. Luckily, people on the right are fighting Communism wherever it rears its ugly head.*

BETSY: *In my thinking, the rigid and prejudiced views of the Far Right are more of a threat to our liberties.*

INTERVIEWER: *You* sound *very upset with folks who don't agree with you and your husband.*

BETSY: *Absolute evil. Despicable enemies.*

INTERVIEWER: *I see. Thank you for your time, Mrs. Kusek.*

The recording stopped and the loose end of the tape flapped until Fletch got up and shut off the machine. There was silence. Cal was drinking a can of a new soda called Diet Rite. The candidate was dressed for a summer night in town in an old madras jacket, a fresh shirt, and blue jeans. He rarely took off his boots nowadays, but did remove the jacket, as it was becoming stuffy in the office. Catching the contagion of distrust that seemed to rise up from the street, they'd shut the windows.

Fletch and Verna were absorbed with smoking their cigarettes. Over the years, Stell's youthful face had not lost its innocence, and she often lightened situations with a cheeky comment, but at the moment she looked bamboozled, as if her pure soul could not comprehend such absolute malice.

"Betsy?" she asked. "Did you really say these things?"

"Of course not! Can't you hear how it's been doctored?"

"But it's your voice."

"The tape's been altered," Cal explained. "To make it sound like she's implicating herself."

"Pretty amateur job," added Fletch.

Cal scowled and tossed the soda can into the trash. "It's good enough to pass."

"But where'd they get it?" Verna asked throatily.

"The principal was taping me all along," Betsy realized.

"Who?"

"Mr. Emry."

Stell's baby-blue eyes widened. "Mr. Emry, the high school principal?"

Betsy explained that she'd been in Mr. Emry's office to talk about Jo's behavior. "He must have had a tape recorder hidden somewhere," she said.

"Why would he do that?" Stell gasped.

Fletch smiled cynically at his wife's naïveté. "Don't mind her. She still believes in the tooth fairy."

"Oh, shut up," said Stell.

"It's not even Mr. Emry!" Betsy was dumfounded. "The so-called interviewer is never identified. Cowards!"

"Just like the Spanish Inquisition," Fletch remarked. "A hood over their faces."

"What a hypocrite!" Betsy said. "And this is the man running the school? I want Lance and Jo out of there," she told her husband impulsively. "We'll transfer them out of the district, I don't care."

"Emry couldn't have pulled this off alone," Cal replied tightly. "He doesn't have the imagination."

"Then who's behind it?" Betsy asked.

Fletch replied: "Has to be the FBI."

"Outrageous!" Betsy exclaimed. "Are we now spying on our own citizens?"

"Hoover's been doing it for years," said Cal. "They're all in it together: Emry, the bureau . . . and Thaddeus Haynes," he added with disgust.

Verna intervened. "Take it easy, boys. Let's not start imagining paranoid conspiracy theories like everybody else around here. We'll get to the truth."

She got up from a chair and leaned her wide bottom against Fletch's mahogany desk. Her stout figure in the charcoal-gray banker's suit dominated the room with businesslike authority.

"Where did you get this tape, Cal?" she asked crisply.

"Scotty Roy."

"Fletch?" Verna asked. "Will you take notes?"

"Right," Fletch echoed obediently. "We should have everything documented."

"Why don't you tape-record it?" sniped Stell.

"Funny." Fletch drew a yellow pad from a drawer and unscrewed a fountain pen.

"What were the circumstances?" Verna went on. "What did Scotty Roy say?"

"He said, 'You should hear this,'" Cal said, and rubbed thumb and forefinger along the vertical creases of his long Nordic face, looking thoughtful at the memory of when he saw his war buddy, just a few days ago. "I was busy in the barn when Scotty drove up," Cal recalled. "He hands me a box and I open it and there's the tape."

"Where did *he* hear it?" Verna pursued.

"A meeting of the John Birch Society at the Roys'. Scotty thinks it's the only copy. He gave it to me in order to put a stop to this nonsense," said Cal. "The Roys got it from Wolf Harrington. The trail stops there, as far as I know."

"People believe this?" Betsy huffed.

"People are idiots," Stell demurred.

"How could Emry have pulled it off?" Betsy demanded, frustrated.

Cal had taken out his pipe and tobacco pouch and begun the pains-taking, maddening ritual of cleaning the pipe, pinching and tamping the tobacco, and striking the match that drove Betsy crazy, especially when she was all keyed up like this.

"Emry made the recording, but that's all." Cal took a long, slow draw. "He doesn't have the motivation or the smarts to take it further. The FBI must have set it up. We know they're investigating Betsy, they've been to the house."

"I don't understand," she protested. "I was interviewed by two FBI agents before we left New York, and they were a hundred percent satis-fied that I quit the party and had nothing else to do with it."

"Well, somehow Haynes must have got ahold of the tape—he's got friends in the bureau—and sent it around." Cal mused for a moment in a halo of blue smoke. "Haynes owns a TV station. He has announcers. He could have done this easily. I'm amazed he hasn't put it on the air."

"We should go to the police," Betsy decided. "You can't just secretly tape someone and then twist it all around! I thought this *wasn't* Russia!"

"Don't trust the police," Verna warned.

"We can trust Randy Sturgis," said Cal.

Verna was unyielding. "Don't."

"Oh, God!" Stell shrieked, theatrically wrapping her arms around herself. "We can't trust anyone! This is like an Alfred Hitchcock movie!"

Fletch was up and pacing. "Troops?" he said. "We need to go on the offensive."

Verna nodded and lit another cigarette. "How are we doing in the polls?"

"Leading the Democratic field by five points," Fletch reported.

Verna blew twin tunnels of smoke through her nose. "Good! We leak this to the press before they do and deny all accusations—"

"No. That would be dead wrong," Cal interrupted impatiently. "We can't accuse them of a smear campaign—it would make *us* look weak. We can't prove rumor and innuendo. So we don't acknowledge it at all. We stick to our position."

Fletch threw up his arms. "They're vilifying your wife in order to undermine your campaign! We have to answer this!"

"Answer who? We're fighting against shadows and they're keeping it that way. *The secret tape with the unidentified interviewer.* It's very cunning, to keep their get-togethers small and off the record, in private homes, inside a web of silence."

Verna agreed. "Gets the gossip mill going. Everyone thinks he's in the know, just itching to tell his neighbor. *Did you hear? Kusek's wife is a Commie!* Then you've got a whisper campaign."

All of this only hardened Cal's resolve. "Haynes et al., they've got no answers to real-life problems," he said forcefully. "All they've *got* is fear. The ranchers I talk to, they see through that, and they're smart enough to smell a rat. The way to win is by winning. Focus on the everyday issues, like keeping nuclear missiles off our land. There's strong backing for that. Do it the way we always have, stressing decency. Voter by voter, handshake by handshake—go back to our supporters and remind them that *we're* the ones making sense!"

Betsy had been quiet. Finally she spoke. "I'm not afraid to talk about it, Cal. Maybe it would be for the better. Face this Communist Party thing and get it over with. Just *tell* our friends this is what happened: I made a mistake in my twenties—who hasn't? Then it's not a deep, dark secret anymore. Really, this has nothing to do with you running for office."

Cal reached for her hand. "Thank you, sweetheart."

"Betsy, you should talk to my bridge club," Stell offered.

"We should talk to everyone," Cal said decisively.

"How do you mean?" asked Verna.

"At a town meeting. Get it out in the open. Challenge Haynes to a debate. The subject: Do we want nuclear missiles in our backyards, or do we not?"

"I love it!" Verna said, hopping off the desk. "A town meeting, right before the elections, when hopefully you'll get swept along with the Democratic vote for Kennedy."

"Now you're dreaming," Fletch said. "This country will never elect a Catholic."

"Don't be a spoilsport," Verna replied cheerily. "This is going to be great. But we have to start rallying our side. Cal and Betsy will go to every rodeo, every barbecue. It's a whole new ballgame. Nothing but confidence, you kids. They'll visit the VA. Host fund-raisers. We'll run a new ad campaign that talks about what Cal's accomplished in the state house—hey! You!"

She snapped her fingers, indicating that Fletch should stop gawking and write everything down. They were going to call for a town meeting to talk about missiles.

Days later, a similar meeting took place just a few blocks away. Over the years, thousands of donations to *The Hour of Truth* had made Thaddeus Haynes rich enough to fulfill his dream of owning his own radio and TV station. It was housed in a building on Fifth Street within sight of the Hotel Alex Johnson, but he no longer was in a rented ballroom with a card table and a microphone. On the street level there was a hobby shop, yarn store, tourist kiosk, and the Hi-Ho Bar. The whole second floor was taken up with broadcast studios, and Haynes's call letters, K-HAY, were painted in cocky yellow on a brick wall overlooking a parking lot.

Thaddeus Haynes welcomed the idea of a town hall meeting, but wasn't taking any chances with a New York lawyer who, someone reminded him, had been on the Yale debate team. When Calvin Kusek took the podium he would be a lone voice; Haynes wanted the entire Mormon Tabernacle Choir backing him up—from behind the curtain, naturally. To this end he called a meeting with two powerful men he had been cultivating for just such a decisive moment, to pool their interests in getting Haynes elected to the U.S. Senate by bringing Kusek down, once and for all.

The co-conspirators met in the second-floor reception area, where Haynes offered each a Cuban cigar. Dutch demurred as it aggravated his asthma, caused by decades of breathing grain dust and chemicals, but Master Sergeant Vance lit up. They gamboled along in a haze of smoke: the large gentleman rancher in his cowboy hat, brandishing his walking stick and wheezing; the air force officer, stepping along in uniform; and their corpulent host, who now dressed in three-piece suits, this one in brown pinstripe with a bright orange tie.

"Here is where the magic happens," Haynes told his accomplices, guiding them past the lab where news photos were processed, the art department where a single illustrator painted all the logo cards for advertisers, the editing bench covered with rattling equipment, the mysterious dark control room filled with flashing dials.

At the end of the corridor they stopped at a small wood-paneled room with glass windows, through which they could watch a country grandma playing a guitar and singing. She wore a starched calico dress and cowboy boots, and stood in front of a white home-movie screen, which was the backdrop for the TV picture. An operator in a shirt and tie, wearing important-looking earphones, steered an enormous General Electric Orthicon camera, which stood on an elephantine tripod that was mounted with a large school clock for the performer to see. The group could hear her yodeling song coming through loudspeakers in the hall.

"Why, that's Wendy-Rose Bixby, from *The Talent Parade Show*," Dutch Roy said, recognizing the voice. "We get that on the radio."

"It's still on the radio, but now we're putting picture to sound," Haynes said proudly, leading them into his office, where a TV set, in a regular console like you'd have in your living room, showed a close-up of the singer's gray hair and deeply lined face at the very same moment it was being broadcast from down the hall.

Dutch roared with laughter. "Wait till I tell Doris! We always thought Wendy-Rose Bixby was a little girl!" he exclaimed. "Got the voice of an angel and she's a fine yodeler, but she sure ain't no spring chicken!"

The office was spartan—a big oak desk, a tall safe, the operator's license for K-HAY on the wall. They sat in leather armchairs around a low modern coffee table, on which there was a heavy glass ashtray for their cigars and a signed photograph of TV and radio star Jack Benny in a frame. It said *"To Tad, Your pal, Jack."*

Master Sergeant Vance was awestruck. "Do you know Jack Benny?"

"The networks send those to all the affiliates," Haynes said with a pompous wave of the hand. "Jack Benny wouldn't know me from a load of wood."

He got up and closed the door, turned to his partners, and got right to it.

"Gentlemen, we need to make the most of this town hall thing. It's a golden opportunity we can't afford to miss."

"What did you have in mind, Thaddeus?" asked Dutch.

"Kusek has a lot in his favor. People like him in spite of his politics.

He's a fast talker and a lot of folks are still on the bench about the missile plan."

"So?"

"So, I say don't let him get out of the box," replied Haynes. "Right off the bat, let them know his wife is a Communist."

"She admits it on tape," Dutch added knowingly.

"We know she joined the party, but what about this name change? She used to be Coline Ferguson and changed her name to Betsy. Why?"

"Fellas, I don't give a damn what some bored housewife did twenty years ago," said Master Sergeant Vance impatiently. "What's facing us right here, right now, in South Dakota is national defense. The air force needs sixty percent of landowners to sign their rights of entry so we can build the silos. We're at forty percent, which ain't good. You send out an inspector, he comes back with resistance, and it's all because of Kusek. That's the problem, and why he has to go."

"Have you read *There Goes Christmas*?" Dutch asked, blinking rapidly. "The Birch Society lays it out for you, the whole Commie plan to destroy the Christian way of life—"

Haynes laid a calming hand on the old cattleman's arm. "Nobody's arguing that."

"Then what're we talking about?"

"How to stop Kusek," Master Sergeant Vance repeated wearily, wiping his face with a handkerchief.

"Coline Ferguson, that'll stop him," said Haynes. "The fact that his wife is a Commie and he's sleeping with her—hell, that's a violation of national security if I ever heard one."

"Plus," said the airman, "we cut off his cash flow."

"That's right," Haynes agreed.

Dutch looked back and forth between his allies.

"You all been talking?"

"Yes, we have," said Haynes. "And this is where you come in."

"I wondered what in hell I was doing here. Hoping it was in order to meet Wendy-Rose Bixby," cracked Dutch, and the others laughed, relieved he was still on the ball.

"Thaddeus tells me you've recovered your losses," said Master Sergeant Vance.

"Yes, sir."

"And you're now in a position, should it come to pass, to supply the base."

"True," said Dutch, lying through his yellowed teeth.

"I can pull Kusek's contract."

"How?"

"On the simple grounds that he is un-American, and nobody will blink."

"That don't seem right," Dutch said, shaking his head. "First of all, it's not him, it's Betsy who—"

"*Coline,*" interjected Haynes.

"Easy, my friend," Master Sergeant Vance told Dutch. "None of this is written in stone. First I need proof you can provide what we need. Second I need your promise to sign the right of entry to Crazy Eights."

Defense of the United States against Russia had recently been built on the jittery policy of "mutually assured destruction"—since everybody had the bomb, nobody would be the first to use it. But if some fool did push the button, it had been decided by the military experts out in California that the barren western states—wasteland anyway—would have to go, vaporized by a thousand Russian ICBMs that were trained on each of America's Minuteman missiles, which meant every ranch that had one was a target.

Dutch could feel his blood pressure rise. "You want to put a nuclear warhead on *my* ranch?"

"Name of the game," Master Sergeant Vance said with a shrug.

Haynes stood up and stretched, casually, as if what he was saying really didn't matter one way or the other.

"You've got a lot of friends, Dutch. They trust you. You're the big chief around here. They'll follow wherever you go. Hell, you're the commander of the American Legion post, am I right?"

"Nobody else would take the job," Dutch quipped, while forcing his mind to roll over the uncomfortable thought of allowing someone to dig a big hole on his property and implant a real live, God-knows-how-big nuclear bomb. Immediately, a black shade of denial came down over that distressing picture. Once it was done he'd forget it was there, like a good-fitting set of false teeth. Nuclear war was never going to happen. Even the Reds had more sense than that. This missile thing was a shell game played by both governments, two sides of the same evil. He saw it dangling in front of him: his last chance. As for coming up with a couple of thousand pounds of hamburger every month—he'd figure that out later.

"Okay. You can build your silo."

"Thank you, sir," said Master Sergeant Vance sincerely, and shook his hand.

"I hate to do it to Cal," Dutch said. "But I guess it's business."

"Business," they all agreed gravely.

Haynes walked over to the safe and spun the lock.

"Now about your friends," said Haynes. "The places you have influence: the Birch Society, the American Legion, the Cattlemen's Association . . . We want them there. At the town hall meeting."

He withdrew several packets of five-dollar bills secured with rubber bands. He placed them on the coffee table in front of Dutch.

"Invitations to the party. Give them out," he instructed, his voice gone hard.

When Haynes and his partners walked back down the hallway, they saw through the studio windows that Wendy-Rose Bixby had disappeared and been replaced by a husband-and-wife accordion team. It was their turn to stand in front of the white home-movie screen with the big camera lens in their faces. A foot-tapping polka came live over the loudspeakers, while back in the control room, the needles on the signal monitors were jumping around like beetles in tall grass.

A sheriff's deputy stood by the nurses' station. Another patrolled the stair-
wells. They'd cleared the fourth floor except for staff and relatives of patients
in the critical care unit. In the public area, an extended family was eating Mexican food from Styrofoam boxes. Jo must have passed them a dozen times as
she paced the floor, waiting for Robbie Fletcher to return with information on
Honeybee Jones. Each time she heard the elevator stop she'd hurry back, and
turn away disappointed, until the doors opened and there was an embarrassed
Randy Sturgis holding a ridiculous number of balloons.

The sheriff's deputy immediately blocked his way. "Do you have a family
member on this floor, sir?"

It was a joke, since they knew each other from the force.

"Hello, Mark," said Randy Sturgis. "Everything okay up here?"

"Yes, sir," said the deputy, smothering a smile.

There were so many balloons of all shapes and sizes taking up the elevator
that Randy looked like his own birthday party.

"Can I help you with those?"

"I brought reinforcements," Randy said.

Jo was coming down the hallway. It was late afternoon. Her hair was
twisted up in a stringy bun. Her skin was oily and her face was drawn. Balloons
weren't going to make her happy.

"What's going on?"

"Look who's here," said Randy.

A tall, imposing woman with teased white hair stood beside him. She
wore a black midi coat and nice boots. She was carrying a shopping bag filled
with Christmas toys.

"I'm Verna Bismark," she said. "I'm an old friend of your parents'."

Jo said, "I'm sorry, Verna. I don't remember."

"That's all right. I think the last time we saw each other was at the trial. Gosh, more than twenty years ago."

"Verna was a bigwig in the Democrats," Randy said.

"Was and still am," Verna said.

She handed the shopping bag to Jo. Inside were teddy bears and a model airplane.

"These are for Willie."

"Thanks, but he's kind of out of it right now."

"Of course, for when he recovers," Verna said briskly, emphasizing the inevitability of when. "They have very good doctors here. I'm so sorry about Wendy," she continued, unbuttoning her coat. "What an awful, awful thing."

Jo was at a loss. She felt overwhelmed by this overbearing person who had nothing to do with her life, yet responsible for whatever Verna Bismark had meant to her parents. How to tell her to leave?

Randy was still holding the balloons.

"What should we do with these?" he wondered.

"I don't know. Give them to those people."

Randy presented the balloons to the kids in the family that was waiting. They were delighted.

Jo took a deep breath. "You guys didn't have to do all this—" she began.

"Us? We didn't do a thing," Verna said. "We're the messengers."

Randy had rejoined them. "Haven't you seen the crowd?" he asked.

Jo shook her head. Verna beckoned and she followed them to the window. A group of people swathed in winter jackets had gathered at the hospital entrance below. Many held candles in the gathering dusk. There was a new pile of toys and flowers.

"It's a vigil. For Willie and Lance," Verna said gently. "They heard it on the news and just showed up."

"Cold out there," Randy said, rubbing his hands.

The darker it became, the brighter the candlelit faces.

24

It was billed as a town meeting so that the public could weigh in on the Minuteman program, but it quickly turned into a lynch mob. Dutch Roy made good on his side of the bargain and Thaddeus Haynes's cash incentive sealed the deal. More than two hundred members of the region's most ultra-right-wing groups packed the low-slung brick Legion Hall building, situated among bleak warehouses on a windswept road that crawled like a lost pioneer out of Rapid City into nothingness.

The landowners who gathered at Legion Hall had been harassed for months to give the federal government right of entry to build silos on their properties, and hauled into court if they resisted. Patriots to the core, many were nonetheless fed up with being singled out by some think tank in California that decided they should make the sacrifice of two acres of land, for which the air force was offering the pitiful amount of $950, in order to plant a missile carrying a 1.2-megaton bomb, equal to 12,000 tons of TNT, within blast range of their houses.

If you had one of these babies, the value of your property would plummet. People might agree the United States needed the atomic bomb for defense, but nobody wanted to live on top of one, or to go around feeling like they had a great big target on their back. Cal had heard plenty of worry from his constituents and was feeling confident as he and Betsy stood at the door shaking hands with supporters, including Verna Bismark, the Fletchers, and the regulars from the Bison Café. Vaughn Anders, the knife-throwing mountain man, was on their side. Shirley Hix and Lucille Thurlow supported Haynes, but Spanky Larson and State Trooper Randy Sturgis were for Cal. There were other familiar faces: school secretary Kay Angerhoffer, Jolene Johnston from the A&J, parents of Lance's and Jo's friends, several of Cal's clients, and Doris Roy in the front row. But meanwhile the militia paid for by their opponents streamed steadily past, and a K-HAY cameraman stood in the aisle taking a reading on a light meter. *Good,* thought Cal. *Let Haynes put it on the ten o'clock news.* He was ready for the fight.

Adding to the mood of discontent in the sweltering hall that night was the failure of the Army Corps of Engineers to master the movie projector. While promoting technology capable of blowing up the world, they somehow couldn't get the sound system to work right, so a propaganda film about the Minuteman program had to play during fifteen minutes of restless silence.

The movie ended. The moderator, a mild-looking tax attorney dressed all in tan named Patrick Bissonette, vice commander of the American Legion post and deacon of the Methodist church, called the town meeting to order. The audience stood and said a prayer, and then, in unison, a sea of blue American Legion caps were removed from white heads and held over white hearts, as they chanted the Pledge of Allegiance.

Before Vice Commander Bissonette introduced the first speaker, air force master sergeant Hayley Vance, he gave the rules.

"We are here for the facts," Bissonette announced. "Politicking will not be permitted."

Master Sergeant Vance, in full dress uniform, marched up the steps to the lectern and gave the air force spiel. He hardly needed to convince this crowd of the imminent danger they saw every day in the news. The Cold War was playing out in Cuba, ninety miles from our shore, and the Soviets had launched a satellite and put a man in space—proof they had the rocket power to lob ICBMs at the United States.

"Most of you are veterans. You've put your life on the line for your country and we thank you," he told the attentive crowd. "Now the United States of America is asking you to stand for freedom once again, and gentlemen, we've got to heed that call. I'm just a Missouri country boy, but I know it when I see it, and Russia is out to get us. Is it a burden to surrender two acres in order to protect your children and grandchildren's way of life? No, sir. It's an *honor* and a *duty*. Even an East Coast liberal by the name of John Fitzgerald Kennedy—"

The hall was filled with hisses and boos. Vance paused, grinning to show he was with them.

"—even Kennedy is telling every family to build themselves a bomb shelter, so this thing is for real. Honor. Duty. Love of country. I think that says it. *Let's show 'em South Dakota is the most patriotic state in the Union and say YES to Minuteman!*"

It was the ideal lead-in for Thaddeus Haynes. The audience gave the air force spokesman a standing ovation, and stayed on its feet for a boisterous welcome to the local TV personality and senatorial hopeful. Without hesitation, Haynes launched his "Coline Ferguson" bomb. It was nothing but smoke, but it made a big bang.

"There's something *evil . . . festering . . . stinking . . .* in this community," he intoned. "I can smell it. Right here in this room."

The audience stirred. Something was going on. Volunteers had appeared in the aisles distributing flyers.

"I disagree with Master Sergeant Vance," said Haynes, stalling until they were passed down the rows. "The greatest threat to the United States is not that Russia has the nuclear bomb. It's the threat of Communism itself. That's what I smell right now. That's what makes me want to vomit."

He waited until everybody was staring at the leaflet. *"Meet Your Enemy—Coline Ferguson"* it said. Underneath was an ominous silhouette of a woman in a trench coat smoking a cigarette.

Legal experts would later admire the way Haynes and his coconspirators used the power of suggestion to *imply* guilt. The veiled threat could have been aimed at anyone. He never identified "Coline Ferguson" by name, although he referred to her as *"The wife of a certain politician,"* clearly implying the shadowy figure was Betsy Kusek. A list of questions left no doubt, especially for anyone who'd heard the tape:

Why did she change her name?

Was it to hide her membership in the Communist Party?

Is her husband also a spy for Moscow?

Why would anyone oppose the defense of our country except a traitor?

When Betsy, standing in the back near the door, got her hands on the leaflet, her knees buckled and she went dizzy. She became incapable of understanding anything except the terror of the hunted that filled her body. She lost track of Cal, the crowd, where she was, until Stell dragged her outside into the heavy summer air and someone brought a folding chair and someone else told her to put her head below her knees.

"Don't cry," Stell said firmly. "Don't give them the satisfaction."

"Pigs!" It was Verna.

Cal was squatting down to meet her eyes, which were fixed on the dirt between her shoes. "Are you okay?"

She shook her head.

"I'm going to rip his throat out," Cal said.

"Put it out of your mind," warned Verna, standing beside them in the mosquito-filled night. She crumpled the flyer and let it drop. "It's a piece of trash. When you get up there, don't acknowledge it, don't refer to it—"

"They can't do this to Betsy."

"It has nothing to do with Betsy," Verna said.

"It's a vicious, personal attack."

"Forget about it. For now. Just for tonight."

Fletch was pacing, distressed. "We'll get the bastards," he promised.

"Stick to our agenda. Don't let them get to you. You're going to be a United States senator," Verna reminded Cal. "These are small-time brats. It's just chump change."

Betsy lifted her tearstained face. Stell gave her a tissue.

"I told you I should have come clean," she sobbed. "A long time ago."

"It's not your fault," said Cal. "You have a right to free speech. You never broke any law."

"What they're doing is mind control," Stell, a fan of science fiction, said wisely. "It's like when they put an electrode in your neck and turn you into a robot, so, Betsy, hon, just . . . think hard and picture a brick wall in your mind and say, *They can't get through this.*"

Fletch stared at his wife incredulously.

"It works in the movies," she said.

They could hear Haynes's voice over the loudspeakers.

"I have serious questions, and you should, too," he was saying inside the hall. "Who is the *real* Coline Ferguson, and why does she turn up now, in western South Dakota? Knowing, as I do, how the Communist apparatus works, I must ask, is she here to use her marital connection to a certain politician to secretly pressure the state legislature to *reject the Minuteman program in a left-of-center coup?*"

"If anyone's to blame, it's me," Cal said bitterly. "For not believing how low they could go."

Betsy was standing. "I'm going in there."

"No!" cried Stell. "The mob will tear you apart!"

"I'm going up on that stage and telling the truth."

"That would be wrong," said Fletch, observing the volatile crowd from his post at the door.

"Friends!" roared Haynes. "We have been called! We have been called to defend our country. And we are blessed. We are blessed because we are the chosen people. *Chosen* to get money and jobs and *brand-new roads* in exchange for our loyalty to the Minuteman program. We don't ask for this, but *it is given.* Prosperity is *given* because His love is free."

The dreary hall was transformed to a bloodthirsty arena, erupting with shouts of "Yes!" and "Amen!" and raised hands.

Verna reached into her purse and gave Betsy a compact so she could powder her face.

"Compose yourself. Cal will handle this."

When they walked inside, Haynes was pounding away. Cheers and applause rocked the room. Faces turned to look at Betsy, but not all were hostile. Betsy straightened her shoulders and followed her husband.

"Have no doubt," Haynes shouted. "We need these missiles. But Communism is more deadly than the atom bomb—and it's right here under our noses. That's why we are correct to ask questions about this mysterious person called 'Coline Ferguson.' Let us hope someone with a Christian conscience will come forth and name the real source of this pestilence!"

Haynes left the stage to a raucous standing ovation. Rather than igniting their western spirit of independence, Haynes's inflammatory speech made them feel that allowing the government to move in on their land was their American duty. United against a common enemy, the crowd rose as one. Cal walked the gauntlet up the aisle with his eyes focused on the microphone, determined to strike back with concise words, to cut through the bloated rhetoric. He saw sympathetic faces in the audience. His trust in the will of the people was firm, and that they would respond to reason. When Cal stepped up and took the microphone, the cheering stopped. He had their silence.

"We do have a plague," Cal declared in a resonant voice. "But it isn't Communism. Nor is it the drought. Or missiles. It's cancer. The cancer of fear that is being spread right here, tonight. The kind of fear that scares men off their rightful land. Men like Tim Ehrlich."

The room stayed quiet. They all knew Tim Ehrlich and were hooked—except for Thaddeus Haynes, who would not give his opponent the courtesy of his attention and kept his eyes down, insolently studying his Bible.

"Tim was a family man. An experienced rancher and a good neighbor. He had bad losses like we all did in the blizzard of '54—in fact, Spanky Larson and Trooper Sturgis and I, we helped pull his dead cows out of the snow," Cal said, making eye contact with his supporters in the crowd. "Tim held on until the air force showed up and informed him that they were taking two acres of his best pasture to build a silo, like it or not, and that he had no choice in the matter. No, he couldn't even choose *which* two acres—that was up to the government. In the process, they cut his irrigation lines and dug ditches that killed his cows. They gave him no recompense. Finally Tim gave up. He sold his ranch and moved to Wall for a job in a cement plant. His grandkids will never know what it's like to grow up free, on a ranch, out in the open. We all face the same choice."

Cal saw Haynes with his head down reading his book, and all he could think about was punching his lights out. He began to lose his footing. He went on with his rational arguments: South Dakotans were victims of the defense industry, run by outsiders. He hit them with numbers: each Minuteman would cost $75 million—all of it lining the pockets of profiteers. The audience looked blank. He wasn't getting the message through. It seemed inconceivable, but nothing could penetrate the paranoid distemper that Haynes had created. Cal's speech was greeted with halfhearted clapping and a few boos.

Moderator Patrick Bissonette took over and asked Haynes if he had a rebuttal. He got lazily to his feet as if awakened from a nap.

"Anyone who's against the missiles, I call them a Communist sympathizer!" he said, to favorable applause. "And anyone who's *married* to a Communist, why, he's in on it, too."

Vaughn Anders stood up, a filthy throwback pioneer figure amid white shirtsleeves and blue American Legion caps.

"How'd you figure that?" he shouted.

"Ever hear of pillow talk?" cracked Haynes.

The crowd roared.

"Now we'll open up for public discussion," Bissonette announced over the laughter.

There was a brief argument in the Kusek camp about who should speak. Verna Bismark raised her hand and was recognized. She made her way to the stage, waving confidently at many she knew who were customers at her bank.

"Hello, everyone," she said cheerfully. "Hello, Verna!" the audience echoed back with mocking chuckles, as they were at the peak of emotional arousal and she was dressed in her usual tight-fitting business suit that emphasized bosom and hips; one of only a dozen women present.

"This is not the Rapid City that I know," she began. "We used to look out for one another, now we're split apart. I've heard people threatening to boycott each other's businesses over this. Tires have been flattened. People don't trust their neighbors. And it's not just because of the Minuteman program. It's the obscene smear and fear campaign against Calvin Kusek that has poisoned the well. In a few weeks we will be going to the polls to choose the next senator from South Dakota, and the speakers here tonight—"

Bissonette stopped her. "I'm sorry. This is not a political meeting, madame."

The crowd's grudging welcome to Verna Bismark turned to hostile applause in support of the moderator.

"Mr. Haynes has certainly been talking politics and making reckless accusations—"

"Just a minute, Mrs. Bismark. We're not going to discuss the candidates here, this is fact-finding only—"

Verna, who had counseled Cal to keep his cool, now lost hers, turning on the vice commander, spitting mad. "Oh, blow it out your barracks bag, Patrick! I'm not going to stand here while you turn this into a witch hunt! You don't get to threaten someone and his wife because you disagree with him—"

There were shouts of *"Throw her out!"*

The K-HAY cameraman, who had been watching from the sidelines, got the signal from Haynes to start shooting. The sixteen-millimeter Eyemo camera held only three minutes' worth of film, and he'd been hoarding it until the crowd came to a boil, which was now. Several men got out of their seats and approached the stage. The room was filled with boos and lewd remarks. The cameraman shoved past everyone and got to the stage.

In the back of the room Cal said, "We have to get her out of there."

Fletch stopped him. "I'll do it. You stay here."

"No—"

Betsy said, "There's going to be a fight."

Cal told them all to get in the car.

"I'm afraid you've stepped over the bounds," Vice Commander Bissonette was shouting over the melee. "We've done everything to remain reasonable and open-minded—"

Two ranchers took Verna Bismark by the arms and marched her off the stage and out a side door. The meeting wasn't over; there was still a lot of milling around and arguing to take care of, but Cal's intention was to save Verna Bismark. He fought his way around the building. When he found her alone, outside in the humid night, he apologized over and over.

"Why are you surprised?" Verna asked, breathlessly lighting a cigarette.

"I didn't see it coming," said Cal. "I made a fundamental mistake. I underestimated the enemy."

"I'm with you. I thought I could get through with my girlish charms," Verna said. "Boy, was I out to lunch." She straightened her back and tossed her head to regain her composure. In the light thrown by a single bulb on a lamp outside the hall, her eyes were moist. "You realize nothing can stop them now."

The cameraman was already on the road. In a matter of minutes he was back in town and had pulled into the station parking lot on Fifth Street beneath the yellow K-HAY letters on the brick wall. Not waiting for the elevator, taking two steps at a time, he arrived at the second-floor photo lab, unloaded the magazine inside a changing bag, rolled the news film onto a developing reel, and stuck it into the processor, where it went through seven different chemical baths while the clock ticked.

Cal and Betsy arrived at the Lucky Clover Ranch a little before the ten o'clock news. In the living room, the kids had dutifully put on their pajamas and were lying on the couch, watching the end of *I Love Lucy* on K-HAY.

"Hi, Dad. How was the meeting?" asked Jo.

Cal didn't answer. He yanked the plug to the TV right out of the wall. Jo and Lance were flabbergasted. The picture on the screen shrank to a dot and disappeared. Betsy walked upstairs and Cal followed without a word.

25

On Election Day, voters awoke to find a plastic bag containing a rock on their lawns. Inside the bag was an alarming message warning them that "new facts" were discovered to prove that "a certain candidate" had "ties to Moscow." The letter was unsigned, but the Ku Klux Klan was famous for tossing plastic bags with rocks and hate-filled tracts at their targets. People took it as a personal threat from sources unknown, which was enough to keep them away from the polls. As a result of this and other inflammatory mailings against him since the meeting at Legion Hall, Calvin Kusek lost the election, with only 28 percent of the vote. John F. Kennedy was elected president, and Thaddeus Haynes was swept into office as the U.S. senator from South Dakota.

Cal had lost in every way. His agenda was in pieces. He was forced to sit by and watch as Minuteman became a fact. Missile fields were quickly authorized across the west and built on a rush schedule. Caravans of armored trucks began to clog the rural roads. Engineers in hard hats and orange vests were everywhere. Backhoes rolled over wheat fields, and if farmers complained, the workers called them "unpatriotic." Construction went fast because the California defense firms that masterminded the project had efficiently broken it down into crews who each performed a single task: excavate, pour concrete, lower the prefabricated silo into the hole, fill in the dirt, and move on to the next.

No matter how he tried to rethink it, Cal's political career was over. *"Twenty-eight percent!"* people kept repeating, either delighted or despairing. No matter which, his reputation had been ruined. The shocking loss had cost the trust he'd built from arriving as a stranger to becoming a community leader. After six years in the state house, dutifully following the trodden path of patience and negotiation, bit by bit making small gains in responsible lawmaking, he'd been chased by a mob of fanatics over a cliff.

For months after the election Cal fell through space. The silence surrounding him was unearthly. He'd go into the law office and sit at his desk and nothing happened. The phone did not ring. No aides called from campaign headquarters, no reporters begged for minutes of his time. He'd open the mail. A letter expressing sympathy could make him cry. Fletch tried to interest him in new clients, but he couldn't concentrate. On downtown streets, instead of reaching out for handshakes, Cal would drop his eyes, ashamed of the mistakes that let his family and supporters down.

He'd gravely misjudged the amount of fear that lay beneath the hardiness of these rural families, and how skillfully Haynes played upon it. Atomic war or endless drought, *"You suffer God's punishment because you have not cast out evil from our midst,"* he'd intoned. Cal had been naive to think that goodness alone would triumph over such malicious nonsense. He should have never allowed himself and Betsy to be put in the role of scapegoats. He should have counterpunched much earlier, with everything he had.

Silence had crept inside the marriage, too. In the evenings, while concertos for piano played on the hi-fi, Cal and Betsy sat in opposite chairs and read, burrowing into the minds of Tolstoy, Machiavelli, Churchill, Lincoln, Brontë, and Ferber, looking for answers. Direct attacks on the Kuseks' loyalty had ebbed, but now they were frozen out by ordinary complacency. People in town, embarrassed by their presence, looked the other way. Even Verna Bismark was saying privately that Calvin Kusek had become "bad meat." Their great adventure had come to a halt.

Jo withdrew from the family and put her head down to get through the rest of high school. Later, when Robbie Fletcher was a freshman at the University of Colorado majoring in journalism, he'd write to her a few times before their correspondence dropped off, but not before driving her crazy with how *"liberating"* everything was *"out here,"* meaning anywhere but South Dakota. Jo spent long, solitary afternoons in the research section of the library, absorbed in the dense pages of the college guide, imagining dorm life in far-off regions, swooning over exciting courses "out there." College seemed like a fairy tale. *All I'll have to do is read!* she thought.

Lance, too, was planning his escape. With Uncle Scotty gone, he'd given up bull riding. It seemed childish to him now. He'd fallen in with a different crowd—students who were fired up about civil rights. They'd been ostracized as weirdo Kennedy supporters, but now they reveled in his presidency, and because Kennedy stood up for Martin Luther King Jr., they did, too. Lance read *Invisible Man* by Ralph Ellison, wore a CORE button, and schemed about sneaking off to join the Freedom Riders in Alabama. His grades improved and he started taking honors classes. One day he completely shocked his father by announcing he wanted to become a lawyer.

It was clear that neither child had any interest in taking over the Lucky Clover Ranch. For the first time the Kuseks considered selling and moving back east. Betsy wrote to Marja about apartment rentals. Cal sent his résumé to New York congressman John V. Lindsay, who years ago had offered him a job, but received a staff-written rejection in return.

Now when he surveyed his livestock, Cal's heart was cold. He wanted to send them all to the feedlot so he didn't have to care anymore. Despite Haynes's promises, Dutch Roy never did receive the air force contract because he couldn't have; it was never a possibility, it had been an outright lie to get him to ride along on the hunt to bring down Calvin Kusek. In fact, Doris and Dutch Roy, former queen and king of the frontier, were now in the same position as the Kuseks. Their son, too, was gone, and they were looking to sell the Crazy Eights.

The only bright spot during those miserable winter months was a new five-year-old purebred quarter horse Cal had bought named Vanity that he was training as a ranch horse. Being a sorrel mare, she had attitude. She'd give off little bucks when he asked her to lope, and head-butt when he asked her to stand, but a bop on the nose would keep her in line, and she was learning to listen.

She loved to run and had good endurance, so he'd take her out to fix fences and look for wolves that had been picking off their weakest cattle. It was late afternoon on a bitter day in December when they reached the edge of spruce forest on the northern side of Bottlebrush Creek, and Cal spotted dog tracks in the snow. They halted and listened. Vanity's ears pricked forward. Cal could hear nothing but the tapestry of bird sounds. He could make out high-pitched warblers and the *whoo-ooh-ooh* of an owl and, deep in the woods, the low pulse of a running creek. He could smell icy water.

Vanity's ears went flat. Her body tensed and she sprang sideways. Fifty yards away a mule deer broke from the trees, running for its life ahead of a dozen gray wolves. Cal pulled the rifle, collected his horse and urged her into a gallop. She took off eagerly, and for an exhilarating sprint Cal was able to keep the wolves in sight, but then the deer darted back into the safety of the woods and the band split in two behind it. Cal wheeled Vanity around to follow the smaller bunch and they took off, nimbly jumping over a thicket of brush—neither of them realizing there was a dry gully on the other side. The horse stumbled into a ditch and flipped over. Cal's heel went through the stirrup and the animal fell on top of him.

The disturbance they made settled and was lost in the endless snowy tracts. Horse and rider lay still, their breath clouds commingling in the freezing air. He was trapped beneath her massive body, just able to move the toes inside his boot. He knotted the reins around the saddle horn so that she couldn't get up, because if she did, the first thing she would do was run, and he'd be dragged to death hanging by the stirrup. She fought the tethers, trying to get on her knees. He talked calmly to her. He stroked her coat, dark and sticky with sweat. After a while she let out a long snort and gave up struggling.

Dusk was coming fast. After dark the temperature would fall below zero. Cal was turned on his side with his right arm torqued beneath his shoulder, his face grazed with scratches. Before his eyes the miniature world grew large. He stared at three fallen juniper berries, big as planets. He could see every grain of forest dust on their skins. The wind swept the evergreens along with cold gray fog, but Cal was insensible, charmed by a single snowflake that had settled on his sleeve. He seemed to be inside the latticework, wondering why he'd never really looked before. Sleep was beckoning, and with it the thought of easy death, of one by one every cell in his body turning into a crystal of ice.

Then he heard the wolves. First the clear horn sound of the alpha male, followed by an answer, then all their voices echoing together with ethereal dissonance. Trapped, Vanity's eyes rolled back in terror. She floundered and kicked, desperate to be free, and with every jolt Cal's leg laced tight with pain. The knife. The knife was in his back pocket. He couldn't reach the knife. He heard the heart-shattering cry of the wolves again, piercing inhuman harmonies followed by a frenzy of yips and barks calling for supremacy.

With his free left hand, he clawed the earth. He seized a rock, a stick, and kept on jabbing and scrabbling until he'd dug a shallow hole. Gritting his teeth, he twisted onto the injured shoulder, raising himself up high enough to get his left hand to his pocket and touch the handle of the knife and tease it from his pocket. He dropped it, found it again, flicked it open, and was able to slice through the stirrup leather, feeling the pressure on his leg release. He spun the reins off the saddle horn and clicked at Vanity, telling her to stand, and as she struggled to her feet, he rolled to safety. It seemed the horse hadn't broken any bones, but her hind leg was curled and hurting.

Cal found the rifle in the bush and fired a booming round into the black woods. The howling stopped but picked up again, undaunted, and he kept the gun cocked and loaded as he led the injured mare across the open meadow. It would be a long, slow trek, and he had a lot of time to think about things as they hobbled along under an infinite blanket of stars. It was past ten o'clock when they made it to the ranch, torn up, weary, and sore, exhausted as prisoners of war. Betsy came running out of the house, frantic.

"What happened?" she cried. "The kids took the truck to look for you. I had the sheriff on the line."

"Vanity's hurt. Call the vet," Cal mumbled, his voice slurred. "I hope it's just a tendon. You're a good old girl," he told the horse, stroking her drooping neck. "And so are you," he told his wife, almost collapsing in her arms.

Betsy ran expert fingers along his arms and torso, examining for breaks and bruises. "Are you okay?"

"I don't know how we made it. We flipped into a gully and she pinned me down. She could have broken her neck. I could have died of cold."

"Cal!"

"God must have a plan," he said.

"What's the plan?" Betsy asked indulgently, as they limped toward the barn.

"I'm going after Haynes. If it kills me, I'm going after him."

Verna Bismark and Randy Sturgis were still in the waiting area when Jo came out of the ICU, accompanied by Dr. Pataki. They stood anxiously.

"Willie touched me!" Jo exclaimed. She was smiling broadly, almost delirious with joy. "He knew I was there!"

Verna clapped her hands together in prayer. "Is it true?"

"I squeezed his fingers and they moved. Right, Dr. Pataki?"

"There was a response," the doctor agreed.

"So there's hope!" Randy exclaimed.

"It's impossible to say for sure, given the severity of the injuries," Dr. Pataki said.

"Well, what are you going to do?" Verna demanded.

"We're going to apply time, patience, and observation. Excuse me, I have surgery," he said, and left.

"I'm going to have a cigarette," Verna said, and followed him out.

Jo flopped in a chair. "Best news all day!"

26

The Pennington County courthouse was built in the 1920s in the Beaux-Arts style, a monument on a grand scale meant to stand for the merits of American government at its most thoughtful and temperate. When the Kusek trial opened in the South Dakota Supreme Court on a wet morning in February 1963, that pale limestone facade had resisted the corrosion of wind and human avarice for almost half a century. As Cal and Betsy, holding hands in the rain, passed the huge two-story arched windows and sober Ionic columns, it was not unreasonable to assume they were entering a temple of justice, where the wrongs against them would be reconciled and the offenders made to pay.

Fletch had repeatedly warned Cal and Betsy against suing Haynes. Getting nowhere, he called in the best trial lawyer in the state, fifty-five-year-old Kurt Lennox, for the thankless job of talking a potential client into dropping a case. The two met at a steak house in Pierre. The trouble was Cal liked Kurt Lennox. He liked the thin white beard that hung inches off his chin and the unkempt gray hair that made him resemble Mark Twain. He liked his showman style—a seersucker suit with a cowboy hat and snakeskin boots—and the fire in his belly for justice, a compadre spoiling for the fight.

Right off Lennox told Cal that no libel case in the country had ever been won if it bore the "pink taint" of alleged Communist sympathies, and no state was more virulently anti-Red than South Dakota. He pointed out that the bias was written into the Republican Party platform, for heaven's sake: *"We pledge a continuous fight against Communism and its influence both at home and abroad."*

Add to that Haynes's sneaky strategy of not *directly* accusing Cal of being a Communist. Haynes and friends had been shrewd in their use of fear and smear to *question* Cal's loyalty ... *question* the truth about his wife ... a precedent set by the McCarthy hearings, in which *suspicion* of guilt was enough to create panic and cause mass firings of university professors and jail time for Hollywood writers. As Fletch had begged him to understand, even the law was stacked against them. Fair comment privilege, conceived to protect free speech, meant that a public official could not sue a person for having libeled against him. Disapproval, denigration, reproach, and blame were apparently considered a normal part of public service, Kurt Lennox reckoned over his after-dinner brandy.

But he was serious as a heart attack when he leaned across the table and told Cal straight up that the worst part of going to trial would be the anxiety and suffering it would cause his family all over again. Every day they would walk up the courthouse steps through a gauntlet of hostility. Cal replied that Jo would be away at Reed College in Oregon, and Lance had only a couple of years before he left for university. They, too, had been victims of prejudice and were ready to make things right. Kurt's frank, pale blue eyes still reflected his concern.

"They won't be spared because they're children," he cautioned.

"They aren't children anymore," Cal said. "Besides, how could it get worse unless they tarred and feathered us?"

The Kuseks had become stooges for every bad thing that had befallen the county in the past decade: the drought, a plague of screwworms and then grasshoppers, the cement plant closing down, Dutch Roy getting into a tractor accident, poor Charmin' Charlie dying of cancer, someone's cattle falling sick, but, scariest of all—and the "proof" of several conspiracy theories naming the Kuseks as agents of the devil—the mysterious disappearance of Scotty Roy.

Nobody had heard from Scotty since the day he showed up at the Lucky Clover Ranch, all scrubbed and ready for the road—*the same day* the Roys realized the tape of Betsy's so-called interview with the FBI was missing from their living room. Weeks had gone by and he'd never called home. His parents heard he'd competed in the professional rodeo in Silver Springs, Texas, but after that nobody knew his whereabouts. Cal volunteered that he might have been the last to see Scotty Roy, and went down to the police station for an interview, which people thought was a calculated gesture, especially now that Scotty's father, Dutch Roy, had been named as a co-conspirator in the lawsuit against Thaddeus Haynes.

The saddest and most shocking revelation to emerge for Cal from the discovery phase of the trial was the uncovering of checks written by Dutch Roy, as well as Haynes, to the printing company that manufactured deceitful letters mailed to voters after the Legion Hall meeting, as well as the "Meet Your Enemy" leaflets. His conspiracy with Haynes against Cal was clear. Dutch Roy had hosted anti-Communist study groups, played the tape, and donated money to Haynes's whisper campaign. Not surprisingly, Master Sergeant Hayley Vance escaped scrutiny altogether.

Cal was torn between his understanding of Dutch Roy as a disappointed older man whose fortunes had turned . . . and the vengeful competitor seeking payback. Cal and Betsy agonized over whether to sue someone who, in good faith, had extended his hand to them, but Lennox insisted that adding the charge of conspiracy gave them a stronger case. Once that was made public, rumors flew that Cal had murdered Scotty to shut him up, or Scotty had chosen to disappear so he didn't have to testify against his dad. Either way, it was agreed that Kusek had bored his way between father and son like a weevil.

After eighteen months of preparation and delays, the trial lasted almost five weeks. The jury looked like someone had rounded up patrons at the A&J market, thrown them in a van, and driven straight to the courthouse. They wore their usual everyday clothes and carried no pretensions. Among them were wives of cattlemen, a uranium miner, a cook at the local Italian restaurant, a druggist, a Lakota grandmother, a retired chemistry teacher, a construction worker. The presiding judge, Harold Wheeler, was difficult to look at: portly, with elongated ears that sprouted tufts of hair, coarse skin, and a thick lower lip hanging loose enough to create a traveling pool of saliva, but he was considered a brilliant eccentric—an author of textbooks on appellate law, as well as a professional beekeeper.

In his opening statement, Kurt Lennox promised that he would deliver proof that Cal's reputation had been severely damaged by the attacks on his character by the defendants, Thaddeus Haynes and Dutch Roy. As a result of a calculated smear and fear campaign, enough people had come to believe that the Kuseks were disloyal to their country to cause harm to Cal's livelihood as a politician.

Lennox summarized for the jury that they were suing in the amount of $200,000 for three separate libels: the radio broadcasts, the doctored tape, and the speeches at the American Legion meeting. In a stunning stroke worthy of that infamous defender of evolution, Clarence Darrow, he broadened the implications of the trial.

"This matter is not about the attacks against one man, but *damage to the whole community,* which has suffered the wounds of suspicion and cruelty as a result of the personal vendettas of Haynes and Roy."

The defense attorney, William Price from Sioux Falls, was a large, lumpy man with slumped shoulders who wore cheap suits—easily underrated, but perfectly in tune with the majority of South Dakotans. He shared the same black-and-white vision of the world as his clients: that Communism was the enemy, a worldwide conspiracy aimed at destroying the United States. Rather than rebut the charges, he kept those emotions alive by repeating the accusations against Cal: he'd deliberately kept Betsy's membership in the Communist Party secret from the public in order to get elected. As leader of the left wing in the state legislature, he'd subversively followed party line. Price flatly denied Betsy's statements that she'd cooperated with the FBI and that she'd left the party. His promise to the jury was to prove that Cal and Betsy Kusek were still, at this very moment, "under the discipline of the Communist Party."

Price had brazenly shifted the focus right back to the Red Threat. His strategy would be to keep the jury in such an anxious state about nuclear war with Russia that it would blur the legal issues at hand. The defendants would emerge as guardians of freedom, and Kusek the agent of threatening, dark annihilation. Lennox countered by depicting Haynes as a lying, ruthless, misguided demigod who had taken advantage of Dutch Roy, a susceptible and feeble old man, with the aim of destroying a good citizen in order to feed his empire of hate.

Lennox set out to take Haynes apart six ways from Sunday on the witness stand. He cut through the claim that Haynes never filed tax returns because he had no income, having dedicated his life to the defeat of Communism, by holding up canceled checks to prove Haynes was currently employed as the owner of a commercial TV and radio station. He questioned Haynes about a statement he'd made in a broadcast that Communists were "highly trained and out to kill us." Lennox pointed to the Kuseks and asked if Haynes was accusing them of attempted murder. Haynes backed off. He meant the "army" of "other Communists" trained to kill us.

Was Haynes aware that Cal had been given top-level navy intelligence clearance? What did that tell him about Cal's loyalty? Haynes replied that he had no knowledge of how the navy decided those things or what they meant.

"So you didn't know what it meant but you accused him anyway?" Lennox asked incredulously.

He played an audiotape of the Legion Hall meeting and called Verna Bismark to testify as to what it was like to be booed off the stage.

"It was the most humiliating moment of my life," she said with her chin in the air.

Playing the tape had been effective. The jury did not approve of a middle-aged business lady being manhandled with audible shouts of *"Throw her out!"*

The trial had become local entertainment and national news. Classes of schoolchildren were brought in to observe the legal process, and TV reporters came from all over the country when it was Betsy's turn to take the stand.

For months Betsy had been nervous about appearing in court, and now it was taking its toll. Since Doc Avery's death, she'd been employed by an agency that hired out visiting nurses. But with all the rumors going around, more than once she'd had the door slammed in her face. That was intolerable, so she'd quit the agency and was working at Mercy Medical Center as a floor nurse giving patient care. It was the emotional fatigue that was getting her down—the long shifts, plus drilling her responses with the endlessly patient Kurt Lennox. She even rehearsed in front of a mirror. But she wasn't used to being in the limelight, and began to perspire the moment his practice questions touched on joining the party. It was decided that Lance and Jo should make their first appearances in the courtroom that day. They would make a strong family showing, and the jury would approve of a daughter who'd just gone on to study at a big college in Portland coming back to support her mother.

Lennox's job was to demystify the party meetings, make them human for jurors who had never seen the ocean, let alone were familiar with the 1930s Progressive movement in New York. He described it as a social club. Betsy testified that there had been only a yearning for a better, more just world. She worked in soup kitchens and collected clothes for the needy. When they met, Cal had no faith in Communists and their egotistical leaders, but he set that aside in his love for her. He would later testify that although he disagreed, he never pressured Betsy to quit.

"I knew she'd come to it in her own way," he said.

And she did. Like a lot of her comrades, she was disillusioned by its impossible and repressive dream. "I stopped paying dues and never looked back. It was a youthful mistake that has nothing to do with who I am today," Betsy said in a clear, strong voice.

Lance and Jo sat together in the courtroom and gave their mom a secret thumbs-up.

The tape of her "interview" was played and she was questioned about her opposition to *Communism on the Map* being shown in school. Asked if she'd ever said those things, Betsy stated yes, in Mr. Emry's office, when she was there to discuss her daughter. But on the stand Mr. Emry had denied they'd ever spoken, and his secretary, Kay Anger-hoffer, backed him up. She had no record of her boss having met with Mrs. Kusek.

Lennox asked Betsy how the contradiction in their statements was possible.

She'd been waiting for this. She located the pale, skeletal face of the high school principal in the audience, looked him in the eye, and replied forthrightly:

"It's simple. Mr. Emry is lying," she stated, shocking the courtroom and sending reporters running for the phones. Lance and Jo could scarcely resist high fives.

After she was deposed, an expert was called who testified that the tape had been altered.

When Cal took the stand he was the picture of dignity and com-

305

posure. Lennox worked to establish his integrity and to emphasize the important projects—"things that change people's lives"—he'd accomplished in the legislature: schools, roads, jobs.

"You're not some phonus balonus, are you, Mr. Kusek? You're a cattleman," Lennox concluded. "You dig in, get your hands dirty, and get things done. Tell me," he said, setting him up, "do you agree with the statement that we are witnessing a war between Christianity and Communism and only one can win?"

"No, sir, I do not," Cal replied. "I believe in the basic values of democracy and free speech as set forth by our founding fathers. As long as there are humans on this earth, the right of freedom will outlast any philosophy."

At this point the defense tactic had become slowing everything down to make the jury forget what it heard. When the time came to consider the verdict, they'd be exhausted, the impact of Lennox's carefully orchestrated moves lost to a "let's get it over with" mentality. To prove the Kuseks'"association" with the party, William Price brought in a tedious lineup of experts on Communism and kept each one on the stand for days. Several swore that Betsy's description of quitting simply wasn't possible.

"They'll assassinate you if you try to defect," claimed a professor.

And nobody gets married without permission from higher up.

"They tell you who to marry," insisted a former party member. "Your mate has to be of the same persuasion."

During the third week of the trial, the defense changed course and brought in razzle-dazzle celebrity witnesses. More chairs were needed for the author of a real-life spy story about his years inside the "Soviet apparatus." He declared Thaddeus Haynes's information to be "correct and fair," and characterized the Kuseks as "part of an underground espionage cell" taught to lie low and betray their country. Lennox attacked the author's credibility, asking how you can tell a Communist from anybody else.

"Suspicion is enough," he replied.

Cal's team realized they had to change the pace of the trial, which was groaning along like a medieval cart down muddy cobblestone streets to the gallows. So they turned to Hollywood and flew in a famous matinee idol who'd joined the party in the 1940s but quit after six months. Then there was a former Trotskyite, who affirmed Betsy's tale of leaving the party with zero recrimination. He dismissed the accusation that the Kuseks were members of an "underground espionage cell," declaring there was no such thing. The chairman of the Political Studies Department at Harvard agreed that espionage was not a group activity.

Like the climax of a fireworks display, Lennox brought in a barrage of experts testifying to Cal's integrity, including the president of the Bar Association, who swore he'd never heard Cal say anything pro-Communist and that he always voted along moderate Democratic lines. Finally there was a no-nonsense naval intelligence officer in full uniform who explained—"For Mr. Haynes's benefit," Lennox sneered— what a top security clearance meant, and that it would have been canceled immediately if there was the slightest doubt about Cal's loyalty.

Lennox pivoted on the heels of his snakeskin boots and shared a cozy chuckle with the jury. "If you believe Mr. Haynes, we can't trust anyone—not even the navy!"

The final assault by the defense was against the Kusek children. As Lennox predicted, they were vilified along with the parents. Jo's high school record—surprisingly made available, although the principal's appointment book had vanished—was dredged up as proof of her subversive behavior. She was criticized for attending Reed College in Portland, Oregon, which Price labeled "a known Bolshevik institution." Doris Roy walked unassisted to the stand and recounted an incident that took place more than ten years ago, when, during a roundup at the Lucky Clover Ranch, she'd stumbled into the henhouse to discover the girl was smoking a cigarette. "She was about to burn the place down," Doris declared. "They raised a little pyromaniac."

Betsy, Jo, and Lance walked out of the courtroom.

Lennox had saved a surprise witness for last. Even the Kuseks hadn't been told so that their reactions would be genuine.

"We call Mrs. Marja Winter," Lennox announced.

The doors opened and Betsy's sister entered the courtroom alone. They hadn't seen each other since her abrupt departure, but were prevented from embracing or even speaking as Marja was marched to the stand. Side by side, Betsy looked work-worn and thin, while Marja— even more the spitting image of their mother—retained a fresh, pampered complexion, a New Yorker in a hurry, clutching an expensive pocketbook, wearing a nubby navy wool suit and red lipstick, speaking quickly because she had to get back on a plane.

Lennox hammered at the charge of secrecy.

"Why did your sister drop her given name, Coline?"

"I was too young to remember."

"Did you always call her Betsy?"

"Yes."

"Why didn't Betsy talk about her membership in the Communist Party at home?"

"She knew our father would disapprove," said Marja. "He disapproved of everything. He was a heavy drinker. If it weren't for Betsy, we would have been on the street."

"Why is that?"

"She supported us in every way."

"Do you have proof?"

"I do," said Marja, and handed Lennox a sheaf of yellowed papers.

"Please tell the court what this is."

"My teenage diary. I was legally blind, so it's written in Braille."

There was a collective gasp from the courtroom. It was a brilliant move. The jury was mesmerized as Marja's fingers traced the words and she read out loud how Betsy was working night and day at Gimbels and going to jail to defend working people. How she'd given up her dream of being a doctor in order to protect Marja, because their father was unable and their mother was gone.

Marja stopped reading. She looked at the courtroom and said, "Betsy always took care of me."

Betsy was overcome with tears. Afterward the family shared only a brief moment in the grand lobby of the courthouse. A car was waiting to take Marja back to the airport. Although Betsy and Cal begged her to stay, Marja seemed skittish, perhaps afraid things might go sour . . . or she might not want to leave.

"Leon doesn't like to be alone," she explained.

The defense rested on Marja's dramatic testimony. Thirty-five days after the trial had begun, Judge Wheeler gave instructions to the jury: "Every man has a right to have his good name unimpeached. Publishing a false and unjustifiable statement which assails the reputation of another is a wrong, for which the law provides a remedy. A libel is a false publication which tends to expose a living person to hatred, contempt, ridicule, or obloquy, or deprive him of the benefit of public confidence or social discourse, or to injure him in his business or occupation."

It was impossible to read their faces as the jury filed out. On a daily basis, over the long course of the trial, the attorneys would assess their score from what they were hearing outside the courtroom, in order to fine-tune their approach to the jury—but now there was nothing to do but wait. Betsy, Cal, Lance, and Jo were staying at the Fletchers' in town, expecting to be called when a decision was reached, which could be at any moment. Robbie phoned from Denver to say, *"Right on!"* He and Jo caught up and promised to be more in touch. Lennox hunkered down at the Hotel Alex Johnson. On the afternoon of the second day there was stirring. The foreman knocked on the door of the jury room and said they wanted to hear the tape recording of the Legion Hall meeting again.

That night Cal's team waited hopefully in the law office until they all fell asleep.

The next day there was another sign: the jury didn't go to the usual pizza place for lunch. Then nothing. By the fifth day Lennox gloomily concluded the jury must be undecided, which would be a disaster. That night they'd pretty much given up and gone to bed early. At midnight Fletch got a call. The verdict was in.

Almost giddy, they all met in front of the hotel and walked together through the cold, deserted streets to the courthouse, linking arms, telling themselves that one way or another this unbearable tension would be over. Even at that hour the courtroom was jammed with reporters, Legionnaires, Birchers, liberal Democrats, Kusek diehards, and court watchers who loved a good soap opera. Fletch squeezed Stell's hand so hard her ring dug into their fingers. The judge called for order and threatened jail time if anyone caused a disturbance. There was a mass intake of breath before the verdict was given. Lance clenched his hat, looked at the sky, and whispered the Cowboy Prayer.

"We, the jury in the above entitled case," the foreman read, "do find for the plaintiff in the first claim against the *'Meet Your Enemy'* flyer for relief in the amount of ten thousand dollars."

Cal got goose bumps. Betsy got the chills. Jo started screaming.

The second claim was against the doctored tape. The verdict again was in the Kuseks' favor—in the amount of $15,000.

The room was buzzing with quiet cheers and loud whispers. *"We won! We won!"*

The third claim was against the speeches in the Legion Hall meeting, and again the jury found for the Kuseks in the amount of $5,000.

Total damages were $30,000, an unprecedented amount for a libel verdict in South Dakota. The jury also found for the plaintiffs on the conspiracy issue, meaning Thaddeus Haynes and Dutch Roy would carry the mark of collaborators in slander. The smear campaign had backfired. Calvin Kusek's good name was restored and theirs were stained forever. Cal and Betsy's vindication was complete.

Judge Wheeler thanked the jurors for their long and faithful service and declared that court was adjourned.

The room erupted in a pandemonium of hugs, tears, whoops, and clenched fists in victory. The other side stalked out in silence.

Beaming and waving, the Kuseks descended the curving stairway from the courtroom to the marble lobby like the royal family, flashbulbs going off, a mob of reporters and frenzied supporters waiting to crush them with joy. Although he'd long ago given up bull riding, outside in the chilly night, surrounded by dancing classmates and friends, Lance got down on one knee, thanked God, stood up, and, in rodeo tradition, skimmed his cowboy hat through the air. It traveled straight and true, coming to rest with finality on the frozen ground.

27

Nine months later, on November 22, 1963, President Kennedy was assassinated in Dallas. Like everyone else, the Kuseks stayed glued to the television set for the next four days as the unbelievable events of the swearing in of Lyndon B. Johnson, the horse-drawn caisson and state funeral for the young president, the burial at Arlington, and the point-blank shooting of the assassin, Lee Harvey Oswald, unfolded live. Cal and Betsy idolized John F. Kennedy and had worked unfailingly for his election. In their vainest moments, they imagined themselves bush league versions of John and Jackie, leading the way to an enlightened society in their own little Camelot on Lucky Clover Ranch.

With Kennedy's death the lights went out on the New Frontier, his vision of prosperity and innovation, which could have been his legacy for America. Instead, the bullet that killed the president released a decade of senseless violence, from the assassinations of Martin Luther King Jr. and Bobby Kennedy to the Vietnam War. At that same moment, of no interest to the rest of the world but with grave consequence to the Kusek family, on November 22, 1963, a child was born named Derek LaSalle.

He came into this world a troubled soul, in a cabin deep in the Olympic National Forest of Washington State. He was the son of Chrissy and Armand LaSalle, with an older brother named Amos. All the males in the family were lumberjacks, and many had grown up in the same camp of simple wood-framed houses built in the 1940s by the timber company as a permanent community for its employees.

On November 22 there was a storm—a deluge of heavy, primordial rain that knocked the power out. Landslides blocked the roads, and because of the national days of mourning, the local clinic was closed. The LaSalles were delayed in getting to the regional hospital, forty-five miles away, where the baby arrived three weeks early and not breathing. When he was miraculously revived, they immediately saw there was something strange about him. As an infant he couldn't settle. He wasn't happy as a child. He bit other children and threw fits. His parents couldn't keep him in school, so he grew up wild in the old-growth rain forest, rigging slings for the company when he was fifteen. According to the locals, the fact that Derek LaSalle, at the age of twenty-two, was fated to murder a prominent family a thousand miles away went all the way back to the odd green eyes that first saw the light of day when President Kennedy was killed: he'd been born under a bad sign.

LaSalle was one year old when Congress passed the Gulf of Tonkin Resolution, unofficially declaring war on Vietnam. The Kuseks, caught up in the antiwar movement, nonetheless felt they had completed their personal mission, and relished the calm that had settled over their lives after the verdict. The missile fields still stood as sentries of the Cold War, and in a few years Vietnam veterans would bring the reality of ground fighting home to South Dakota. As the state's children served and fell, the plow of history dragged on, overturning the battle of the Kusek trial and burying it in a consecrated field of valor.

In this new and shining day, Calvin Kusek emerged a hero. He'd stood up to the enemy and won. You might not buy his politics, but you couldn't argue with the dollar amount of the prize! Thirty thousand was a big number, big enough to prove—as many now admitted—that he'd been right. The tactics of the other side had been dirty pool. He'd been ambushed, but he fired back, protecting his honor the way any true patriot would. The jury had been right. The judge had been right. On the street, people went out of their way to chat, and Cal and Betsy savored the paradoxical wonderment of having been vilified as traitors and now held up as champions of freedom.

They abandoned all thoughts of moving back to New York City.

They were true westerners now, especially since while she was at Reed College, Jo had fallen in love with the wooded squares in the city of Portland and the gorgeous rivers that crisscrossed the state. Her next stop would be the University of Oregon for a degree in landscape design. She didn't know where that would take her, except she was inspired by the innovative culture of the Northwest. If her parents wanted to see their daughter, they'd have to travel there, because she rarely came home.

The Fletchers and Kuseks continued to be close friends and law partners. Being convicted of slander had no effect on Thaddeus Haynes's political career. He was reelected to a second term in the Senate, and by 1968 had bought two more local TV stations, creating the Haynes Broadcast Network.

When Lance left home for Northwestern University, Betsy started working full-time at Mercy Medical Center. Two years later she was promoted to floor supervisor, but after a while began to wonder if she'd taken on too much. Getting up at five a.m. to do ranch chores was becoming harder. She dreaded the drive, especially in bad weather. She felt tired in the mornings and found herself calling in sick more than she'd like. It couldn't be age, she told herself, she was only forty-seven. Stell urged her to quit or at least take time off, but Betsy felt so responsible for everyone—patients, coworkers, animals, and family—that she kept on pushing.

A nasty cold was going around the hospital. Along with the usual sore throat and stuffy nose, Betsy had symptoms of lethargy and loss of appetite, which was par for the course for the virus, but over the next few weeks, food itself became less interesting. She began to avoid it, cooking for Cal but taking just a tablespoonful for herself. He joked that she certainly didn't need to diet. But not eating was making her weak in the head. It was hard to concentrate, which worried her, because as charge nurse she had to check everyone else's work. She kept bumping into things and getting bruises, then having no memory of how they got there. She drank more coffee and doubled down harder.

Mrs. Galveston was a patient on Betsy's floor who had her gall bladder removed and was recovering normally. On her rounds, a nurse's aide noted an alarming decrease in Mrs. Galveston's heartbeat, and that respirations were down to four per minute. Her blood pressure had also dropped precipitously, to 80/40. The aide quickly summoned the doctor, who discovered the patient had been given twice the dose of morphine indicated. He immediately administered Narcan to reduce the effect of the opiate. Mrs. Galveston recovered, but Betsy Kusek was called on the carpet. It turned out she had administered the morphine, and in the correct amount, but failed to note it on the chart, causing the next nurse on shift to repeat the same dose within a half-hour period.

It was a serious mistake, which required official intervention. Betsy was well liked and respected, but the doctors had been concerned about her. She'd been forgetful, didn't have her usual energy, and was losing weight. Before any kind of disciplinary action, they insisted that she undergo an examination and take a blood test. Betsy didn't share this with Cal. She was certain it was a recurrence of the flu, or maybe late-life anemia.

The results were devastating. Betsy was diagnosed with acute myelogenous leukemia, the same bone cancer that had killed her mother. The oncologist offered a bone marrow transplant, but Betsy didn't want heroic measures. She realized she'd been in denial all this time and didn't want to prolong the inevitable.

"I just want to go home," she'd said.

She was fine for the next few weeks, then turned feverish, and Jo and Lance came home. The children learned how to give morphine injections. A hospital bed and IVs were set up in the living room so Betsy could be where she belonged—in the middle of things. Stell was there to hold the bucket when she vomited. Cal would go outside to weep but soon gave it up, and they all cried together almost all the time. He could not imagine life without her. His mind was stopped at an impassable wall.

Beside the bed they made a little altar of Betsy's best-loved things: her mother's jewelry. Ceramic ashtrays Jo and Lance had made in grade school. Eagle feathers she'd picked up, the medicine wheel Doc Avery had given Cal, fresh sprays of lavender from the prairie. She told Marja not to come out. She didn't want the burden of her sister's grief. They called each other every day and made a point of saying not good-bye but "Talk to you tomorrow."

The parade of ranch wives bearing casseroles began. There was no rancor left against the Kuseks; it had all been swept clean like the smudge sticks of sage they kept burning to purify the room. Stell brought magazines and they'd talk about silly things, hairstyles and manicures. Jo was in on these discussions. She'd become a grown-up woman now.

"I had a dream," Betsy told her husband three weeks before she died.

He was sitting on their bed, feeding her chips of ice. She moved the bowl away.

"I saw my mother."

"Yes?"

"She was floating on the ceiling," Betsy said, indicating with an emaciated hand. "There. She was wearing a nightgown and that robe she had at home, in Scarsdale, when we were kids. She had long hair, just flowing. It was light outside, and the light was so beautiful. Do you know who was next to me?"

"Who?" asked Cal, eyes brimming.

"Ruby."

"Ruby, the little calf?"

Betsy smiled. "Yes, the little red calf who died. But he was here, so calm and trusting, right next to the bed. He was waiting for me."

Cal's eyes overflowed. "I know."

"He had a crown made of flowers."

Cal touched her dry cheek. "I'm glad you had such a beautiful dream."

After that Betsy began to sleep a lot and barely took a sip of water. She stopped speaking. When Jo, overwhelmed, threw her arms around her mother, Betsy turned her head away. She was detaching from this life. The most profound change of all was the look in her eyes. Even at their worst moments, Jo had always found protection in her mother's eyes. Loving and open, they'd always said, *You are precious to me.* Jo needed that reassurance right now more than anything, but Betsy had been transformed into a separate being. Her eyes said, *This is serious, take note,* but they could have said that to a stranger. She had no more to give. The stare was uninhabited by the mother Jo had known.

The day they buried Betsy Kusek beneath the cottonwoods on the Lucky Clover Ranch, the skies broke open and it poured. The drought was truly over, but their mourning would be unending. Cal was lost. His soul just wandered. Comically, he'd immediately become the most desired widower in Pennington County. Shirley Hix appeared at Betsy's funeral all gussied up, admitting to having a crush on Cal the moment he set foot inside the Bison Café almost twenty years before.

Cal was having none of that, but he needed to stop walking around in circles and crying in the barn. *Kusek v. Haynes and Roy* had set a new standard in libel law. Over the years he'd been invited to speak at conferences and to teach a course at Yale but always declined. Now he hired a ranch manager and some hands, and went back to New Haven for a semester, which turned into a year. And another year. And another.

When she was first diagnosed, Betsy had told him, "You go on and live another life." As unthinkable as it had been, three hard years of grief passed, and another life was opening up for him in the long-ago pleasures of university life. He wasn't on a tenure track, so he had nothing to prove. As long as Yale kept offering, Cal was happy to accept the role of guest lecturer. He loved being with students. He'd forgotten how young was young.

He made the rounds: sailboat races, cocktail parties, bookstore readings, weekends on Martha's Vineyard, dinner parties in Manhattan with the most exciting minds in law. To the East Coast cognoscenti, Calvin Kusek's sojourn on the western plains could not have been more exotic if he'd joined a colorful troupe of Mongolian horsemen, living in tents, drinking the blood of their ponies as they swept across the windy steppes, subsisting on boiled lizards. He'd gotten used to the skeptically raised professorial eyebrow: "North Dakota sounds god-awful."

Cal would smile, no offense taken. "South Dakota," he would say. "And only when it gets below minus ten." He'd abandoned all efforts to explain the art of bull riding.

He was pursued and fell into a couple of short-lived affairs, which always seemed to end over sugary cocktails in a seafood joint with a disappointed thirty-five-year-old professor dressed in black. Jo and Lance and Betsy's memory, it endured. And the white farmhouse from Sears that had been set too close to the road. All this he wanted back.

When Lance graduated from law school he, too, came back home. He joined the law firm of Fletcher and Kusek and married a sweet-natured, down-to-earth woman he'd known as a student at Northwestern named Wendy Justin, who taught elementary school. They bought a saltbox house on West Boulevard and painted it bright blue. Their son, Willie, was born in 1975.

Cal was living at the Lucky Clover Ranch and coming into town to work, but the child became his world. Willie's first sentence was "I want Grandpa." When Nelson Fletcher retired from the practice, Cal and Lance went on together. They built an addition to the saltbox house and moved their office there so that Grandpa could see his grandson every day—when they weren't out on the ranch together, which was every weekend.

Cal was blessed with seven beautiful years with Willie. Too soon, he passed peacefully in his sleep at the age of sixty-nine and was laid to rest beside Betsy under the cottonwood trees at the Lucky Clover Ranch.

At a memorial service attended by more than three hundred people, Lance and Jo spoke of their father.

"Calvin Kusek was a hero in war, a hero in the fight for personal liberties, a hero as a husband, and always my personal hero as a dad," said Jo.

Lance added that he'd never felt as proud as when he and his father became partners in law. He recalled the day they hammered in the sign on the front lawn so it faced West Boulevard: KUSEK & KUSEK—LAW OFFICES. It was colonial-style—white, with blue lettering that matched the color of the house.

When she remembered that Verna Bismark owned a bank, Jo realized she had misjudged the lady. Verna had been a female pioneer, as she told it, putting up with ridicule and lewd remarks when ranchers sat down to discuss their loans, expecting a little flirtation to go a long way, which it did not.

"Your dad was the exception," Verna said. "Never blinked an eye."

"He was plenty happy at home," Randy Sturgis added.

Verna rolled her eyes and Jo felt consoled to be sitting between these two kindly relics, almost in place of her parents.

"Cal and I, we got right down to the business of politics," Verna said, "and we had great success. Those other morons, they would've gotten a lot further in life if they hadn't been driven to distraction by a double-D, and I'm not talking about a ranch, honey."

Jo laughed through a fog of exhaustion that was suddenly scattered by the neon-orange flash of Robbie Fletcher's parka as he strode from the elevator, clutching a reporter's notebook. She could tell from the look of professional distraction that he had news. He greeted Verna and Randy and they exchanged sympathies.

"Take a walk with me," he told Jo.

When they were alone at the end of the hall he said, "They've eliminated Honeybee Jones as a suspect."

Jo became angry. "Why?!"

"He's a witness. He's cooperating with the police."

"What's he telling them? It has to be a pack of lies."

"He says he knows who did it," Robbie said.

"He does? How?"

"My source says he came down to command headquarters and named the killer off a police sketch. The guy they're looking for is a drifter. Honeybee claims he stole his gun."

"Claims he stole his gun," Jo said derisively.

"I don't blame you," Robbie said. "Tyler Jones always was a wiseass."

"That's putting it mildly."

They headed back to the waiting area.

"Don't spread it around," Robbie said. "What I told you."

"I don't care." Jo flashed him a tired smile. "Willie touched my hand."

"Oh, hey, that's wonderful!" Robbie Fletcher said.

"It is wonderful," said Jo, her smile vanishing.

His arms flew open and he held her as she cried.

FOUR

NIGHTMARE

28

Derek LaSalle was being dive-bombed by a murder of crows. He shouted at them and waved his ax, but crows are territorial, and they continued to be quite bothersome. He decided he'd have to put up with it, being two hundred feet aboveground and with a tricky job ahead. He was to chop the top off a tall, straight Douglas fir and, by skill and calculation, cause it to fall in such a way that it did not kill himself or the crew in the landing zone below.

At six feet four inches and 230 pounds, LaSalle had grown up to fit the Paul Bunyan image of the Northwest logger—a big man conquering big trees. He was almost twenty-two, strong, and unusually limber for his size, which gave him the endurance, using only gloved hands and spiked boots, to free-climb the tree, branch by branch. Anyone respectful of what could happen if he miscalculated, or if the wind blew the wrong way, would have done the normal thing and tied himself to the trunk using a lanyard, but Derek LaSalle had a peculiar numbness when it came to fear of any kind.

He was also not good at resisting temptation; he had what a police psychiatrist would later call, in a grand understatement, "poor impulse control." There were all those enticing branches; he couldn't stop himself from starting up. It was extremely hard physical work, scaling a ten-foot diameter, but it made him feel best to be alone up high with vantage points and views that other people never get to see. He'd describe it, somewhat shyly, as a Superman kind of feeling. Right now he was looking through a clearing the lumber company had made at a lake that was miles away, silvery fog clouds hanging low. With the sun poking through the shining boughs of the evergreens nearby, everything was beautiful with nobody around to spoil it. And it always smelled like Christmas.

The crows had given up. They knew he wasn't going anywhere. LaSalle determined where to crack his notch with the ax and how to place the back-cut, so the top fifty feet of the Douglas fir would fall cleanly to the ground where crews were waiting to trim the limbs. Immediately after he'd made his cuts he realized that he'd misread the setup. Not by much, but just enough to tilt the delicate interaction between the living tree and a level breeze from the west into an unstable danger zone.

The tree had a little bit of lean to it, and the moist wind picked up just enough to edge the top in the wrong direction from his notches, so when it did drop, the piece was ninety degrees off from where he'd planned. Instead of falling all the way down, it got hung up, landing against the crowns of other trees. And it was still attached to the Douglas fir in which LaSalle was sitting.

He calmly appraised the new situation. It was catastrophic. A massive chunk of foliage, fifty feet long, was hanging by a neck of splintered wood ten feet across, pulled by a different set of forces than he'd anticipated. It was not only gravity acting on the enormous weight of the thing, but the halfway-fallen piece pushing hard on the canopy of neighboring trees, as well as against its own trunk, that had formed a giant spring that could snap in any direction. LaSalle, with nothing to anchor him, would be swept off his perch twenty-five stories up and die. Men and equipment in the landing zone would be flattened, and the value of the wood would be lost.

He felt no responsibility for the mistake, moving on to the next logical step, which was to get the tangled branches free. Like Superman, LaSalle found himself to be the only one who could master the impossible. The solution was to lower himself on the trunk and do it all again. He reread the vectors, made a new notch and a back-cut that would top the tree off in the new location, hoping he didn't have to dodge a mass of rolling thunder on its way down. On this second try the severed crown came loose, crashing to the ground with a roar that rumbled through the forest.

When his boots touched down, the superintendent of the logging camp, a wiry, square-jawed company man of forty-five named Bill Danvers, who wore horn-rimmed glasses and neat leather suspenders over his hickory shirt, was already yelling his face off.

"What the hell do you think you're doing, climbing again without your lanyard? How many times have I told you not to do that?"

"It was the wind," LaSalle told him, stomping past. He'd fixed it; what was the problem?

"I can't have this!" Danvers shouted over the booming roar of heavy equipment. "You're my fastest climber and maybe the most productive, but you're also the most dangerous. You don't know when to stop. You put my hires in jeopardy and I just can't have it!"

He didn't have a good temper, but neither did LaSalle.

"I told you, boss. The wind shifted," LaSalle shouted back. "Happens to everyone. I know what I'm doing. Get off my back!"

"No, buddy, not this time. This has been a pattern with you. You just don't listen. I'm not going to wait until you kill yourself or somebody else. I'm going to have to let you go."

"Oh," said LaSalle, thick brows rising. His eyes were unusual, crystalline green with dark lashes. "That so?"

"Truth be told, it's a relief to get you out of here. You're way too reckless and immature. You want to show off, go race cars or something. This isn't kid stuff, Derek."

LaSalle held his ground; the only sign of the annihilating rage coursing through his body was his right hand resting on the head of the ax still on his belt. Danvers wasn't going to wait for the kind of explosion he'd witnessed before from this guy. With a flick of the head he alerted the nearest crew members, two Cat drivers, who climbed off their machines and began to walk toward LaSalle. This all took place in a bubble of silence inside the screaming chorus of chain saws echoing a thousandfold in the empty space they'd ripped from the forest.

LaSalle's response was to smile laconically and flash Danvers the peace sign.

Danvers spat. "Punk."

Nobody else knew he'd been fired and there was nobody in particular to whom LaSalle gave a damn about saying good-bye, so he ambled through the camp and turned onto the road. The parking lot for the crew was a mile and a half away, usually serviced by a bus, but the bus wouldn't be making its run until the end of the day. He'd walk.

Now that he was on the ground, he was no different from every other bum. Mild afternoon sun lit up green pastures behind pipe fences where dairy cows grazed. The bucolic scene was lost on LaSalle. The company had taken away the one thing that mattered to him: being alone up in the trees. A logging truck whizzed by with a full load, sounding its horn in greeting. LaSalle still looked like one of them, but no, he wasn't. He'd decided to quit working the Northwest woods. He would get a job in the Amazon jungle. Washington timber country was bad luck. That hanging snag—it'd never happened before. Luck could turn on you like that, and when it did, you had to act fast. Crossing the blacktop to the employee parking lot, he spotted his favorite snake—a beautiful two-foot-long boa—dead, flattened by the rig, and that sealed it.

Even at this distance he couldn't escape the angry drone of the chain saws. It played on his nerves. Then he saw Bill Danvers's Ford pickup. On impulse, he power-lifted the log that served to mark the parking space from its rut in the dirt, heaved it over his shoulder like an Olympic javelin thrower, and rammed two hundred pounds of solid wood through Bill Danvers's windshield, so one end rested on the driver's seat and the other stuck out of the broken glass like a great big dick. Then he turned to his own beat-up Camaro and was halfway inside when a golden beam of excellent pure luck struck his eye. It was the sun reflecting off the key in the ignition of a black Toyota 4x4.

The truck had been pampered. It was filmed with sawdust but there wasn't one dent. He opened the nice, solid-feeling door. Inside you had all the comfort of a passenger car—carpeting and an AM/FM stereo radio. The interior was neat as a pin, and a dangling air freshener made it smell like lemons. The owner probably kept it in the heated garage of a brand-new development where you could eat off the driveways. He hated people like that. Stuck on the dashboard was a photo of two kids. He turned the ignition. They were his kids now.

. . .

In the parking lot of a Motel 6 a hundred miles north of San Francisco, Derek LaSalle stole the license plates off a Buick and switched his out. (The Toyota came with a complete tool set.) In Sausalito he flipped the old plates into the bay and feasted on an obscene breakfast of scrambled eggs, smoked herring, and pancakes with whipped cream and strawberries in a joint overlooking the boats. He drove across the bridge and didn't even mind the morning rush-hour traffic, just turned up the stereo and cruised in comfort into San Francisco, gleaming and fantastic, like something off a psychedelic record album cover. He made his way to the Haight-Ashbury district. Working shop by shop, LaSalle pawned everything he'd found in the back of the truck. It looked like the yuppie owner had been about to go on a camping trip, because it was *loaded* with brand-new stuff, including a camera bag with a Nikon and two lenses. He walked away with $476 and a lid of weed he'd scored on the street.

LaSalle drove to the suburbs and hit the appliance stores, gorging on items that would bring him good money—Epson pocket TVs, Polaroid cameras, Casio watches, VHS players, and a Walkman for himself—using the credit cards Mr. Toyota had considerately left in his wallet in the glove compartment. He bought two bags of jeans and shirts at the Gap, a pair of Ray-Bans, a Nike tracksuit, and Converse sneakers, size fourteen. He'd never paid for a haircut in his life, and he was laughing out loud to himself when he walked into the place in the mall, but he had to admit when they got through that he looked a lot like the golden boy in Duran Duran.

He planned to spend the night with an old girlfriend named Taylor, and sell the truck for an awesome score. Then he'd hang out with Taylor until he got a gig cutting big trees in Brazil or maybe Costa Rica, where he'd have enough money to veg on the beach for the rest of his life. He looked her up in the phone book and she was still in North Beach, so he headed that way. The evening rush-hour traffic wasn't so much fun this time, and it was a bitch to find a parking space. This city was not cooperating. He had to trudge uphill to the triple-decker Victorian, still as seedy as he remembered it, and her balcony, on the second floor, was still jammed with wind chimes and macramé junk, which raised his hopes that everything would be just like five years ago, until he saw her coming up the street pushing a baby stroller.

It was definitely Taylor: long deep-honey hair and skinny legs, a plain-okay face, wearing one of her crazy thrift-store outfits—go-go boots, a dead person's dress, a poncho, a straw hat, who knew what—squinting suspiciously up the street like someone might be lying in wait on her doorstep, who happened to be LaSalle.

"Derek!" she said, instantly on guard. "I thought you were still in prison."

"Nah."

Five years ago the sight of him would have caused a panic attack. Now she was stronger. She inspected his clothes and sandy-blond hair layered to the shoulder, not trusting the transformation. His eyes hadn't changed—the shiny bright green eyes that never seemed to settle.

"You look good," she said, pacifying him.

"You look exactly the same," he said approvingly. "I see the neighborhood hasn't been yuppified."

"Yet."

LaSalle was pleased that they could still agree on some things.

"This is Kyle."

Taylor maneuvered the stroller so Derek could see the baby. It was sleeping. It had kinky hair and dark brown skin. Derek was repulsed. No, they didn't agree at all. How could she do it with a black guy and raise his half-breed?

Taylor saw his disgust. "I'm married," she lied. "What about you?" she asked, challenging him with an unblinking stare.

"Oh, I'm married, too." Derek whipped out the photo of Mr. Toyota's children. "Want to get something to eat?"

"Are you serious?"

"I'm good now. I'm in rehab."

Taylor did not believe a word. She pushed the stroller toward the steps of the weathered porch as quickly as she could without looking like she was trying to escape. The last thing she wanted was for Derek to run into Kyle's father upstairs.

"Can I help you with that?" LaSalle offered.

She jumped between him and the child. "No!"

"Don't freak. I'm just back for a visit. I need money," he added plaintively, even though by tomorrow he'd have thousands.

"There's an ATM at the supermarket," Taylor said.

LaSalle's lids drifted down over pleading eyes. "Can you help me out?"

She hesitated, then decided it was worth it to get rid of him. She wheeled the stroller around and flew down the hill. By the time LaSalle had trotted after her, she was withdrawing fifty dollars from the machine outside the market.

"This is all I can give you."

"I'll walk you to the house."

"No, don't."

The doors to the market opened automatically. Taylor seized the opportunity to get away by pushing the stroller inside.

"Don't you say good-bye?" LaSalle called after her.

The threat in his voice made the hairs stand up on the back of her neck. The doors closed and she pretended not to hear. She strongly suspected he was violating parole and considered calling the police, but was afraid to start the whole thing all over again. The restraining order. The long months of counseling. White as a sheet, she watched through the window until Derek LaSalle was gone, shaking so violently that a stranger stopped to ask if she was okay.

LaSalle walked six blocks to the truck, thinking that San Francisco might be a better idea than Brazil. North Beach was crawling with nude bars, and Berkeley would always be ripe with chicks. He could rent a place, take a breather. Go to a Giants game. Who else did he know from his dealer days that might still be around? Just as he was ticking off the list he came to the spot where he'd parked the truck. It was no longer there. In its place were a vacant curb and an Asian guy in a red jacket standing under an umbrella. Now he noticed the fancy Chinese restaurant and realized that he'd ended up in the worst bad luck parking space in the Bay Area. For Christ's sake, a dragon in the window? Everything the color red? He was in deep shit.

"I'll bet you own a black Toyota," the parking guy said. "Sorry, man. It just got towed. After six it's valet parking." He pointed to a street sign that said as much. "Do you want me to call a cab? Cost you maybe fifteen bucks. The police station where they take it isn't that far."

For all sorts of reasons, reclaiming the stolen truck that contained his stolen fortune was not feasible.

"Truthfully, it belongs to a friend," LaSalle admitted.

"Bummer for him."

LaSalle went into the nearest bar and stayed until daybreak. There were many, many things wrong, chief of which were Chinese and blacks taking over American jobs. He was a fountain of hurt and betrayal, but a lot of people agreed with him, and he made some good and lasting friends. Someone took him, as requested, to the Greyhound station, where LaSalle was able to clearly announce to the ticket man that he was going to Bozeman, Montana, to see his brother, Amos. The man told him to wait on the bench. The next bus would leave in six hours.

BOZEMAN, MONTANA

LaSalle awoke in a magical place. He was in an alley, but not just any alley. It was the back side of an old building with signs painted on the rose-colored bricks, beautifully faded words over words from days gone by, like pictures in a dream—STORE OF THE NG BORAX DELICIOUS MOON PIES—and yet there were also rows of windows with curtains and shades where people were really living. The insides of the windows had been painted bright orange. There was newer graffiti that had been rubbed away so the present was even more faded than the past. You could stare and stare at that ghost writing and never see all the parts of it.

LaSalle gazed at the wall a long time until the scent of marijuana caused him to look to his left, where a black man was sitting beside him, leaning against the chain link and smoking a pipe. He could have been anywhere from forty to sixty years old. He wore a yellow beanie and a blue coat with the tattered cuffs of different shirts showing underneath. LaSalle would have gotten up and moved, but there was something psychic about this guy. His eyes were closed and he had long, innocent lashes. His soft wide lips, surrounded by a thick black goatee, were curled around the stem of the pipe, and he was taking it all in, not just the smoke, but something else, like music. Like he was playing silent music on the pipe. Behind him were a warehouse and a row of white trucks, concrete loading bays. The dude was tranquil and still.

His street name was Buzz. He told LaSalle the reason he got high was because he had been wounded in Vietnam. Once he sat, he was down for the count. Walking was a trial. LaSalle took the pipe when it was offered and sucked greedily. He noticed another drifter, maybe twenty, wearing a hunting cap, who eyed him hungrily while he smoked. Generously, LaSalle passed Buzz's pipe to the young man, explaining that he was a Christian.

At this, Buzz pulled a small, supple Bible from the pocket of his ragged peacoat and waved it in LaSalle's face with a gold-toothed grin. They exchanged black power handshakes and LaSalle affirmed that he, too, was "a brother." Buzz said he knew where the shelter was. It would be serving lunch. LaSalle helped him stand and saw that his buddy was in bad shape, one leg longer than the other. It took them a while to get there—the Salvation Army Center of Hope—and it was a raw, freezing day.

It wasn't hard to act grateful. It just poured out of you when you got into the warm and took your place at the end of an orderly line of men. LaSalle chorused in with the exclamations of "Thank you, *Lord*!" as they filed past a folding table laid out with paper bowls of chili, brownies, and potato chips. A woman and her two girls stood behind the table with cheerful greetings. The mother wore a calico prairie dress down to the floor with a sweater underneath it and plastic gloves. The girls were twins, squeaky clean, wearing dresses, with their hair neatly parted and pulled into braids. *"Want a brownie? Take two!"* they chirped, not at all afraid of the grubby men who shuffled by wearing cowboy hats and fishing caps, leather jackets and parts of cast-off suits. The men kept their heads down and didn't smile or chatter like the little girls.

LaSalle followed Buzz into a large utility room with blank walls and a soda machine. Folding chairs were lined up, and that's where the men who already had their food would eat. LaSalle told Buzz he'd been "set up" by his brother, who promised him a place to live, but when he came all this way from California, it turned out Amos had moved or died or disappeared.

After they ate the chili, they got into another line for a ticket to get a bed, and waited outside against the building in blowing flakes of snow until it opened again at five. The room was stacked with narrow bunks barely two feet apart that looked as if they'd arrived in the days of the railroad. The iron frames were peeling paint and there were no mattresses on the springs.

"Just like the beds you see in some of those jailhouses," Buzz remarked.

Buzz was hoping for better days. He was on his way to Rapid City, South Dakota, because they had an air force base down there that had "a big hiring going on," especially for veterans. It was the easy life, he said. You could live on the base and they fed you, too. Buzz heard they were giving vets first preference, which is what they deserved. LaSalle agreed. He was a vet, too. He'd enlisted at Fort Lewis, which was the first place that came to mind. Buzz said he was out of there as soon as his old Chevy got fixed. Presently it was on the street with a disabled fan belt. Buzz wondered idly if LaSalle could contribute in exchange for a ride. LaSalle's mood rose like a rocket.

"Fan belt, hell!" LaSalle exclaimed. "I can cover that, brother."

It wasn't just the fan belt, as Buzz well knew when he lured the white kid in. He figured that fool would be good for something. It turned out the car needed hoses and a water pump and a new battery, plus a full tank of gas, so by the time they left Montana, LaSalle had $267 remaining of his bonanza from San Francisco. Two days later, they arrived at Ellsworth Air Force Base in Rapid City, ready to go to work, but the carefully groomed and shined cadet at the gate, who looked about sixteen, told them there was no "big hiring" going on, not since they built the missile silos back in the 1960s. In fact, they had their hands full right now with the hippies come from all over, wanting to take the missiles *out.*

LaSalle felt like a clown, standing in the noonday sun outside the gate with this useless codger, who'd purposely taken them 666 miles to the middle of nowhere. Then a voice told LaSalle to kick himself—666—how could he have missed *that* sign? For about the millionth time, Buzz had to use the "gents'," as he called it in his quaint, old-fashioned way. They stopped at a gas station with pink and yellow bunnies smirking in the windows because it was Easter. LaSalle followed his friend inside the single restroom, grabbed the old man by the neck, and banged his head against the tile wall, counting to six, six times in a row. He let go, then squatted down, observed eye movements behind the lids and blood from the nose. Buzz had wet himself. Pathetic, thought LaSalle.

He washed his hands and flicked the light switch. The room went dark as a TV screen, and LaSalle forgot all about it.

He got into the Chevy and drove off, reaching for the pipe in the glove compartment. By the time he'd hit the interstate he was doing ninety-five, thanks to the last of the crack, a new kind of high that made cocaine look like peanut butter. This, coupled with the dimensionless space of the prairie, caused an agoraphobic reaction in LaSalle. Seized with panic, he kept looking for trees. Cacti. Anything but nothing. Arrows of sun zinged through the windshield directly into his brain. LaSalle gripped the steering wheel and shook it with all of his 230 pounds, howling, *"Ray-Bans!"* in agony over everything that had been taken away from him, until forced to hit the brakes before he rear-ended a line of vehicles stopped at a state police roadblock at Exit 152.

"Oh, sweet Jesus," he gasped. "They're waiting for me."

No they're not, asshole, answered LaSalle's inner voice. *Open your eyes.*

RAPID CITY, SOUTH DAKOTA

A gathering of about a hundred people was following a priest down an access road into the open plains. One group sang church songs in fervent harmony. They looked like they were in some kind of happy trance. Then he saw the banners: BLESSED ARE THE PEACEMAKERS and NO HIROSHIMA EVER AGAIN.

Stalled drivers were angrily honking horns. LaSalle leaned on his, loud and long. He rolled down the window because it was getting hotter and hotter in the car. The air-conditioning wasn't working for a change.

"God bless America," said a gruff voice at the window.

LaSalle almost jumped a mile. "What the hell?"

It was a burly, friendly-looking older guy with long gray hair and a big belly, wearing a red, white, and blue Uncle Sam hat, baggy jeans, and red suspenders over a shirt patterned like an American flag.

"I'm the voice of reason," he growled.

LaSalle didn't know what to make of that. Then the guy handed him a leaflet wrapped around a cold can of Coors and LaSalle realized it had been a joke.

"Are you for real?" he asked, grinning.

"Don't drink and drive," the dude advised, moving on.

"Hey, wait a minute."

Since he was stuck there anyway, LaSalle got out of the car, surprised to find the dry prairie air so bitter cold. "What's going on?" he asked.

"A bunch of faggots protesting the fact we've got a defensive missile system in place to protect our country from a surprise attack by Russia. Yeah, good luck. They're going over to E-5 but they'll be arrested," he said with a world-weary sigh. "And you and me'll foot the bill for their pansy meals in jail. Not too early for you?" he asked of the beer.

"Just in time," LaSalle agreed, chugging, even though the brew froze his teeth. He looked at the words in big type on the leaflet. "What are they—Communists?"

"Oh, definitely. Without a doubt. Last time they cut through the chain link and sat on the silo lid."

LaSalle guffawed. "Like it might go off?"

"Pretty weak, if you ask me."

"So what are you?" LaSalle asked, reading from the pamphlet. "The New Pioneers?"

"We're a local group," the man said with the same sigh, the burden of righteousness on his shoulders, "working to keep strangers out of here, along with troublemaking fags and hippies—something wrong with your car?"

Piles of steam were spurting out from under the battered hood of the Chevy. LaSalle reached in and turned off the ignition. The smell of burning rubber hoses stung their noses.

"I put good money into this thing. Never trust a nigger," LaSalle added with disgust. He received a sympathetic shrug.

"Got a truck. I can give you a tow."

"That would be much appreciated, sir."

The red, white, and blue guy offered his hand. "They call me Honeybee. Honeybee Jones."

"Derek," answered LaSalle. "Hope I can do something for you one day."

They shook on it.

. . .

Honeybee liked to talk and LaSalle liked to listen. While they were driving, the Chevy lashed to the tow bar of Honeybee's truck, he described the interstate as a cash pipeline. The flow went from the Colombian cartels to Florida, Georgia, and across the West. Quaaludes, weed, synthetic cocaine. Honeybee told LaSalle he'd "been into a lot" and done time, first in South Dakota for stealing cattle when he was a youngster, later in Wyoming for robbing a bank, but in his old age he'd finally figured out the way to get by was slow and easy. A couple of transactions now and again were enough to keep body and soul together, and "Rapid," as he called it, was a righteous home base because everyone was too stupid and stoned out of their skulls to pay attention, and he could live for free in his mother's old house.

LaSalle didn't say much, which after a while spooked Honeybee out, wondering if he'd just spilled his guts to a fed, but he decided the big kid was stressed by his car breaking down and whatever. They left the Chevy on the street. It fit right in with the scruffy working-class subdivision: muddy trucks and broken-down RVs in the driveways, and rows of mailboxes on posts stuck in buckets of cement along the sidewalks.

Honeybee lived in a dirty white rectangle with greenish aluminum awnings over blind windows. Nothing grew in the yard except trash. There were things in there that had nothing to do with him—blow-up kiddie pools and abandoned pet cages. Over the years, neighbors got in the habit of dropping their crap in his yard, despite the furor of three large mongrel dogs throwing themselves against the fence.

Several years ago, Honeybee had come home after a stint in jail to find his alcoholic mother dead in an armchair, still attached to her oxygen tank. Nothing had changed before or after her demise. Joints, cigarettes, sewing stuff, little baby dolls his mom collected, and odd bits of hardware littered the coffee table. The big TV was always on. In the kitchen, cats had the run of the counters, where piles of dishes moldered for days, and the top of the refrigerator was a wonderland of empty liquor bottles. The cabinets were sliding off the wall; in fact, the entire house sat on a slant.

"Smells like crotch in here," said Honeybee, as if he'd never noticed it before. "You can have the sofa."

Honeybee gestured toward a sunken piece of furniture covered with old blankets and crusted with dog hair.

"Could I trouble you for a snack?" LaSalle asked politely.

"Help yourself."

LaSalle went into the kitchen and opened the refrigerator. He found a carton of milk that was still okay and was about to pour cereal flakes into a bowl, when a .40-caliber Glock fell out of the box.

"Yeah, the guns," Honeybee remembered. "Let me show you."

There was also a semiautomatic M1 carbine under his bed and a .38-caliber pistol on the windowsill above the toilet. Day-to-day he lived like a slob, but he was well organized for the apocalypse. In a lean-to beside the back door he'd neatly stored and labeled a month's worth of water and dried food, along with a tent and ammunition. This he kept under lock and key and did not mention to guests.

After a couple of days of getting high and playing their favorite video game, *Dragon's Lair,* Honeybee's hospitality dried up. He sat down on the couch next to the young man and asked about his goals. Offhand, LaSalle couldn't think of any. Honeybee said if he didn't contribute he'd have to leave. LaSalle came up with an idea about the pipeline. One thing he could do is drive. What if he helped Honeybee out sometimes with a delivery?

"I have skills. I can fix your place up," he offered, and told about his life in the trees and how—*here's a goal!*—his plan, he remembered it now, was to save enough money to get to Brazil and cut trees in the jungle. Honeybee didn't know much about Brazil, but it had to be close to Colombia, so maybe this could work out. LaSalle bolstered his argument with exaggerated claims of his criminal background, making him sound like a jack-of-all-trades, from burglary to homicide.

LaSalle put on his Boy Scout face, eager to please. He did a huge sweep-out of the rotten little house, carrying truckloads of decaying stuff to the dump. He cleaned out the junk from the backyard and made a place for a bench and a set of weights he found in the garage; got the vacuum cleaner fixed, threw out disgusting things in the kitchen, spent days at the Laundromat watching blankets go around, and got on Honeybee's nerves with all this endless straightening up. But that was cool because Honeybee drove LaSalle nuts with his constant yakking. Still, by molding himself into a docile shadow, LaSalle fit himself into Honeybee's lifestyle of drinking at a biker bar, lifting weights, cruising chicks at the pool hall, letting the dogs out, and occasional meets at a

Wal-Mart parking lot to pick up a kilo of coke for delivery on the West Coast, with LaSalle doing the all-night driving. Honeybee didn't mind getting some sleep.

The New Pioneers turned out to be the best part of LaSalle's week. Every Tuesday morning four to eight fat old dudes—even older than Honeybee—turned up at the Kaiserhof Kafe, a German family restaurant, where they got special treatment and were seated in a private room in the back. The walls were covered with murals of medieval castles on the Rhine, painted in lurid, mind-altering colors that made LaSalle feel like he was Dirk the Daring, hero of *Dragon's Lair,* rescuing Princess Daphne from Mordroc and Singe, finding himself on the brink of a life-and-death decision between eggs Benedict with Black Forest ham and the big Jack omelet, all of which he found hilarious.

The meetings of the New Pioneers would start with everyone standing for the Pledge of Allegiance, a long boring reading from Scripture, and sometimes a moment of silence for friends who had passed. Then they'd let loose on a rampage that made fascinating entertainment for LaSalle. Sometimes it was the Jewish international banking scheme or insane welfare programs. It could be "keeping Rapid white and free" or the immoral federal income tax. They kept copies of the Constitution on plastic cards in their pockets and made LaSalle stick one in his.

The elders' mantra was about "justice and the value of human life." They said everyone is born with "human capital," although some have less value than others, like Mexicans, blacks, Communists, and Jews— nevertheless, if you killed one of them, you automatically gained their capital, like a bank, *ka-ching.* The New Pioneers insisted they weren't a violent bunch, although they did enjoy shooting guns. Honeybee would go out and unload five hundred rounds from the pistol into a target twenty-five feet away, "just to put the fear of God into them." With his gift for mimicry, LaSalle was able to chime in with these beliefs right on key, but it was the "human capital" idea that stayed with him, tucked away, because it made such obvious mathematical sense. The grandpas treated LaSalle like family. They called him "the big kid" and paid for his breakfasts.

One clear morning in October everything changed. You might

say it was the first sign of the End of Days that was long predicted to happen. A book had just come out called *Loyalty*, written by Harold Wheeler, the judge in a famous trial twenty-five years ago. It was famous because it was the first time a politician had sued a member of the public for libel and won. The politician was a state legislator named Calvin Kusek. He'd brought a lawsuit against one of their idols, Senator Thaddeus Haynes, and received $30,000 in damages. A lot of the New Pioneers had been around at that time, and they were still incensed by the verdict.

Calvin Kusek, they explained to their youngest member, was a liberal Democrat married to an avowed member of the Communist Party, a sick combination, and if he thought Communists were gone he was dead wrong. The enemy was still among us. Cal Kusek, who lived in a fancy house on West Boulevard (you could see the sign), was "regional director of the Communist Party"—right under our noses. Haynes was some guru type they all worshipped, LaSalle figured out, who, sadly, was in his nineties and gone in the head with dementia. Back in the day, according to the elders, he was as great as Senator McCarthy, whom LaSalle had never heard of, but okay. Senator Haynes had pointed the finger right at Kusek but nobody would listen. Honeybee had known both men pretty well and agreed the whole thing was a perverse travesty of justice.

The group chipped in for a copy of *Loyalty* and passed it around. For weeks they couldn't get off the subject. The Kuseks still lived in town, two miles away but a world apart from Honeybee's. LaSalle didn't understand how a blatant enemy could be allowed to live out in the open. Well, they explained, he was a lawyer, tied to the banking conspiracy—what do you expect? Like many things, Calvin Kusek slipped from LaSalle's mind, until he had cause to remember.

Around Thanksgiving, Honeybee told LaSalle he'd have to start paying his share in cash money or move on. Tree topping wasn't an option in the prairie, and he had no other prospects. LaSalle really didn't want to go back to living on the street. That raunchy sofa was the sweetest place he'd ever known. He wanted to prove to the New Pioneers that he was a good soldier. In that case, Honeybee would be proud of him and let him stay. He decided to kill Calvin Kusek and his family.

29

Every morning on his run, Lance Kusek made sure to go by the ball field. He ran on a median between two wide streets, empty at six a.m., just the lonely slapping of his shoes on wet pavement and the pleasant hot-cold sensation of sweating skin and freezing air. On gray wintry mornings, it gave him a lift, in a melancholy way, to pass the field where his dad had taught Willie to hit a ball. Passing it was like saying hello to Grandpa. This would be the first Christmas since Cal died that anyone really felt like celebrating.

Lance reached the halfway point in his run and realized he had no awareness of where he was. He'd been ruminating on Christmas at the ranch when he was a kid, how they'd had to wait to open presents until the cows got fed, but Mom always had hot cocoa with peppermint sticks for when they came in. He passed the silent infield, where the unbroken banks of snow flecked with breaking sunshine brought a memory of how on Christmas Eve they would scatter oatmeal in subzero weather to feed the reindeer . . . and the golden sparkles he and Jo would find the next morning, proof that Santa had been there. The cheerful idea hit him that he and his wife, Wendy, could do the same for their boy. They left cookies for Santa; why not oatmeal for reindeer? That would be radical!

Lance felt happier then, comforted by the thought of a family tradition rolling forward in time. He'd found himself sentimental lately. The season brought wistful recollections of how much Willie had meant to Cal. Given him new life, really. Lance was amused to remember how his intellectual father had been transformed into a clown with a repertoire of goofy faces, and a regular customer at Who's Hobby House downtown, never showing up without a Matchbox car for the boy's collection. When Willie was four, he'd even gone so far as to dress up like Santa Claus. There was a knock, and Lance and Wendy swooshed Willie toward the door with excited whispers, *"Who can that be?"* The boy opened it and stared up at the figure wearing a red nylon costume and fake beard.

"Ho ho ho, little boy!" said Santa.

Willie eyed him suspiciously. "You're not Santa."

"Is that so?"

Willie frowned. "You're wearing Grandpa's shoes!"

Lance smiled to himself and said a blessing for his dad, to let him know that he was here with them, at the blue house, where he would be pleased to see tradition carried on. On the front door was the same wreath with a gingham ribbon they bought every year from the same lady at the farmers' market. He pushed the door open and the sweet pressures of the holiday fell on him like gifts from a closet. He had to call his sister in Portland, and he still hadn't bought something nice for Wendy. The moment he entered, Willie jumped all over him, begging to go out to the ranch and go sledding. Lance told his son it was Christmas for the caretakers, too, but they could go the next day, and besides, guests were coming for dinner.

"What about *Santa Claus: The Movie*?" Willie demanded. "You said we could see it."

"That, too," Lance promised. "You have a whole week off from school."

LaSalle had begun to prepare. A phone book supplied the address for the Kusek law office on West Boulevard. Several times he took the bus to scope out the scene at different times of day. He walked around the blue house and saw there was an alley. He observed that the garage door didn't have a handle. That meant he'd have to somehow get in through the front door. It was a rich neighborhood, and he concluded this Kusek must have a lot of cash lying around, enough for LaSalle to get out from under Honeybee.

Things had been going downhill. Uphill or downhill, depending on how much crack cocaine LaSalle could get his hands on. Honeybee often made the north-south run along the interstates with a kilo hidden inside a panel of his truck, but he kept a stash at home. LaSalle had found his drug of choice. It was like a hydrogen bomb in his brain raining Halloween candy.

LaSalle was high when he bopped over to the hardware store. He examined several types of rope and engaged with the clerk for quite a while, boasting loudly about his tree-climbing techniques. After that, he still needed more supplies—chloroform, handcuffs. To finance the mission, he pawned the stereo set in the living room. Honeybee wouldn't care when he found out a soldier for America had wasted the Commies.

On Christmas Eve, LaSalle was again high, and making a real pest of himself. Honeybee was smoking a joint and trying to watch *The Twilight Zone* marathon while LaSalle was describing how their enemies were going to be taken care of by the ThunderCats.

"Shut the fuck up!" Honeybee roared. "I'm sick of your rants. I told you weeks ago to get the hell out."

"I'm trying."

"Doing what? You are out of here tomorrow, I don't give a shit how."

"Just chill," LaSalle told him, taking a hit. "I'm good now."

"Yeah, that's you being good. Fuckin' nuts." Honeybee stared at the TV. "Do me a favor and die."

LaSalle sniggered at the joke. No way his buddy really meant it, and even if he did, he'd get the picture soon enough. Derek LaSalle left the bungalow and took the bus to West Boulevard for the final time. He was so fried from coke and weed that with all his planning, he went to the wrong address on West Boulevard, a brick-and-stucco Tudor English. He realized his mistake when he saw a different name on the bell. It was too late. A woman surrounded with a bunch of kids in Christmas pajamas opened the door with a smile.

LaSalle put on his charming face. "I have a delivery for Mr. Kusek," he said, holding up his plastic bag filled with supplies.

"I'm afraid you have the wrong house."

"Oh."

The lady cocked her head at his disheveled looks, but took pity on a young man trying to make a buck on Christmas Eve. "You'll want the little blue house, two blocks down."

"Sorry to bother you, ma'am."

"That's all right."

The lady closed the door but stopped to wonder. She didn't remember seeing a car. She hadn't seen this delivery boy before, and he looked a bit scruffy. After arguing with herself while the kids went crazy begging to unwrap gifts, she decided to go ahead and call the Kuseks and give them a heads-up, but the line was busy.

It was cold. LaSalle hurried along the deserted sidewalk and crossed the street. Then he saw a sign on the lawn, KUSEK & KUSEK—LAW OFFICES, and the blue house behind it, just like the lady said. He was confident and shining. The worst was behind him. He was here. He rang the bell.

Lance Kusek opened the door and stared at the young man on his porch—big, possibly homeless. Lance felt none of the compassion of his neighbor up the street. The guy was a drifter looking for a handout.

"Mr. Kusek!" announced LaSalle. "I have a package for you."

In the kitchen, Wendy was talking on the phone to her mom in Illinois. She put Willie on to say Merry Christmas to his grandma and then hung up. Immediately the phone rang again. Wendy was flustered. She had guests arriving in twenty minutes. She picked up the receiver.

Poised in the doorway with the freezing wind at his back and the warm room with a fire blazing before him, LaSalle had struck a moment of perfect balance on the threshold of two realms. Inside it smelled like freedom, like being up in the spruce. Ahead of him were swirling bursts of color—colors he couldn't name. Behind him was darkness.

"Who are you?" Lance asked, gazing in wonder at the stranger. As if he already knew.

As if he knew that past and present had come together, face-to-face.

The stranger whipped a gun out of a plastic bag, grabbed Lance by the shirt, turned him around and stuck the barrel in his back. Willie bounded out of the kitchen followed by Wendy.

"That was the lady in the brick house up the street," Wendy began, but her voice tightened when she saw her husband's white face and the terrifying person behind him.

"We're going to help this gentleman out," Lance said slowly and meaningfully. "Do whatever he says."

"Y-yes, of course," Wendy stuttered. For a split second she almost told Willie to run, but her husband's eyes said, *No.*

LaSalle's mind had entered a featureless void like when he was up there in the intergalactic distance between branches, but at the same time inside the infinitesimal space between each pine needle, a shape-shifting vacuum that ordinary humans couldn't survive. There was a boy. He didn't know there would be a boy, but he was into it now, he could be identified, so the soldier pushed the gun deeper into the man's back and kicked the door shut behind them. It seemed to close without sound. He ordered the man and boy to lie on the floor. The man offered cash money and the soldier said, "Yes, everything you've got. Credit cards, too." The man said, "Guests are coming at seven thirty." A clock said 7:10. The woman stood still. She was wearing a dress. She was ordered to lie facedown next to her husband and son. The soldier tied their hands behind their backs. The room smelled sickly sweet, like cinnamon. It was becoming hot. The soldier took his equipment from the bag and soaked a special rag he'd brought in chloroform. He pressed the rag against each person's nose until they shut up talking. The clock said 7:20. The soldier searched for a weapon. He opened a broom closet and found a clothing iron. He went back to the three figures and began to hit the father's skull with the point of the iron, four or five times. Then he beat the lady in the dress with it, and then the boy. But the lady was still scratching with her fingers, so he went into the kitchen and picked up a small, thin knife, the kind you'd use to cut meat off a bone. He went back into the dining room and saw that it was wildly splashed with blood. His shoes picked up blood, and when he knelt to stab them in their brains, the knee of his pants got soaked with blood. The woman had stopped breathing, but a distant alarm had begun to sound in his mind. He was exiting the void and hearing the wail of self-preservation. The guests would be there any minute. He took the man's wallet from his pocket and pulled out credit cards. Then he turned out the lights. In his panic, he couldn't locate the back door. He ran blindly through the darkened house, tracking blood. Finally he found the stairs to the basement, groped his way down and out another door. He hit fresh air. He ran through the backyard. A giant shape was lurking in the shadows.

He ducked sideways like a deer, but it was only a canoe turned upside down to protect a pile of firewood.

None of the guests could get inside. The doors were locked, the lights out. Someone went to the next house to call the Kuseks, but there was no answer. The guests went around the side and peeked through the dining room windows. By the light of a fire blazing in the hearth, they saw three bodies on the floor. The police arrived and determined that the father and son were still alive.

Derek LaSalle realized he couldn't take the bus because his clothes were covered with blood. He had started to walk in the direction of Honeybee's house when he remembered that he'd left the handcuffs behind with his fingerprints all over them. He turned around and jogged back to West Boulevard, but by the time he got to the blue house there were lots of people and cop cars, and the snowy streets were alive with dizzying red lights, so he kept on walking. It was damn cold and starting to rain. As he wandered off alone, the streets grew quiet and deserted, with more elaborate decorations, people going nuts with light-up snowmen, that kind of crap, their fancy snowmobiles loaded onto trucks and campers parked in driveways. The wind was blowing right through him and he became desperate to find shelter. The thought arose that nobody would be checking their camper on Christmas Eve. After several tries, he pulled on the door of a Winnebago and found it unlocked. It was nice inside, and in back there was a big long seat where he could sleep.

Special Agent Robert Dolan arrived in Rapid City just before midnight on Christmas Eve. He'd received the call for assistance from the local police on a possible multiple homicide at nine p.m. and driven from Pierre in blustery snow at seventy miles an hour. Following in a separate van were assistant detectives and a sketch artist. When they got to West Boulevard, the two surviving victims had been taken to the hospital and were receiving medical care. Police vehicles and a coroner's van blocked the street. Yellow tape surrounded the house. Inside, a brief conversation with the coroner affirmed the female had been killed by blunt force trauma and the weapon had been a steam iron.

Dolan crouched in the doorway and surveyed the dining room. It looked surreal, but all crime scenes had that weirdness. Normal and not at all normal at the same time. He saw the well-appointed house of an upper-middle-class family. The fire had burned down and the lights were on while a photographer documented everything. Dolan took note of the blood splatter sprayed across the walls, meaning an attack of great force. An earnest young sheriff's deputy was posted near the body. She was facedown with hands bound behind her back. The dress across her legs looked untouched; no obvious indication of sexual attack, but that would be confirmed by the autopsy. He crouched down and peered at the knots. Double loops. Unusual. He took a cheap pocket magnifier from his jacket pocket. There was no grit in the fibers. The edges were cut, not frayed. The rope looked new. He directed the deputy to check the garage and workshop for similar material. When he reported none, Dolan asked if there was a hardware store in town.

"Yes, sir."

"Call the guy."

At two in the morning, Jarvey Bennet, the sixty-five-year-old owner of Bennet's Hardware, was unlocking the front door and turning on the lights. Dolan was there with another detective.

"A kid was in here the other day. Knew exactly what he wanted. One-eighth braided polyethylene." He led the detective to the spools of line. "This one here."

To Dolan's naked eye, it looked exactly like the one at the crime scene. "Did he say why he wanted it?"

"Said he was a tree trimmer."

Agent Dolan asked the hardware store owner to come over to the sheriff's office and talk to the police artist.

"I'll tell you, it was a Christmas I'll never forget," Bennet said later.

Honeybee hadn't moved from the couch where he'd passed out the night before. On Christmas morning the TV was still playing and the local news was on. He was smoking a joint and waiting for the basketball game when Derek LaSalle appeared on the screen. He thought he was hallucinating. He punched up the sound. It was a police sketch of

LaSalle, all right, implicated in a murder at the Kusek residence over on West Boulevard.

Honeybee reeled into the kitchen to get a beer and saw the cereal box had been dumped out all over the counter and the Glock was gone.

"He took my gun!"

If that lunatic had used it to kill someone, it would all come back to Honeybee. No matter what, the kid had been living here, the doo-doo was about to hit the fan. Honeybee did a quick sweep of the house for drugs and called the cops. Next thing he knew, TV vans were pulling up and cameras were in his face.

When the owner of the Winnebago, forty-one-year-old car mechanic Emmet Johnson, came out of the house to get the camper warmed up, he didn't notice the brownish smear on the door, too wrapped up in dreading the drive over icy roads to his in-laws' in Gillette for the holidays. He sat in the driver's seat for several minutes with the engine running before going into the back, where he found cans of food opened up and empty beer bottles scattered around, the suitcases they'd packed for the trip opened and rifled through. His good jacket was missing. He stiffened with rage. Someone had been in here and had the gall to leave a note. It was carefully written on a brown paper bag with one of his daughter's markers. "I am sorry for what I done. I am the person you are looking for. I am the only one. Do not blame anyone else." When he carried the thing inside, his wife had the TV on, and it was playing the same news over and over about the Christmas Eve massacre that occurred just blocks away. Johnson notified the police, but they'd already been called to the Kaiserhof Kafe, where a disheveled man wearing a new hunting jacket had told the bartender that he'd "killed a hotshot in the Communist Party." A waitress recognized him as a regular with a radical group called the New Pioneers. LaSalle was arrested in the restaurant without incident.

One year later, Derek LaSalle received the death sentence, later commuted to life in prison without the possibility of parole. In a jailhouse interview for a TV documentary on psychotic killers, he was unconcerned about having murdered three people.

Asked if he felt remorse, LaSalle replied, "I don't feel much of anything."

His emerald eyes with the strange shine to them roved around the cell, never once looking at the interviewer.

"I wish I could cry," he said, "like I used to."

Lance Kusek suffered a stroke caused by swelling of the brain and went into cardiac arrest. He died at 8:46 p.m. His sister, Jo Kusek, was present.

The vigil outside the hospital for his son had grown to several hundred. Candles were still burning. Flowers were laid at the entryway. Notes of condolence were slipped into the chain link bordering the snow-covered grass. Someone brought a guitar and people prayed together.

Three hours later, Willie Kusek died of his injuries. It took just forty-eight hours for the boy to join his parents.

TEN YEARS LATER

PEACE

The old cowboy is bent against the sky. Bowlegged and half crippled, he hops along slowly, one leg dragging. After a lifetime of riding bulls and wrangling horses, his body is broken in a hundred ways. His spirit, too. He's no longer a seeker of trophies. His outlook on life has hardened around one thing: the land on which he was born and raised. The rest is a waste of effort.

Scotty Roy, age eighty-two, slides down the hill on worn boot heels, arms flailing to keep his balance. Those watching from below know not to offer help. He prides himself on still running cattle on the open plain. Such as it is. In his youth, at this time of year, the prairie would have been opening to summer with banks of magenta bee balm flowers against yellow bristlegrass, delicate Indian ricegrass, sage-colored wild rye, and swaying tussocks of orchard grass among lush miles of natural forage. Few now living could picture it.

Jo Kusek is the first to step forward and embrace Scotty Roy. She feels she has a right. He's as old as her dad would have been, and was "Uncle Scotty" to her brother. She's emotional; he is shy, but true. Stops, grips her arms, and looks her in the eye to say how sorry he's been all these years for having left Lance without a good-bye. He'd gone off without a word to the boy, then was too ashamed to make it to the funeral. Jo tells him that she understands.

When Dutch and Doris passed, Scotty said the hell with it on the deal with Monsanto. Just couldn't stomach it. When Lance and his family were murdered, Jo turned the Lucky Clover Ranch over to caretakers. Now they'd come back to make peace and heal the land.

Scotty shakes hands with Jo's husband, Warren, an easygoing, clean-cut, and straightforward fellow. The cowboy's knees crackle out loud as he squats down to say hello to their six-year-old daughter, Nicole, and baby, Alice. The girls are tired because they've driven three days from Portland, but when Scotty promises fireworks, Nicole perks right up.

Warren carries the baby in the backpack and Jo takes Nicole by the hand. They follow Scotty over the hill. The wind is dry and searing. The low, constant wail gives Jo a chill, even though the July day is sunny and warm. The former missile site is a quarter mile from the Roys' house. After all that hoopla, the Strategic Arms Reduction Treaty was negotiated in 1991 and the missiles decommissioned. Nuclear warheads were pulled out, leaving a thousand empty holes. That same year, the Soviet Union collapsed, and all that remained of the Cold War in western South Dakota, and everything that came with it, was the wind.

A party's going on. There are picnic tables covered with tablecloths. Jo feels nervous—will she remember the names?—but soon she's enveloped by laughter and welcoming arms and everyone saying it's a great day. A happy day. Robbie Fletcher is there, along with his wife, Sherry, and their three boys. He never did leave Rapid, still works for the *Journal*. His parents, Fletch and Stella, are visiting from Arizona. They look tanned and healthy. Stella's gone gray, and Nelson is sprightly; he's been working on his second humor book of lawyer jokes. They both are wearing shorts.

Jo and Warren are pleasantly surprised by the mix of people who show up. Portland does not have a lock on eccentrics. There are old hippies. A country fiddler. A grandma in an electric wheelchair with a parrot on her shoulder. Straight ranching families, churchgoers, liberal types who loved her dad and speak in soft voices of "that terrible time," a young priest, a biology teacher, hip restaurateurs breaking into Rapid City.

They've taken down the chain link and antennas, leaving a circle of concrete and a shaft that goes three stories down, where the charges will be dropped. Warren, along with another firefighter and some Gulf

War veterans, goes over to set the explosives. Jo is proud of how easily he fits in, tossing horseshoes and talking fly-fishing, minding other people's kids—that rare grounded person who knows what he's about. Jo and Stell sit on a blanket eating homemade strawberry-rhubarb crumble. Nicole's made friends and is playing Hula-Hoop. Baby Alice is content in her carrier nearby. Jo looks up at the lofty blue sky filled with gentle white clouds, and smiles. In Portland it is raining all week.

Scotty comes by and says it's time. When everyone quiets down, he and Jo make their little speech. "Before we blow this thing up," they say, "we have an announcement to make." The two of them, surviving heirs to the Crazy Eights and Lucky Clover, have decided to combine their ranches and buy the land in between. They're going to put the properties together in order to create a continuous space of more than four thousand acres of open grassland that will become a wildlife sanctuary. They'll plant switchgrass, bluestem, Indian grass, and woody cover for migrating birds. Wildlife will flourish in its natural habitat. Waterfowl, antelope, painted turtles. Eagles. Badgers. Pheasants. Prairie chickens. Burrowing owls. Wolves, elk, grouse. Scotty will sell off the herd to help finance the deal, and instead of cows, they'll run native bison.

Hoots of joy erupt, prayers of exultation. Anyone with anything that can make noise does. Clapping, fiddling, yodeling, pounding on the lids of chili pots. But the biggest noise is to come. The men tell everyone to step back. Nicole clings to Warren's leg, turning up her elfin face and saying she's scared. Warren puts his big hands over his daughter's ears.

They give Scotty a remote detonator. He yells, "Fire in the hole!" and presses the button. The sharp crack of an explosion booms underground. A geyser of dust shoots up a good thirty feet and everybody cheers. For one brief moment a hole appears. Then the sides collapse, the hole craters, and the earth closes in upon itself.

On this land, Jo thinks, nature will repair itself. It will grow stronger as seeds are sown and seasons come and go. Animals will mate and birth and suckle and die in the ungroomed wild. There will be no owners. There will be nothing to buy or sell. There will be no ideas. No purpose. There will not be one thing more important than another. There will be only this. Jo can feel her parents and her brother standing close beside her in the long grass. It had been theirs for a while.

Author's Note

When a novelist falls in love with a story there is no letting go—on either side. The story takes root, and soon it is hard to tell if you are writing it, or have merely become the host for a living thing that demands to see the light. That is what happened when I first heard of the Goldmarks, an East Coast family that moved to Okanogan, Washington, in the 1950s to start a new life as cattle ranchers. It was during the height of the McCarthy era, and their liberal views made them the victims of a local smear campaign that cost John Goldmark, a rising political star, his career. In a groundbreaking trial, he sued his attackers and won. But that wasn't the end of it. The legacy of hate seeped into the next generation, resulting in a sensational multiple murder that was widely covered in the press. As a novelist, I had to write about this, but needed to go deeper, behind the headlines, to create a fictional world in which I could dramatize my own understanding of these extraordinary human events. To start, I radically changed the location, choosing South Dakota for its open plains. I invented a new cast of characters and their stories, but it was the clash of opposing worlds—idealism and fanaticism, city and prairie, sensibility and insanity—that first captured my imagination and remained the inspiration for writing the novel.

Acknowledgments

I am grateful to the Overnell family of Concrete, Washington, for my first contact with cows during my stay at their historic inn. Thanks to Craig Vejraska, owner of the Sunny Okanogan Ranch, who shared his knowledge of raising Angus. In Bucklin, Kansas, I spent long, happy days with Joe and Nancy Moore on the Moore Ranch, riding, branding, sharing chores—and meeting their amazing red heeler, Whiskey, who has a cameo in the book. Marilynn Moses, coordinator of the Okanogan County Historical Society, graciously provided research materials. For legal arguments I relied on *The Goldmark Case* by William L. Dwyer, and its transcripts of the trial. Much appreciation goes to Evan Levinson for access to the archives of her father, Paul Sherman, who wrote movingly of his experiences in New York during the Depression. For medical expertise, thanks to Kelly Coffey, M.D., and Michelle Abrams, R.N., and gratitude to Jim Arnett and Elaine Kogan for early reads.

Benjamin Brayfield, former photojournalist for the *Rapid City Journal* and coincidentally our son, was my guide to the ins and outs of that town, and Emma Brayfield, our daughter, was the expert on animals who kept things real. Each of them accompanied me on field research.

Fashioning these experiences into a cohesive narrative was solely due to the genius of my editor, Carole Baron. Thank you also to her talented assistant, Ruthie Reisner, as well as the brilliant staff at Knopf. None of this would have come to fruition without the continuing support of Sonny Mehta; my wonderful agent, Molly Friedrich; and my ever-encouraging husband, Douglas Brayfield.

For more information on the research visit www.aprilsmith.net.

A NOTE ON THE TYPE

This book was set in Celeste, a typeface created in 1994 by the designer Chris Burke (b. 1967). He describes it as a modern, humanistic face having less contrast between thick and thin strokes than other modern types such as Bodoni, Didot, and Walbaum. Tempered by some old-style traits and with a contemporary, slightly modular letterspacing, Celeste is highly readable and especially adapted for current digital printing processes which render an increasingly exacting letterform.

Typeset by Scribe,
Philadelphia, Pennsylvania
Printed and bound by Berryville Graphics,
Berryville, Virginia
Designed by Soonyoung Kwon